LET ME LOVE YOU ANYWAY

HOLLYWOOD

LET ME LOVE YOU ANYWAY

JORDYN BARNES

THE HOLLYWOODLAND SERIES
BOOK ONE

First Published in 2024

Orlando, Florida, USA

For more information, please visit jordynbarnes.com

Paperback: 979 8 9905034 1 0

Ebook: 979 8 9905034 0 3

Library of Congress Control Number: 2024912445

No AI tools were used in the writing of this book, its contents, or any artwork including the cover.

Edited by: Horn & Ink (@horn.and.ink on Instagram)

Book Cover and Illustrations by: Jordyn Barnes

LA skyline, filmstrip, color book graphic, and palm trees by Freepik.com and Vecteezy.com

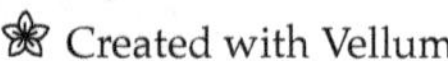

CONTENT/TRIGGER WARNINGS

This book is a romance, and it does end with an HEA, but there are some heavy topics. If you're not sure about the warnings, reach out to me at any of my social media platforms or my website jordynbarnes.com. I can make sure this book is right for you. Take care of your mental health and don't be ashamed to ask for help if you need it. You're not alone out there.

SA (on-page; not between MC's), Discussions of SA, Religious Trauma, Child-Abuse (discussions/memories), Drug Use (marijuana & prescriptions), Domestic Violence (not between MC's), Panic Attacks, Depression & Self-Doubt, Toxic Families, Loss of a Parent (off page), Gaslighting, Body Shaming, Grief, Emotional & Physical Parental Abuse, and Explicit Sexual Scenes.

This book is intended for an adult audience.

Please read responsibly. If you would like a list of chapters that these triggers appear in, please contact me.

For everyone who understands
that in order to see the light of the stars,
there must be darkness.

*

* Also, for that AP English teacher who said the journalism department's work was only worth using to mop up water from the floor. Thanks. And fuck you.

*"Tell me every terrible thing you ever did,
and let me love you anyway."*

EDGAR ALLAN POE

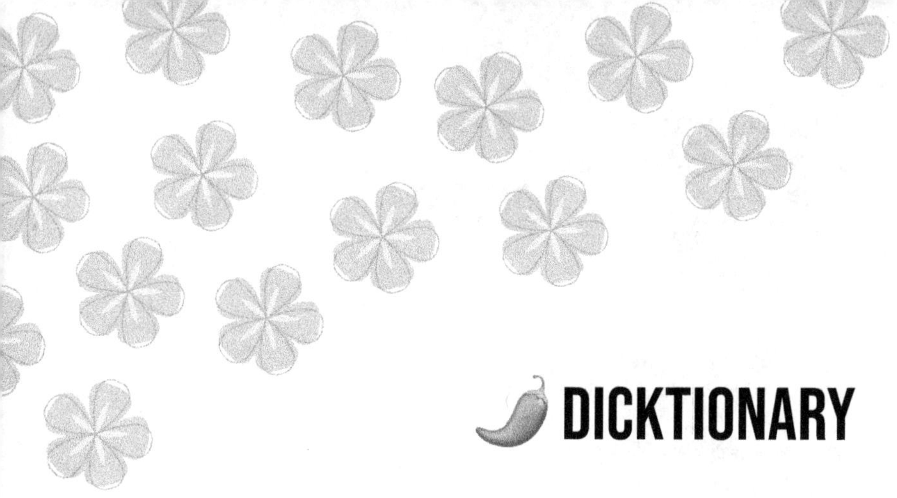

DICKTIONARY

Want to find (or avoid?) the open door chapters? Here is a list, and you'll find a pepper at the start of each of these chapters as a reminder.

Chapter 10
Chapter 17
Chapter 18
Chapter 20
Chapter 21
Chapter 22
Chapter 28
Chapter 30
Chapter 31
Chapter 34
Epilogue

CONTENTS

1. Under Presure 1
My Chemical Romance & The Used
2. Honeybear 9
Yeah Yeah Yeahs
3. I've Just Seen A Face 19
Jim Sturgess
4. Heads Will Roll 33
Yeah Yeah Yeahs
5. Tear In My Heart 43
Twenty One Pilots
6. Some Nights 57
Fun.
7. Tongue Tied 69
GroupLove
8. Stupid Girl 77
P!nk
9. All The Good Girls Go To Hell 87
Billie Eilish
10. Arms Tonight 99
🌶 *Mother Mother*
11. Fade Into You 111
Mazzy Star
12. Into You 123
Ariana Grande
13. I'm Not Okay 137
My Chemical Romance
14. Brown Eyed Girl 143
Van Morrison
15. Smells Like Teen Spirit 155
Malia J
16. Nothing's Gonna Hurt You Baby 169
Cigarettes After Sex
17. I'm On Fire 185
🌶 *AWOLNATION*
18. First Day of My Life 199
🌶 *Bright Eyes*

19. Pictures of You 213
The Cure
20. True Love 227
🌶 *P!nk, Lily Allen*
21. Just Like Heaven 241
🌶 *The Cure*
22. Cherry Blossom 257
🌶 *Lana Del Ray*
23. Time After Time 271
Iron & Wine
24. Beverly Hills 285
Weezer
25. Sympathy for the Devil 301
The Rolling Stones
26. Just The Way You Are 313
Billy Joel
27. The Sharpest Lives 325
My Chemical Romance
28. Season of the Witch 337
🌶 *Lana Del Rey*
29. Hurt 349
Johnny Cash
30. All I Need 365
🌶 *AWOLNATION*
31. Across the Universe 377
🌶 *Fiona Apple*
32. Paint It, Black 389
Ciara
33. All Apologies 399
Sinéad O'Connor
34. Till Forever Falls Apart 411
Ashe, FINNEAS
35. Take My Breath Away 423
🌶 *EZI*
Epilogue- Loving You 435

Mental Health Resources 444
Mantal Health Resources pt 2 445
Acknowledgments 447
About Jordyn 449
The Hollywoodland Series 451

BOOK ONE:

JAMES + ALEXIS

HOLLYWOOD

James

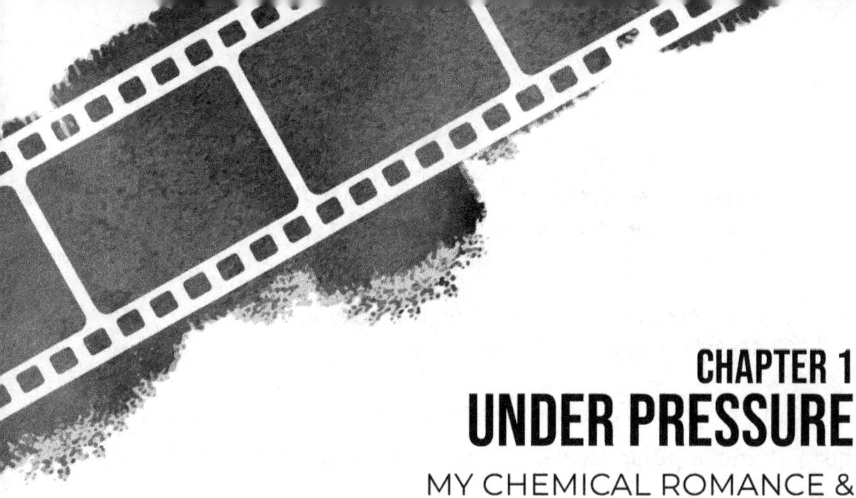

CHAPTER 1
UNDER PRESSURE

MY CHEMICAL ROMANCE & THE USED

THE SCREEN'S bright light draws me like a moth as I doom scroll under the covers, phone clutched firmly in hand, waiting for the buzz of the morning alarm—so much for sleep.

I toss off the two blankets I'm huddled under and instantly regret that decision. It's too fucking cold for California. I grab my hoodie from the foot of the bed and shuffle over to my laptop, flipping up the screen. I don't expect an answer yet, but the 'what if' tickling my brain demands appeasement. The Wi-Fi searches for a network, then takes its time connecting to Beaches_LUV_my_WIFI. It's my neighbor's, and he's a tool, but he's been letting me use his connection.

Spam, sales, bill notifications—not what I'm looking for.

"You knew it wouldn't be there, dumbass," I mumble to myself.

My neck cracks as I roll my head and wipe the sleep I didn't even get out of my eyes. When I sent in the application, they said it could take a week to sift through all the candidates and respond. But when your entire life is hinging on one email, a week can be longer than a year. I pick up my phone again and re-read the message from an hour ago.

SAM

Hey buddy, we got the okay to run with your photos AND the client wants to buy the rest.

SAM

Can you come by today and drop them off? Check will be waiting for you.

Sam is my one constant client. Over the last ten years, I've been doing regular freelance gigs for his company, so I'm not surprised to hear from him, but I am surprised he wants me to come in. I shuffle through the paperwork on my dresser and find the envelope of prints he's asked me to bring in. I pick up the prints and frown. Apparently, I was using them to cover up the pile of bills with the red stamps that scream at me for money I don't have.

If there's something I need right now, it's money and a distraction. Besides, people are always saying I should get out more. This counts, right?

The aroma of fresh coffee pulls me out of my wandering mind and down the stairs. I pour out two cups, stop myself, and dump one back into the pot. While heading back upstairs, I spot a bong, rolling papers, and an empty jar of weed. Also, my friend Trey passed out on the couch. I guess we hit that a little harder than we'd planned.

"Hey, man. Coffee is ready, and I'm leaving in a bit."

There's a shuffle and mumbling under the blankets, and I don't wait to see if he's alone. My home is on the verge of being rezoned as a frat house since I started letting Trey crash here.

Back upstairs, I dig through my closet for clean clothes and make a mental note about picking up some detergent. I hold the phone between my shoulder and ear, and somehow I manage to pull on a pair of pants, finding five dollars in my pocket just as Dani answers. Jackpot!

"Hey, Dani!" I'm trying to sound chipper to match her energy, but it's not working. "Sam wanted me to bring the rest of the prints for that real estate agency. I should be able to get those together and be there in about an hour. Will that work?"

There's movement in my periphery, and I spin around, finding something far worse than an intruder—a mirror. I stare into it and scowl while Dani talks to me. With a scrunched-up face, I watch a deep line form between my brows. I'm a few months shy of 34, I have a face that's closer to 40, and a body that thinks it's 106. This isn't normal for my family.

After Dani says something in my ear, I remember that I'm on the phone. "Yeah, cool. I'll make sure I grab you something on the way."

Leaning in, I scrutinize the man who looks back at me in the reflection. New lines have appeared on a face I don't recognize, along with dark bags that have become ridiculous. Who the fuck am I?

The splash of cold water on my face helps wake me up before I change into a white button-down with a grey vest. I go to reach for my tie and it's not there. Shit. When I'm out shooting, I like to keep it friendly and casual when I can. It's easy to move in and isn't intimidating to camera-shy people. When I'm meeting clients, especially one like Sam, I try to step it up a bit, which should include a tie. At least, that's according to my father.

I search under clothes and in the closet, but no luck. When I check the dresser area, I uncover the large envelope that's been sitting on my desk for two months. I turn it over so I can't see the giant URGENT stamp glaring at me. God, I hate red. I tear through the room until I find a blue tie and my dad's old grey paddy cap. I give myself one last glance in the mirror. Yikes.

I need a haircut, and I haven't shaved in a few days, but there's no time for that now.

Instinctively, my hand reaches for the knob of the door to Dad's room to tell him I'm leaving. I stop, looking down at the white knuckles of the hand gripping the knob. I thought I'd finally broken myself of this habit, but evidently not. It's the smallest things I'm having the hardest time getting used to.

"Sorry, Dad. Still working on this," I mumble to the door. The silence that follows is heavy, and I'm not ready for it. I should be by now. "Wish me luck, Pops."

"Yo, man, you leavin'?" Trey calls out from the kitchen.

With no signs of any college girls with him today, I feel some relief. It's both unusual and a welcome change from the last few nights.

"Yeah, I got a meeting. The kitchen is fair game, not that there's much. Just, you know, save me a beer, okay?"

Trey was my weed dealer in high school; now, he's my budtender at the dispensary. It has its perks—like the free weed last night—but after his girlfriend kicked him out last week, he's couch-surfing. Well, less surfing since he landed on my couch. I'm too damn nice to kick him out.

It also helps the house feel less empty and cold.

"Spare key is where it always is, so just lock up when you go."

"Will do, man. I think I'm hittin' the pier today. See if I can find me a—"

"Don't bring her back here. Please?" I yell back, headed down the steps.

"Nah, it's totally cool, bro. Hopefully, I'll be in the lovin' arms of a sexy, tan babe tonight." I listen to him slurp his coffee and force myself to flash him a smile when I glance back. He's standing on my porch in just his boxers and sunglasses. "Banging on your couch is super weird anyhow. They don't seem to dig it."

Fuck. Maybe it already *is* a frat house.

I don't have time to react to Trey's comment as I hear a familiar noise while I sling my bag into the Jeep. Ding. I stand there debating with myself if that was the chime assigned to texts or the emails I've been waiting on. Fumbling a little, I pull the phone out of my pocket without spilling the coffee or dropping the keys. Miracle.

New email notification

"Oh, shit!"

I'm scared to open it in case it's about the grant I applied for when I found out the teaching position I planned on starting had fallen through. This could be it. This could be my shot to do something real and fulfilling with my life instead of sacrificing my soul to the corporate machine. I hold my breath and open the email.

> *Dear Mr. Barton,*
> *We have reviewed your qualifications and samples, which exceeded expectations for a grant like this. However, we regret to inform you…*

"No…no…shit."

> *…that while your work is impressive, we have decided to go in a different direction at this time…*

My shoulders slump, and I hold on to the roll bar to keep myself upright. I've read rejection letters from six universities, four grants, and ten art shows—all in less than three months. Rejection is a normal part of being an artist, but this is worse.

This signaled the end of everything I'd worked hard to accomplish—the end of the life I'd desperately hoped for. Who knew six months was all it took to thoroughly dismantle my life and dreams?

Who was I kidding? It wasn't six months—it was six seconds. I've just spent six months trying to fix a life that's beyond repair. I stare up at the empty window and the pain intensifies when I recognize the corner of a canvas I haven't seen in months. A canvas I could sell quickly for a few more months with a roof over my head. But it won't.

Rereading the letter, skipping the polite request to try again next year, my stomach does a few Olympic-level flips. The number of bills on my dresser is the only reason I don't head back inside and hide in my bed for the rest of the week. I toss the phone into the Jeep and pull myself into the driver's seat. I can drown myself in a bottle tonight. Right now, I need to get paid.

HOLLYWOOD

Lexi

CHAPTER 2
HONEYBEAR
YEAH YEAH YEAHS

PUSHING MY CHAIR BACK, I stretch my arms to the ceiling and feel my back cracking all the way down. If I stare at the screen anymore, I'll fall asleep. I shouldn't be this tired, but then, I also shouldn't go out on terrible dates on a work night.

The tap on my shoulder spooks me and I jump, whipping around. "SAM!" I shout, pulling one of my earbuds out.

"When you go deaf listening to music that loud, don't come see me about it. What are you working on?"

"Did you say something? I couldn't hear you." I flash him a snarky grin and a wink. "Seriously, I don't even get a noise warning on my phone; it's fine. I was in the zone cleaning up these logo files. What's up?"

He hands me a flash drive. "Everything in their files needs to be uploaded to this. Do you have time to tackle that? I'm meeting with the client tomorrow, and I really want to hand them the files and walk the fuck away. Idiots. That photographer of theirs is a no-talent hack."

The flash drive is the wrong way when I go to plug it in, so I flip it. Somehow, it's still the wrong way. Finally—on the last try—it's the right way. "100% of the time. Fuckers."

"As soon as the meeting is over tomorrow, we're firing them and I'm banning that woman from ever working for us in any capacity. I'm never doing that shit again. We have our approved photographers; they either get the work with one of them, or they go somewhere else." He checked his watch, mid-rant. Sam loves to rant, but half of what he says is bullshit. We'll take clients regardless of their photographer; we always have. "Shit, speaking of, I've got to get on with a potential client and hopefully be done with them before Barton is in with the prints for Amanda."

"Cool. Once the files are loaded, I'll shoot you a message."

"Thanks; you're a lifesaver. Now, go back to your dancing—or whatever all that flailing around was."

With my tongue sticking out, I slide the earbuds back in. I love my job. Sam hired me years ago, and I've never regretted it, or considered other jobs. He's less interested in pumping out more work as fast as we can than most businesses. Instead, he wants us to pump out the best work, no matter how long we take. Exceptions happen, but even those aren't bad. It also helps that I have a great relationship with Sam and his wife.

Once I drag the files over to the drive, I wait for the transfer to start. The timer starts at six hours, but quickly drops to slightly over fifteen minutes. Not terrible considering these files are huge. I check my watch—perfect.

While the files are saving, I grab my phone, building keys, the case to my earbuds, and my wallet—in case the mobile pay isn't working today. I'm almost at the door, but stop as someone shrieks my name from the other side of the room. Kennedy. For a split second, I consider going through the doors without acknowledging her, but she'd inevitably run and catch up anyhow. Alone time escape plan foiled once again!

"What's up, Kennedy?"

"We're going next door, right? Ugh, thank god! I'm like, so dying over here!" She's overly dramatic, and the vocal fry adds an extra edge to it. "Seriously, I'm going to fall asleep on the keyboard if I keep staring at these fucking logos. I'm also starrrrrrrving."

It's phrased as a question, but she's not really asking permission to go; she never does. Her giant purse is already on her shoulder and she's ready to go. I wonder what she'd say if I said I was going somewhere else. I don't bother testing it—more than likely, she'd still want to tag along and I'd be stuck finding somewhere else to go.

"We're getting java, Silva!" I yell out as we pass the empty desk in the lobby.

"Roger, Roger!" comes a voice, yelling from somewhere in the back. "Okay, don't worry about me!"

"Hey, did you hear about the new club that opened up a few weeks ago in WeHo?" Kennedy asks as we step outside and we're both blinded by the mid-day sun.

"Fuck, my sunglasses are at my desk." I squint and keep my head down as we're walking. "Yeah, I went already. It's fine, but I'm not sure it will last. They're overcharging, and the whole place is trying too hard to be different, but really it's just more of the same you'd see in other neighborhoods. The branding is way off-target. It's a glorified sports bar."

"What if we go there to pick up guys? Like, the best part of sports bars is the guys." she says, pushing my shoulder like it's supposed to be cute. "Let's check it out!"

"Kennedy, it's in WeHo, which means it's a fucking gay bar. Most of the guys there don't want you, *and* you're straight, so the woman are out, too."

"Lame! What if they turn it into a straight bar in WeHo?" In her mind, this is the most brilliant idea ever. My eyes roll back so hard they might pop out. I'm grateful that she changes the subject. "So, there's a party this weekend in the hills. I might go, but Michelle from accounting said Tony from sales is going. God, he's so boring. He just wants to talk about some new tech toy he bought or whatever."

"I always thought Tony was cool." He's a bit of an asshole until you get to understand his sense of humor. He's also something of a man-whore, but not an absolute dick about it. "Wait, didn't you and Tony—"

"Oh, we did, like two weeks ago in the bathroom. That's kind of why I don't want to go. Since he's, like, been calling me and stuff, wanting to hook up again. Like, the guy doesn't understand how a fling works, and now he's obsessed with me. It happens all the time!"

I'm half tempted to text Tony and see what he says, but something tells me I already know. Kennedy talks a big game and throws herself at everyone, but she's about as trustworthy as a Trump with factual details about her life. He's probably called her once—if that.

Kennedy stops by the entrance, still pretending to be engrossed in her phone, until I open the door for her. The scent of fresh coffee hits me, and I'm drooling like Pavlov's dogs. Life in Los Angeles comes with plenty of options for vices. Mine is coffee. I need coffee before I can function appropriately in the morning. If I'm offered coffee or a cocktail, I'll choose coffee in every setting but a bar. At the bar, I'll drink people under the table thanks to college life and growing up in North Carolina.

"Oh my god, why is there such a fucking liiiine," Kennedy whines, laying on the valley vocal fry extra thick and flicking her hair.

"It's not that bad. At least the lunch crowd has died down," I defend the shop and wave to Zack behind the counter. I've got a soft spot for this place since it's become something of my escape. I've spent more money and time in the corner booth in the back than I care to admit, but I enjoy the place's kawaii vibe and fun pastel colors. Besides, it's one of the few places around here built with lots of seating and plenty of outlets for the nerds.

My phone rings, and I tell Kennedy not to save my spot since the line is moving. I read the name on the screen, and I'm sure the groan is audible since several people glare at me. I answer my phone when I get to the back of the shop.

"Hello, Marc." My voice oozes sarcasm right from the start.

"Oh, Alexis! Hi! I, uhm, I thought you'd be working."

I've told him a million times not to call me that; I've never been fond of my full name. "I am working, Marcus. I took a break to get a coffee. We're allowed to do that in the twenty-first century, assuming the warden allows for it."

"Sounds, uhm, nice."

Marc isn't my type. He prefers church services and volunteering for the Boy Scouts to my bar hopping and pride rallies. He's also somehow stuck in the nineteen-fifties, even though he's in his early thirties. To appease my mother, I agreed to give him a shot, which we agreed means three dates. Total. So far, Marc and I have been on two dates. They were the worst dates I've ever been on.

"Something you need, Marcus?"

"Look, Alexis, I just…I've had a pleasant enough time with you, so please don't take this wrong or anything. I just…" He takes a breath and his next words come in a deeper, authoritative tone. *"I need to step back and sort of rethink the nature of our relationship."* I force myself to hold back the snort-laugh. Especially when he sheepishly adds, *"If that's okay with you."*

YES! I want to shout with my excitement, but I keep it all inside. My sigh of relief is loud, and I'm not even ashamed.

"Your refusal to grow spiritually and insistence on fighting conformity is too much for me. I understand that our mothers meant well, but you're...uhm..." His voice trails off. I picture him turning bright shades of red, like he does when he's put on the spot. I bet his mother is standing behind him, feeding him lines. It takes a lot for me not to laugh into the phone, considering the first date was a shitty wartime movie he picked, and the second was an open mic night for Jesus. Fun. He was less than excited about the rainbow boots I wore that night and the pin with my pronouns listed as she/her/they/them. I'm sure I'll be hearing about *that* next time I talk to my mother.

I'm a rebellious teenager stuck in a thirty-four-year-old body. At least that's what I tell myself.

"I'm what, Marcus? Exceptionally smart, fun, full of life, spirited, open-minded, and not a total tool?"

"I mean, yes. But, look, I talked to the pastor about my concerns and he—"

"You talked to Ronnie? As in my stepfather?" The air deflates from my balloon of fun.

"Pastor Ronnie, yes. I was concerned about your behavior, and I don't think it's very—"

"What did he say to you?"

"Alexis, please listen. We're just worried about your well-being, is all." He sighs into the phone so loud it sounds like a hurricane in my ear. I can feel the warmth moving up my neck and to my cheeks as he talks. *"Pastor Ronnie and I agree that I'm probably not the right man to tame you. I tried to show you more appropriate ways to handle yourself, things that won't leave a stain on your eternal soul, but I don't think you're catching on. The drinking, the tattoos, your swearing—"*

"*Tame* me? I'm not a fucking animal, Marcus." I don't miss

the irony in me growling that into the phone, but I also am having a hard time keeping my voice down.

"Alexis, you're right, and this is why I guess we should move on. God has even told Pastor Ronnie that he has someone else who will bring you to the light, not me."

"Hey, Marc. I only went on those dates because my mother asked me to in the harshest terms possible. Everyone at that congregation pities you because you're a sniveling, whiny, mama's boy with no sense of humor, no tact, and no taste. You're blander than white bread and you know I was the last available choice for your sorry ass. You want a subservient little housewife to keep locked up at home and do whatever depraved bullshit your disgusting mind comes up with. You're right. I'll never be that. But at least we don't have to waste any more time, *right*?"

"Wait, are—are you breaking up with me?"

"I'm gonna get my coffee now, Marcus. Good luck with your search for your obedient, brainless house slave."

He tries to say something about my stepfather as I hang up, but I don't care. I'm a little upset I didn't throw in a good old *Hail Satan* at the end for kicks. A temporary sense of relief floods through me, even though I'm sure this will come back at me sooner than later. It doesn't matter right now, and I'm going to live in the moment of joy. No more excuses or canceling on him to do better things like playing video games, dancing, and reading as many smutty books as possible. All the things a well behaved god-fearing girl shouldn't do, apparently.

Kennedy slides up next to me as I rejoin the line, blocking Marc's number as I do. She's twirling her hair and trying to look cute and innocent, but I know better. "Hey, uhm, so I forgot my wallet, but he said you could totally pay for me, and it wouldn't be a big deal, okay?"

I stare at the giant purse, pointedly. "Fine."

Turning on her heel, she heads to the door, waiting impatiently like I was holding up her life, not buying her fucking coffee. I text Dani the good news before it's my turn to order.

LEXI

Marc is out of the picture. Finally.

🦄D💗

OMG! Seriously? DETAILS!!

LEXI

As soon as I get back. At the Boba place.

You sure you don't want anything?

🦄D💗

Hurry! I need all the tea!

Not the literal tea...

I take a deep breath of relief as the line moves and smile at Zack, who waits for my order. Fuck calories, carbs, Marc, and Kennedy. I'm going to have an amazing day, and it will involve a sugary milk tea and a giant chocolate croissant.

HOLLYWOOD

James

CHAPTER 3
I'VE JUST SEEN A FACE

JIM STURGESS

THE RECEPTION AREA is empty when I get to Sam's office, so I take a seat and wait. Traffic was a nightmare, but what did I expect coming through Hollywood from Pasadena during awards season? I'm doing everything I can to not think about the rejection letter, which means all I'm thinking about is the rejection letter.

"Jamie!" comes a voice from down the hall. Dani runs toward me as I'm setting her coffee on the desk. It doesn't matter what time of day, Dani is always a firecracker.

She has her curly blue and purple hair pulled into her standard bun, and her bright makeup matches the crazy patterns on her clothes. I'm convinced she was single-handedly doing her best to revive retro neon fashion trends. A giant pink bubble pops as she jumps on me, wrapping me in a big hug. Even on the darkest days, Dani could be a beam of sunlight reminding me to keep my head up.

When she finally lets go, I reach into my satchel and hand her a small box wrapped with a cute pink bow. The unmistakable warm, buttery smell wafts up and makes my stomach growl. It's more than I could afford at the moment, but seeing someone else's joy—especially Dani's—is worth it.

"Ahh! Oh my god, you are the best!" She unwraps the box like it's Christmas, tossing the bow aside and pulling out the pastry. She pouts when I decline a taste before she's diving in, melting with euphoria. "Oh, holy fuck. I missed you."

"Yeah, you missed the pastries more, but who could blame you? Those things are pretty damn amazing." We'd been on a date once a few years ago and quickly realized we make much better friends than partners. We haven't seen each other much in the last few months, but she's one of those friendships that picks up right where we left off each time.

"Boo! Seriously though, how are you doing? Still going through the mopey phase?"

I shrug. "I'm pretty sure that's my standard personality, Dani. Sorry." I guess I should accept it now since brooding artist mode is very on-brand for me. "Is Sammy in?"

"He's on a call with some big client he's trying to scoop up before Strax gets their hooks in them. But it's fine. I know exactly who needs the prints." She takes my hand, pulling me toward the large double doors.

I've never been to this department before, but I've seen it from the window in Sam's office. The room is enormous, like an open warehouse with no floors above it. Four floors of offices line one side, all with large windows looking out over the pit of designers. Giant skylights soak the cubicles with California sunshine, trying hard to make it cheerful instead of corporate. Neon lights and garish colors decorate the walls along with motivational posters covered in phrases like 'The Future is Yours to Create'. It's suffocating—like a zoo for artists. Soulless artists.

All the necessary evils of making a life as a creative in the business realm—squashing any natural talent to turn people into production machines. I'm bombarded by everything I hate, which is about to become exactly what I am—a soulless artist.

I have been fighting hard against joining this kind of place, and now I'm destined to fall victim to the corporate 9-to-5 world out of necessity. I can't imagine there's much comfort in knowing these people pay their bills on time and have full refrigerators. A full-service coffee bar in the back of the room and a pool table certainly seem like perks to selling your soul. But I want to make something that matters. These people settle for making things that bring paychecks. I don't blame them or think any less of them; I just never wanted to be one of them. No one does until they have to.

"So that project is one of Lexi's. You've met her. Right? She's been with us for like ever. Cute, funky hair, kind of cheerful goth vibe to her." She turns and must recognize the blank stare on my face. Her jaw drops open, and she clutches imaginary pearls. "Seriously? Fuck, I swore you met her at a party."

"I don't really get to talk with your creatives much. Most of the time, it's Sam and I with the occasional person or two from sales joining us." I scratch the back of my neck. It's obvious what's coming next if this Lexi person is single. With any luck, she's blissfully married with ten kids. "And I haven't been out with you in a while."

"I hope she's here. You'll love her! She's one of our best and so much fun and—"

Although I try to hide the sour expression, she catches it. She knows me too well. Her shoulders sag as her face turns sympathetic before she blows another bubble.

"I still don't need a matchmaker, Dani. I'm good."

"Whatever. At least meet her before you shoot her down, big guy. She could be your soulmate, or she could be a really cool person you add to your list of cool ass people to hang out with.

Like me." She spins around and bounces toward the back. I wish I had her energy and her outlook on life.

While walking by display mockups and product samples hanging from the walls of each cubicle, I can't avoid noticing a mixture of personal touches added in for fun. The company works on everything from pet products to luxury vehicles, and Sam has a silver tongue for selling their services to anyone and everyone. How else could he afford to have ten designers on staff, a giant building in LA, and a handful of other creative types waiting by the phone for freelance work? He's smart enough to say no, where other companies brag they don't know the meaning of the word.

"Shit, that's a lot of toys. I'm guessing someone's really into pop vinyl figures," I mumble. It shouldn't surprise me when it's the cubicle Dani stops at, tossing the prints down on the desk. I already considered a thousand ways to get out of the conversation that Dani would inevitably drag me into trying to set us up. But looking around at the toys and comic book artwork, I realize I'm a little curious.

"Woah, is that—"

"A signed Captain America shield from the set? Yes, it is. Someday, ask her about it and you'll get a dissertation on superhero movies, casting, and how long it took her to save for this thing. She waited to get Chase Cooper's autograph for four hours. Four! He's not even the lead!"

"Did you not tell her you have connections, or was this before she worked here?"

"She was new! She still doesn't know, because it's weird, okay? Saying shit like 'the guy I dated one time used to be roommates with the guy you think is fucking amazing in movies' is crazy."

"Dani, you and Coop have gone out drinking together on

more than one occasion. He's your friend. You've been to his house, for fuck's sake."

"Fine, well, you luck out for now since she's not here." Dani taps her watch, and the voice of Mickey Mouse informs us the time is a few minutes past two. "Fuck. I guess she's still on break. Next time, Jamie, I am absolutely introducing you to her. She's really sweet."

"It's probably better for her that you don't." I pull my phone out and hand it to her. "I got the response about the art grant this morning."

"What? That was fast! Why don't you seem happy about it? They didn't say no *again*, did they?" She takes the phone, and another pout forms as she reads it. She looks up at me and wraps me in another hug. "I'll talk to Sam. There's got to be a couple of jobs we can throw your way soon to get you over the down season."

"Hun, when the down season lasts six months, it's time to move on. I'm okay." She doesn't look like she believes me. "The house is almost paid off and the guy who owns it is working with me to keep the price down, I have options. If I keep helping with his odd jobs around the other properties, he'll knock the rest due down even more. It's still going to take a while to get it fully paid off, but once that's done, I'm considering leaving California."

"You're going to finish fixing the house so you can buy it back, and after that, you'll leave? Where are you going?" Dani sucks in a breath, and her eyes grow wide in fear. "Not your mom's, right? You can't do that, Jamie! You're a brilliant photographer. You hit a rough patch, that's all."

"The offer isn't off the table. In fact, it's still sitting on my dresser, unopened. It doesn't matter, though. It's not like she'd welcome me with open arms or anything." I shrug and shove my hands in my pockets. "I want to try to keep the house, but I need a better job for that. Maybe I could rent it out and move somewhere cheaper. A place I can pick up more stable work."

"I really wish Sam would hire you already. I would love to stare at your face every day in the creepiest way I can. We could give you an office next to mine." She smirks. "Or put you right over here next to Lexi." Her wink looks more like she's got something in her eyes, but I laugh anyhow.

"Eh." I look around the room, and reality sets in hard. "I don't think I can do this, Dani. A few gigs are one thing, but a full-time corporate job? I'm better off finding some kind of maintenance work. If nothing else, I can paint houses."

"You're not that kind of painter, Jamie. Why don't you show your pieces again? Give it another try?"

"I'll think about it, Dani." I won't think about it. She knows that.

"Well, I hope you got that deal with the landlord dude in writing. I don't trust that guy." She digs around in her pockets and pulls out a crumpled wad of cash. "I heard your stomach growling. You have got to stop doing nice shit for other people when it means you're not taking care of yourself. Sam wants to meet with you before you go, but he'll be in this meeting for a bit longer, so swing by next door and get yourself some coffee and something to eat."

"I'm not taking your money. But yeah, I guess the morning slipped away from me."

"Whatever. Use it to get me another coffee. Now go before you start making me cry. I don't want you to leave."

"Thanks, Dani. Be back in a few."

I walk out of the office and into the blinding afternoon sun. It doesn't matter the time of year or how cold the nights get, Southern California can't decide whether it wants the day to be early summer or late summer. I roll my sleeves to my elbows and look up and down the street to spot this coffee shop. Barely three steps out of Sam's office, and my phone buzzes.

SAM

Did Dani ask you to stick around? Need to talk to you about another project.

JAMES

Yeah, I'm grabbing a coffee. Want anything.

SAM

How the hell do you people sleep when you drink that stuff this late in the day?

JAMES

You assume we sleep.

Not surprisingly, it's a boba shop. There might be more bubble tea places in LA than Starbucks. My friend Steve likes spreading the rumor that they're all fronts for some crazy mafia operation. I think he's nuts. I flip through my phone to make sure I have enough money in my bank for this. Dani was right; I'll spend $5 on a pastry for her while I have empty cupboards back home and an even emptier bank account.

I barely glance up as I walk in, trying to squeeze past some stuck-up blonde blocking the door while texting. I read my pathetic bank balance, and I find the end of the short line. I should leave; it's not like I want to be around people right now, anyhow. I glance up to check the menu to find out what I can afford, but before I can, my breath gets knocked right out of me. In front of me stands what might be the most beautiful woman I've ever seen. I've lived in the Los Angeles area my whole life, a land of plastic and high beauty standards, and this woman was outshining every one of them.

She's a few inches shorter than me, probably around five

nine, and she's wearing skinny jeans that, for once, look really damn good on someone as they hug and accentuate her soft curves. Her grey sweater hangs off one shoulder, leaving the thin strap of her tank top showing. When she turns, I spot a tiny piece of a tattoo on her pale skin peeking out from under the sweater. She wears her bubble gum pink hair in cute little space buns with some loose strands that I want to tuck behind her ears. I can't see all of her face, but it's enough.

The guy between us steps out of line to take a call, so I hurry to close the distance between myself and the angel in front of me. As I do, the sweet scent of strawberries and cherry blossoms smacks me in the face. It has to be her body spray or her shampoo. Either way, it's making my mouth water.

I'm trying hard not to stare like an absolute creeper, but I want to talk to her. I can say hello and hope that goes somewhere. Maybe I'll ask her out for coffee and to marry me. Except I remember we're already in a coffee shop, and I'd come across as an idiot. I'm not even sure she'd hear me with the air pods in.

She's playing with her phone as she bops to the music in her ears. Fuck, I have to close my eyes to stop staring at her ass as it sways. My brain is in overdrive, trying to figure out what to do. I have to say something. I can't simply let her order her tea and walk out of my life forever. You can't do that when an angel stands so close you can almost feel her. I can picture her with wings.

I glance down at my phone, but I can still see her. She has hips I want to squeeze and thighs that—Shit. I don't even remember when I last noticed a woman with thighs like hers in this town. Not those thin little things that might break if she sneezed, but natural, beautiful, thick thighs that I wanted to sink my fingers into while she…

Jesus, man. What the fuck are you doing? You need to get out of your own head right now before you become the perv your brain is turning you into. Don't be Steve!

My eyes are closed, and I almost don't realize when she steps away from me and approaches the counter. I can't tell what she orders; I only hear the music of her soft, sweet voice. My heart is thumping so loud I'm sure everyone in the shop can hear it. Worse than that, though, is how that thumping pushes all that blood south the longer I stare.

I've turned into one of *those* guys. Fuck.

Then it happens—my opportunity.

The guy behind the counter hands her a big drink and two small bags, and I can see it coming from a mile away. She's trying to hold too much and is about to drop her drink or phone. My hand shoots out on instinct, giving me only a split second to hope that if it ends up being the drink, she ordered something cold.

I'm a little relieved when I stare at the phone in my hand, black with a hot pink skull and crossbones stickers along the back. She's still cringing. At first, I'm worried she's freaked out about me having her phone, but I realize she's still waiting for the phone to hit the floor and smash to pieces. The scrunch of her face is adorable, and my heart is skipping.

"Excuse me." I didn't even recognize the softness of my voice. "I uhm, you dropped this." *Son of a bitch, is that the best you have, Barton? Idiot!*

Finally, she opens her eyes and sees me holding out her unharmed phone. She stares at me for a while, like she's trying to figure out why I have her phone and how it's still in one piece. She has the most beautiful deep brown eyes that sparkle in the shop lights, like looking into two pools of Dr. Pepper. Maybe I should cut back on the soda.

"Oh, I, oh my god, how did you catch that?"

"Reflexes are pretty good, I guess." I wasn't about to admit that I had been staring at her since I got in line. I'm not that much of a fucking moron.

"That's amazing! Like Spider-Man or some shit. Thank you so much!"

When she reaches out for the phone, her soft fingers brushing against mine, sending a jolt of electricity through me. She's captivating, and I'm not sure she even knows it. My father always told me I had the mind of an artist and a dreamer. I've always seen people for their beauty, both inside and out, and used to love showing it through my art. Watching her, I instantly visualize her beauty on canvas; this woman might be my muse. I mean, if I was ever going to get back into art.

Wait, did she call me Spider-Man?

The soft pink on her cheeks is getting darker now, and I watch the embarrassment take over. "I should, uhm, I should probably…"

"No, no, let me. It's the least I could do considering how full your arms are." I don't even remember how little money I have when I tap my phone against the reader. I barely even register the sound of the machine as it pulls the last pennies from my bank, too busy drowning in her eyes again. She can take everything I have—I won't stop her.

Neither of us has looked away yet.

In an unblinking gaze, our eyes linger until I eventually give up and lower my gaze to her full lips and shy smile. In a rom-com, this is where we'd kiss, and a year from now we'd come back and get married right here in this boba shop. I've never wanted someone as badly as I want this woman, and I don't even know her name. This is LA; she could be a tourist, and I may never see her again if I don't do something.

But she doesn't look like a tourist. I wonder if she works nearby.

"Alexis!" The screech from across the cafe pulls us back to the harsh reality of the busy shop around us. It's the blonde, who is *still* blocking the door and texting. I hate her so much right now. "Are you coming or what?"

The quintessential valley girl has given me something, though. *Alexis*. I couldn't have picked a more perfect name.

"Hey, uhm, so thanks for the coffee. Oh, and for catching my phone." She walks backward toward the exit, biting her lip nervously and trying to fight the smile. "I really appreciate not having to order a new one. I really need to be more careful."

"No problem. Just your friendly neighborhood Spider-Man."

Her giggle is ethereal, and I feel the pull of my half-smile on my mouth. These are the moments when I wish I had any game at all. I've become entirely dumbfounded and unaware I'm still in line as I watch the sun hit her hair when she opens the door and disappears. She's gone, and my heart sinks as someone clears their throat.

"Uhm, so are you going to order something or what?" The kid behind the counter is glaring at me, bored and unimpressed. I'd forgotten other people existed.

"Shit, yeah, yes. I'll just, uhm, coffee. Do you have just coffee?" He rolls his eyes, judging me. I must be some kind of brand-new alien who'd never been in a boba shop before. This is why I don't leave the house. "Just give me the biggest, cheapest thing you have with caffeine." I glance at his nametag. "Okay, Zack?"

I use my emergency-only credit card to pay because this is essentially an emergency. Then, an idea pops into my head. As he hands me a large coffee, I blurt out, "Hey, does she come in here often?"

"The one whose pants you were trying to get into, Mr. Good Reflexes?"

I close my eyes and force a smile. Smug motherfucker, but I had earned that, hadn't I. "You know what, never mind. Sorry." I pull the wrinkled bills Dani forced me to take from my pocket and stuff them into the tip jar. Broke, enamored, and embarrassed, I leave as quickly as possible.

HOLLYWOOD

Lexi

CHAPTER 4
HEADS WILL ROLL

YEAH YEAH YEAHS

I DON'T STOP. I rush back to the office, even though Kennedy complains the entire way that I'm going too fast and her feet hurt.

Blue—such a pretty blue. It's not like the sky or a baby blue, but steel, almost grey. Sad.

"Oh, man!" Dani yells out as I barge through the door. "Lex Luthor, you have the absolute worst timing, I swear!" Our receptionist announces the obvious as I stumble back into the office. She sees me juggling things and runs around the desk to help while eyeing the utterly clueless Kennedy as she parades in.

"Shit, did I miss something? Did Sam need something?" I check my watch. The download should still have another few minutes, so it shouldn't be that.

"No. The guy I've been trying to hook you up with for fucking months was here." She takes a few things until I can get a better grip. "Tall, handsome, great ass—ringing any bells?"

I roll my eyes and ignore her, hooking the keys around my finger and adjusting my grip on…life.

"He said he was coming back. Please let me introduce you to him," she begs, batting her eyes like that will win me over somehow. "Oh, and I left those new prints by your desk. Sam's been waiting on them, but that's way less important."

"Sam's waiting on them, and that's less important than you getting me to meet some dude? Silva, your priorities are fucked."

"Uhh, yeah!"

"What dude?" Kennedy asks, not looking up from whatever she's posting online.

Dani has been determined to find me someone to date. I told her a million times that I wasn't interested and didn't have the time. I've dated a little on and off since moving here fifteen years ago, but nothing ever lasted past a few dates. I've resorted to quick and easy hookups through apps, but that's rarely ever worth it or satisfying. The people here are far too shallow or next-level creepy; there's no in-between that I've found. Sometimes, I wonder if I even fit into the Los Angeles scene. I still go out for the pointless one-night stand occasionally, and I have a drawer full of electric boyfriends who don't complain and do a far better job than any real man.

Besides, real guys eventually learn who I am. When they find out I'm the stepdaughter of the preacher for one of the largest evangelical churches in Southern California, shit always goes downhill. Either they're super turned off by who I am because it must make me a prude—or, worse—they're super turned on by the idea of fucking me in the church. Some even assume I'm rich.

I've never understood the whole religious lifestyle, it's never fit who I am. When I need to, I can pretend—for my mother's sake. Also, their church is modern, so there's no altar or confessional to get kinky and defile. I wouldn't necessarily say no to a little fun in the church for the right person. Maybe I've read too many fanfics.

I don't even know if evangelicals do the whole confessional

thing, and you lose a little bit of the dirty, kinky, fun side of things when it's just a stage with a podium.

"So can I?" Dani's voice pulls me out of my inner ramblings.

"What?"

"Can I introduce you to him? Come on, he's really cute. You sure you're okay?"

"She's busy daydreaming about the guy who was drooling all over her; we'll need a bucket and a mop if they ever meet again," Kennedy cracked. "Actually, I may go back there because I would climb that man like a fucking tree."

"Kennedy, there aren't many men in Los Angeles you wouldn't climb," I hit back.

"Rude. I have limits!"

"Yeah, but have you actually found any of them yet?" Dani cackles at her joke so hard she flops back down into her chair. "So, tell me about this mystery man!"

I nod toward the pretty box with the bow on her desk, still trying to ignore her. "Please tell me it's not your birthday, and I forgot, and if it is, take this cookie as a down payment on a real birthday present. Actually, take it either way since it's for you."

"Not my birthday, but yes, please!" She snags the bag with the cookie and holds up the pastry box. "This is what I'm trying to set you up with, girl!"

"An empty pastry box?"

"No, the delicious man who delivers the hot pastries! Wait… you know what I mean!"

"So he's an Uber Eats driver? Less hot," Kennedy deadpans.

"He's not an Uber Eats driver, you moron. He still brings me delicious pastries when he comes by, and we're just friends." She dramatically clutches the box to her chest. "Like, what would he do for someone he was banging? He probably eats pu—"

"I don't want a guy who buys gifts for *you*," Kennedy points out as she sips her iced coffee. "Wait, is he rich? I could make an exception."

"Shut up, Kennedy." Dani rolls her eyes, then cackles again. "Shit! In thirty seconds, we found two boundaries you actually do have!"

"Whatever. I don't know why you're wasting your time trying to hook her up." Kennedy flips her hair annoyingly. "Don't you, like, have to marry Jesus or some guy your mom picks out for you or something?"

"I...what? What the fuck does that even mean?" I ask, shaking my head. Seriously, I need this girl to cut way down on the caffeine. She found some flyers I made for my mother on the copy machine a week ago and hasn't let it go since.

"Wait, does all this mean you're a virgin or, like, you were born again or something? I thought you made out with that guy at that party?"

"Kennedy, how are you actually this dumb?" Dani asks as I continue to stare, dumbfounded by the stupidity.

"Although I saw your stepdad on TV the other day. More like step*Daddy*! Right?" She makes a terrible growling noise and moves her hand to mimic a big cat's paw. "There's another man I'd climb like a tree."

"Inappropriate, Kennedy!" Dani balls up a piece of paper and throws it at her. "To be fair, even Jesus would approve of the photographer you desperately need to meet."

"Too late. She's got the guy in the coffee shop now."

"KENNEDY! I'm seriously going to throw a stapler at you next! Wait, what guy in the coffee shop?"

"Whatever. Look, if Lexi doesn't want to be dicked down by the hot Uber pastry guy, pass him my way."

I'm saved from the stupidity when Kennedy's phone dings. I

finally say, "I'm going back to work. This is giving me a headache."

"Hey," Kennedy stops me, reading her text. "The guy at CyberSales wants to know if we're coming to the industry mixer tonight. Do you guys want to go? There's free booze until eleven and food."

"Is that the one at the new brewery?" Dani asked, grabbing her phone to look. "Oh, it is; come on, Lex, you can fucking WALK there from your place. I could crash after, and we can watch those stupid movies you love."

"I'll think about it. Which actually means I'll think about a way to get out of my prior commitment." I used my butt to push open the door to the creative department, trying to run away from this conversation. "It's a solid maybe, okay?"

"Come on! It's a work function and you can be out by like eight. You need a few drinks to deal with your mom, anyway." I wave, wishing the door would close just a little faster. She knows about my life outside of work and how crazy my family is. "What does Jesus need on a Thursday night from a hot single chick living in the middle of Los Angeles's art district?" She yells as the door creeps to a close. "I'll be at your place at five!"

I stop just inside the door and take a moment to soak in the blessed silence. It's been a long week, and I just want it to be over. I take a few deep, calming breaths and head to my cubicle, dumping my stuff onto my desk while not spilling my coffee.

Kennedy clamors in behind me and bee-lines it to the new guy's desk. Her fake giggle grates on my last remaining nerve, and I'm sure I hear her invite him out to the mixer. Good, maybe there will be enough guys to keep her company, so she leaves us alone. With any luck, the guy Dani wants to set me up with will get sucked into the Kennedy vortex and leave Dani and I to do all the drinking and dancing we can.

I slide into my chair, enter my password, and open up a file I'd been working on all morning.

I'm playing around with color variations when my mind drifts back to the coffee shop and how weird the timing of all that was. One minute, I'm breaking up with Marc the Narc, and then I'm looking into the prettiest steel-blue eyes I've ever seen. I snicker and shake my head. I don't know why I'm bothering to daydream about him. I'll never see him again, and I don't have time for that right now. Kennedy can try her shot with him if she wants to go hunt him down.

Sometimes, I wish I *did* have time for things like meaningful relationships. My dating life has been one train wreck after another. I doubt I could land anyone who looked like that guy, and if I did, he'd be a dick. Those soft, sad eyes and a pretty smile, though. Maybe I should have given him my number. He's probably married with three kids and cheats on his wife. Besides, even if he is single and interested, it would lead to heartbreak and sadness—especially once he met my family. Daydreaming is fun, though.

"Oh good, you're back!" Sam yells out as he jogs down the stairs. He's a health nut, and even though his office and the meeting rooms are four flights up, he insists on jogging up and down the stairs whenever he needs to talk to us. Some days, I wonder if he knows how the speakerphones work.

"Yeah, went to my dealer next door," I say without looking away from my screen. I hold up the flash drive for him, and he laughs as he sits on the edge of my desk. "Dani left the prints here. Is that a new project I'm taking on or just because my desk is the first one you hit?" I point him to the large envelope sitting beside him.

"Awesome. Let me see what we're working with." He rips

open the envelope as I continue to work. "I'll be putting you on this job since it's a higher priority."

"Do you want me to stay on the branding for the weed company at the same time? No big deal either way."

"We'll put the cannabis company on the back burner for right now; the owner's still deciding on the name. I'll update that in the system tomorrow."

He flips through the prints, stopping on a few to give them a little extra attention, then sticks a business card to the edge of my monitor. *Barton Photography*. Boring name, but it's to the point—terrible logo, though.

"Should have used Silian Rail."

"Huh?"

"Nothing, a movie quote for super nerds."

"Another papyrus joke I don't understand? I don't think you've worked with much of Barton's stuff yet; he's good and a good guy. The website and password to download the shots and anything he didn't print off are on that card. Keep it with you in case you work offsite."

"Yeah, 'cause I do that all the time. I'll put those on the client database." I turn back to the computer and then look back at Sam. "What about the tasks already on my radar?"

"I might hand your open tasks off to Kennedy to close out, at least the ones where the design is approved. The rest will go to the new guy to give him a turn in your crazy layouts." He turns and looks across the room at where Kennedy is continuing her flirty giggle that could peel paint off the walls. Sam rolls his eyes so hard that his hat nearly falls off.

"Kennedy, do you have that presentation done yet? Because if you don't, I'd appreciate it if you take your social life off-hours and stop scaring the new guy."

"God! I'm just trying to make him feel welcome!"

"And I'm just trying to run a business, not a dating site."

I cover my mouth to hide the giggle as I watch Kennedy stalk back to her desk. This is why I love Sam. He's cool enough to let us get away with a lot, and if one person is ruining it, he doesn't let it affect how he treats the rest of the team. He's right on the cusp of sixty, so it's a surprising mentality. Then again, he grew up around the Los Angeles art scene.

"So, what *is* the new project?" I ask, taking another drink and tucking the business card into my desk drawer.

"We're creating a multi-part presentation and trade show graphics for an event they're hosting next month and a bigger conference in three months. After that, they want a boatload of other work, assuming they like your work."

"Our work."

"Speaking of, the first one is a tight turnaround, and I know you're going to hate this, but you can't fly solo on this one." He holds up his hands. "Don't worry, the help isn't for the graphics. There's a lot of information, and they have a thicker brand guidebook than a phone book. They're also firmly against using stock photography." He stops, narrowing his eyes at me through his round lenses. "Do you even know what a phone book is?"

"Jesus, Sam. I'm not Kennedy-young. I know what a phone book is and how to use one. They're for boosting kids up in their seats, right?"

"Ha. Ha. I forgot you're older than you look. No offense." He checks his watch and then taps out a quick message on his phone. "Okay, meet us upstairs in the big conference room in five. The freelancer is here, and I want to review assignments, timelines, and expectations. That way, if either of you needs more help, we're ahead of it."

He hops off the desk, envelope under his arm, and looks at my screen.

"That's a really nice color for that logo. I wouldn't have thought to go that way with the blue-grey, but I think they'll love it."

"Yeah, thanks." I stare at my screen. I hadn't even been paying attention when I picked this color earlier, but I could see exactly where my head was when I did. "It, uhm, came to me at the coffee shop earlier. Total surprise."

I wait for Sam to leave before I let out a long breath and drop my head to the desk. Overtime and working with a freelancer. Great. This is going to suck.

I'm already getting enough heat from my mother about how little time I spend with her. She keeps pressuring me to come to services and begging me to meet the *nice boys* she thinks would help me become a better woman. Not. Happening. Her version of a better woman would make a Stepford Wife seem inadequate.

There's some big conference of crazies coming up soon, and my stepfather wants to make a 'tremendous impression'. He's an asshole, but he's not dumb, and he understands that marketing is what brings the money in. It was supposed to be a few handouts and a poster, but now it's snowballed into a second job. Unpaid at that.

I know I'm juggling too much and putting too much pressure on myself, but I like to keep people happy.

"Oh well, goodbye to my meager social life. My liver will probably thank me for that," I mumble. Then I get a message from Dani. I don't bother to open it because it's just her telling me to go to the party tonight.

I've already decided I'm going, no matter what my mother or anyone else says. Now, I just need an excuse.

I take another deep breath, plaster on my happy, smiling face, grab my stuff, and head up to the conference room.

HOLLYWOOD

James

CHAPTER 5
TEAR IN MY HEART
TWENTY ONE PILOTS

I TEXT Sam that I'm on my way back to the office.

Sam is one of those rare clients who doesn't make me anxious when I meet with him. He won't lowball me or change the pricing at the last minute, which is why I come in when he asks.

It also doesn't hurt that he and my dad worked together a few times, and Sam has always treated me well for the ten years I've been freelancing with him. He's my most reliable client. He's also the only client who genuinely gives a shit about the talent he employs. He's become more of a friend than I'd ever expected.

I'm still nervous because I have to ask him for more money. He's generous and is one of the few businesspeople who understands paying your people what they're worth, and it's never been a problem before. He won't question it, which makes me feel more guilty about asking. The last gig was a pretty fair price, but since I didn't get the grant, I'll be short. My mind wanders to my dresser back home and the pile of bills with their red stamps. I'm reminded of the large envelope mixed in with them that could probably solve most of my financial issues—or make them worse.

"Oh good, you're back. Come meet that designer I want you to—" Dani starts the second I pull the door open and step inside.

"Woah! Down girl. I've got to meet with Sam first, and by the time I'm done with that, I'll find some other excuse to not ruin her life and meet her. Besides," I make sure none of the sales guys are within hearing range, "I may or may not be busy sitting in that cafe next door for the next week."

"The cafe? The food's good, but what are you talking about?" I should recognize the tone of her voice. It's the one she always uses when she's trying to be shady. But I'm too distracted. She holds up her hand before I can answer and leans in close to say, "James Barton, is that…a smile?"

The heat rising in my face sends my heart racing again. I'm biting my bottom lip, realizing how much I'd forgotten this feeling. How much I missed this sensation. Hope. Attraction. Fuck it—love.

"Dani, I've just seen the most beautiful woman on the planet, and I have this absolutely stupid idea that if I wait there for her, she'll walk in the door again." I shake my head, laughing. *Laughing*! "I have to wait there and drink a lot of tea and eventually hope that I'll be rewarded with the sun hitting that dreamlike cotton candy pink hair that's set my soul on fire."

"See, this is why I love dating artists. Every woman is the woman of your dreams and gets you to say stupidly poetic shit." She shakes her head and stops. "You know, I should totally keep an eye out for her. You said she was at the coffee shop? And she has pink hair?"

"Yeah, and she called me Spider-Man, which sounds dumb, but only a nerdy person does that and—" I stop myself and snicker. My choice of words and what I'm planning makes me seem like an idiot. "Who am I kidding? I'm surprised someone like her even gave me the time of day. I mean, she didn't, yeah… never mind. Not important. I'm going to meet with Sam."

"Wait!" I finally notice that she's up to something; I can tell by her grin. "Jamie, you know how you owe me that favor? Well, I'm calling it in. Come out tonight. Some people are going to this little mixer they're having in the arts district. Nothing big, I just, uhm, need a not-date."

"Tonight? Why? Please tell me it's not the woman from the spa you met months ago. If it's her, I'm…busy."

"Don't you dare act like you have plans beyond going home, turning on a movie, ignoring your art, and jerking off to free porn on your neighbor's internet. Do not leave me hanging, James 'JimJam' Barton."

"Ouch. Only Coop gets to call me that." I pretend that I'm hurt, putting a hand on my chest and spinning on my heel dramatically as I back away. "Besides, I don't need free porn tonight." I spread my arms out wide, spinning in a circle as I yell back, "I have the cafe goddess of my dreams who will probably never say anything beyond 'thank you' to me. That's all I need!"

"Gross, Barton!"

I'm not completely jaded. I could stalk the cafe for a month and I'd never go beyond admiring her from a distance. I'll never again work up the nerve to approach her. I'll have a million excuses lined up before she walked in the door. With my luck, she'd walk in on the arm of some buff movie actor boyfriend. Fuck, she's probably already dating Chase Cooper somehow.

"So that's yes?"

I walk back over to her desk, pretending I'll turn her down and knowing I likely won't. "Possibly. Let me see how this meeting with Sam goes and if I can somehow avoid telling you her name."

"You have her name?! What is it, you fucker?" She leans over her desk, trying to grab for my tie, but there's not enough showing and I dodge her.

"And that's why I wear a vest. To thwart your grabby hands."

She huffs at first, but it's followed by a cackle of a laugh. "You and your poetic bullshit. I promise it will be worth your time tonight. Meet me there; I'll text you the address. We'll talk about your boba girl."

"She's so much more than a boba girl, Dani. She's my muse." I stop, cognizant of the idiotic grin on my face. "My damn fingers are itching for my sketchpad. It's been a long time since I've wanted to make something, but now? I can't shake it!"

"This is why I told you to carry that thing with you. You're a terrible artist, dude."

"Hey! I left it in the damn Jeep. I didn't think I'd need it for a drop off." I check my watch. "Shit, I really need to get back there before Sam hires someone else."

"Sam wouldn't do that to you, dummy." She rests her hand on my arm and gives it a gentle squeeze. I love Dani, and in another life, we could have been fun together—under extremely different circumstances. But our friendship is still pretty special. She's like a sister to me now. An annoying, nosey, matchmaking sister.

"Grasp the opportunity, Jamie! You really should ask him about a full-time spot. I get that you're worried about the design programs, but he wouldn't hire you for that. Plus, we have all these great people here who would absolutely help you if you wanted to learn them."

"Yeah, I'll think about it, Dani." I lean in and give her a quick peck on the cheek.

"Barton code for not going to happen. What about tonight?"

I back away toward the elevators, "Can't really go out drinking if I'm broke."

"Free drinks till eleven! It's a creative mixer, so plenty of people to help you find more work." She leans around the corner and shouts, "Plus, Sam is extending your contract, you idiot! So you better come out and live a little, loser!"

"Thanks, jerk!" I disappear around the corner with a wave before she can yell anything else.

"Jamie, you good, man?"

"Huh?" I glance up from the check in my hand. I wish I knew how he did that. Considering I never got the chance to ask for more money. It's like he knows, and I'm now sure he has my house bugged.

"I asked if you had any issues with the list of shots they wanted to get. I'm well aware it's a bit scattered, but this is LA, baby, and it's the right time of year. A few hours in either direction and we can go from sunsets on the beach to snowboarding. Right?"

"Oh, yeah." I stare down at the piece of paper in my hand. Beach Daytime, Beach Early Morning, Aquarium, Wild Marine Life, Mountains Distance, Mountain Road, Rivers, City Life Daytime… the list continued on and on. Stock photography sites would have plenty of these images, but they want original. So, who am I to argue? "I, uhm, I might need to travel overnight for a couple of these so I can get to multiple locations in one day."

"No worries, we've got that covered. You can book the hotels in advance, have Dani book them, or you can always invoice me after." Sam laughed. "Don't forget to make sure you book two rooms. I want Lex to go on some of these trips with you to get a solid appreciation for these places. I'm looking to make these mood boards more than pictures on a wall for this, and she's got a great eye for interactive elements. It's got to look better than a google search, more authentic."

My brain has done about fifteen record scratches DJs do. *Did*? I'm not sure that's even a thing they do anymore. Outside of a wedding or two, I try to avoid places with DJs.

Sam expects me to work with someone? Shit.

"Fantastic."

Sam goes over numbers with me; I'm not listening, already lost. Sam has become accustomed to me phasing out during the budget discussions. I'm not a numbers guy, and I'm not a negotiator. It's why I'm a terrible freelancer and can't make ends meet. A job I should charge two grand on will lowball me at five hundred, and I'll shake their hand and fucking thank them for it. It wasn't always like this, but working a job to make ends meet as an artist takes a toll. Like most things in my life lately, I've given up the fight.

"I'm taking you out for dinner and drinks after work today, buddy. You look like you're about to pass out."

I shake the thoughts out of my head. "I'm sorry, Sam. It was a rough night. Too many thoughts and not enough brain cells."

"Out partying with Coop?"

"Nah, he's off somewhere. Toronto, I think he said."

"Tell him to bring that new dog of his by sometime. She looks sweet as hell. I heard his brother got called up to the pros."

"Backup goalie for Pasadena, yeah. Want me to get you some tickets?"

"Absofuckinglutely. No shitty seats, either. I should get a box." He leans forward on his giant desk, folding his hands as his face turns serious. It makes me nervous. "Hey, I heard about the grant falling through. I'll get a feel for who has jobs coming up. If I can pull some strings and get you a few more gigs once this one is over, I'm sure it would help. Shit has been rough for you lately, but hang in there, and if you ever need someone to talk to, I'm here, man."

"Thanks, Sam."

He means it, even if I never take him up on it. Hell, I won't even ask him to hire me full time, even though I'm sure he'd take me in a heartbeat. He shuffles through a desk drawer, pulls out a card, and hands it to me.

A therapist. Fantastic. Sam covers insurance for his freelancers, so he's not leaving me with a lot of excuses to get out of this.

"He's really good. Went to school with my wife before he took off for Paris for a while. If you don't want to talk to me, try talking to him. I'll cover the cost."

"Sam, you don't have—"

"I have the resources to care for my people, so don't argue with me. Anyhow, don't worry about how you get nervous around new folks. I think you'll get along wonderfully with Lex. She's weird as hell sometimes, and I can't figure her out, but she's excellent. You two will have fun making this money."

Dani must have made me paranoid. If I didn't know Sammy well, I'd be concerned about his motives—is this meant to be a date or a project? Neither would surprise me, especially with Dani involved. I wonder if they're in on this together and it's some elaborate—

"—It would be nice if you were doing that again. At least a little more than you have been, anyhow."

Shit. I phased out again. "Wait, doing what?"

"That's exactly what I mean. You're way too damn stressed. You're gonna burn yourself out like this, kid. When was the last time you hit the town and enjoyed yourself? It's Hollywood, baby!" I laugh, but Sam's not kidding. "Jamie, you gotta live a little. You don't even come out to Dani's gigs anymore, and you used to be a regular. You're too young and talented to lock yourself away like this. Enjoy life again, man."

"It's got to give me something to enjoy first." It's possible it already has. I stand up with Sam and gather up my stuff. "Don't worry, I won't scare her away with the brooding artist routine."

"What? I thought women were all about that whole moody, starving artist scene?" He claps me on the back while he throws his head back, laughing. "Come on, let's introduce you to my little vampire. When you said you might be busy, I was going to stick her with Lorenzo. She probably would have chewed his ass up and spit him out."

I smile, holding in the anxiety running through my veins. I can do this. Meet this Lexi person, go back to the coffee shop, and become a part-time creeper. Perfect. There's the potential that I'll find her again and realize she's a daydream and nothing more. Or worse, she's got the personality of a rock.

Sam's talking about money again as he holds the door open, and when I finally regain my focus, my heart stops. Across the table, working on her laptop, is my coffee queen. She's still beautiful. The ethereal wonder that came and went before my eyes. But now she's here. In Sam's office.

Wait. In Sam's office?

Lexi.

Alexis.

Sam mentioned her name earlier, even before this project. Dani said her name earlier when I dropped off the prints. I'm a fucking idiot. I try to check with Sam. Maybe this is a joke; I even blink a few times to make sure it's not all in my head. But there she sits, the woman who lit a match to the dying embers of my soul.

Of course, this also means I have to talk to her. Words less moronic than 'you dropped this' and 'you're the most beautiful woman I've ever met, please run away with me' are now necessary—this plan is failing already.

This could be the best or absolute worst three months of my life. Based on my current track record, there's a depressingly high chance it won't end up as the former.

This is a disaster. This is terrible. I'm about to be working with her! She can't be the woman of my dreams and my co-worker. Shit. Dani planned this whole thing somehow. That's what she was hiding when I mentioned the pink hair and the coffee shop. We inevitably had to cross paths. I fell into her trap without her doing anything beyond mentioning that I was hungry. Is that why Dani invited me out tonight? I can't go to the mixer! Lexi might think I'm a loser!

I am a loser.

Dani's devious little plot was brilliant—likely exceeding her own expectations. Especially when I waltzed in like a love-struck Shakespearian Romeo going on and on about his Rosaline. If Rosaline looked like Lexi, there's no fucking way I'd give Juliette a second glance.

I'm so fucked.

"Okay, have a seat, Jamie..."

I shake my head back to reality and sit down in the nearest chair I can find, which is hard to do when I still can't really take my eyes off her. Of course, I nearly drop all my stuff, solidifying my place in Lexi's mind as an idiot.

Don't say I love you. Don't say I love you. Don't say I love you. Don't say I love you.

"...and we'll have a card setup..." Sam is talking, and I'm catching every few words and nodding like a bobblehead doll.

FOCUS!

She's married…shit, no ring. She's absolutely got a boyfriend. Girlfriend? Both? She smells like fresh strawberries in the summer.

Her sweater slides off her shoulder again, and I follow her clavicle, letting my gaze drift lower. Realizing what I'm doing, I screw my eyes shut as my cock strains against my pants. I grab my bag, desperate to find anything I can use to distract myself.

"I've already told Jamie about the hotel rooms. I want you to experience the vibes of the places and really let this stuff get into your soul."

"I'll still need to work around my other schedule for the time being."

"Absolutely. Jamie?" My head snaps to Sam's voice. "Make sure you double-check on dates before you book anything. Lexi has some side hustles you'll need to work around."

"Side hustle implies I'm making money from it, Sam," she shoots back. "More like a side headache."

I nod to Sam and try hard to remember what he's said. I lose every word when I catch a glance of Lexi in my periphery, sliding on a pair of black-rimmed glasses. Kill me now—my nerdy little muse.

"So you two will be the team." Sam's voice brings me back to reality yet again.

"Go, team," the sarcasm is unmistakable, and it makes my heart sink a little. "Okay, so we've got the schedule, paperwork, releases…"

My heart is racing. Her voice is soft but with an edge to it that would sound utterly perfect as she says my name—screams my name. Those perfect glossy lips—I can't help but picture them wrapped around my—STOP! The pencil in my hand snaps and they both turn their attention to me.

"You good, Jamie? Seriously, man, you need to relax. I should give you a card for a masseuse instead of thera—"

"I'm good!" I cut him off before he can say it. "It was an old pencil and I'm eager to get to work." It takes everything in my face to keep me from cringing at what I said, wishing I could take it back.

"Okay," Sam draws out every letter. "Cool. How about we get out of here? I'll take you both out for an early dinner as a thank you because you'll be working some overtime for this one. And because I'm hungry."

"No can do, Sam. I've got a hot date," she says, and my heart crumbles to pieces. "With your receptionist."

But his receptionist is…Dani?

"That industry mixer?"

Oh. That kind of date.

"Yep. I'll get you a stack of business cards to add to your dragon's hoard."

"You should go to the mixer, too, Barton. Work out some of that stress on the dance floor. If you're lucky, pick up some new clients or a date while you're at it." He playfully elbows Lexi. "Both of you."

That should embarrass me, but I'm way too excited because I'm already going to that fucking mixer. So, I watch the soft pink dusting of a blush spread across her cheeks, highlighting the constellation of tiny freckles that decorate her nose and under her eyes. I want to count them, but I keep getting distracted by those eyes. The sun turns her eyes into glasses of whiskey I could stare into for days on end. In fact, I'll never again look at a glass of whiskey and not think of her. The soft light diffused by the windows catches the honey-gold flecks.

"Huh? Oh, yeah. I, uhm, I don't know if I can make it out tonight, but thanks, Sam."

"Alright, what do you say to tacos and beer before the mixer? Come on! I'm starving, and I'm paying."

"I uhm…yeah. Sure, Sam, but I can't stay long."

"Yeah, whatever. Not my fault you live in Pasadena. Like I said, go to the mixer."

I glance down at the photo list again, and it's transformed into something so much more now. It's an open invitation to, at the very least, get to know her. The things Sam talked about earlier come flooding back into my very horny brain. Hotels. Overnight travel. Working late. Diners. For the first time in a long time, I'm happy about what the future is bringing and every second I'm about to spend with her—even if it goes nowhere.

HOLLYWOOD

Lexi

CHAPTER 6
SOME NIGHTS

FUN.

I'M the first one in the conference room and listen to the sound of Sam talking to someone in his office. So I set up my laptop, make sure my pen has ink, and turn on my tablet. Sam teased me about being over-prepared when I started working here. He called me the Doomsday Meeting Prepper for a while. I usually stick with the boring *'better to be prepared'* response, but I've always been this way. Now, Sam comes to me after meetings to get copies of my notes. I'm just thorough, I guess.

While I wait, I think about the mixer tonight, debating internally if I should go. I kind of owe Dani anyhow since I've been turning her down for months and still have only ever made it to one of her shows. She's my best friend, which also means she forgives me and understands how fucked my life has been lately. I slide my phone out and shoot her a quick message saying I'll go, but reminding her she needs to come over early and help me pick out something to wear.

"Alright, let me introduce you to the lead designer." Sam's voice is just outside the conference room. I shift to get a better look, but I only see cuffed sleeves and part of an arm with a tattoo. Tentacles, I think. "You rarely work directly with the designers, but this is a special case. I've already told her that overtime is very much on the table. You're not on the actual payroll, and it isn't in our contract, but I'm still going to offer you the same deal, so anything over our regular hours gets higher pay, okay?"

"Thanks, Sammy. I appreciate that."

The voice sounds familiar, but I can't place it, which isn't that surprising since Sam's Rolodex contains around twenty freelancers for various positions. *Rolodex,* I giggle at myself for even knowing that word. It's likely that Sam doesn't think I know what a Rolodex is. Someday, I'm going to buy him an old card catalog cabinet and watch his head explode.

Okay, I'm laughing at jokes that make me seem old. My own jokes. I'm glad I'm going out tonight. I wonder for a moment if she'll try to set me up with the guy from the art show a few weeks ago. I hope he's not going.

The door opens, and I almost fall out of my chair as my phone-catching boba guy walks in the door behind Sam. It wasn't my imagination earlier; he's still drop-dead gorgeous. He stops as soon as he sees me and stares. The slightest hint of a smile forms at the corner of his mouth, which somehow triggers my entire face to heat up.

What the fuck is the boba guy doing here? Did he follow me? Did Kennedy do this as a joke? To fuck with me? How many years will I get for murdering her and is it worth it?

I smile back hurriedly and duck into my computer. His eyes are too damn pretty.

"Alright, Lexi, this is James Barton. Jamie, this is my top designer, Lexi Strauss."

My brain finally catches up with the rest of the world, putting the clues together. Sam doesn't just have photographers drop off prints unless he needs to see them in person. To him, that would be a waste of time, and hates that. Dani had already told me the photographer was around, waiting for Sam. Boba guy is the photographer. Boba guy is Dani's pastry hook-up.

Oh. Fuck. I'm like a character in an old crime drama. I'm waiting for the detective to lay the evidence out nice and slow for the morons to understand. I'm the moron!

"You two will be working together for the next few weeks at least, more if we land the gig. So long as you're still interested when that happens, Jamie."

"Uhm, yeah." We emerge from our stupor around the same time, and he finally looks away.

"We've kind of met," I say, giving him only the slightest smile before looking back down at my computer. "At the coffee shop next door."

"So you two have met already? Perfect!" Sam stops as he pulls a chair out for himself. "Have a seat, Jamie. There's a coffee shop next door?"

Jamie drops hard into the seat in front of him like this is a twisted game of musical chairs. I'm still staring at my laptop, waiting for an escape hatch to open up so I can disappear through it.

"Yeah." His voice is both gravelly and airy simultaneously, and it's mesmerizing how he does that. I also can't figure out why my heart is slamming against my rib cage like a salsa beat. "She, uhm, we—It's not really…"

"It's the coffee shop I've been going to for a year now, Sam. I bring you cupcakes from there all the time to tempt you to the sugar-filled dark side," I say as I finally find my voice. Thankful that it's kept its sharp, snarky edge. I hold up the cup with the logo facing him, shaking it until recognition dawns on him.

"Right, your dealer."

Sam is smart, but Sam is also too busy for mundane details

like another coffee shop in L.A. I've always seen some irony in a man who is too busy for insignificant details around him opening a marketing firm. Those little details are the keys to successful design. But that's why I'm here.

I'm not sure if it's bold or stupid, but I flick my eyes toward the new guy. Sure enough, he's staring right at me; our eyes lock, and my brain empties. I can feel it just oozing right out of my ears as my spine turns to sponge and I melt into a puddle under the table. I just hope my mouth stays shut and I don't ramble like an idiot.

Wait. Shit. I told a complete stranger, who can't keep his eyes off me, that I go to a specific coffee shop every day. This is how people get unalived! *Shit. Shit. Shit.* What if this pastry-loving photographer is some kind of creeper? What if he's the next Buffalo Bill, feeding people delicious treats so he can slice off their skin and make a dress out of it? I can picture my story being used by my two favorite podcasters as they tell listeners that this is absolutely not how you stay sexy and don't get unalived!

I hope they don't interview my mother. I should warn Dani about the news crews. I make a mental note to find another nearby coffee shop with boba. That really shouldn't be difficult in Los Angeles. I also make another mental note to lay off the true crime podcasts for a few days.

Sam kicks off the meeting, and for the next hour, he introduces us to the client who will run our lives over the next few weeks—potentially months. This job will be bigger than any of our usual clients. Which has me wondering if Sam is taking on more than we can handle. He could sell you your own house, but he doesn't have a grasp on the inner workings and intricacies of design.

While he keeps explaining and laying out the deliverables

and dates, the reality that I am undertaking this task with someone else settles in. I have flashbacks to school projects and past jobs.

What if tall, sad, and handsome is one of *those* people? I had spent the better part of my high school and college years being part of group projects where I carried the load. I was an overachiever. Hell, I *am* an overachiever. I'm also a perfectionist. Until this project, Sam essentially let me work on my own, occasionally giving me a junior designer to lord over if the workload was higher than normal. Regardless of my opinion, this is still a group project. Mr. Coffee Shop and I are on equal footing and we're about to be spending a lot of time together.

"Well, we don't need to work like that if it's not your style, Mr. Barton," I interjected, hoping like hell he would take the life raft I was tossing at him. "We could always just work through email. That way, you don't have to worry about coming here daily."

This is a nightmare. There's no way the guy across the table can change my mind. No matter how his arm muscles bulge a bit with his sleeves rolled up. Or how good he looks in that damn paddy hat.

"Oh, about that." My heart sinks, and all I want to do is slap my hand over Sam's mouth for ruining my one hope. "You're both going to have freedom in this one because I trust you. I won't ask you to pull all-nighters here in the office—that doesn't make sense. But on that same note, I do want you to work close together. I think Jamie has a great eye for photography, and Lexi, you're a born layout designer. The two of you together could be an unstoppable duo, and honestly, that's what I'm counting on."

"What do you mean, not coming here to work?"

"Most of this project will be out in the field. You'll work off laptops and tablets, and we can get you some more monitors or whatever you need for whatever you do from home."

"Home?" I'm a little surprised this James guy hasn't said much yet. Is he actually okay with this? He is. He's probably calculating the money he'll make while he's slacking off and watching porn, and I do all the work. Batting those blue eyes at me while he tells me he couldn't get his part done, so here's some half-assed work and expecting me to fix it.

"Or wherever you want." Sam held up his hands. "There is no stock photography. That means I need you both out there helping each other get candid shots, ensuring the model releases are signed, and whatever other paperwork we need. We don't really have time for reshoots, so Lexi, if you're in the field with him, you can give your feedback and get the shots you need. It also means you have free rein over when and where you work. Here, hotel, coffee shop, I don't care."

This is now my worst nightmare. If my mother found out I was working from home, she'd be at my door daily checking up on me. She'd drag my step-father along and they'd find me there with this Barton guy and make assumptions. It won't matter that I'm 34, they just care about how it will affect their reputation. It doesn't matter how many women Ronnie fucks, but it absolutely matters how many beds I hop between.

"You have the keys for the office, so if you need the equipment here, the door is open as always. But I'm not going to be keeping tabs on where either of you are for the next few weeks outside of a handful of progress meetings to see how things are going. It's a tight deadline, and I trust you both."

This was all too confusing for me. It's a dream job, no doubt. Avoiding morning traffic and being left alone with my creative brain. But was I really being left alone? Was this guy supposed to be my babysitter? Was I supposed to be his?

"I've had Dani set you guys up on a new expense account. I'll give you one of the company cards in a bit. If you need anything during the project, use that and just submit the receipt later. That will include dinners if you're working late. I don't mean hit up the steakhouse and order the biggest slab of meat they have every night, but I also don't mean McDonald's, either. If it's running late and you're still working, get food. Get drinks, too. Whatever you need."

"Sam, can I ask how much this client is going to be paying you for all of this? Seems like a lot since they're not even signed up for the full contract yet. Hell, you didn't even go this crazy when HummingBird was here trying to hire us to clean up their brand."

"HummingBird is a bunch of dicks. But these guys, yeah, they didn't even balk at the number I threw at them, which had a lot more zeros at the end than our standard clients. It's also a five-year contract, so all said and done, we'd be clearing over fifty million in the next five years. Big, Lexi. As in, you're both getting a few damn nice bonuses from this."

Sam winks at me, and I glance at the coffee shop guy, and he's just staring at me like he hasn't heard a word of this.

"Oh, not you two working together like this for five years. All this is just to get the first project out of the way; then, we'll return to normal again with you dancing in your office."

"Cubicle. Unless you're saying I'm getting an office out of this." Sam laughs at my joke, but it doesn't help my panic.

I try to let it sink in. I don't read the contracts for the jobs I'm on. Honestly, it doesn't affect me, so I never care what the client is paying so long as I get my paycheck at the end of the week. This is a far bigger undertaking than we've handled in the past. Which explained Sam's willingness to take this task to the extremes.

"Okay, well, uhm, Mr. Barton, I guess we should start getting things arranged and figuring out the schedule for what we need done."

"Oh, actually," Sam interrupts, which I appreciate since I don't think the new guy is mentally in the room with us anymore. "I got you both tickets to the big convention in Long Beach this weekend. I only got you two tickets for tomorrow, so if you need more days, just put it on the card."

"You want pictures of your niece?" Barton asks. Has he met Sam's niece? Which niece?

"Okay, maybe that too. I'll text you the booth number."

"It's, uhm," Barton clears his throat, and I glare at him. "It's actually a solid idea—the conference tomorrow. There are usually some pretty large corporate sponsors and vendors. It's also really out of the box for what your client would do, so we'd get shots and graphic ideas no one else would think to use. Large crowd shots, too. It ticks a few of the boxes."

"Yeah! Yes! That!" Sam shouts, clearly happy that James came to his rescue.

My mouth is wide open, but I can't seem to close it. Not only is he already throwing out ideas that make sense, but he's actively taking part in the decision-making and the work. This looks far more promising than I expected and leagues above where my college group project mates had left me.

James and Sam start talking about the convention when my phone buzzes on the table. I tilt the screen to check the message, and my stomach clenches. Her timing is impressively awful, as always. Is there ever a right time to deal with my mother?

👿 SATAN 👿

Where are you?

I heard you broke up with Marc. Why would you do that?

LEXI

I'm at work. A big project has come up.

😈 SATAN 😈

Alexis, don't avoid the question. This is embarrassing. He was a nice boy!

Margaret is coming for dinner, so I can't have you over tonight.

You'll have to come over tomorrow night.

I would ask her about her son, but you don't want to come across as a hussy, Alexis.

LEXI

I can't make it tomorrow night. I'm sorry.

😈 SATAN 😈

Alexis, stop playing games and get your priorities straight. You're letting that silly job take up so much of your time. You have responsibilities and commitments to your family.

Your father is a highly regarded man. He can't attend events coming across as a fool simply because you can't accept your calling from God.

I'd like to remind her Ronnie isn't my father and that my priorities lie with my actual job, not her shitty husband. I want to point out to her that all the work they were having me do should cost them a pretty penny, but they won't pay me a dime for it. Thoughts and prayers don't pay the bills. She'd never leave me alone if I tried to say any of that to her, so I try to compromise.

LEXI

> I will pick up the measurements at the church office when I can. Send me pictures of the arrangements, and I'll design the custom tablecloth so it won't clash. I have to go now.

"You good, Lex?" I put my phone down and smile at Sam. I've clearly missed something, and my phone is still buzzing in my lap. Thankfully, Sam just smiles back.

"I could pick you up tomorrow if that's alright. It would be better than both of us being stuck in traffic in separate cars," Barton suggests, and I'm surprised at the amount of words coming out together without him tripping over them. Good for him.

"You two figure it out," Sam announces as he stands. "I'm going to grab my stuff. James, I'll meet you downstairs. Lex, don't let her get to you. Have fun at the mixer tonight."

I watch Sam walk out the door, not waiting for any further responses. I'm too nervous to look at James, and he seems too nervous to talk to me. Guess I have to break the ice or neither of us will.

"Did you know about all of this during your Spider-Man deal at the boba place?" I try breaking the ice, but I know how brash that sounds and wish I could take it back the instant I say it. God, he's pretty.

"Nope. I should have known something was up when Dani sent me over there." He rubs the back of his neck and it makes his arms flex and my butterflies swarm again. "I was just here to drop off some prints and pick up a check."

"Dani sent you there?" I could smack her. This was a perfect example of a Dani trap. Setting us up before without us even knowing.

"She said they had excellent coffee. She didn't mention the

incredible view, though." He doesn't say it with that cocky Los Angeles flair. Instead, he practically mumbles it. "I'm getting the feeling we're kind of being…set up?"

I look up, and his sad, beautiful eyes lock on mine. Faint traces of hope dance on the edges, along with the soft beginnings of crow's feet. I desperately need to hear him laugh, mostly to prove that he can.

"You're an unwilling client of Dani's matchmaking services, too, huh?"

"For the last five years, yeah." He chuckles. Close, but not the laugh I wanted. Some of his sadness fades away briefly. "So, would it be okay to pick you up, or would you rather go separate?"

"I think I'm okay with carpooling, but Dani knows where we're going, so if you end up being a mass murderer or some shit, just know that." I can't hold back the snorting giggle noise I make, but instead of looking at me like an idiot, he laughs.

"I'll keep that in mind, but I'd make a terrible mass murderer." He shrugs as he tucks a notebook into his satchel. "I'd probably apologize through the whole thing."

I'm a sucker for self-deprecating humor when it's done right. "Good to know. Uhm, here's my number. I'll text you the address."

HOLLYWOOD
James

CHAPTER 7
TONGUE TIED
GROUPLOVE

SOME OF THE best places to eat in Los Angeles are little more than small, mom-and-pop style joints, which is exactly where Sam takes me. Bright colors decorate the room along with a handful of tables and mix-matched chairs. There's an extensive selection of tequila behind the bar, which has my hopes up for a decent margarita. It looks like they stay pretty busy, so I'm glad we get there just as someone gives up their table inside so we're not stuck at a sidewalk table.

"Order whatever you want. This is a business meeting, so I'm expensing it, anyway. Including the pitcher of margaritas!" Sam laughs as he tosses his jacket on the bench and ducks out to take a phone call. I slide into the booth and glace at the menu before I pull out my phone and see a missed text.

DANI

Where are you, fucker? I wanted to hang out before the bar!!

JAMES

You… I trusted you, and you betrayed me!!!

DANI

No, I simply kept my mouth shut for once while you waxed poetic about pink haired goddesses.

JAMES

Evil.

DANI

YOU LIKE HER!

JAMES

I didn't say that, Dani.

DANI

SHE'S MY MUSE, DANI!!!! Those were your words, big shot. Admit it!

You still coming tonight?

James Barton, get your mind out of the gutter! But also, absolutely keep dreaming of her naked so both of you can get LAID tonight!! 🍆💦😩

JAMES

You suck.

Send me the address. What time are you getting there?

DANI

[Image Attached]

I juggle my phone, nearly dropping it into the pitcher. She's with Lexi; they're sticking their tongues out and making silly faces. Lexi's lost the sweater and looks like she's still trying to wake up, or she might be a little stoned. It's hard to tell. Her eyes are half closed and my mouth goes dry at the sight of her lopsided smile. The angle going right down her top isn't doing a damn thing to help, either. What it *is* doing is making my dick hard again. *Fuck.*

DANI

I told her that was for Sam. 😉

You're totally putting that in the spank bank, huh? 🍆💦

JAMES

It's your mind that's in the gutter!!

DANI

What?! Her tits look great in that shot! She's got a nice 🍑 too…which you probably already stared at today, huh???

I fumble the phone again as Sam slides back into the booth. "Alright, let's get some food to go with this booze. It's cheat day, and this is only the pre-game before date night."

"Cheat day on date night? Is that irony or…?"

"No! But I can save a little money if I fill up on tacos here." Sam flags down a server, and we order more food than either of us will eat. He's doing this on purpose because he thinks depressed means I don't eat. He's not entirely wrong, but I'm too fucking nervous to eat right now.

We talk about the new gig and work-related matters for a while, avoiding the elephant in the room for as long as we can. The food comes out right as we run out of shop-talk and I think I'm safe, but Sam uses the lull in conversation to jump into my personal life.

"You're going tonight, aren't you?"

My phone buzzes again. I glance down, expecting more of Dani's antics, but I'm met with a message that makes my stomach drop instead.

UNKNOWN NUMBER

Why do you bother? You can't keep a job, so this won't work out, either.

"What?" I ask Sam, my voice cracking. I clear my throat and flip the phone over. It continues to buzz and Sam glares at it, so I stuff it into my pocket.

"The mixer? You're going because if you tell me you're not, I'm driving you over there myself and dumping you on the doorstep. You can't lock yourself in that house forever, James."

I laugh nervously. Sam would actually do what he's threatening. "Yeah, Dani conned me into going."

Sam and Dani want the same outcome, and it has nothing to do with me dating. They want me to bring my walls down, come out of hiding, and let go of the ghosts of the past. It's so much easier to say than do, and they both have watched as I try. Admittedly, I don't try very hard. I've always had the brooding artist to fall back on, but there was a time when I could laugh without crying and enjoy a night out with my friends without spending half of it in the bathroom, avoiding a panic attack. I haven't found a way to tell them I've accepted the darkness, and it's comforting to me.

Or maybe I've just given up.

"Two warnings. One is Kennedy—she works for me—you won't be able to miss her, and Dani will do her best to keep her away from you. She's a bit…well, she's a lot. I have no problem with what she does in her free time, but watch yourself around her. She's got the love 'em and leave 'em game on lockdown." He takes a huge bite of a taco, the lettuce and guac dropping off onto his plate.

"Noted. Is she the blonde, typical valley girl?" Sam nods to my question as he chews and I purse my lips, remembering how she blocked the door. I get the feeling she doesn't like being told no. "She was with Lexi at the coffee shop. She seemed… preoccupied."

"Yeah, her parents have money and when she started wasting

too much of it, they told her to go get a job. She got through college and unfortunately, I golf with her dad." He takes a drink and laughs. "Which brings me to warning number two, Lexi. Don't try to sell me some bullshit about how I'm crazy. I saw how you looked at her today. You haven't had that sparkle in your eyes since Natalie. I'm not blind."

"Sam, I—"

"No, trust me. Lex is amazing, and I hope you make that move. This isn't me being a cock blocker in HR clothing. I'm here as a friend, and I'm on board for any woman—or man—who can put that joy back on your eyes and the paintbrush in your hands." He fills our glasses from the margarita pitcher. "Just, you know, don't go ruining my big payday project with your dick, okay?"

"I wouldn't do that, Sam. Like I told Dani, it's better for me to stay away from people anyhow."

"Bullshit. You told her Lexi was your muse. Yeah, she told me about that."

"Fucking Dani," I mumble while he laughs, loud and hard.

"Anyhow, my warning isn't actually about Lexi. Whatever does or does not happen is between the two of you. You're both good kids, and if she doesn't like you, she'll straight up tell you." He stops laughing and leans in closer. "Listen, if she tells you about her family, keep in mind that she's not blowing it out of proportion. I've had her mom escorted out of the damn building before."

Sam knows my past and about some of my family issues, so his warning hits differently. It also makes me curious for long enough to remember that I'm trying to avoid being interested.

"Thanks for the heads up, but you really don't have to worry about any of that. No matter what Dani says, I don't have a shot with Lexi, and I intend to keep this all on a professional level."

"Sure, whatever you say." Sam winks at me and I feel my neck turning red. I almost tell him that I don't believe myself either.

"Why aren't you going tonight? You and Tish used to hit these things all the time. Did she finally get tired of all your shmoozing and networking?"

"Careful! No, we've already got reservations that I will not break for free drinks and too damn many young kids like you. We're too old for that shit. Now, we do what every self-respecting old couple does. We eat dinner early, watch Jeopardy, and go to bed."

"Sam, you're not *Jeopardy* old. Not by a long shot. I also have it on excellent authority that you're never in bed before two in the morning. Excellent authority being my cell phone text log."

"Old enough to be your—" He stops himself before he can say it. "well, let's just leave it at old enough." He tops off our drinks even though they were only half empty. His expression tells me he's about to go where I had hoped to avoid, and I'll need the drink to get through it. "So, have you been in the garage yet?"

"Nope." I pop the 'p' hard and then take a big ass swig, trying to numb any emotions before they even have a chance to surface. It's the middle of happy hour, though, which means watered down drinks. I won't get numb with these, but luckily, I have a joint on me. I can't get out of this conversation, but at least I can handle the crowd later. "I haven't had the time."

"You're going to have to go in there at some point. You don't have to face it alone, Jamie. Any of it."

I've known that for six months. It doesn't change the fact that I'm terrified to open those doors and look inside. In my pocket, my fingers brush against the card Sam gave me earlier, and I think about calling the guy. I won't, though. There's nothing left for me in that garage, nothing left of me. That part of me is gone, and no therapist is going to bring that back. I may have the itch to draw again, but it's a passing phase and as soon as I get Lexi to think I'm an asshole and truly unworthy of her time, it will fade again.

"Yeah, I will. Once things settle down a little."

Sam takes another phone call and while I sit at the table, I pull my phone out and read the texts I've been ignoring.

UNKNOWN NUMBER

The house looks like shit. You should tear it down.

I may be in town again soon. I can help. 🔥🔥

I delete the messages and distract myself by looking at the picture Dani had sent earlier. I shouldn't go tonight. I can tell Dani I drank too much with Sam. Even as I try to convince myself of that plan, I know it won't happen because I can't stop looking into those eyes. They're haunting and beautiful, and they're bringing something in me back to life. It's terrifying. Somewhere deep down there's the spark of hope trying hard to grow inside me, and I need to find a way to stop it. Hope is the worst thing in the whole fucking world. Right next to love. They both hurt so fucking much.

UNKNOWN NUMBER

Aww, you don't want to come out and play?

Not even going to ask why I'm coming to town?

You're fucking pathetic!

I can't ignore them, so I turn off the phone for now and wait for Sam to come back.

HOLLYWOOD

Lexi

CHAPTER 8
STUPID GIRL

P!NK

I GRAB a can of soda out of the fridge, surprised there's even one in there since I can't remember the last time I bought soda. Or took a trip to the damn grocery store. I crack it open, half expecting it to explode all over me, and take a long drink that makes my eyes water. The caffeine surging through me will hopefully calm the headache that's already scratching at my brain.

There's a knock at the door, but before I can even say *come in*, Dani is pushing through, tossing her bag on my couch and kicking off her shoes.

"Do you think Sam will murder me if I call in sick tomorrow? I want to get absolutely shit faced tonight and crash on your couch," she asks, walking through the apartment like she lives here. Checking the fridge, she finds it empty except for the barbecue sauce and an emergency pack of Reese's peanut butter cups. She knows better than to eat the candy, though. That's grounds for murder. Slamming the door shut, she grabs the can of soda from me, gulping half of it down without batting an eye. "Seriously, Lex? Dude, they clean dirty grills off with this shit. Also, how do you not even have chips in this house!"

"Yes, seriously. I've been…busy." I snatched the can back from her. "Besides, it was part of my emergency food stash. Caffeine and chocolate. And peanut butter."

"Sweetie, you are aware grocery delivery is a thing, right? You don't even have to talk to them. They'll leave it right outside your door." She makes a face at the taste of the soda. "This stuff should only be used as a mixer. Where's the booze?"

"This was the only mixer I had. So now, we have to drink straight whiskey, which you complain about every time."

"It's not my fault you don't keep limes in your house! Or anything else, for that matter! Just split what's left." She tugs the freezer open and rolls her eyes. "You don't even have ice?"

My head falls back as I sigh, heading over to a small cabinet in the corner and grabbing the half-full bottle of Jameson. All I do here is sleep and shower. I don't keep food here because I pick it up on the way home or walk out and get something. Food would mean cooking, and I hate cooking for myself. "Wait, why are we pre-gaming when they have free booze?"

"Because I have a secret! It's about the guest list for tonight, and I'm not going to tell you about it. All I will say is you should drink up." She spins on her heel and heads out of the kitchen, skipping toward the bedroom. "Pour those, and I'll meet you in the living room; I need to pee."

Since she drank most of our mixer, and I'm already dreading what comes next, I pour us both doubles. She doesn't have to pee; she has to go through my closet. Which means she's about to find the two bags of awful clothes my mother dropped off last week. I take a drink from the bottle to prepare myself. I think about her guest list comment and realize Kennedy must be who she's talking about and take another long pull.

As I expected, Dani parades out of the bedroom a few minutes later. She's holding a dress from the bag my mother brought me in front of her. It's beyond hideous. There's a floral pattern reminiscent of a tablecloth, a neckline that goes to the eyeballs, long sleeves with puffy shoulders, and a pleather belt to tie it all together. My mother's taste is very *religious martyr in spring*.

"I do declare!" She says in the worst southern accent I've ever heard before fainting on the couch. "Oh, lawd, I've got the vapahs! Oh, Rhett! What shall I do? Mrs. Daisy, oh lawd! The scandal of it all! Why, they can surely see mah ankles in this abomination of a frock!"

I push her legs off the couch, and she cackles, hugging the dress to her chest. She laughs so hard that she falls off the couch and starts rolling around and kicking her feet.

"Shelby! Drink your damn juice!" she yells from the floor, and I roll my eyes until I laugh equally hard.

"Get the fuck up, asshole. Here, drink your own juice." I thrust her drink out to her, and she snags it. We both take a drink as she stands, holding the flowery, springtime corporate chic monstrosity in front of us. It's one of those things where the longer you stare at it, the more you find wrong with it. If I knew where my mother found this stuff, I might just have to burn it to the ground. However, there's a solid possibility one of the women from her church donated these, and by the looks of it, the previous owner likely died in the eighties.

"I take it good old mommy dearest went shopping at the old folks' home again?" She side-eyes me. "Alexis, your closet is the house of Satan! I'll save your soul through fashion by house Mormon! I wonder what she'd do if we poorly hid some whips and giant dildos in there for next time. Quick! To the internet!"

"She'd make a terrible Mormon and you're not ordering giant dildos. Mom dropped the clothes off the other day with a note while I was at work. Said something about these looking more…feminine… appropriate…other words," I hear my voice trail off as the rest of the letter plays back in my head. Dani knows those weren't the words my mother used. I skipped the ones that hurt. More attractive to a man of faith. Less like a whore of Babylon. Better fitted to my larger than necessary frame.

"Do you have scissors? God, my mother dresses better than this and she's like seventy-six." She doesn't wait for an answer, hopping up and running into the kitchen. She returns a few minutes later, victorious in her search, and flops down next to me. Once she takes a big swig from her glass, she looks me right in the eyes. "Fuck this dress and fuck her. Come on, we're doing this."

A shiver runs up my spine as I nod slowly. I can always tell my mother the dresses didn't fit or something when I throw them into a donation box somewhere. Dani picks the spot to make the first cut, then stops and holds the scissors out to me. I stare at them like I've never seen a pair of scissors before and couldn't touch them.

"I can't do this." I push the scissors away and I remind her, "This whole fashion thing is your gig. I'll fuck it up."

"This cut isn't about fashion, Lex. This cut is about freedom." She pushes the scissors into my hand. "We're going to turn this into a sexy, fun kimono and you're going to wear it tonight. You're going to drink, have fun, and meet the man of your dreams, all in rebellious defiance of that cunt who is absolutely unworthy of a daughter as badass and exceptional as you. In fact, I hope you get laid in this monstrosity. Repeatedly. Tonight!"

Sometimes it's easy to forget where Dani comes from. She's always happy and full of spice, even though her home life was never a walk in the park. Her father died when she was young, an accident at the factory he worked in. The payout from the company was a joke and it left her mother with six kids and no job. They made it work, though, and now, Dani, her sister, and her mother live in a cute little house near Silverlake. Or that's how she describes it. I've never even been to her house.

I hold the ugly fabric in one hand and the cold steel shears in the other. I shouldn't do this, and eventually I will end up paying for it when my mother finds out. But fuck if Dani isn't right. The sound of the blades slicing is beautiful, and the way they slide through the material is therapeutic.

"Ah! You did it! So proud of you. Now, take off your sweater so I can get this thing sized up. Hurry!" She grabs her bag, and of course, she has a sewing kit and supplies with her. She gets to work cutting and ripping as fabric flies around her. I can tell she's concentrating hard because her tongue is sticking out, so I hand her glass over now and then. She stops long enough to take another drink and get back to work.

I thumb through my phone for a few minutes, get bored with social media, and turn on the TV to some horror movie I've seen a dozen times or more. The whiskey is warm and Dani's humming is soothing. Soon enough, I'm closing my eyes and letting it lull me to sleep.

"WAKE UP!"

I bolt upright, "What? What happened?"

"Nothing, smile. I'm sending a pic to Sam. Stick out your tongue or something cute." She snaps the picture and sends it off as I stretch and rub my eyes. "I'm almost done. Go dig through your closet. White tank top, black shorts, and those cute ass boots you rarely wear. Oh, and fix your makeup. Either go all in on the raccoon mask or don't. You can't half-ass it tonight."

"Okay, okay!" I trudge into my room and stare longingly at my bed. I can tell her I have a headache; it won't be a total lie since I *do* have one. It just isn't bad enough to bail yet. Deciding against the idea, I glance over my shoulder and watch her finishing her project. I throw on the clothes she told me to wear and fix my makeup in the mirror.

Dani slides up behind me, and I put on what was formerly a dress and is now a boho-style duster. She's cut slits in the arms and even added pockets. Fuck. I look damn good. Curves and all. She could probably sell this thing for a decent amount at a thrift store or clothing exchange.

"Your mother would hate this because of how fucking sexy you look in it. Does she even know about all these beautiful tattoos?" She arches an eyebrow at me in the mirror, and I shrug and shake my head. "She'd also hate James. So let's go piss her off."

"James? What about him?" I remember the conversation from earlier and gasp. "Oh fuck, he's coming tonight, isn't he? I can't dress like this!"

"Yes, you can. You can dress however you want, look amazing! So let him stick his big—"

"Dani, I don't think that whole hook-up plan is a good idea. We're supposed to work together. Work togeth—wait, how do you know he has a—"

"I don't, it's a guess. Are you kidding? By the end of the night, I'm hoping he tears your clothes off, and this duster ends up in a pool at the foot of a sleazy motel bed."

I don't have time to change my mind or my clothes as she grabs my hand and drags me out of the apartment, leaving the shredded remnants of the dress on the floor for me to clean up later.

The bar is only a few blocks from my apartment and it's still daylight out, so the walk is a kind of refreshing. I can't stop myself from looking around as we walk and pulling the dress closed every time I notice someone. It hides some of the skin I'm showing, except now that it's a duster, so it just keeps fluttering open with every step. I don't mind wearing revealing clothes, but not around guys I'm supposed to be working with. I shouldn't have let myself get so carried away with Dani.

I don't get this nervous going out, especially to a bar with Dani by my side. If I'm honest with myself, it's not the clothes; that's just what my brain has decided to focus on. What I'm really worried about is spending the next few weeks working my ass off with James in tow. Traveling with him, staying in hotels, working weird hours. I barely even know him. I'd sure as hell *like* to know him, though. Nothing long-term, but it's possible Dani's right. Temporary co-workers with benefits could do me some good.

"Why are you freaking the fuck out on me, Lex?" Dani breaks me out of my private headspace.

"What if he thinks I'm weird?"

"You are weird, Lex. It's why we love you." She pinches my cheek and pops her gum. "Besides, the worst thing that happens is you both get to work out your sexual frustrations with each other!"

"I have to work with him over the next few weeks. How about we stick to that? Just, you know, work. No hooking up or fucking or whatever."

"Yeah, but imagine how much fucking you're going to do if you hit it off tonight! I mean, even if you don't hit it off, you can still bang."

"Working! Not fucking!"

She stops and stands in front of me with her hands on her hips while I sigh. It's honestly comical and I should be laughing. I'm a good six inches taller than Dani, even in her heeled boots. So while she's trying to be serious with her arms folded and giving me one of her looks, it ends up looking like a kid is angry with me.

"Where's Lexi? My Lexi? Not that shy, self-conscious girl you become around your mom." She digs through her purse until she finds her cigarette case, pulling out a joint and handing it to me. "I didn't invite Alexis out, even if you are wearing that fucking dress she bought. I invited Lexi, my ride-or-die. The bitch who gets drunk with me and dances on the tables before turning the guys down. The chick that chants at pride parades and takes exactly no shit from anyone? Now, let's smoke this and go be the badass bitches we are!"

"You're right. You're fucking right." I light the joint and take a slow, deep inhale. Feeling the haze settle in my mind, I let my whole body shake off the stress and worries. When I open my eyes again, I grin at her. "Let's go get drunk, dance, and maybe even screw. If that doesn't happen, we can end the night getting even higher and watching horror movies at my place. I'll even make out with you on the couch."

"That's my girl!"

HOLLYWOOD

Lexi

CHAPTER 9
ALL THE GOOD GIRLS GO TO HELL

BILLIE EILISH

THE SOUNDS of music and talking spill out of the building when we open the door. There's already a massive crowd, and it's not at all the atmosphere I expected for a brewery. The open industrial ceiling and giant brewing tanks are the only signs that this was usually a laid-back place with burgers and beer. Tonight, though, one of the host companies rented it out, and someone obviously paid top dollar to have the space redecorated for an impact. Two full bars are already slinging drinks, and trays of finger foods make their way around the room. To keep it semi-professional, they've got a few tables off to the side with literature about different creative groups and places to sign up for job fairs. A DJ setup has transformed the cozy bar into a nightclub and she already has the party very started.

"Oh shit! Okay, this is amazing. I need to get the contact info for whoever did this and hire them for Sam's next event," Dani shouts over the music. She points to a group in the corner near the dance floor. "There's Kennedy."

I'm not sure if that's meant as a warning or a direction to follow, but Dani grabs my hand, and we move through the crowd toward the table where Kennedy is holding court. At least four guys are drooling over her, and she's absolutely in her element. She's changed out of her work clothes and into what I can only describe as a college party girl club dress. Before, I was feeling too exposed. Now I think like I'm dressed for a totally different party. I'm so glad I'm high.

"Oh my god, I forgot you guys were coming!" Her voice is even more grating as she screams too loud. "Guys, these are my friends from work. This is Dani. She's amazing and is in a fucking band. She's also single and looking to mingle. You'll love her! Oh, and this is Lexi. What the fuck?"

It's like she's looking at me for the first time, her jaw dropping open as she stares. I glance down at myself, expecting to see a giant spider or a space vortex opening, but it's only me. Standing there like an idiot.

"WOW! Oh my god, you should dress like this more often so you're not permanently alone for the rest of your life! That outfit is so cute! And look! You have legs!" She slaps the table and the guys around her take the cue and run with it, laughing their fake little laughs. "Seriously, you're going to need to go to confession or whatever after this. What would Jesus think?"

I flip her off and hand my bag to Dani, motioning that I'm headed to the bar. A spot opens as I walk up, so I take it, and a cute blonde takes my order. I think about flirting with her because I'm a flirt when I'm high, but she's too busy. I pull out my phone while I wait, texting the one person I trust more than Dani.

LEXI

I think I'm about to do something stupid and so very you.

💀 BEXXUS 💀

WHAAAT?! Not you!!

Wait, no, seriously…what are u doing?

LEXI

I didn't think you'd answer. Aren't you in Amsterdam?

💀 BEXXUS 💀

Yep, still adjusting to the time change.

TELL ME!

LEXI

I'm out drinking with Dani, and she's invited a guy…

💀 BEXXUS 💀

TELL ME MOOOOORE!

LEXI

She's been trying to set us up for a while. But I work with him now. He's…cute.

💀 BEXXUS 💀

Baby, you're in Cali. They're all pretty boys.

Get railed, little sister! You deserve it. Unless he's an asshole, then just get him to eat you out in the parking lot and bail.

LEXI

Your ridiculousness is why I love you. He just seems… nice.

💀 BEXXUS 💀

Okay, so if the sex is good, marry that man. What are you wearing?

I take a quick selfie and shoot it to her.

💀 BEXXUS 💀

HOT FUCKING DAMN! He's more than nice… you're dressed too good for nice.

Shit, I gotta go!!

Miss you! Stay out, party, and don't let the snake woman get in the way!

Also, if he doesn't work out, go fuck the guy standing behind you in that picture.

The bartender reappears before I can scroll back up. She puts the two drinks I'd ordered down and winks, so I wink back. Before I can even thank her, she's already nodding her head to get the next person's order. Open bar at creatives function? They're going to be exceptionally busy tonight.

"Hi. Can I get whatever she's having?"

I roll my eyes and prepare for the onslaught of awful pickup lines, but they don't come. Someone sits beside me, and I peek over next to me. Oh shit, boba shop boy is here already, and he's giving me puppy dog eyes. Wait, is that who Bex saw in the picture I sent?

"Hey, Dani sent me. I think it was to keep Kennedy away."

"Sounds like a solid move on her part."

"What did I order?"

"Jack and coke. Double." I'm keeping the answers short and trying to remind myself I can't get involved with him, no matter what Dani says.

"Thank god. I was worried yours was the IPA she brought over, and I'd have to drink that shit to look cool in front of you."

"No, that's for Dani. I can't drink that shit either." I laugh. I want to say more but don't want to come across as desperate. I also don't want him getting any ideas that this will be a thing. We work together and happen to be at the same party for creatives. That's all. Okay, maybe a little more than that.

"You, uhm..." he stutters and swallows hard before licking his lips. He has pretty lips. "You look—"

"JAMIE!" Dani yells and comes running up to the bar and jumps on him. I sip my drink and turn away because there's this strange sensation in my gut. It's not the drink; it's more like some weird part of my brain is unhappy about how close they are. I can't be jealous over someone I met a few hours ago, can I?

"I finally got a chance to break away from Kennedy and her entourage and give you a proper hello," I hear her say, and I slide her beer over to her. "Come on, we've pushed a couple of tables together over there so you won't have to sit next to the Queen Bitch."

"I'll be right there, waiting for my drink." Jamie answers, flashing me a half smile.

That weird uneasiness in my stomach grows as she loops her arm through mine and pulls me away from the bar. Away from him. I don't understand why, but I don't want to go. I turn back and he's looking right at me. He mouths one word, and I almost drop my drink. *Amazing.*

"Oh, and aren't you already a flustered mess!" Dani says in my ear as we near the tables.

"Shut up!" I peer back over my shoulder again, and now he's smirking at me. Smirking. "Oh my god, I can't stop looking at him! What the fuck is wrong with me?"

"Uhh, you're sexually repressed with a history of shit boyfriends and a family full of bible thumping drama queens that you can't seem to escape. This coming from a Mexican, no less."

"Jerk."

"Just telling it like it is, *chica.*" She over-emphasizes the word and her grin reminds me of the Cheshire Cat. All she needs is some stripes and for her head to pop off and start floating around the room. "So, you like him? Don't bother lying, because

Bex told me you do. She texted my like thirty seconds ago ratting you out."

"Bex? *Seriously?* She wasted no time. Okay, fine. He's fucking gorgeous, but he's so out of my league. Like, that's supermodel dating material there. I mean, at the least, Hollywood B+ list." I take a drink and sigh. "He deserves to be railing Kennedy all night, not me."

"Stop selling yourself short and enjoy yourself. Besides, Jamie is about as down-to-earth cool as an artist can get. Well, when he's not dreaming of his new muse." She winks at me like she knows something, or at least tries to. Dani can't wink to save her life. "Oh! Here he comes, and he looks like one very hungry wolf eyeing up his dinner. Rawr."

I concentrate on the ice in my glass as he joins us. I don't bother looking until he slides a fresh drink in front of me. Out of the corner of my eye, I can see him give Dani another beer and I'm not altogether sure how I should interpret any of this. I should have stayed home.

"Aww, trying to get me drunk, Jamie? That won't work! You've seen me drink." Dani turns to me and yell whispers, "It's safe, you can drink it. He used to bring me my drinks when I was on stage. I trust him."

"Hey!" Kennedy yells, the slur already apparent in her words as she joins the conversation. Evidently, she's been here for a while. She points a crooked finger with a long, sharp, hot pink nail in his direction. "Aren't you the guy?"

James looks at Dani and shrugs. "I mean, I'm *a* guy."

"You are! You're the coffee shop phone guy! Are you like stalking me or something?" She wiggles her shoulders as she speaks, like some kind of deranged mating dance.

"Kennedy, you idiot," Dani smacks her arm. "This is my

friend Jamie. He works for Sam as a freelance photographer. He's working on that project with Lexi."

"No shit! WAIT! You're also the Uber pastry guy?!" Her mouth drops open in fake surprise and I'm forced to watch as her figurative teeth come out. She knows I'm interested—or whatever I am—so she wants a piece of him before I have a chance. She leans forward to push her boobs out a little more and flashes her bright white smile. "Well, tell me next time you swing by the office. I could give you a very special private tour."

"Gross, Kennedy. Gross," Dani says, smacking her arm.

"Oh my god, this is my song!" She holds her hand out to James expectantly.

"Oh, uhm, I'll pass. Thanks."

"Ugh, whatever!" She grabs the hands of the two guys next to her instead and drags them to dance in the crowd.

The three of us talk for a while and order more rounds while Kennedy dances with a new guy every few minutes. By round four, I'm hitting right about tipsy levels and the numbness is settling into my body. Dani and James have been cracking jokes back and forth for a while now, and they're having fun, but I'm bored. I feel a bit like a third wheel. Fourth if you count Kennedy.

"Hey, I'll be back," I tell Dani, and head out onto the dance floor. I let the music take over, and the world outside of the beat slips away—no projects, no work, no guys, no parents. It's only me and the bass line.

I catch a glance at Dani and see a round of shots hit the table. Dani waves to one of the girls at another table, and I recognize her as someone she's hooked up with before. Good for her. I had just started getting into the music when someone bumps into me *hard*. I spin around, and of course, it's Kennedy.

"Oh my god, I'm so sorry! Fuck, I need a drink. Come on!"

She grabs my arm and pulls me back toward the table. Dani and James stiffen up at the sight of her, and I brush Kennedy's hand away.

"I'm gonna stay out here." She huffs. I don't need to be there while she climbs all over James. She's just mad because she wants to rub it in my face. She waves me off and slithers up beside him, her hand on his arm, and then on his thigh. Her boobs pushed against him. My stomach drops when he laughs along with her. Seeing the way she's hanging on him makes my insides crawl. She always does this when we're out, so it shouldn't surprise me. But this time it actually hurts.

"Hey! Lexi, right?" comes a voice from behind me. I turn and while I recognize him, I can't place him. He must see the blank stare on my face because he keeps yelling at me. "I'm Shaun! I work at Sintax! We met a few months ago at LACMA."

Oh shit, I do remember him. We might have made out in one of the side rooms of the last mixer I went to. These things always go one of two ways. Either it's a snooze fest and everyone is talking business and sipping on lite beers. Or it's a nineteen eighties corporate holiday party where it's guaranteed someone has done a line of coke off the tits of a coworker while photocopying her bare ass.

"Shaun! Hi. Did you cut your hair or something?" He's not terrible looking, but he's not James. Besides, he was hotter with longer hair.

"Yeah, that's why you didn't recognize me!" Or it's because I never cared to remember you.

Fuck this. I don't need this shit. "Wanna dance?" He nods eagerly, so we dance. He wastes no time before he's grinding on me like a drunk monkey, but I don't give a fuck. I'm drunk, I'm high, I'm pissed off. Why shouldn't I enjoy myself? Maybe, if I act interested enough, Kennedy will swipe this one up in her talons and fly away.

I can't hold a candle to Kennedy. She has that supermodel-level body that matches James's good looks brilliantly. If they were together, people would say things like they'd make cute babies or whatever bullshit they say when pretty people inevitably hook up. I know I'm too thick in all the wrong places. I wear glasses, and my sense of fashion is comfortable cat lady minus the cats. She could be on Baywatch; I could be an extra on a documentary about creepy swamp witches—which suits me just fine.

Dani motions for me to come back to the table, but I ignore her. When I glance back at her a few minutes later, I get the evil eye of doom and know shit isn't going well. Kennedy winks at me and scoots forward on her chair so that he's standing between her open legs. He's not my problem. He's a big boy. I turn back and see that my short-term dance partner has moved on. Against my better judgement, I head back over to the table.

Kennedy looks over her shoulder. She knows I'm right there and that I'll hear her when she says to James, "You've got really pretty eyes. Ever had your dick sucked in a bar bathroom before?"

James coughs, choking on his drink, as Dani grabs Kennedy and pulls her away. I step into the space that has opened up between them out of habit. We do this whenever we're out with Kennedy because we know she'll eventually cross the line. We take turns on who gets to babysit and who gets to dance with the guy she'd made very uncomfortable. I guess it's my turn to have fun.

"Do you want to dance?" I yell over the noise as he stares at me with wide eyes, wiping his drink off his chin. He points to himself and looks shocked, like no one has ever asked him that before. "Yes. Do you dance? Or you could just stay here; I don't really care."

"He's busy," Kennedy blurts out, trying to push her way back in, having somehow escaped from Dani. "Besides, isn't dancing like, against your religion or something?"

"Kennedy, shut your fucking face before I rearrange it. Don't think I won't tell Sam exactly how you're representing his company. Now sit the fuck down and drink some damn water." Dani's voice is stern, and Kennedy responds instantly by pouting and throwing herself into a nearby chair.

"So, do you?" I ask him again, ignoring the situation nearby.

"Fuck yes," he grins, and I grab his hand, pulling him away from the table and Kennedy, who sneers as we walk away. I hear her say something about leaving room for Jesus, but I ignore her. It's Dani's turn to deal with her.

When we finally stop on the other side of the crowd, he offers me a sad smile. "Thanks for the rescue."

"Yeah, no problem." I shrug and lean against a nearby pillar. "We don't have to dance if you don't want to. It was more of an escape plan than anything. Give her five minutes and she'll forget about you and move on, then you can go back. Otherwise, the exit is a straight shot from here."

"Oh, yeah. Uhm, okay." He looks around, confused. I'm close to believing this guy's standard state of living is confused. When he looks back at me, he's got that smirk from the bar again. It's like I can watch his confidence turning on and off again like a switch. "What about a third option?"

"Third option? What's that?"

"What if—"

A man steps between us, cutting James off. "Hey! Happy un-birthday, uhh," he looks at the slip of paper he's holding with two shot glasses. It gives me enough time to recognize that he's working the party, not a drunk asshole trying to hit on me. "Lexi! Your friend sent you some shots to celebrate. Cool, un-birthday, huh? Fuck yeah."

"Uhm, yeah. Thanks!" I feign surprise and excitement. James and I take the shots and stare at each other awkwardly. "Don't worry. It's a cue that the storm known as Kennedy has been spoken to sternly and promises to be on her best behavior." I scoff at the thought. "Dani's just—"

"Being Dani," he laughs.

"Bottoms up?" He nods, and we both knock back the shots. I close my eyes and embrace the full body shiver I get from the alcohol slithering through me. "So, you should be good to go back now. She'll stop acting like a cunt for at least ten minutes."

"Is she always like this?"

"We like to call her an acquired taste at the office, and then we hope no one has actually acquired a taste for her." I'm mortified when I giggle, and a snort sneaks out.

"Fuck, you're adorable." I expect to see panic at what he's said, but there isn't any. We might be drunk. He takes the shot glass from me and puts them both on a tray as it passes by. "Sorry, I forgot to tell you the third option I came up with."

"Oh yeah? What was it?"

"It's the option where I don't go back to the table, and I don't leave." He grins, and if I believed in the devil, I'd be reasonably certain this was him. "We dance."

"You actually wanna dance?" I ask. Maybe the devil isn't so bad. My mother would hate him, and that makes me want him more.

HOLLYWOOD

James

CHAPTER 10
ARMS TONIGHT

MOTHER MOTHER

WHERE THE HELL did that come from? What did I just do? It's not that I hate dancing, it's fun. But what surprises me is that almost sounded like a smooth line. Almost.

This entire night has been chaos. First, Kennedy's drunk ass steamrolled over every opportunity I had with Lexi. Then Kennedy tried to grope me, finally succeeding while making my skin crawl. If that wasn't awful enough, some other guy danced with the girl of my dreams. I was so sure Lexi already hated me I was ready to leave this stupid party. But fuck, I can't take my eyes off her, and now she wants to dance?!

While I follow her deeper into the crowd and closer to the DJ, I remind myself she's not some random chick I picked up, I have to work with her. If I can keep my head screwed on straight and my dick in my damn pants tonight, this might end up being enjoyable. The problem is that at some point, I won't be able to hide the fact that staring at her all night has made me rock hard. I hope she knows it has fuck all to do with Kennedy.

She stops and steps toward me, putting her hand on my chest, and I think I am going to implode. I watch longingly as she tucks her bottom lip between her teeth, biting down the way

I want to. She gradually drags her teeth over her lips and I'm suddenly dizzy. Does she have any idea what she is doing to me? I'm drunk. I must be. Normally I would tuck tail and run, but I can't move away from her.

Because we're both a little unsure of ourselves or each other, we're clumsy at first. But we find a groove and I'm lost in the way her body moves. Her hips are rolling, her arms brushing against me, the way her head rolls back and exposes her neck—fuck, I want to lick the hell out of that damn neck.

Every song is background noise, and I don't care how many people are dancing. Nothing in the world has the power to pull me out of this moment, or make me see anything but her. But I can tell you every single way her body moves. I can paint each and every curve of her with my eyes closed. The room is empty except for her and I.

Based on the way she's moving, the songs are still upbeat, and I'm thanking the universe that she isn't grinding against me. I want her to, god damn I want her to. I want her body all over me, but it's a horrible idea. I'll screw up and scare her away. I'll lose any chance with her and my job. I need her. I need my job. I have to keep my shit together, but I'm already failing.

As if the DJ can hear my thoughts—and hates me—the tempo slows, and the music is heady and full of bass. Unexpectedly, her eyes open and I can't stop looking between them and her lips. I want to taste her. All of her. Every fucking inch of her. Her hand slides over mine and suddenly there's not enough oxygen to breathe. She smiles and my heart drums to the music that is her.

This is so not me. I'm way out of my element. I'm the wingman. I'm the one who tries to date the cute friend so his buddy can date the hot chick. I'm not even cool enough to be the last kid picked for kickball—I'm the shy kid who doesn't get picked at all because I'm in the nurse's office with a broken nose. But she's done something to me.

I haven't craved someone like this in a long time. Hell, I haven't had sex in months. No, that's wrong. It's been over a year ago and I'm not even sure it counts as sex. Neither of us were in our right minds. I was working a freelance shoot in San Diego with a new client. A day at the beach, women in tiny bikinis, and too much weed later, and I found myself at a bar with some coworkers. Someone decided we should shoot some pool and I remember a blonde coming over and talking to me. Rubbing on me. We had shots, and we drank a few beers together. It was fun, until it wasn't.

The next thing I know, I'm on a bench outside the bar, and she's on top of me, moaning someone else's name as she bounces up and down until we both get off. Romantic. A woman I knew from the shoot found us outside not long after we finished and when I could barely stand or say my own name, she ended up taking us both to the hospital.

Some dickhead spiked the blonde's drinks…the ones I shared with her. And people wonder why I have trust issues. Her attitude toward the entire situation made me realize I'd dodged more than one bullet that night. She considered herself fortunate, fucking the nice guy while drugged instead of the wrong guy. At least I left her alive and felt like an absolute asshole. I've never gotten over that guilt or the shame. The police took our statements at the hospital while we had our stomachs pumped; the doctors discharged us, and we walked away. They never found the guy who dosed us. It could have been so much worse for both of us, but a year later, I still struggle with what happened.

We stayed in touch long enough to know we both tested negative and she wasn't pregnant. I never told my dad. He just knew I wasn't myself after that. I'd lock myself in the garage and paint for hours, only to cover the whole painting in black and throw the canvas away. It reminded him of when I first started painting to deal with my trauma.

I almost called her a few times in the last six months to see if I could fuck the pain away, maybe replace the shame with something good. Instead, I tried several women I didn't know. One passed out as we got in the cab, so I made sure she got home safely and left. Another time was with this beautiful redhead. I made sure she got off like six times, but I kept having flashbacks to San Diego every time she touched me. I cried a lot and stayed in bed for a week after both encounters and then I gave up trying. I do that a lot, though. Depression is a never-ending cycle. It doesn't give a fuck who you are. It consumes you, gives you a glimmer of hope, and pulls you back into the darkness over and over until you rot.

Lexi turns her back to me, and my mind snaps back to the here and now. I hold my breath as she moves her hips, pressing that beautiful backside up against me. I can't stop the moan as my eyes roll back in my head, and I find myself praying that she can't hear it over the music. She doesn't move away, though. Rolling her perfect ass against me. She has to feel that. I take hold of her hips as she sways, and my head drops down until I'm nuzzling against her ear. The music is gone now. It's just our breathing and our hearts beating.

Now that she's standing, I can see the tattoos on her bare legs. I want to touch them, hell; I want to lick them. My fingers walk down her hips and graze against her bare skin next to the ink. One leg is full of comic book characters I recognize, the other has references to video games. Instead of running off the dance floor, she's leaning her head back onto my shoulder and wrapping her arms around my neck.

That's when I realize she doesn't have on a bra—her tits are perfect. I gently nip at her hot skin and watch her pebbled nipples pressing against the tight fabric of her shirt. I'm practically drooling at how much I want her, but I close my eyes and try hard to get my head out of the gutter and her pants.

She smells like dessert. Cherries...no. Strawberries. I close my eyes and leave a trail of soft kisses up her neck when her hands start to play with my hair. I suck softly on her pulse point and I feel the vibration of her moan. One of her hands finds mine and leads it between her legs and my hips thrust involuntarily. She's soaking wet and wants to make damn sure I know I'm not the only one turned on.

As if I'm in some kind of weird dream, she turns around to face me again, leaving her arms around my neck and leaning in close. She licks the shell of my ear and says just loud enough for me to hear her, "Let's get out of here."

I nod. I must look like a lovesick puppy as she weaves us through the crowd and down a hallway to the bathrooms. She pulls me into the women's room and I am thanking whatever designer decided on the private stalls with full doors as it shuts behind me with a click.

My head is spinning, and the world is moving too fast when she pulls me to her, directing my head back to her neck. My hands want to touch all of her. Fuck, my heart is slamming and I'm trying hard to remember if I even have a condom with me. I fumble with the button on her shorts like an idiot, then I give up and slide my hand up her leg.

She purrs—fucking purrs—against me when my fingers slip under the silky panties and tease at her entrance. My other hand grabs her tit and I roll her hard nipple through her shirt. Her back arches when I find the sweet spot, and she starts riding my hand with a moan. The fire in me is raging now, and I push the long, flowery blouse off her shoulders and pull her top down, exposing her breasts to the cool air of the bathroom. I lean over and flick her nipple with my tongue before wrapping my lips around it.

"Oh fuck, just like that!" she coos.

I want to see her—no—I need to see her when she comes apart. I need to have that memory of her face in ecstasy so I can hold on to it forever. I want her to have my name in her mouth when she comes. I pull away from her breast and stare at her.

"Fuck, you're—"

"Don't stop!" She grabs my vest and I'm tripping backward, my head slamming into the door behind me as a string of mumbled swears comes out of my mouth. That's going to hurt later, but her hands are fumbling with my buckle as we both share a drunk laugh and hunt the release together. I tuck a strand of her hair behind her ear, watching my own fingers slide along her lips. I want to kiss her.

"You're—" I don't even get to finish before her lips ghost mine. At this point, she could be sucking my soul out, and I wouldn't give a rat's ass. I pop the button on her jeans and shove my hand in for a better angle. My thumb rubs circles around her swollen clit and I slide two fingers into her; she's so damn tight and fucking soaked. Her moan is angelic. Her breath tastes like whiskey and cherries. I think it's my new favorite combination. I'm just about to kiss her when she gasps and throws her head back.

"James! Oh fuck, I'm gonna come."

When her head rocks back and our eyes lock, my mind flashes to the blonde on the beach. Then to Sam telling me not to let my dick fuck this up. Shit.

"Lexi, I… this is…we can't do this. I can't do this."

She lets out a whine and my dick is screaming at my brain as I pull my hand out of her shorts.

"Motherfucker, seriously?"

"Sweetheart, you're—you're fucking phenomenal. But—"

"But?" she scoffs, then pulls her top back up. "Fine, I'll finish it myself, asshole."

"Wait!" I grab her as she reaches for the door. "It's not you. You have no idea how badly I want this. I want you."

"Yeah? But what?"

"I…" My mind races for any excuse I can grab onto. "I'm too drunk. I drank too much. I…I can't."

She stares at me with a raised eyebrow, then looks down at the bulge in my pants and I realize how dumb that sounded. She knows I'm already hard, and I just left her right at the edge of her orgasm. I go to say something, but her phone buzzes and she lets out a low groan as she pulls it out of her back pocket.

I need to fix this. I can't let her leave. I need to tell her the real reason I can't do this right now.

"Fuck." She looks at the screen, then up at me. Her eyes are cold daggers driving through my broken heart. "This was probably a stupid idea anyhow. I gotta go."

I follow her out, getting a few looks from people that I don't care about while I button my pants. Once we're clear of the door, she bolts for the patio without a word or a second look. I've already fucked this up.

Fuck. FUCKFUCKFUCKFUCKFUCK!

"Hey, lover-boy, where'd you two disappear to? Like I need to ask," Dani teases as she stirs her drink and tries to give me an over-the-top wink. Her arm drapes over the woman who was buying the table shots earlier. Once she sees the expression on my face, Dani slides her drink over to me and watches with a raised eyebrow while I down it in one big gulp.

"Don't." I lean over the table and bury my head in my hands, rubbing my temples with my thumbs as hard as I can stand.

"What happened? Where's Lexi?"

"She went outside, to the patio. We were dancing. Everything seemed great. We…we kind of..." I run my hands through my hair. I don't want to say anything, but it's Dani. I trust Dani. "We were making out in the fucking bathroom, and I realized how drunk she was and—"

"San Diego?" she asks, and I nod.

"I didn't want her to regret it later, so I stopped it. She looked pissed off, but in the middle of me trying to explain, she got a text and took off." I slump down into a chair. "This is why I tell you not to set me up, Dani. I'm a fucking train wreck. One day, and I've already messed up, and she hates me, and now, she has to work with me."

"You're a cute train wreck who's a decent human being, Jamie." She rests a hand on mine, trying to console me. How many guys in this bar right now would stop sucking her face in the bathroom because she's drunk? You. You're the only one."

"I need to call Sam and tell him to take me off the project." I reach for my phone but stop when I realize how late it's gotten, and that my head isn't in the right place. "Listen, does she have a ride home? She's wasted, and I'm a little worried about her."

"I'll get her home; it's not far. Do not call Sam—you idiot—she doesn't hate you. Hang on and I'll go find her and get to the bottom of this. You two were hitting it off so well. This is just a bump." She nods toward Kennedy, who pushes her way through another crowd of men to head this way. "Will you be okay for a few minutes?"

"I think I should go. I've done enough damage for one night." I rock my head back and groan when I remember about tomorrow's assignment. "Fuck! Dani, I have to pick her up tomorrow morning, and she hates me. This is never going to work. I really should just call Sam."

"Chocolate croissants."

"Huh?"

"She loves those things, so bring her one. Oh, and coffee. It's a peace offering that I don't even think you need. I think she likes you, Jamie. I'll text you later and tell you what she says, because I bet she's fine and you still totally have a chance. Maybe you both need to sleep it off and try again fresh in the morning?"

"Doubt it. Especially after I flat-out turned her down. Shit," I grumble, and Kennedy takes the spot she had before, her legs wrapping around mine.

"Back so soon? There's no way she took care of you that fast, right?" Kennedy slides her hand to my ass and stares down as if she can see my dick. "Uh oh, she didn't even get you off, huh? Walk me to my car, big boy. We can get high, and I'll take better care of you than she ever could."

"Oh, knock it off, Kennedy. You're a sloppy drunk, you know that?" Dani scolds her, and I'm glad she didn't leave to find Lexi yet. I need to get out of here. I move away from Kennedy, but she's not taking the hint.

"How much do I owe you?" I go to grab my wallet, but Dani shakes me off.

"Nothing, hun. It's paid for. Call me when you're home, okay?"

"I didn't mean to fuck this up, Dani. I swear. The second I noticed how drunk she was, I shut the whole thing down. I didn't want to hurt her."

"I know, Jamie." She smiles. "I just want to make sure you're okay."

"Thanks, D."

I turn, and I'm staring right down at Kennedy. She'd be cute if she weren't so annoying. She's got big blue eyes and gorgeous lips, but I'm absolutely uninterested. She pushes her large, barely covered breasts against my chest and grinds against me. All I can think about is how perfect Lexi felt in my arms and how fast I can get the fuck out of here.

I've thoroughly fucked this whole thing up. Lexi and the gig.

"You look a little drunk, big boy. You wanna ride?" Kennedy yells to me as she empties her drink. "Why don't you take me with you, and I can ride you all night long, Daddy?"

She's on her tiptoes, throwing her arms around my neck before I realize what's happening. Her mouth smashes into mine and the world tumbles straight into the regret I still have over San Diego. I grab her by the shoulders and stumble away from her. I can hear Dani yelling at her, and I take that as my cue to leave.

I want to stay. I want to find Lexi and find out if she's alright. I want to dance with her until I can't my legs fall off or they throw us out of the bar. I want to kiss her. I'd give anything to hold her against me again. Instead, I'm going to sober up, go home, get high, and pass out. Tomorrow, if I'm lucky, I can work alongside her and not come across as a starving wolf or anymore of an asshole.

HOLLYWOOD

James

CHAPTER 11
FADE INTO YOU
MAZZY STAR

I'M STANDING in the parking lot, looking at my Jeep, realizing there's no way I'm capable of driving but can't stay in the club either. Not with Kennedy's total lack of regard for personal space and boundaries. I can't get the flavor of her fucking lip gloss out of my mouth and I hate it. I want it to be Lexi's. I'm such a fucking idiot for messing this up so damn fast. My phone buzzes; I want nothing more than to smash the fucking thing. But it wouldn't do any good. She finds me no matter where I am.

UNKNOWN NUMBER

Come on, Jamie, I'm bored. Play with me.

I promise no one will drug your drink…at least not this time 😇

I just want to fuck up your life a little more unless you're already doing it yourself. Then I just wanna watch.

It's too much. It's all too damn much. My head is throbbing, my heart is breaking, and I've lost all hope. A diner sign across the way flickers against the dark night sky. At least I can hide there while I sober up. I sure as hell don't have any money for a ride share. I take a step toward my new destination when I hear someone nearby sniffle and let out a soft sob.

I search the lot, and it takes me a second to find her, but eventually I spot the bright pink space buns over by the bar's patio. There's another sniffle, and I'm sure she's the one crying. As I approach, I try to shuffle my feet and make a little noise so I don't spook her.

"Lexi, are you all right?" That's a dumb question; of course she isn't.

"James?" Lexi stammers as she stands, wiping her face. "Shit. I'm… I'm sorry…fuck!"

"What's the matter?" She's shivering, and my instincts kick in before I even think it might be me that caused this. I'm the reason she's breaking down in a parking lot. I wrap my coat over her shoulders without hesitation before I lift her face and wipe tears away with the pad of my thumb. "Please tell me this isn't my fault—"

"No, I just, uhm. It's nothing."

"You're a beautiful woman standing alone in the middle of the arts district in a shitty parking lot, crying outside of a brewery party—it's not nothing."

She sniffles and tries to lower her head, but I won't let her. "Look, I, uhm, I'm sorry I came on so strong, and I…I shouldn't have thrown myself at you like that. I drank too much, and my stupid brain thought that—fuck—it doesn't matter."

"That was all on me; it was my fault. I drank too much, and I don't want to fuck this up." I wonder if she thinks I mean the job, when in reality, I mean any shot I have with her—if I have a shot. I offer her a pathetic smile. "You shouldn't be out here alone."

"I can take care of myself."

"I believe you, I do. But it doesn't mean you have to. Where's Dani?" I glance around, but there's no one. "She was supposed to come find you."

"She's probably still running damage control. I needed some air after…" she huffs and rolls her eyes, tucking her phone away and not bothering to finish the sentence.

"Damage control?"

"You two make sense. Go on, get back in there. I'm sure she's waiting with legs wide open for you. She might have a black eye, but I'm sure you won't notice while you stare at her fucking tits. I'll see you tomorrow for work."

"Are you talking about Dani?"

"You don't have to hide it. Everyone was there. Hundreds of witnesses. But fuck it. I don't care. Why should I? You're just another asshole I have to work with. So, I'll meet you in Long Beach. Don't worry about picking me up."

"Saw—fuck, you mean Kennedy?" She rolls her eyes. "No, come on. Kennedy was—"

"You fucking kissed her not five minutes after you rejected me. She told me you were taking her home. I guess you thought it was two for one night—" Her head rocks back, and I can see new tears forming in her eyes. When she looks at me again, all I can see is disappointment, and it's directed right at me. "Just don't let her fuck up any of our work. In fact, I can talk to Sam tomorrow and try to get Kennedy to take over the project. I have enough shit to deal with, and I certainly don't need you added to that." She pulls free and shrugs off my jacket, holding it out to me. "I should go back inside. No, I should go home. I wouldn't want to waste any more of your time."

"Is that it?" I stare hard at her, ignoring the jacket she's still holding out to me.

"What?" She pulls back, clearly not expecting the bluntness of my question.

"Is that it? Did you get everything you needed off your chest?" She nods almost imperceptibly, but her face scrunches up as she sniffles. I step closer again. "Good, because I don't want to do anything with Kennedy. I don't ever want to see her again, if that's possible. I wouldn't go out with her for a million dollars and I sure as fuck don't want to work with her, either."

"But? Why were you kissing her?" Now she's confused, and I can't say I blame her.

"I didn't kiss her, Lexi; she kissed me. I told Dani to check on you and that I was leaving. When I turned around to go, Kennedy grabbed me. I promise you, it was not reciprocated or enjoyable." I wipe her face again. Despite the nagging compulsion to kiss her, I want to make this right between us.

"Why were you leaving?"

"Because I thought I messed this all up, and apparently, I was right, but for the wrong reasons." I tuck my hands into my pockets. "I'll call Sam in the morning. I'll take myself off the project."

I turn to walk away, but she calls out and grabs my elbow. "James? You really didn't like kissing her?"

"No. In fact, I was looking to syphon some gasoline while I'm out here to get the taste out of my mouth." My face scrunches up like I've bitten into a lemon. A chuckle escapes her before she can stop it, and I brush that same piece of hair behind her ear again. "Put the damn jacket back on. You're shivering."

Reluctantly, she allows me to help her slide it back over her shoulders. I like the way my jacket looks on her, and I realize I'm grinning like an idiot. Especially when she curls her fingers around the edges and pulls it tighter. "You're… fuck. Lexi, I haven't gotten you out of my head since the coffee shop. Kennedy's a dumb kid trying to figure shit out, and that's not what I need in my life. That's not what I want."

"What the fuck happened in the bathroom?"

I bite my lip and lower my head. "I've had some fucked up things happen to me when alcohol was involved. It, uhm, left me with a lot of anger, disgust, and regret. You were drunk, and I didn't want to be the face of your regret tomorrow morning or any morning thereafter."

"Shit," she groans.

"Yeah," I whisper, closing the small gap between us. I take a risk and I press my forehead to hers. "There was only one woman in all of Los Angeles who could get me to follow them onto a dance floor, let alone into a bathroom. She's an angel with the prettiest pink hair and a thing for coffee."

Her mouth moves, but she stays silent. Maybe I broke her.

"If you let me, I'd like to take you out sometime. Somewhere without the crowd, and probably fewer drinks in both of us. Not for work, and not on Sam's dime." My hands drop to her hips, and I can't help but stare at those beautiful, pouty lips. "Hopefully somewhere with nicer bathrooms."

"They have very nice bathrooms here, sir," she smiles up at me. It's soft, with a hint of an apology that I don't need or deserve.

"We could go back in and confuse a lot of people by giving the bathrooms a second chance. Take it a little slower." She bumps my nose with hers and my legs turn to jelly. She's all I can feel, all I can see. Even the smell of her is intoxicating and making my head float more than the weed I smoked earlier. I want to bottle this scent so I have it forever and I don't give two shits about how creepy that sounded in my head.

My pulse quickens because we're about to kiss. I feel her

phone buzz in her pocket, and she steps away again like we're teenagers getting caught making out. I miss her body and how it fits so perfectly against mine. I'm hopeless, and I'm going to absolutely let this woman break my heart a thousand times over, if that's what it takes.

"Uhm, I don't know. I should probably just…uhm…I need to go. Dani's friend is taking us home, and I … I'm…"

"What did I say? Please, tell me." I am seconds away from dropping to my knees and begging her for a chance. What the fuck is wrong with me? She deserves better, and I should let her go. But I can't give up. Not yet. "Come on, you were right there with me, and now you're practically running to get away from me."

I need her to blame me, to throw my words back at me and make me feel like a fucking loser. Otherwise, I'll let my brain overthink things, and I'll convince myself there's still a chance. She looks like she's on the verge of a panic attack. I can recognize the symptoms. I've had enough of my own to know, and now I feel like an even bigger ass.

"It's nothing. I should…go."

"Alexis?" I stare into her red-rimmed eyes. The tears are back, and I realize these tears aren't from my dumbass not taking care of things in the bathroom. It's something deeper that she doesn't want me to figure out. This is raw pain; someone hurt her between her leaving the bathroom and now. "What happened in there? When you ran. Did someone hurt you?"

I'll never forgive myself if someone laid a hand on her because I let her go.

"No one touched me. I'm… it doesn't matter.

"Who did this, Lexi? Who hurt you? Was it Kennedy? What else did she say to…" She looks up at me again, recognizing the fire in my eyes behind all the pain. I'm ready to burn the whole fucking building down to find out who did this, and that's when I figure it out.

The text in the bathroom. The phone call she got as she ran down the hallway. She doesn't want me to see her phone either, that's why she tucked it away.

"It's nothing, I don't matter."

I don't matter. It wasn't a slip. Families are such a bitch sometimes, and somehow they always know right where to hit us. They have a special way of cutting too deep, knowing they'll never let you recover from it. That has to be what's gotten to her.

"You do matter. I won't push you for what's going on, but you shouldn't be alone." Her chin trembles, and it's breaking my heart. She lets me pull her close and trusts me enough to hold her. "Let it out, darlin'." Her body fights back sobs as I kiss the side of her head.

Rage like I've never felt before is growing inside me, and I have this urge to protect her from anyone and everyone. Protect her like no one had done for me all those times.

"What can I do, Lexi? How can I help?" I whisper in her ear, and she pulls away just enough to see me. We're both inches away from making more bad decisions as she stares at my lips and starts moving closer.

"You don't even know me, James."

"We can change that. Say it again, please?"

"You barely know me?"

"No, my name. It sounds fucking beautiful when you say it."

"James." It's breathy and sexy and perfect as her lips graze mine.

"Lex Luthor! Are you out here?" Dani's voice pulls us apart again as the night of near misses continues.

"Shit," she says as she slips away, dabbing her eyes on the cuffs of my jacket. She winces when she remembers the jacket is mine and tries to take it off again, but I stop her. She smiles at me, hugging the jacket a little closer. "I should go."

"I should, too," I whisper, not meaning it. I don't want to let her go. "If you need to talk, I'm a good listener."

"Okay, I'll see you in the morning?" She starts backing away slowly. "I uhm… I'd like to do that someday, the going out somewhere thing. I think that would be great."

"Yeah?"

She bites her bottom lip and nods. She's beautiful.

"Ah ha! Found you!" Dani screams as she runs over and looks between us, trying to figure out what's going on. "Oh shit, am I interrupting?"

"No," Lexi smiles back at me as they walk away. "I'm hungry. Let's go home and order a pizza."

They're about halfway across the parking lot when I yell out, "Hey, Angel?" She turns around hesitantly, "What do you take in your coffee?"

"Silky and sweet, just like her!" Dani yells back.

"Extra Cream and sugar," Lexi clarifies. She flashes a bashful smile before turning around and hugging Dani, glancing back one more time before they disappear around the corner.

It's around one in the morning when I sober up enough to head home. I trudge up the stairs and sit on the floor outside my dad's room, leaning against the door. The aroma of incense, art supplies, and old lumber fills my lungs, replacing the cherry blossoms and strawberries. Closing my eyes, I rock my head back. The dull sensation of a bruise forming on the back of my head makes me laugh at the memory of how it got there.

"Dad, I um…" Stuttering and unable to find the words. "Shit,

I guess it's been a while since I did this. I met someone today. She's smart, funny, and a damn knockout, too. You'd like her right off the bat because she's got pink hair. Like really pink, right out of a pack of bubble gum. I know it sounds dumb, but I think I'm falling for her. Hard."

I miss talking to my dad, and he was always on my ass about putting myself out into the world and letting people get to know me. I always fought him on it, saying it was better for everyone if I didn't. I understand now that he only wanted me to be happy again. Chase Cooper is my best friend, but my dad was something more. I'm still mad he's gone. I bet if I told a therapist I talk to him like this, they'd say I'm an idiot. It's probably why I left my last therapist.

"She makes me feel, Dad. I almost went out into the studio tonight instead of coming up here, and I haven't been in there since—" I stop myself and sit in silence as the pain passes. "She just might be my muse, Dad. I miss being around her already.

"Remember that last girl I brought home? It was right after the divorce, and you managed to trick me into going out to the studio to get you something before I took her up to my room." I run my fingers over the scuffed-up wood floors as my mind wanders. "I came back in, and she was long gone. You never told me what you said to her, but I don't think I ever thanked you enough for that. You knew I wasn't ready, and she wasn't right. I don't think you'd chase this one out. I would run after her and bring her back if you did."

I tell him about the coffee shop, job, dinner, and dancing. I tell him how alive she makes me feel and how I'm going to dig out my old sketchpad and bring it with me tomorrow. At some point, I must have fallen asleep because I woke up to my back hurting like a motherfucker and my phone alarm going off.

I look around, trying to remember why I'm on the floor, and

then it hits me. I grab the phone and realize I slept through twenty minutes of alarm noise.

"Shit!" I jump up, shower, and change; no time to shave. I'm out the door in fifteen minutes, headed to Lexi's with the biggest smile I've had on my face in years.

HOLLYWOOD

Lexi

CHAPTER 12
INTO YOU
ARIANA GRANDE

I CHECK the mirror one last time, questioning myself and the makeup. I don't normally wear makeup beyond a little base powder or something with SPF and my standard black eyeliner. This morning, though, I woke up and pulled out my bag of random cosmetics, and went to town. Okay, that's a bit of an overstatement, but it's more makeup than I wore yesterday. Most of it hides the bags under my eyes from this fucking hangover.

Glittery eyeshadows in an array of purples and pinks coat my eyes before I line them in black, as always, with a swipe at the end. My dark burgundy lips make me worry for a second if I'm overdoing it with the makeup. Then I see the all-black clothes in the mirror and laugh. I'm too much of a 90s goth reject to overdo it with the makeup.

Wash that off your face. What are you, Satan's whore? That's a whore's color. What kind of man finds a fat clown like you attractive?

I slam the lipstick down on the counter, snapping the bracelet around my wrist while I try to block out my mother's voice from my head. When it passes, I grab a few necessities and shove them into the backpack I've loaded with my tablet and anything else I might need today.

My phone buzzes on its charger, and I dart across the room and grab it.

JAMES

Be there in five

"I still can't believe I tried to have sex with you in the bathroom," I mumble to my phone, laughing. I was unprofessional and drunk; he was there and willing. That's all. But I can't stop thinking about it—I even dreamt about it.

LEXI

Great, I'll be right down!

I study myself in the mirror again and groan. If there's nothing between us, why am I wearing makeup? I finish packing everything up in my backpack and glance at the jacket hanging off the back of my couch. If he doesn't like me, why would he let me borrow his jacket? I should bring it downstairs and give it back to him. Instead, I slip it on, letting the smell of whiskey and spice pull me into a daydream. The one I had in the shower after Dani left this morning. The daydream where his fingers don't stop and…

JAMES

Parked across the street

Really hope you're hungry 😉 Might have overdone it.

I stare at the winky face. Is he flirting? Was it weird that a guy would use a winking emoji? I nearly convinced myself that booze was the root cause of everything we said last night. The good and the bad. But now I'm not so sure. Maybe he meant what he said in the parking lot. Or, it's just an emoji.

"Okay, you fucking weirdo." I mumble to the empty room. "Enough overthinking for now!"

Professional. I'm going to keep it professional today. The smell of his cologne hits me again, and my heart flutters as the butterflies wake up and start their antics again.

D

Have fun today… I miss you at the office already!! I may need you to help me bury Kennedy in the desert somewhere.

You'll be fine today!

But you two looked SOOOO fucking CUTE together last night!!!

I sling my bag over my shoulder and scoop up my keys before running down three flights of stairs. I fly out the main door of the building, spotting him right away. He's leaning with his foot against a blue Jeep that looks like it's both well-used and well-loved. He doesn't see me as he laughs at his phone with a cup of coffee in his other hand.

I stop and stare. With so much happening, I never stopped to check him out beyond his face. Which is a little weird, because he looked—and felt up—every inch of my body while we danced. I bite back the wicked smile, remembering how he felt when I moved against him. Based on what I felt, I bet he looks phenomenal naked.

He's dressed down today, a t-shirt instead of a button-down and no vest. I can't stop staring at how tight the shirt is around his chest and biceps; it shows me he hasn't missed arm day in a long time. Not bulging, body builder muscles, but just that right, thick, sexy as fuck appeal. He's got a tiny waist, so the bottom half of his shirt is baggy and so are the shorts that hang off his hips. I get a little jealous momentarily, wondering if he's smaller than me. Fucker even has the audacity to have nice legs. Rude.

I don't want a relationship. But I sure as hell wouldn't complain if this guy broke my back a few times. What did Dani say? We could mutually relieve stress?

I watch his tongue slide over his lips and realize I have no idea what he tastes like. We didn't kiss. I mean, he kissed my neck, and we had a few near kisses. We were so busy trying to get into each other's pants it never happened. Now, as he pulls his bottom lip between his teeth, I'm regretting—

PROFESSIONAL! I let out a slow breath and collect myself again before I head toward him.

"Hey, good morning." His smile is bright as he spots me. He reaches into the Jeep and hands me a giant iced coffee milk tea with boba and I forget how words work the second our fingers touch. "I, uhm, I went to the shop by your office and asked the kid what you usually order."

"Oh," is the only thing my brain and mouth can agree on saying.

His scruff is a little thicker today, perfectly framing those pretty, full lips I'm trying not to stare at. He's wearing sunglasses and a backward baseball hat, which still looks good, but I secretly wish I could see his eyes again and that soft, fluffy hair with its slight curl to it.

"I've got some Tylenol in my bag if you need it today. I'm sure I will."

"Are you saying I'm a hungover mess, Mr. Barton?"

He smiles and pushes his sunglasses up his brow, and they stay there, defying gravity. His steel-blue eyes are breathtakingly gorgeous in the bright morning sun and just as distracting as they were yesterday in the boba shop. Forget words—I don't even remember how to stand anymore.

"Hell no. Definitely not saying that." He stares too long before remembering something. "Oh, and I brought you a little something for breakfast. Okay, several little somethings. They're in the Jeep."

I smile back, and he darts around the car, holding the door open for me. He even offers to take my bag. It's warm this morning, so I shrug off his jacket and he puts it in the back.

"Oh, uhm, I didn't even know guys still did that. Thanks."

"If they don't, they should. Hopefully, they made the coffee how you like it, foods in the center console."

I open the bag, and the scent of butter and chocolate hits me hard. "Holy shit! Is that like six chocolate croissants?! What's the deal with you and pastries?"

"I didn't think flowers would be your thing, at least not yet, since I have no idea which ones you like. And the bakery by my house is pretty amazing." He smirks, and I'm wondering if he's still drunk because he's giving off some severely cocky vibes that he didn't have last night. "So, which ones do you like? Flowers, I mean. For tomorrow?"

He doesn't give me time to react before he jogs back to the other side. I sit there, drooling at the bag of croissants, while trying to think of flower names, any flowers. Flowers, breakfast, holding the door open—who is this guy?

Honey, maybe you should lay off the sweets. No one wants a pig for a wife.

I take a deep breath, quieting the voice again. I hate days like today when it's louder than usual.

He climbs in and starts the drive, and I glance at the GPS on his phone. "Are we going to be late? I should have just said we could take the metro."

"Don't worry. It's not that kind of convention. No one will even notice if we walk in a little late. Hair and makeup professionals don't really worry about things like that, and half of them are hung over from a big party the sponsors hosted last night."

"Ugh, I know the feeling. Wait! Hair and makeup? Fuck! God, they're going to see me and think I'm a fucking idiot." I dig through my bag, looking for anything I can find to clean my face. Out of nowhere, there's a hand on mine, and my eyes meet the soft blues that keep making my heart skip. "How do you know so much about hair and makeup convent—? Never mind, you're a photographer."

"It's fine."

"I get that you're trying to be nice or whatever, but no." I'm blushing so hard I wish I could find a rock to hide under. "My makeup is on par with a toddler who broke into the drawer of markers and glitter and wanted to play dress up. I'm too old for this anyhow. I—"

"No, I mean it. I think…I mean…what I'm trying to say is…" He licks his lips and pulls his bottom lip through his teeth slowly as he thinks. He can't stop looking at my mouth. Is it because I have clown makeup or there's chocolate on my face?

Fuck. Does he want to *kiss* me?

"Angel, you're…stunning."

I stare at him. A strange feeling fills my stomach and makes my head spin. Stunning. Not pretty, not beautiful, not even just adorable. Last night he said I looked amazing, and today I get stunning. Me?

"I…we should probably go…the light's… uhm, green," I barely even hear myself think the words, let alone say them. He nods and goes back to paying attention to traffic while my brain continues to slosh around. I mean, how often does a hot-as-hell man in this city tell someone like me they're stunning?

Never. It's never.

And he called me Angel. He's also called me Alexis a few times now, and I hate that name, but when he says it, it sounds so…different. I have got to get my head back in the game. Even if I did like him—or he liked me—I don't do relationships.

We drive away from the city's high-rise buildings and down the freeway, heading toward Long Beach. If traffic cooperates, the drive isn't horrible. But the traffic is rarely cooperative in L.A.—except for weekend mornings before ten. I watched the GPS moving closer and closer to the river of red we're headed for. The roaring wind from the topless Jeep provides a serene escape from conversation. Once we hit that wall of cars, though, all we'll have is time to talk.

It's so much easier at a club or out with friends, where everything becomes a distraction and loud music makes it hard to talk.

My mind drifts back to last night. The feel of his mouth on my neck and the way he held me. We shed our awkwardness, even if for only a few stolen moments. I giggle to myself, thinking about how that moan and the high-pitched whimper that followed went to my bones. Most guys I've been with don't make a lot of noise, or if they do, it's nothing but terrible attempts at dirty talk.

"I'm sorry if that was too forward earlier. I didn't mean to make you uncomfortable," he finally says as the Jeep slows and we join the long line of commuters clogging the roads. We should be fifteen minutes away. Instead, we're going to be another forty-five at least.

"Oh, no, it's, uhm, fine. Really."

"Look, I know we've been doing a hell of a job starting on some weird footing, but I just wanted to tell you that I'm *really* excited to work with you."

My stomach lurches, and I wonder if this is the part where

we return to promises of professionalism. The part where he tells me the alcohol did all the talking last night. I drop the remaining half of the croissant I'm working on back into the bag and roll the top down on it. I don't need croissants anyhow. Or cute guys complimenting me.

"Sam showed me some of your work yesterday—before you and I met—it was spectacular. Some of the best layouts I've seen in a while. You've got a real eye for it."

"Thanks, you take really good photos." I'm staring out the windshield when I say it, and already wish I could take it back. That was so insincere. From what I saw while loading his images yesterday, his work isn't good; it's gorgeous.

"No, my work is borderline stock photography. Or, well, at least it has been for the last few months." He turns and looks at me, and my heart quickens. I hope we can go back to pretending there's something between us—even if only for a few more minutes. "This sounds kind of weird, but I'm psyched to be doing this project. To make something and be inspired again with someone like you."

I nod, and we fall into silence again, this time much less comfortable. Someone like me? The rumble of a large truck lurching next to us on the way to the port draws my attention out the window to the sea of cars and semi-trucks.

"Have you always wanted to be a photographer?" I blurt out, desperate to fill the silence.

"Kind of? I've done a lot of stuff—painting, writing, pottery, sculpting. Photography is the quickest one to make money with, so it kind of supports the others. Or, well, supported." His brow furrows, and the grip on the steering wheel tightens. "I've become a part-time handyman, too. Which, honestly, sucks. Gotta make ends meet somehow here in California, huh?"

"Handyman? That seems like a leap, but I'll keep that in

mind," I laugh nervously. You would think that as a designer, I'd have art hobbies, but I don't. "I took a photography course once, and I just sat there confused and eventually gave up. I don't think I could paint a stick figure. People always think I can draw."

"You get that, too? People automatically assuming you can illustrate, edit a video, and build a website? Yeah, I've seen a little of that. So, what about you? Was this pursuing a dream, or are you one of the many who came here to work in film and then realized how hard that is to get into?"

I don't enjoy telling people about me or my life; it's led to too many people trying to trauma bond with me. Who I am in private differs drastically from who I am in public. I'm outgoing and fun, and I never miss out on a party, unless they get a glimpse of the real me. Then they learn I'd rather be in a secluded place with a book. That I'm hiding in plain sight from someone who knows exactly which buttons to push to send me into a tailspin.

So, I find a safe answer.

"I thought about film, but it wasn't a priority. We came out here for school and better jobs—to start a new life. I think if I had gone into the film industry, it would still have been as a creative, behind the camera role."

"We?" It isn't accusatory, like he thinks I'm hiding a secret husband or something. I wonder if Sam or Dani gave him a heads-up about my mother—or stepfather.

"My sister and I. We moved out here together after we turned eighteen."

"Nice. It's better than coming here and not knowing anyone." He tips his coffee cup all the way back, trying to get the last drop, and I notice a scar on his wrist near a small tattoo. I want to ask him about it, but then I'd have to open up about my life. "I could teach you some photography tricks."

"Yeah, that would be cool."

"Excellent!" He grins like that is the best answer he's ever heard. There's a pause, then he asks, "Where are you from? You said you moved here, but you never said where from, and you don't strike me as a California girl."

"I'm that obvious?"

"I'm asking too many questions, huh?"

Yes.

"No, but should I work on my vocal fry to blend in better? Wait, I don't have some kind of telltale accent or drawl, do I?"

"No, nothing like that," he laughs, glancing over at me before turning his attention back to traffic. "It sounds cliché as hell, but you're just different."

My therapists used to tell me I need to get closer to people and let people meet the real me. But why should I when they'll just leave? If they don't leave because of who I am or who my parents are, I'll push them away because it's better for everyone. So I just let them all think I'm allowing them in on my secrets and keep my disguise on.

"Because I'm still desperately clinging onto my high school goth phase? Or is it the hair?"

"No, and I love the hair." His brow furrows as he thinks. "It's like you're two different people, but not for any superficial California reasons. The person I met at Sam's office and the one from last night outside the club are two very different women. Like two different sides of the same shy coin."

I stare at him while he drives, my mouth hanging open. Has he already cracked my code? Is he a mind reader or some shit? How did he do that?

"Oh, I'm not shy." I watch him intently, hoping he believes

me. "Yesterday was just a bizarre day. Between Sam's project shuffling and Kennedy being, well, Kennedy, it stressed me out a little. Last night was just a build-up of tension and alcohol. I'm not usually like that."

I'm talking too fast and I can't help it, that's my nervous tell. When someone gets too close to me, to who I'm trying to hide away, I talk faster to try to throw them off. Or to get out of the situation faster.

"Mmm, are you sure? Shy usually has a keen eye for spotting other shy people."

"Wait, you're saying you're shy?"

"Angel, you have no idea."

"You didn't show it last night. Especially in the bathroom." I turn in my seat, bringing my leg up so I can face him better. If I'm going to throw him off the scent of my secret self, I need to rely heavier on the public act. "Oh, and from what I heard—and felt—while we were dancing, you sure didn't seem shy. More like a man who had a pretty damn good idea of how to get what he wanted."

I watch the red creep up his neck as he looks out his window, trying to avoid looking at me. He's blushing so hard right now, and all I can do is giggle. Not only does he make noise, he blushes. Fuck. He could be fun in bed. The guys who blush like this are usually the ones who will bend over backwards to please a woman. Sometimes literally. I should wear shorts next time I'm in his Jeep—or, as crazy as it sounds, maybe a skirt. I wonder what he'd do to me right now if I let him.

"So, what's your excuse for not being shy last night, huh?" I let the last word drip off my lips in a whine, giving it a hint of sexual tone.

His laugh is nervous, and his grip on the wheel tightens again. He shifts in his seat, and I'm pretty sure that little noise I made worked and has him turned on. He takes deep a breath, trying to collect himself, and that's when I catch it. He's a mess. This isn't an act for him. He is a nervous wreck. The more I come on to him, the deeper into his own head he goes. Interesting.

"I didn't mean to—"

"I was distracted," he blurts out, his knuckles still white as he stares holes into the car in front of us. "Last night, I was... distracted."

"I thought you said you weren't into the bubbly blond with big tits." I smirk, remembering Kennedy wrapped around him. I guess I'm still jealous about that. I mean, she got to kiss him before I did.

"I'm not," he laughs and shakes his head. He's struggling to find an excuse, and I'm worried I'm tanking this conversation. "It was... blonde is so... boring."

"Boring? I should tell her that when I see her again. Blonde is boring."

"When there's a spell-binding woman I'm desperate to impress instead, blonde is, well, overdone. I've never really been into the blonde craze. Pretty sure I'm screwing *this* up, though. Again. Anyhow, I like pink hair. And brown eyes. Tattoos."

I feel the warmth of my skin, and I'm pretty sure my red face matches his. That wasn't what I was expecting.

"I have trouble keeping my mouth shut, so something stupid eventually falls out of it—like it's doing right now. You can tell me to shut the fuck up. It won't be the first time a woman has when I'm trying to compliment her."

"At least you're self-aware." My voice is soft and strange-sounding to me.

He laughs. I was right; he has a charming smile that sends my butterflies fluttering.

"Not sure if Sam warned you, but I'm not really a people

person. Dani's been trying to get me to go out with the group for a while now. I'd just rather stay home and, uhm, work."

"*Work?* That didn't sound very convincing."

"I work, a bit." He chuckles. "I do the editing and developing at home when I get gigs. When I can't get gigs, I get so stoned I don't have to think about it. It's easier."

"I get that. I like the solitude and being able to hide in the back of the office."

"See?" He grins. "Shy can spot shy."

"Yeah, but that's just work! I can't be shy. I like going out and partying with Dani and some other people. I got you to dance with me. I'm pretty sure I was leading the charge to the bathroom last night, no less. How is *that* shy?"

He glares at me over the top of his sunglasses, and I have to look away. Is it possible to have eyes that are too pretty? This isn't happening. Is it?

"When you go out, do you spend the next three days trying like hell to avoid all human contact? Is today's huge conference full of people making anxiety creep around the edges of your well-trained facade? Wouldn't you rather be anywhere today but stuck with all those people in that building?"

My jaw drops, and I laugh a little louder than I mean to. "Oh, whatever, fine, I'm an occasional introvert, but I don't think I mind today at all. I've got the right company for it."

"So we're both going to be a hot mess today, huh?" He laughs deeply, and his eyes wrinkle a little. "I'll make sure to keep the next few days as people free as possible—for both of us."

"It's fine, I'm prepared." I dig through my bag and pull out a small pouch of edibles. "I'm also kind enough to share with a guy who prefers to stay home alone and get baked."

"Fuck, you're also brilliant."

HOLLYWOOD

Lexi

CHAPTER 13
I'M NOT OKAY

MY CHEMICAL ROMANCE

"I'M gonna make you work for it, though." I giggle, taking a peanut butter cup out of the baggie and hold it between my teeth.

"Work for it?" His smirk should be illegal.

"Yep. Especially since traffic isn't going anywhere. I figure you owe me this much after last night." Shifting in my seat, I leaning as far over as the seatbelt will allow. I can see his Adam's apple bob as he swallows hard, leaning over to meet me. Without looking away from my eyes, his hand finds my knee and slides up my thigh.

I can feel his breath on my face when my phone chimes the toll of doom and I jump away to grab it with a loud groan. "Sorry, I should have… anyhow, here," I stumble over the words and hand him the candy as I read the onslaught of texts. I don't even look to see if he eats it.

😈 SATAN 😈

Why aren't you answering your door?

Your car is here, Alexis. Come out here and answer your door.

I look like an idiot standing in the hall.

LEXI

I'm working, Mom. I'm not home.

I'm going to a conference, and we carpooled

😾 SATAN 😾

Don't lie to me. Were you drinking again last night? Are you hungover?

LEXI

No, mother. I'm not home. I swear.

😾 SATAN 😾

Where are you? I'll come get you. You should know better, Alexis.

The phone rings before I even reply, and I cringe. "Sorry, I should take this or she won't stop calling."

"No problem," he smiles, slipping the peanut butter cup back into the baggie before his hand is back on my leg, squeezing. If I wasn't already slipping into my *deal with mom mode,* I would probably jump this man.

I haven't even said hello, and she barrages me with questions.

"Alexis, what do you mean, a conference*? Don't lie to me; you're home, I'm sure of it. Just answer the door. I can't believe you were out boozing and debauching again last night. What is the matter with you, Alexis?"*

"Mom—"

"Please tell me you at least didn't black out and wake up in a stranger's bed. Where are you? It sounds like you're in a car. Whose car are you in? I'm going to send your father to get you right away. We've talked about this kind of behavior, young lady. Send me the address. My lord, this is embarrassing. Do you understand how embarrassing this is for us?" She doesn't stop to breathe.

"Mom, calm down. Everything is fine. We just, we're going to Long Beach and—"

"Long Beach? Are you high, Alexis? You can't go to Long Beach! It's full of drugs and homeless people, and you're just gallivanting around there with some strange man? This is Danielle's fault, isn't it? I told you she was no good and a terrible person. All those rainbows and flags, shoving it down our throats. She's turned you to the devil's side, just like I knew she would."

She's not expecting answers to any of these questions—she never does—but I try, anyway.

"Her name is Daniella, Mother, that's not—"

"Why can't they just have normal names?" She mumbles, and it's difficult not to hang up on her. Some of her worst traits are racism, sexism, and homophobia. If I try to correct the behavior, she attacks me more and I can only handle so much. *"Why do you do this to me, Alexis? Why do you insist on being just like your sister and bringing shame down on your father and me? Why do you have to run around this den of sin, whoring yourself out to anyone willing?"*

"Mom, I—" I'm shutting down. It's hard to breathe even though I'm in an open Jeep with plenty of air.

"I'm calling your father and sending him to come get you. This is absolutely ridiculous. He's a busy man, Alexis. He can't be babysitting you while you live out these ridiculous fantasies of yours."

Traffic, the Jeep, James, none of those things exist anymore. The world has swallowed me whole as I slip inside my mind to find a dark corner to hide myself. My mother sets off all the warning bells in me, turning me into the person I try desperately to hide away. My extroverted slash introverted Jekyll and Hyde act is cute, but the third me is why I've been in and out of therapy since I was fourteen.

"Please, mom—" My voice sounds pitiful and I barely get the words out.

"Should I have him bring one of our sheriff's office parishioners with him? Did that boy touch you, Alexis? I swear to the baby Jesus himself, if he got you pregnant I'll—"

"STOP IT!" I scream, holding the side of my head and pulling my legs up to my chest. The line is silent and the seconds squeeze my lungs tighter.

"Excuse me?"

I want to scream, but all I can do is bed in a childish whimper, "Please don't." the breath I take sounds like I'm some kind of asthmatic. I shouldn't have yelled. It's exactly what she wanted. "I'm sorry, Mother. I'll be home later, and we can discuss this when I'm home. Please don't send Ronnie."

The silence that follows is a deep, dark sludge and I'm trapped waist deep. Silence around her is more terrifying to me, as my entire body stiffens as I wait for what's coming, but I can't stop shaking. Then there's a warmth as his hand wraps around mine and he squeezes. I can't even look at him. I don't want him to see this version of me.

"I want you to call me when you get home to let me know you're alright." She flips on a dime, and abruptly, the poison in her voice turns to honey. *"You know I'm just worried about you. There's no need to yell at me like that when all I want is for you to be safe."*

"I'm sorry."

"Did you get to work on that project for your father?" Each word is calm and calculated. I email her updates on the project daily; she knows how far along I am. She's taken me to the edge and pushed me over like she planned. *"That's your priority and your penance. Your service to God to amend for these sins you insist on committing."*

"Stepfather."

"Alexis, don't start with me." She's back again, coiled like a snake, ready to strike. *"You're an adult; act like one."*

"I'm sorry."

"Fuck this," James says under his breath.

"Who was that?"

James's hand lets go of mine and grabs the back of my seat as he turns to check traffic, then zips into the lane for the off-ramp. The noise from the wind now that we're moving again is deafening, and I barely hear my mother freaking out and screaming at me.

"Alexis Strauss, what is all that noise? Oh my god, are you on a motorcycle?"

"I gotta go. It's really hard to hear. I'll call you tonight. I love you, Mom."

I end the call and close my eyes. I'm ready to break down and crawl back into bed. I want to hide. I'm sure I'm about to throw up when his hand returns, this time on my knee. He wants me to know I'm not alone, but I am. I hide my face, turning toward the window.

HOLLYWOOD

James

CHAPTER 14
BROWN EYED GIRL
VAN MORRISON

"ANGEL, can you open your eyes for me?" The wind quiets as we slow down and I pull off to the side of the ramp. "Come on, just long enough to breathe with me for a bit, okay?"

I'd heard enough from Lexi's mother, so I used one of the oldest tricks in the book for a Jeep owner. I find the gap in traffic and punch the gas, heading for the coming offramp. Earlier, when the wind kept us from talking, I had cursed myself for leaving the top off. Now I'm glad to have the roaring wind tunnel to shut her mother up.

Lexi's blocking out the world around her by shutting her eyes tight against it. I don't blame her; I would, too. I have.

"Angel?" I keep my voice soft while I gently stroke her arm with my knuckles. If she doesn't want to be touched, even a soft brush could be enough to send me off the edge of a cliff. Her. I mean *her*. I wonder how much more we have in common.

She chokes on a sob she doesn't want me to hear, "I'm okay. Can we…can we just go?"

"Yeah, whatever you need, sweetheart." I pull back out onto the road, my mind racing to find some way to fix this.

I understand why Dani was trying to match the two of us.

Lexi understands trauma, and while that should make me believe I'm not alone, and we share things in common, it makes everything worse. My beautiful muse hides her scars on the inside. Her broken pieces of armor glued crudely around her, trying to keep her safe from the demons. I don't want that, not for her. The urge to protect her is even stronger than last night. I wonder if I saw something that reminded me of myself, that tried to reveal her broken pieces. Misery loves company, but I thought she was my rainbow, not a matching cloud.

"Thanks for the noise," she mumbles.

I look over, surprised that she's even talking yet. "It sounded like you needed a bit of an out on that call. I hope I didn't overstep. I don't want to cause you trouble."

She's chewing on her nails and staring timidly out the window. She's probably trying to figure out if I've kidnapped her, given that she's already warned me not to be a mass murderer. "Where are we?"

"I opted for the scenic route. I figured we could use a break from the 405." I flash her a wink.

The acidic tone of her mother's voice put me on edge, so I can only imagine what it's doing to her. I wanted to grab the phone and toss dear old mom out the window into oncoming traffic. It all hit a bit too close to home for me. Too much familiarity. Not in the exact words, but in their meaning—the painful lash they inflict.

That old saying they tried to teach kids about sticks and stones? It's utter bullshit. Words have fangs. They sink into the skin and burrow deep in the mind. They gnash and claw at happiness and confidence. Like a spell or mind control, these words give the speaker a power only they can control. The closer to your heart that person is, the more pain their words inflict.

"No, that was...appreciated. Thank you." She tries to smile, but it doesn't last long. I don't want her to be locked in this shell, but I don't want her to have to pretend either. "Did, uhm, you hear any of that?"

"Nah. I was way too busy watching traffic and thinking of how next to embarrass myself in front of the pretty girl next to me." She doesn't need to know I heard every damn word. I wish I could tell her I understand, but somehow, that feels hollow—like I'm trying to make it a competition. 'Whose mom is the worst' isn't a game I'd care to play with her.

"Okay."

Her entire demeanor has changed, so I'm treading lightly for now, trying to find a crack in the shell she's hiding inside. The speed at which she shut down isn't foreign to me. We're too much alike, and that scares me. I want to hold her, to whisper how badly I want to help her. I'll open my own wounds and pour out my soul if I thought it would help heal hers.

As we drive, I remember something from last night. It's small, but it might help. I reach behind her and pull my jacket out, laying it over her. She instantly snuggles into it, and I can see some of the tension loosen its hold on her. I'm not taking her to the conference like this. I need to give her somewhere safe, somewhere she can hit the reset button and tuck away the insecurities her mother brings up again until Lexi can deal with them on her terms.

"Hey, uhm, there's this excellent breakfast place up this way. What do you say we start the day over with better coffee and the closest thing to home-cooked food you can get from a restaurant? It's better than convention center food."

"Can I leave my phone in your car?"

"Do whatever you need to, Angel." I glance over at her while we wait for a light. She doesn't flinch when I reach over and wipe the tear from her cheek. "I thought you might appreciate a little comfort food and time to shake that call off. We can probably get a table away from anyone else."

"Okay. Yeah."

When I park down a crowded side street near a golf course ten minutes later, Lexi is confused. For whatever reason, she's trusting me and I'd like to keep it that way. Inside the house-turned-restaurant, memorabilia and framed pictures of different water skiing events from years ago decorate the walls. The place has a comforting atmosphere of someone's lakeside home with pictures of real people on the walls instead of those ugly corporate paintings of fruit.

She slips her arm through the jacket sleeve and into my hand as a man walks toward us with a big smile. I squeeze her hand twice. Once to tell her I've got her. A second time to tell her I understand. She tucks her head against my shoulder, as if she gets what I'm trying to tell her without words.

"Hey, hey! Long time no see, pal! And a good morning to you too, young lady." The man's bright white smile is flashy but kind. He owns the place and takes pride in running it. It's why it wins all sorts of local awards. "End of the patio?"

"Yeah, please." He walks us outside, and after Lexi takes the seat facing the road, I slide into the patio-length booth across from her.

"If you order the cappuccino or anything with foam on top, that guy comes out and draws a little duck in the drink. It's kind of his schtick."

"Guess you come here a lot?"

"Enough. My dad and I came to this place as much as possible when we lived closer. He and the owner would talk each other's ears off about anything and everything under the sun." Realizing I should veer the conversation for my own good, I change gears. "Do you like muffins?"

"Uhm, I dunno. I mean, coffee's fine."

"I'm not convinced. What if I order one, and if you want, you can try it? I promise only healthy stuff in your half. All the calories or glutens or whatever people say is bad are in my half. Okay?" I want to see her eat something, but I've got a feeling her mother is why she's not.

She nods reluctantly, right as the waitress steps outside and rounds the corner. "Hey, hey, stranger! I haven't seen you and your pops down this way in forever!"

"Yeah, it's been a while." I order one of their giant muffins and coffee for both of us, flashing Lexi a smirk and a wink as I do. I wait for the waitress to leave before I ask, "Would it be better if we talked about work?"

"No, I'd probably get annoyed with myself that we're here instead of at the convention." She looks at her watch and then at the menu. She simply wants the day to end. She needs to be in her safe space, hidden away from the pain. Mine was in the closet as a kid; in bed as an adult. "Do you bring people here often?"

"No. Only you."

"Only me?" She bites her lip and I can tell she's trying to come out. Struggling to resurface. "And all the girls you try to flatter after making out with them in a bathroom and bailing?"

"Ouch." I lean forward and gaze into her eyes; it's like staring into a strange mirror, like seeing all my hurt in someone else's eyes. I want to take it all from her, but I know that's now how it works. "I've never brought anyone here. Not dates, not friends, not even clients. Because this is mine, this is a secret place I could go to when I needed reassurance that I'm in a safe place. Well, it's not very secret; the place is packed on weekends."

This was a private getaway for my dad and I. We'd sit for

hours after my therapy sessions. I would sketch and work through my issues while he talked to people and made sure I ate. When I tilt my head and peek through the window, I spot Dad's sketch on the wall. A waterskiing duck. It's cartoonish and silly, not his typical style, but I can see him in each pencil stroke. He loved sharing art with people, making them something unique. He also loved bringing me here. Something about the place always helped me.

"Oh!" she gasps. I get the sense that she finally sees something familiar in me. "I, uhm, I thought that…never mind."

"Anyhow, I figured you could use somewhere to escape for a bit before we dive into too many people and not enough oxygen. Give your edible a little extra time to kick in." I lean back. "Did you even take one?"

"You know you didn't need to do this, right? It's not your problem, and I'm sorry if I'm being difficult."

"You don't need to be sorry; it's not your fault." I'm throwing darts in the dark to find a way to help her. I've known her for less than a day. That's not enough time to learn how to pull her out of this headspace, but I keep trying. "Is she who called you last night?"

"How could you tell?" There's a trace of sarcasm in her voice.

"It was something in your eyes. You've got it now; it says you'd rather hide under the covers than be wherever you are." I bite my lip, hoping I'm not going too far with this. "Besides, your co-worker hitting on a guy you've known for a few hours wasn't enough to set someone like you off. I'm sure I didn't help, and I was hoping it wasn't just because I'm a dick. It seemed like there was something more wrong."

I can't stop looking at her. I'm trying, but I simply can't. My hand is twitching again; I would give anything for a pencil and a piece of paper. Fuck, give me some chalk and a bit of clear sidewalk—I don't care. I need to draw her. The sensation should have faded by now, but it's growing stronger.

"Yeah, well, I did a lot of things wrong last night. Going in the first place, everything I did with you, smacking Kennedy in the face. None of that was very professional or normal for me."

"You smacked her? Well, Kennedy deserved it after how she treated you. As for what we did, why was that wrong?" I lean forward and stare into those two deep amber pools. "I think we should finish what we started. Possibly a few times."

She looks surprised and lets out a fake laugh. "No, you don't. It's okay." A small strand of hair has fallen out of her ponytail. I wait, giving her long enough to fix it herself. When she doesn't, I reach over and gently tuck it behind her ear, letting my fingers linger on the shell of her ear as our eyes meet.

Fuck. Her hair is so soft, and I want to run my fingers through it while I kiss her. I have a hunch she tastes like candy.

"Here you go, kids, one fresh giant muffin!" I pull my hand away from her and sit back. Lexi also pulls back, bringing her knee up to her chest, fixating on something off in the distance.

I nod and smile at the waitress. As she walks away, my head rocks back until I stare at the ceiling. The longer she stays quiet, the longer I overthink everything. Right now, I'm focused on how she's wishing last night hadn't happened while I desperately hope it happens again. Keeping it all out of my head has been…difficult—her smell, her warmth, how in control she was. I rub my eyes, trying to clear my mind.

"The muffin is really good."

I watch her rip off a chunk from the side and take the tiniest, mousiest bite. She licks the sticky caramel off her lips, watching me the whole time, so I know she sees how hard I swallow. Is she flirting? Coming on to me? After all that? How can I complete a three-week project with her if I can't stop daydreaming about how she tastes and what her lips feel like?

We're interrupted again when the owner drops off our drinks, pulls out a toothpick, and draws a duck's head in the foam. Just like I'd described—he's no Picasso, but the thought behind it counts.

"Tell your pops I said hi, and you kids don't be strangers, okay?" As he leaves, my phone buzzes.

UNKNOWN NUMBER

Why aren't you answering me, Jamie?

Have you got a pretty new toy for me to play with?

I hope it's not the blonde. She was way too easy, wasn't she?

"Okay, you were right. It's cute," Lexi comments, pulling me back to the here and now before I turn my phone over. She's looking down into her cup of coffee. "I mean, I almost don't want to drink it, but it's probably twice as offensive if I don't."

I nod, barely hearing her as I frown into my own cup and watch the figure slowly melt away as I stir it with the spoon. Why did I come here? I close my eyes and take a few deep breaths, keeping myself from spiraling into the memories. I want to be there for her—but fuck—this hurts.

"North Carolina."

"What?"

"You asked where I was from and I never answered you. I'm from North Carolina."

"Oh," I answer flatly, still watching the swirling liquid and rising steam but unable to focus on them. She's nervous and I know what's coming next, but I won't stop her. I understand why I came here now. To be somewhere familiar and close to my happier memories. It's okay; she shouldn't be interested in a mess like me.

"Look, I don't know how to say this, but uhm…I'm not the girl for you. I think you're really…great…but we should just work together. Keep it professional."

"Yeah, I know." I nod, dropping my eyes to catch the last remnants of the melting duck figure. "I knew that at the coffee shop when I first saw you. I hoped Dani finally got one right, but it's fine. You're so out of my league, not even in the same sport."

"No, I'm not," she says defensively, before laughing. "I'm nothing like that. I'm a normal, boring girl with issues and a weird family. You're the hot, mysterious photographer, slash artist, slash handyman. I'm sure you'll be fine even if you are shy."

I should let it go. Normally, I would. I'd take this as a sign that this isn't going to happen, and I'd move on. I glance back through the window and see that picture my dad did, and it's like he's here behind me, pushing me forward. Maybe there is an afterlife, and he heard me last night at his door. Maybe that's why I picked this restaurant, of all places, to take Lexi. He really would have liked her.

"Alexis, anyone who thinks you're not the most intelligent, fun, stunning, incredibly talented, most amazing person they've ever met is lying." I'm blushing; I can feel it. "I know that sounds stupid and desperate because I've known you for barely a day, but I don't care."

"It doesn't sound stupid, I'm just… I'm not those things."

"You are. Those things and so much more, and I wish you could see how incredible you are—how I see you."

"James."

I drop my head and close my eyes. I think I've run out of

ideas and steam. "Thanks for not throwing the coffee in my face or calling me creepy."

"Why would I waste perfectly good coffee messing up a perfectly good face?" Her half smile makes the butterflies start a Conga line in my stomach. "So, you're not upset? About not wanting to, you know, go out or whatever?"

I shake my head, knowing that if I talk, my voice will betray me.

"I didn't mean to hurt you. I just, there's a lot of chaos in my life right now."

"I get it. I've got a lot of baggage and no trunk to store it in." This is the part where I'd make a joke and walk away. Letting go early is less painful than dragging out something that won't go anywhere. But I can't do it this time. "Can I ask you something?"

"Yeah, sure."

"Why did you say you're not the girl for me instead of saying you're not interested in me?" My hand is so close to hers I can feel the sparks that snap between us, and I want to know why she can't or won't. For once, I feel like this is one to fight for, one to push at least a little to see if I can break through those walls. "It's like you're afraid you'll disappoint me, or yourself."

"I…I don't know, really. I mean, I guess I just don't think it would be a great idea since we work together and everything. I don't really date." She picks at the edge of the table, a nervous habit. "I get what you mean about the baggage. Not many guys stick around for long when they finally see mine."

I can't help but think that her mess and my mess would make the most beautiful art. I think back to the studio for the first time in months, and I can't fight the urge to bring her there. To sketch her, then strip her naked and take my time worshiping every inch of her. I want her covered in paint and moaning my name while her fingers play in my hair. I want to tear apart every piece of her armor and find the soft angel hiding inside.

"Don't shut the door."

"What?"

"Leave the door open. When we're done working together, no strings attached, no expectations, and only when and if you want to, I'll take you out. Then we can try to convince each other that we'd be terrible together." My finger slides along hers, and she doesn't pull away. "I'm not afraid of your baggage, Lexi. If you can get past that, please let me carry it for you, even if just for a little while."

"How about we order some food, get high, get through today, and leave it at maybe?" She takes out the baggie of edibles again and tosses them on the table with a smirk.

"Deal."

HOLLYWOOD

James

CHAPTER 15
SMELLS LIKE TEEN SPIRIT

MALIA J

THE CONFERENCE BUSTLES with crowds and noise, just as we expected. We spend most of the day taking reference pictures, collecting more postcards and free trinkets than I've ever seen, and occasionally ducking into a panel to check out the presentations. It's less about what's being presented and more about how. The company we're working for is young, but it has a lot of potential. They don't want the same old shit people have done over the years; they want to break molds. Of course, every company says that, so how broken those molds get remains to be seen.

I was worried our conversation over breakfast would make things weird, but Lexi got back to feeling like herself again and I pulled myself out of my spiral. There was a little banter, some harmless flirting, and by the time the day was over, I knew that no matter how this went between us, I was madly in love with her. It's the dreamer artist in me; I fall fast and hard. I only hope that this time, I can get a softer landing than usual.

I keep getting harassing text messages until I eventually turn off my phone. Blocking the number doesn't matter, she just text from another number; they're all burner phones or computer systems anyhow. Lexi has noticed, but so far, she hasn't brought it up. I'd rather not bring more drama to the day.

We leave well after dark, and the drive back takes us no time since rush hour has long ended. There's an open spot up the street from her building, so I pull in, jump out and run around to the other side to open her door for her.

"You really don't have to do that, you know."

"I most certainly do." I reach behind the seat and pull out her bag and the oversized tote full of random things we collected throughout the day. Our hands brush together as I hand it to her, and she hesitates for a minute.

"Do, uhm, do you want to come upstairs and go through the shots from today? You don't have to. I still have all this energy and, ugh, never mind. I'll start going through this bag of crap and organizing everything. I'm sure you have better things to do."

"If you're okay with me coming up, getting a little deeper into the project sounds fantastic." I would take any excuse to spend extra time with her, even though I'm making this harder on myself. "I'm a night owl, so I was planning on heading home and looking through the shots anyhow. Having company wouldn't suck."

"Yeah?" She tucks her hair behind her ear, her smile beaming in the glow of the streetlamp.

She leads me down the long, dark alleyway that heads to the back of her building. Only one light still works, or tries to, as it hopelessly flickers against the night. I'm immediately concerned that this isn't the best situation for a single woman in this neighborhood. I'm confident she can handle herself, but Los Angeles can be rough. People can get desperate when they're lost and find themselves forgotten by a system that was always meant to fail them.

We round a corner, and she lets us into a small, dimly lit room with an ancient elevator opening on one wall and a door to the lobby on another. She hits the button, sending a screeching, rickety elevator down to the first floor to greet us. The elevator doesn't have an actual door, nothing but a rusty metal grate and cage.

"The elevator is some kind of antique from one of the old studios, which should scare the hell out of me," she says after she sees my hesitation. She pulls back the grate and motions me in. "But really, it's kind of cool. It makes me think of old classic movies and gives the building some personality. Everyone is afraid of it, so it doesn't get used much."

"Hey, so long as it works and isn't haunted, I'm game." I tilt my head to the side before she can hit the floor button. "Do you mind?" I take her hand, place it on the grating, and pull out my camera. I quickly adjust the settings and start taking pictures while she watches me.

"Sorry, it's a photographer thing. It looks too damn cool to pass up."

"Yeah, but you ruined it with my hand."

I've never been so glad I have my digital camera. I flip the screen over and pull up the last few shots as we let the elevator slide shut and start its journey up.

"Your hand is beautiful, and the way your rings bring in the extra contrast, it's perfect. So much at odds with one another."

"What do you mean?"

"Okay, so the metal grate is cool looking on its own, but it's old, rusted, and dull. Your rings are shiny and smooth—a juxtaposition of textures. The picture could be fine like that, but your hand," I take it and rub my thumb along the back, "is beautifully pale and exquisitely soft. It's a texture you can't make from manipulated metal."

"Wow, see, this is why I could never be a classical artist."

"Eh, it's just words. At the risk of you kicking my ass onto the street, I think I like this one the most." I hand her the camera, a dangerous move since she could delete the picture before I can stop her. The elevator grate with her hand is in the foreground and out of focus, framing her face while she watches me. Her eyes are dazzling, and the old, yellowed light gives her a spellbinding Old Hollywood vibe. She stares down at the screen in surprise.

"That's, uhm, the best picture anyone's ever taken of me, and I had no clue you were taking it. It looks…" she fumbles for words. "Creepy? But in a cool way. I didn't know you could shoot digitally in black and white. I thought that was something you did in Photoshop or Lightroom later."

"Monochrome settings. Not all cameras have it, but there's really nothing like shooting in black and white. Okay, 8mm might be a little bit more fun. No, a lot more fun."

"You listen to vinyl records, too. Don't you?"

"Guilty. Does that make me a hipster millennial, old soul, or just someone who's mentally older than they physically are?"

She holds the camera up, takes a picture of me, and looks down at the screen. She's smiling as she hands it back, and the air thins as her fingers slide over mine and up my arm.

"I think they're calling us Elder Millennials now. I dunno." She reaches up and plays with the ends of my hair at the back of my neck. My knees are weak, and I'm not sure my heart can beat any faster. "If you grow the hair out a bit more and maybe a little more beard, I think you'd make an excellent hipster. I bet you'd be even hotter with longer hair."

I smile like an idiot and realize that, like her, I don't know how to take a compliment—I never have. The elevator stopped a while ago, and she finally turns around and pulls the grates open again, the loud screech pulling me from my daydream. She leads me down the hall and to her door, and I wonder if she can hear my heart or if it's only me.

She opens the door and drops her bag on a nearby couch. "So, this is my place. The bathroom is straight through there; no snooping in the medicine cabinet. The kitchen is over there, but it's probably pathetically empty unless there are such things as grocery fairies." She pulls my jacket off and her baggy sweater, tossing them both over the back of the couch. I'm trying not to stare at the tight tank top that's hugging her body the way I want to.

"I've got more edibles or there are a couple of joints in the box over there by the tv if you want. I know I work better that way." She turns to me; I can see her chest rising and falling nervously as she steps toward me. "How about we order something for dinner? My fridge is kind of empty."

"Yeah. Yeah, that's a great—" I jump when someone bangs loudly on the door and jiggles the handle, trying to get in. I look at Lexi with an eyebrow raised, and I can feel the panic coming off her. She knows who this is, and so do I. She told her mother she'd be home tonight.

"Would it be better if I hung from my fingertips by the fire escape or something?"

"I'm so sorry. Uhm, let me try to get her to go away. She probably watched us come in, so hiding wouldn't do much except make her tear the place apart looking for you. I'm sorry for anything she says. She's…"

"Hey, it's alright." I offer her a smile as I lean against a wall, preparing for the oncoming storm. I want to stand with her. I want to hold her and tell her we can get through this together, whatever happens. I squeeze her hand gently. "Only what *you* say matters to me, Angel. Not her."

I see the slightest twitch at the corner of her mouth at the name. She hasn't asked me to stop using it, so I haven't. She walks over to the door and timidly places a hand on the deadbolt. The Lexi I'd come to know over the day is gone, replaced yet again by a scared child who's afraid to open her door to a monster she knows all too well. Home is not her safe space, which explains why she works so much.

She barely gets the door unlocked, and she's pushed backward as the woman who could only be her mother comes in like a locomotive. She's taller than Lexi and thin as a rail. She looks like she's stepped out of some conservative magazine from the 50s, her blonde hair pinned up neatly and a buttoned-up neckline under the sweater.

"Alexis, how do you expect me to get in when you've locked the deadbolt? I've brought the—"

I keep still, wondering if she's realized I'm here.

"I thought we talked about this, Alexis. You can't be wearing these kinds of things out in public, and your hair is a mess." She pulls at the hem of Lexi's shirt like she's a child. "This style isn't doing anything to help hide your figure, dear; it's far too tight on you. Did you get those pills I sent over? I can't believe you really go to your job like this. Come on, I want to go through your closet and get rid of these things. I left you new clothes the other day, and you still wear clothes that make you look like a—"

She doesn't take two steps before she notices me. Immediately, her eyes become daggers, and her face hardens. My jaw ticks, and I'm trying not to let my lip curl into a snarl. I give her a curt nod, daring her to finish that sentence. She scoffs and spins so fast that Lexi flinches. Seeing that reaction makes my blood boil. There's only one reason someone would react like that.

"Mother, please. This is James. We work together."

"Oh really? At this hour? In your *home*? Well, since you're practically undressing in front of him, am I to assume you've started working at a whorehouse?" She spins, focused on me again. "Come on, Alexis, what kind of idiot do you think I am?"

"Mother, I—"

"And you," she spins on me, wagging her finger, but not stepping any closer. "What kind of man intrudes on an innocent young woman's home at this time of night? Are you here to take advantage of my daughter? It's obvious you are with how she's dressed. Clearly asking for it, so I suppose I shouldn't blame you?"

Her words are poisonous, not protective. She barely gives me a second glance. My fists clench in anger, and I want to throw her the fuck out, but this isn't my home, and Lexi is begging me not to with her eyes.

"Two more minutes, and he'd be defiling you right here on the couch. Is that what you want, Alexis? Should I put a sign on the door advertising you to the entire neighborhood? The Strauss Whore House."

"Mother, that's not what happened! I just got home. I was on my way to get changed. I swear." She grabs her sweater off the back of the couch and pulls it back on. "Please, go home."

Her mother grabs Lexi's arm and pulls her close. I go to move, but Lexi shakes her head, staring right into me. Her mother thinks I can't hear the next part, or at least pretends to think that.

"How dare you, Alexis? You're done up like a damn harlot, and I find you alone in the home we provide you with this lecherous older man? I bet he's married. Home wrecking slut." She sneers. "You lie to me so you can bring this filthy man into your bed to spread his depraved seed? Why do I even bother with you? You're just like your rotten sister. Is this what you've been doing all day? Lying on your back for him?"

"Mother, I—"

She's staring Lexi down hard. "I should have never let you move out alone. I told you that you couldn't handle the responsibilities and temptations. God is testing you, and clearly, I have failed you as a mother." She's a pompous windbag, looking down her nose at the child she's tormented for too long. "You've brought the devil into your home, welcomed his seduction into your bed, and stained your eternal, lust-filled soul. I won't have a filthy daughter claiming me as her mother."

"Please stop!" Tears stream down her face as she holds her stomach. I won't stand by anymore. I move behind Lexi, sliding a hand to her back to tell her I'm here for her. Her mother literally clutches her chest as if she's having a heart attack.

"You're done here," I say, feeling Lexi press against my hand.

She gawks at Lexi, then at me. When that doesn't get her anywhere, she scoffs at us. "Are you seriously asking me to leave you alone with this…this… pig? Your father is going to hear about this. Where did we go wrong with you, Alexis? I gave up so much for you and your sister, and this is how you treat me? It hurts me, Alexis. It hurts that you do these things to me."

"Please, mother? Please, just go."

It comes out as a whimper. My hand finds hers while my eyes don't leave her mother's. No one deserves this, especially not from a parent. I hope being here keeps her physically safe for now, but I don't know what tomorrow will bring. I've been there, I've been in this situation, and it's utterly helpless from her position.

"You are so dramatic. You had better be at the church and on your damn knees in the morning. Your father is going to want to talk to you about this. About what Jesus thinks of whores like your sister. I will not have a Jezebel for a daughter. Do you understand me?"

"No, mother, you can't tell him. Please? I haven't done—"

My hand comes up, catching her mother's arm in mid-swing, inches from Lexi's terrified face.

"Lexi has asked you nicely to leave. Go. Now." My voice is a growl, and I'm careful not to squeeze her wrist. I could already see the police report now, and I'm not about to put Lexi in that situation.

"How dare you touch me!" She pulls her hand back and rips the door open. "This conversation is not over, Alexis."

The door slams shut, and I grab Lexi, holding her tight. "I'll let go if you tell me to, Angel. You're okay now," I whisper as I rub her back and let her sob into my chest. "I'm sorry if I've made things worse, but I wasn't going to let her hit you."

I don't hush her or tell her not to cry. I don't lie and say everything will be okay. I hold her, rocking her gently until she pulls away on her own, trying to wipe her face.

"It's alright. I'm so embarrassed that you had to be here for that—for her."

"Lexi, you have nothing to be embarrassed about. She does, you don't." I wipe away her tears. That's two nights in a row I've done that. I'll be damned if it will be three. "How often does she hit you?"

"It's not…it's not like that. I should have known better than to—"

"Hey, look at me." I tilt her chin back so she has to look. "*No one* should ever hit you. Do you understand? I'm not going to let her touch you again. No one will touch you like that again."

In an instant, she buries her face in my chest again and she finally lets out the sobs she tried hard to hold back. Strawberries fill my nose from her shampoo as I kiss the top of her head and whisper her reassurances that she's alright for now.

"I should have known; I should have known she'd do something like that. I shouldn't have had you come up here. I did this to myself."

"No, that's her gaslighting you. There wasn't a single thing you did to deserve any of that. She's wrong about you, Lexi."

"You don't know me."

"I don't have to know you. You didn't deserve that. No one does, Angel." My hand slides up and down her back, and I feel her arms around me, clinging to me. "You were very brave, standing up to her the way you did. That isn't easy. Mothers can be…a tricky situation sometimes."

"She wasn't always like this," she mumbles. "She only gets mad when I do something wrong. She doesn't mean it."

I pull back a little and slip my hand to her face. I want to tell her how soft and perfect she is, and that she doesn't need the walls up around me. I want her to realize that even with puffy, tear-soaked eyes, she is still a vision of beauty that I would protect with my life.

"I have an idea."

"Uhm, I… I don't know. I think I should just go to bed."

"Nope, that's the worst idea. Please?" She hesitates, then nods. I pull her jacket off the hook and slip it over her shoulders. "I promise you won't regret this. Come on, we can walk it from here."

"Walk?"

"Don't worry, I'll keep you safe." I mean those words in every way possible.

When we leave the building, she immediately scans the streets to see if her mother is still lingering nearby. I honestly don't know what I'll do if she is. I'm not sure I'll be able to keep my mouth shut if she tries to come near her again. Thankfully, there's no sign of her, so we walk up the empty street.

The night has a little chill to it, so when I see her shiver even with her coat, I pull off my hoodie and drape it over her, then wrap my arm around her and pull her close. Her skin smells like cherry blossoms. I never want her far from me again. I've never felt like this for anyone, especially not someone I've just met.

My dating life, as minimal as it's been lately, includes too many one-night hookups at bars and a few relationships that lasted into the month's range. Only once had I been with someone for over a year, but she was my high school sweetheart, and it felt like we would be together forever. It's strange to think that tonight, as we walk down the dark streets of Los Angeles, I feel that way again with Lexi.

"Are you going to tell me where we're going?"

"Well, it's a safe bet that if you haven't already guessed by where we're walking, you haven't been there before." I'm a little surprised she hasn't pulled away or told me to get lost yet, but I also understand what it's like to just really need someone around—especially someone who isn't judging you for how someone in your family acts. Every family has at least one person they're not exactly thrilled to be related to. "Do you not like surprises?"

"Sometimes. I guess it just depends on what it is and why. Surprise visits from my mother. Yeah, not so much. God, I'm still so embarrassed you had to see that and the way I broke down. I'm not like this all the time."

"Oh, this is going to be way better than surprise visits from her. Don't worry. You don't have to be embarrassed about that, sweetheart; I'm not going to think any less of someone as incredible as you over something out of your control like that."

"It should be in my control, though. I should be stronger and tell her to fuck off."

"Woah! Hold on now, you mean to tell me that a woman as sweet and pretty as you has a dirty mouth, too?" I'm relieved when she smiles at my piss-poor attempt at humor.

"You have no idea, dirty mouth, dirty mind. Guess I'm one of those weird kids that was sheltered by church life only to turn out to be messed up and a mess."

"You're not the first person a cult has messed up, and you won't be the last. But you really need to stop talking so badly about yourself. As the reigning king of self-deprecation, I know something about being a big old mess." Reaching around her and into the pocket of my hoodie, I pull out a joint and hold it out to her. "No pressure, obviously. It helps my nerves when I'm in a bad way."

"I can't picture you in a bad way. You're so confident and sure of yourself most of the time." I flick the lighter as she inhales. "I wish I could be more like that. Stupid stuff doesn't even seem to bother you at all. Meanwhile, I'm having internal panic attacks because we were late to a conference we weren't really even a part of." Her head hangs low.

I stop in front of her and put my hands on her shoulders, "Lex, look, I know I'm still getting to know you and that first impressions can be misleading. Yesterday, when you dropped your phone, I was one hundred percent certain I'd just met the most brilliant, confident, amazing angel in the entire city. My opinion of you hasn't changed a single bit since then."

We talk more as we continue our walk, passing the joint between us and letting the weed take the stress away.

"It should have." She says a few minutes later. She holds the joint out for me, and I take a hit while she holds it. "Changed the way you think about me."

"It hasn't," I say after I hold the breath in. I cock my head to the side. "I'm confident about absolutely nothing in my life. Okay, not true. I'm confident about one thing, but only one."

"What's that?" She asks, already giggling as she blows a smoke ring.

"Pie."

"What?" She looked up at me, confused.

I turned to the side, revealing the sandwich board sign for The Pie Hole. "Pie. It makes everything better. And their apple pie is absolutely freakin' worth it."

Her eyes narrow and her face scrunches up, "You watch Supernatural?"

"Hey, don't knock my boys. I love those guys. They're like brothers I never had. Dad and I used to watch it all the time in the studio."

She giggles again, and to my surprise, her arms fling around me in a hug. Just as quickly, though, she dropped her arms at her side and bit her lip, apologizing.

"Angel, you can hug me any time you want. I'm never going to turn that down."

"You're kind of ridiculous, you know that?"

"What can I say? Being around someone like you just puts me in a good mood. Which is impressive. I haven't been in a good mood since at least my late teens. Come on, let's get to business on this completely unhealthy coping mechanism."

Lexi

CHAPTER 16
NOTHING'S GONNA HURT YOU BABY

CIGARETTES AFTER SEX

I DON'T KNOW where he's taking me, but for whatever reason, I feel safe with him. I would voluntarily follow him into a dark alley—no questions asked. It's rare that anyone is around to help me through these situations with my mother, not since my sister left. There's always pain, hurt, and anger, but this time, I'm not sitting alone and allowing these emotions to consume me. It's…nice having someone else here, and while he may not be who I expected, I'm realizing I was far too quick to judge him earlier.

My mother's wrath is never over, and I'm still convinced that she's lurking behind one of these cars or around a corner, just waiting to pounce on me again. She's waiting to finish what she started so she can push me down further into myself until I break and give in to whatever she's decided my life should be. I check over my shoulder again.

"Here." He pulls me from my thoughts as he strips off his hoodie and wraps it around me.

"I already have a coat."

"Yeah, and you're still shivering, so you need the hoodie more than I do."

I hadn't even realized I was shivering, and I doubt it's from the air since it's not that cold out. I dip my head down just enough to breathe in his comforting scent while I wonder why he's still here. It reminds me of sipping whiskey in a dark room only accessible through a hidden door in a bookshelf—a mystery wrapped in leather, weed, and warmth. He didn't have to stay or look after me.

Sam is the closest I've had to someone watching over me since Bex left. I was lucky to find Sam when I did, and I won't deny that he helped fill the void when my only protector couldn't take it anymore. Sam has an excellent mental health plan for his employees. He added it about six months after I started working for him, and I let him think I believed his reasons. He knew how badly I needed to find someone I would open up to. My therapist likes to tell me about boundaries and safe spaces when she's not trying to convince me that drunken sex isn't what she means by opening up to people more. Apparently, sex isn't actually a healthy way to validate my self-worth or silently fight my demons. It's easy to dream of a different, stable life. But when it's time for reality to make an appearance, the plans and hopes slip through my fingers like sand on the beach.

"So, are you on some kind of weird group text?" I nod toward his phone. "The only time my phone buzzes that much is when Dani puts me into a group text with half her family."

"What? Oh, no it's, uhm. It's junk. I think I signed up for a gym membership somewhere and they sold my number or something. I dunno." He turns it off and shoves it back in his pocket. There's something he's hiding from me, but I can't tell what it is or how bad it is. No one gets this many texts from spam numbers in one day, not unless it's election season.

"Well, are you going to tell me where we're going?" I ask, giving in to the magnetic force that's pulling me closer to him.

I should pull away. I should go home. It's not right of me to use him after I've pushed him away, and that's exactly what I'm doing. Using his protection and kindness is a slippery slope that could lead me to exploiting him to feel good again. Like a drug.

I laugh quietly, thinking about how this must look to an outsider like James. If you boil it down to its most basic elements, I'm a single woman walking at night in Los Angeles and of all the things the world tells me to fear, it's my mother I'm worried most about. I take a quick glance at James, and I wonder what's going through his mind. I wonder if he regrets telling me this morning about his feelings or asking me last night to go out with him sometime. I should give him an out, an escape. I don't want to hear some idiot excuse from him later, like the other dates I've had. But if I'm being honest with myself, I like him here next to me. It's comforting knowing that someone will fight my demons when all I can do is stand there, frozen in place, as they attack me over and over.

He lights a joint for me and the minute I inhale, my mind eases and my muscles relax. We walk, smoke, and talk. The smile on his face is foreign to me and I can't wrap my head around it because it's genuine. He's not pretending to care or even asking me a million questions. It makes me wonder what happened in his life, that he gets it more than anyone else ever has.

"I'm so sorry you had to see that. You don't deserve to be attacked like that."

"Neither do you."

Oh, but I do. I'm just another disappointment in a long line of failures in my mother's eyes. My sister and I stole our father from her and have done nothing but take from her since we were born. She reminds us of that frequently.

"Can I ask you something?" His voice is soft, like he's afraid he'll scare me away. I nod. "Is she why you hold back? Did you say you weren't the woman for me because you're worried I'd be scared off by her?"

"No. Yes. It's…complicated." I shake my head, trying to get the words sorted before I say them. "You're a nice guy, James. You deserve a good person who doesn't come with baggage that includes an unstable mother who's out to embarrass me and everyone I ever…"

I bite my lip before I can't finish the thought because he doesn't need to know the rest. Knowing the rest could give him hope that anything is going on between us. He's making it hard not to like him, though—especially how his eyes sparkle whenever he looks at me as if my mother didn't just call him horrible things and he didn't watch me crumble under her wrath.

"Lex, it doesn't matter if it's as friends or if it's more, your mother isn't going to do a damn thing that will scare me away from you. No one can." He stops and pulls his hoodie tighter around me. I can see in his face that he's holding something back. "I, uhm…I know what it's like, and I'll never blame you for her actions because they're not your fault. I stand by what I said earlier. You were very brave. I…couldn't have done that."

"I should be able to tell her to fuck off, though. To leave me the fuck alone."

"You already know it wouldn't help. She'd probably be offended by your choice of non-Christmas words."

"Non-Christmas words?" I almost choke on the words and the weed.

"Yeah," he laughs, his face scrunching up around his nose. It's adorable. "I accidentally swore at a friend's house once. His grandmother was there cooking us dinner because we'd been out of town for Christmas. She heard me and I thought I was in for it, but all she said was *'well, that's not a Christmas word'* and moved on."

Suddenly, he stops. Pie. The man has brought me to one of the best known pie chains in Los Angeles to help me get over my mother being a controlling, manipulative bitch. I was terrible to him last night, then reject him today. She insults him and embarrasses me. He brings me out for pie.

Maybe I'm wrong about him. What if I am his type of girl, after all? His baggage might go with mine.

It's past nine on a Friday, with most of Los Angeles creating chaos at clubs and parties, but this place is packed. After we order, I pull out my phone, and James stops me before I can pay.

"James!"

"You can only pay for cheer-up pie when you're cheering someone else up or if you're alone. Those are the rules."

"But you paid for breakfast." That's the only argument I can think of. It's weak and sounds more like a whine than an argument against him buying.

He shrugs and says, "Sam paid for breakfast. I'll dig through the couch for coins before I let you buy your own cheer-up food, Angel."

We find an empty table outside as another couple leaves. The restaurant converted a few parking spots into a little patio area with tables, lighting, and a canvas tent covering. They've even put down fake grass and potted ferns to help you forget you're basically sitting in the street. It's cute, and I'm kicking myself for never having come up here before tonight.

"Thanks for, I dunno, not bailing after the whole mom thing."

"I mean, I could have ditched you while you were crying, but then I'd have to come out for pie alone. Where's the fun in that?"

"Fuck, I had just forgotten that I totally broke down in front of you like that."

He breaks off a piece and holds the fork up to me, smirking. "This is one of my favorites, so I'm really curious what you think of it."

"Sugary kid's cereal is your favorite kind of pie?" I smirk, and he chuckles. I even see a slight pink rise in his cheeks. I wrap my lips around the fork, and the sweetness hits instantly. I'm looking into his eyes, and I know how wrong and sexual that must look, but I can't hold back the moan as the flavor bursts in my mouth. I'm transported back to our living room in North Carolina on a Saturday morning. I can practically hear the cartoons playing.

"Holy shit," I don't even care that my mouth is still half full of sinful goodness, "that's the best thing I've ever put in my mouth."

He tries hard to bite back the laugh. I can see him struggling and how his nose scrunches up as the laugh grows. "I'm sorry, I promise. I'm not laughing at you. Sometimes, I'm just a fucking stupid teenager trapped in a grown man's body."

"Oh, don't worry, I'm laughing at myself! I know what I just said, and I mean it!" I'm so wrapped up in the moment that I can't stop the inner dialog from coming out as I add, "Besides, that's a pretty damn spectacular body to be trapped in."

His face cycles through several shades of red as he runs his fingers along the side of his nose. It makes me want to compliment him more to see if he does it every time. It's adorable, but a little sad. Someone like him should receive compliments often enough to know how to handle them.

"Oh yeah, there she is," I laugh, reaching out for the other fork and holding it up for him this time. "Queen of saying embarrassing shit out loud! Okay, I want to try this, but I'm kind of scared. Sometimes, I'm too white for Mexican chocolate. I know that sounds dumb, but—"

"I get it, but I won't be the best judge for you. I was raised in Los Angeles, remember?" His voice drops as he leans forward, eyes locked on mine, and he winks. "I like things a little…spicy."

My smile melts, and my heart skips as I watch him the way he had watched me. His full lips wrapping around the fork isn't accidentally sexual—it's blatant, and his eyes darken as they lock on mine. I have an urge to climb on the table and let this man have his way with me, but part of me is still hearing my mother's voice screaming at me from earlier about being a whore.

I think, just maybe, I could be a slut for James Barton and those steely blue eyes and cheesy pickup lines.

"Why are you single?" I shrink away after the words escape. "Sorry, I didn't… I mean…fuck." I take a big bite of my pie while he watches me. I realize it's far too hot for my taste too late, but I try to hide it.

"I, uhm, I don't have much to bring to the table when it comes to relationships." He holds my coffee up, tilting the straw toward me and I take a huge drink, trying to stop the fire in my mouth. "I'm shy, nervous. I don't really like people. Most people in LA like the whole night life scene, but I'd rather stay in. I'm also a dick."

"Dani told me you were nice."

"No, *Dani* is nice. I'm a panicky, overthinking mess that constantly gets compared to that grouchy cat picture on the internet. I'm on medication that I consistently forget to take. I freelance because I've been rejected for every solid job I apply for, and our boss gave me the card for a shrink yesterday because I'm such a mess."

"None of that describes the guy I've been hanging out with for the last couple of days. Hours. Whatever."

"No? Because I'm pretty sure I'm making it all worse now." He winces. "I just can't help it. I'm sitting in front of a pie shop telling all of this to a beautiful woman I can't get out of my mind."

I blush and bite my bottom lip, debating on whether I should tell him how loud I screamed his name in the shower this morning. I may have to tell him that someday, but I think it would melt his brain right now.

"Fuck, I'm so bad at this. Did I mention I have absolutely no game at all? Guess that's what I get for being the permanent wingman."

We talk and laugh together long after the pie is gone, and I can't help but notice that the longer I'm with him, the quieter my mother's voice in my head becomes. He's unlike any man I've ever dated before—and most of the women. According to my sister, my type is dumb, toxic, and only around for a good time, not a long time.

But Jamie doesn't fit those descriptions. He's got the kindest eyes and the sweetest smile…when he smiles. He's also smart, charming, and witty, even if his jokes are dad-level lame.

I barely even notice when the employees start closing up, and we're still outside talking. I could listen to him talk for hours, or until someone shuts off the lights.

"Shit, guess they're kicking us out." He laughs as our eyes adjust to yellow streetlights, and we finally head back.

As we walk, his fingers graze mine. I convince myself it's happening by accident, but it's hard to fight the urge to grab hold of his hand each time. Until he wraps his pinky around mine. Neither of us says anything or looks at the other as he threads the rest of his fingers with mine. We walk together in a rare, comfortable silence.

We're back at my building too soon, and I gaze at the door that marks the night's end. I should have walked slower or taken a longer route. I don't want this night to end, and I don't want him to leave. I'm already addicted to the safety and protection he offers, but there's more to it than just safety.

"I can run up and bring your stuff down. Save you a trip," I offer him a way out while praying he doesn't take it.

"I should come up and make sure the coast is clear, if that's okay with you."

At some point, while we were walking and talking, I somehow forgot about my mother and what she'd done earlier. I was so focused on James and how he was making me feel. Something tells me that had been his plan all along, and I can't help but wonder how he knew to do that with such ease.

"I know a few more late-night dessert places we can hit if your mom wants to go for round two." He squeezes my hand, reminding me he hasn't let go yet. "If you want to call it a night, that's fine, but I'd like to know you're upstairs and safe before I leave."

"I think between my mother and the sugar, I won't be going to sleep anytime soon." I catch the smile he tries to hide, but I can't blame him—I'm smiling too. I want to stop being afraid. I want to stop pushing people away. I want to let someone in for the right reasons for once. "Any chance you like movies?"

I've never invited a guy to my apartment on a first date, and now, for the second time tonight, we're walking to my door. I keep reminding myself that it's alright because this isn't a date. It's two co-workers hanging out together—maybe friends—perfectly innocent. What isn't *perfectly innocent* is the fact that I want him to stay. I want to listen to him talk into the early morning hours. I want to stare into those pretty eyes until one of us is forced to look away. I want him to wrap me in his strong arms and tear my fucking clothes off.

Flipping on the lights, I hang up my coat and his hoodie on the hooks by my door while James gives a low whistle. I panic, thinking my mother is back or worse, but when I turn to see what he's looking at, I find him staring around the apartment with wide-eyed surprise.

"Wow, nice place."

"I guess you didn't really get a chance to see it before." I cross my arms and lean against the back of the couch while he continues scanning the room. "It's alright." I pick up a candle and sniff it before lighting a long match.

"You have the whole place to yourself, no roommate?" He purses his lips and shakes his head, "Wow, that didn't sound all serial killer or anything, did it?"

"Well, at least if you're going to kill me, you got me pie first," I giggle. He's staying across the room, keeping some distance between us. Maybe neither of us trusts ourself to be alone together. "I do live by myself, but don't spend much time here. My mother and stepfather own it, so the rent is cheap. She claims it's helping me out, but she just wants to keep me firmly under her thumb. I was just dumb enough to fall for it. Now I'm kind of stuck here."

"You're not dumb, Lexi. She's manipulative. It's hard to get out from under that kind of thing." His head tilts to the side as he looks at the three large art pieces leaning against a wall. "Did you make these? They look like your style."

"Yeah, they were an art project I started in college that grew into those three monsters," I gush proudly, like I'm talking about my kids or something. "They're mixed-media, so I collected pieces along the way and created them over the years to keep my mind off things. I just finished the redesigned RENT poster last year; I've been working on it for seven years total. That one took the longest."

"Weird place to keep it," he frowns as he looks over the mantle and the blank walls around it. "Why not there where it would be easier to see? A focal point?"

"I'm trying to figure out how to get it to Sam's so he can put it up there. I'm worried my mother or stepfather would take it down and burn it if they found it hanging up. They don't approve of that…lifestyle."

They don't approve of me.

"That's too bad. It's a great play. I've seen it five times, I think. This is beautiful and really captures the complexity of the message. It's brilliant. Like you."

"Fancy words for saying it's alright. It's not that special, but it makes me happy."

"You do that too much."

"What?"

"Play yourself or your work down. You're talented. Not in the corporate, boring, stuck-in-a-box kind of way, either. You've got some amazing skills." He bites his lip, and his eyes soften. He steps closer to me, and I feel myself stop breathing when his hand comes up. He wipes at the corner of my mouth. "Pie."

"Oh." My knees try to give out as I watch him lick it off his thumb.

"Lexi, I'm sorry they disapprove of you and your work," he says in a low, gravelly tone. "They're wrong, and it's not fair to you."

I breathe again and blurt out, "So, still up for a movie?"

"I'll take any excuse to spend time with you. What kinds of movies do you like?"

"Uhm, you're going to think I'm weird, but uhm, Action-

Adventure, Horror, Science Fiction. I'm team *blow things up and make me laugh about it*. Dani calls it disaster porn."

"You have got to stop being so incredible. Favorite Science Fiction movie?" He's leaning against the arm of the couch now, a little more relaxed again.

"You can't ask a girl that! Probably Alien or The Martian. Yours?"

"Both excellent movies. I gotta go to classic Star Wars, though." He narrows his eyes and asks, "Thoughts on Starship Troopers?"

"What? Why that movie?"

"I've learned a lot about people from their answer. My buddy Steve thinks it's cinematic gold."

"Okay, it's fucking stupid, but decent when you're high and just want to watch something dumb."

"Right answer. Steve's a fucking moron. So, do you have a movie collection or just streaming?"

I lead him to the cabinet where I keep my stash of DVDs. I like to display books, but DVDs are like strange relics from a long ago past—or just a few years ago. Thanks, streaming service. So, I keep those neatly tucked away.

He moves next to me, his hand on my hip, and part of me wonders if he's actually reading the titles or using them as an excuse to be near me. I'm okay with either answer.

"Wait! Do you like horror?" I turn to face him, and the reality of how close he really is pushes my heart into overdrive. He nods, but I'm not sure he even knows what I just asked him. "H-Have you seen this one about the cute guy who ends up being some kind of crazy cannibal serial killer living a double life and selling people meat to the rich?"

He slowly shakes his head and for a moment, I think he's about to kiss me.

"I, uhm, I think that's become one of my favorites." I'm stuttering, and the words keep leaving my mind before I can say them. "Or they just put one out about the Queen Mary, and we were right there today. Although I heard it was only good if you're really baked."

"Still got those edibles?"

"Yeah," I squeak out.

"Both."

"Both? Wait, you want to watch both movies?" I try hard to act surprised instead of giddy. I don't think I should come across as too desperate, but deep down inside, it's precisely what I am. "I mean, it's just, it's pretty late."

"I'm a night owl, and like I said, I'll take any excuse you give me to spend time with you."

I take a minute to float back down to reality. I want to kiss him. I want him to kiss me. I would really like him to throw me on the couch and ravish me. But neither of us does anything but stare until we eventually sit beside each other awkwardly.

"Do, uhm, do you want popcorn or something to drink?" I ask, handing him my bag of edibles. I shouldn't be this nervous, especially since I practically dared him to take one from my damn mouth earlier today. But that was before. He shakes his head with a smirk. "Good, cause I don't actually have anything to eat."

We're a little over an hour into the movie when I try to shift and realize my foot has fallen asleep. I hiss at the pain from the pins and needles, and before I know what's happening, he's pulled my leg up into his lap and is giving me the most amazing foot massage I've ever gotten. I should be freaking out; I usually hate when people touch my feet.

"Oh, that's not good. Don't do it, girl," he says to the TV, which I haven't even looked at in the last two minutes since he picked up my foot. He glances over at me. "Can't trust men. We're the worst."

I can't even speak; I just nod at those blue ponds, staring at me and asking me to drown in them. After a few minutes, he puts my foot down and motions for me to turn my back toward him. As I turn, he takes my hips and pulls me backward so we're closer. "It's okay, Angel. I only bite if you're into that." He chuckles. "I swear I have got to be racking up some kind of record on terrible lines today."

"I think it's funny," I giggle. It's true; he's had me giggling like a teenager all day. I didn't know I still remembered how to giggle. Laugh, sure, you can fake those if you need to. But a giggle is real; it's pure and innocent. It also feels good.

"Okay, take a deep breath and let it out slowly."

I do as he says, and as I breathe out, his large hands on my shoulders squeeze my muscles, pushing down with his thumb. "Oh, my god."

"Nice to know I still have the touch." His warm breath tickles my neck, and I know he can feel my heart racing as he gently massages my shoulders. This man could take a knife, cut out my kidney, and sell it on the black market. I'm willing to take the risk so long as he keeps touching me. When he's done, he lays back, pulls me down on his chest, and starts watching the movie again. "Do you want anything? We walked a lot today, and you might be dehydrated."

I shake my head, and he nuzzles against my head. I'm going to die right here from an emotional overload. Time ticks by, and my eyes are getting heavier. I'm losing more and more of the movie, so I know I must be dozing off. I curl against him, too comfortable to fight the urge to let sleep take me.

"Promise you won't kill me in my sleep," I mumble against his chest, his arm wrapping around me.

"Why would I kill the most perfect woman I've ever met?" His words are barely a whisper as he brushes through my hair with his fingers.

I'm sure that was just part of the movie I misheard as I drifted to sleep.

HOLLYWOOD

James

CHAPTER 17
I'M ON FIRE
AWOLNATION

AN ANGEL IS SLEEPING in the arms of the devil tonight.

She's been asleep for about half an hour, and the whole time, I've been debating whether I should leave. Whenever the thought comes to mind, I realize I'd have to move, which would mean waking her up, so I stay. I'm watching her and have no idea what's going on in the movie playing in the background; I'm too busy watching how her nose scrunches up just before she nuzzles into my chest. Carefully, I take off her glasses and set them on the table.

She's beautiful.

My eyes are getting heavy, and the slow rhythm of her breathing is lulling me to sleep, so I give in, lean my head back against the couch, and fall asleep with her in my arms.

When I wake up, it's dark, and I take a second to remember where I am. The TV has gone into sleep mode, and her thick curtains block out any street lights. I'm still holding Lexi, but she's twitching, trying to fight someone away—that must be what woke me. She yells and lashes out.

"Hey, hey. You're okay, Angel," I say in a soothing voice, running my fingers up and down her arm, barely ghosting her soft, pale skin. I hope this will wake her slowly or at least help pull her out of the nightmare. "You're okay, sweetheart. I've got you."

She sits bolt upright and gasps as she looks around the room like she's waiting for someone to pounce on her. I'm about to say something so she can remember who I am, but she beats me to it.

"James?"

"You were having a nightmare. I wasn't sure what to do." She wraps the blanket tighter around her while her eyes adjust to the darkness. "Do you want some water?" I hand her glasses to her.

"Coffee." She takes the glasses and sets them to the side. "Thanks. I don't need them all the time."

"Oh, uhm, I can get you coffee!" I go to stand, but she grabs my arm and stares at me, eyes wide with fright. Whatever she saw in the nightmare refuses to let go of her, so neither am I. I'll show her and her demons that I'll fight for her. "Or I can stay right here, whatever you need."

"I'm sorry," she winces, wiping the sleep from her eyes. "Fuck. This has been the weirdest day for you, I'm sure—pie, my mom, me crying, nightmares. I told you I was a mess. Ugh."

I brush her wild hair out of her face and smile, able to make out the eyeliner smudged around her eyes even in the dark. Her lips are pouty and begging for me to kiss them, and it's taking everything in me to hold back. I forget whatever I'm about to say when she reaches up and touches my face. I doubt I could get a solid caveman grunt going at the moment. I'm far too enamored with her fingers softly brushing against my scruffy beard.

"You…stayed?"

I nod, "Yeah. I hope that's okay."

"Why?"

"I…uhm…You were asleep…and I didn't want to wake you."

"I don't get it."

"I thought you could use the sleep after the shit your mom did." She's moving closer to me, and I realize I've started blinking faster. "You, uhm, you looked so peaceful, and I," I stutter and trip over every word I'm trying to say. "…I wanted to make sure you didn't have more company. I can leave if you—"

"James?" Her voice is raspy, and fuck, it's sexy. My mind is on the fritz as her hand slips down my chest. The air in the room is gone and my skin feels hotter than a desert. "Is yesterday's offer still on the table?"

"I think so," my voice breaks like a fucking teenager. Shit. "W-which one was that?"

"The one where you and I go out sometime. I think…I think I changed my mind." She swallows and climbs on top of me. "Although, right now, I might just be dreaming."

"I know I'm awake, even if you are an Angel."

"What are we doing?" We're just a breath apart.

"You're asking me questions."

"What are you doing?"

"Wondering what you taste like."

Our eyes have stayed locked on each other the entire time, and my heart is about to break a few of my ribs. My brain tries to pump the brakes, tossing every bad thought it can muster at me. *What if she doesn't like you? What if I'm not enough? What if I fuck this up?*

"Can I kiss you?"

"Yes, James."

"I like it when you say that. Say it again."

"Ja—"

She jumps back to the other side of the couch as her cell phone vibrates off a counter, hitting the floor just as a cop somewhere down the street whoops his sirens. She covers her face and starts laughing, and I let my head fall back on the arm of the couch. So close.

She jumps off the couch, and I'm watching her ass as she bends over to pick up her phone. When she looks back up, I glance quickly at my watch; it's just before six in the morning. I look at the windows and see the sun making its way up for the day.

I look back at her just in time to see her holding the phone to her ear and ducking into the bedroom. She closes the door behind her and I cover my face and groan.

"Son of a bitch," I sigh before picking the blanket up from the floor. I bury my face in it, breathing in the cherry blossoms. It makes my cock twitch when I think about her on top of me, how close her lips were. So damn close. I can't help but wonder who the fuck needed to call her this early. I also wonder what part of last night I did right. She's considering going out with me—or at least that's what I hope she was talking about when she asked if the offer was still on the table.

What if it wasn't? Wasn't she just about to kiss me? It had to be that, right? Yeah. But what if?

I hear the shower turn on.

"Okay. It's fine. It was just…it was nothing. We didn't kiss. Everything is fine." I'm mumbling to myself as I walk to the kitchen. "She wasn't awake. Nothing happened, it was all in your head. Give her some fucking space, man."

Making my way into the kitchen, I swipe through my phone and see a series of texts that came in late last night from my best friend, Chase Cooper.

JACKASS

Dude, be home tomorrow afternoon. Beers?

Oh, and Mini Cooper is moving into my place two weeks from now.

Are you asleep or jerking off?

Nothing? Dude, are you getting laid or something?? 🤣🤣

I go through the cabinets until I find coffee, filters, and the coffeemaker. I'd make her breakfast if she had more in her kitchen. Waffles, French toast, eggs, anything she wanted. I could go to the store while she's showering, or order groceries. I need to get a hold of myself. It was a kiss. No, an almost kiss. Why am I freaking out over an *almost*-kiss?

JAMIE

I'll be there tomorrow for beers.

JACKASS

So, what's her name?

JAMIE

Fuck you, man.

JACKASS

So she's French? Kidding. You better spill it tomorrow, Jimbo.

Someone clears their throat behind me, and I spin around, bumping my head into the cabinet and dropping my phone.

"Oww!" I grab my head and she rushes over, running her hands through my hair. I should do that more often.

"Sorry, I was trying not to sneak up on you since you seemed like you were kind of in your own little world!" She continues checking my head and trying to act concerned as she hides her laughter. "Did you find the demon in my fridge? The fucker keeps bailing on rent and overcooking my eggs."

"What? No, I was, uhm, I was gonna make coffee." I hold up

the package of grounds and shrug while I wince. "You said you wanted coffee, didn't you? Wait, who cooks your eggs?"

"Relax, I was trying to be funny. Do you have a concussion or something?" Her smile is soft, and the sun lights her wild hair like a pink lion's mane. The silky bathrobe clings to her glistening, wet skin. She's not wearing a top, and her nipples are getting hard—so am I.

Good morning, butterflies. It's nice to know you're still around.

"I think I died, actually." There's no doubt that my grin is goofy and uncool, but I can't help it.

"Head okay?"

The ten-year-old in me giggles because of where my brain is. Thank fucking god I'm not high right now. I probably do have a concussion. "What? I mean, yeah, I uhm, I would make you breakfast, but—"

"I have no food. I know. I keep heading to the grocery store and ending up at parties with Dani. It's crazy."

She hops up on the counter, and my eyes follow the fabric as it slips off her bare shoulder and down her arm. The opening, barely covering her breasts, dives to her soft stomach. The air is thick and I feel like I just ran a marathon.

"So, you okay?" My voice strains. I clear my throat as she grins and fixes her robe, "I mean, the nightmare."

"Hmm? Oh, yeah. I get nightmares sometimes. Thankfully, I rarely remember them once I wake up."

There's a familiar twitch in her eye when she says that, one I barely even catch. She's lying. She remembers all of her nightmares. I know how that can mess with someone's head. It's strange how much we have in common, and not much of it is good.

"So, uhm, do you have plans for today?" She asks with an

eyebrow cocked, "Or are you just going to stand in my kitchen all day staring at me while holding up stale coffee grounds and filters?"

"No. That's all I have planned for the rest of my life. How about you?" I'm laughing again, and it's such a strange sensation. It's easy, not forced, not fake, just as natural as breathing—which I still have trouble doing when I'm near her. Everything seems easier around her—everything except breathing and talking.

"I thought we could get some of the beach shots they wanted out by the pier. It's probably not too bad this early. According to the weather app, we've got clouds for most of the morning." She slides off the counter and her hand brushes against mine as she reaches around me and presses the button on the coffeemaker that I had altogether forgotten about. This attempt at making her coffee is going as smoothly as most of my life.

Forget butterflies; when she moves, her body presses against me, and I'm hard as a rock. I'm trying to stand still and I'm not sure that's helping. "T-that would be great. I need to check my Jeep to see if I have any clean clothes—"

"Take off your pants," she whispers into my ear.

I'm glad I'm leaning against the counter, because my knees just gave out. Or I *did* just die.

She crosses the room and I somehow catch the heap of fabric she tosses at me, still trying to wrap my brain around what she's asked me to do. She laughs hard, doubling over when she realizes I'm not moving away from the counter. I follow right along with her, shaking my head at the sweatpants she threw at me. This should be uncomfortable. I should be embarrassed, but I'm not. Everything about right now—about her—just feels so right.

She gestures to the sweatpants., "I figured you could shower and then wear these while we toss your clothes in the washer." She nods to a stacked washer/dryer unit at the other end of the kitchen. "I can order breakfast, and we can go through the photos from yesterday while we eat. Then possibly the beach."

"Shit," I whisper as I stare at the laundry machines. "I was going to try to tempt you out to my place with the promise of a private, free washer and dryer. Guess I have to do better than that now, huh?"

She bites her lip as she looks at me. For a second, I think she might wait for me to strip out of my clothes right there in front of her, and I seriously think about it until she steps aside and says, "Leave your clothes on my bed. There are towels on the counter for you. I'll finish the coffee and then start the laundry when I hear the water turn off. I'll try to find you a shirt, too."

I nod, or I think I do. I've gone full zombie on my way to the bedroom until I'm standing next to her bed with my clothes in my hand. Part of me wants to call Coop and ask him what the fuck I'm supposed to do. This is his thing; I'm just the wingman. He's the one meeting stunning women and being smooth enough to land a date or whatever. Although, his luck with women has declined in recent years. Calling him is definitely off the table.

Instead, I pull up my dad's number and wait. I listen to the voicemail greeting, hang up, and take a deep breath to center myself.

Standing in the shower, I let the water cascade down my face and hair as I try to pull my head out of the clouds. I spot her body wash and sure enough, it's cherry blossom scented. I think about popping the lid open, but that smell won't help this hard-on. In fact, it would make me do things I don't want to do in her shower. At least, not without her. I turn the hot water off and let the blast of cold hit me until I'm shivering.

The sweatpants are a little tight, but they'll do for now. I check the bed and I don't see a shirt anywhere. For a split second, I contemplate checking her closet, but then change my mind. Her voice comes from the kitchen as I emerge from the bedroom. I listen, and once I'm sure she's on the phone, I grab my hoodie and head for the couch.

"The sweats are a good look on you." She's chipper and sweet as she joins me.

I avoid looking down to draw attention to the outline of my dick when I realize what I'm wearing. Tight grey sweatpants—clever girl. The smirk on her face says she knew exactly what she was doing. It also makes me want to throw her over my shoulder and smack that round ass while I carry her into the bedroom.

"How far into the second movie did you get?" She leans across me to put my coffee cup on the end table beside me. I close my eyes and pray to no one that I make it through the morning without making a total ass of myself. Somehow, I avoid looking down the opening of her robe.

"Uhm, oh, I didn't turn on the second one. Guess we were, uhh, tired."

"Good. We could, uhm, watch it later."

"Later?" My eyes shoot open and find hers. She's sitting beside me on the couch with a pillow over her lap and her hair up in a messy ponytail. Her makeup is gone, and I can see the constellation of freckles decorating her nose and cheeks. There's a soft dusting of pink from her blushing, and I know I'm doomed to be forever haunted by those dark brown eyes staring back at me. This woman could ask me to rob a bank, and I'd ask which one.

"Yeah, hopefully tonight? If, you know, you're free or whatever." A buzzer goes off somewhere in the kitchen and she hops up and starts walking away while talking. "I mean, if you're not busy—which you probably are—never mind. I should probably…work. Or…something…"

She doesn't wait for an answer, disappearing behind the wall and still mumbling to herself. I'm off the couch and following her in an instant. When I round the corner, she's on her tiptoes, her long legs stretching and the robe no longer covering her ass. She's trying to reach a basket at the top of the laundry closet while she does *my* fucking laundry and I'm standing here ogling her like a fucking asshole.

I reach over her, causing her to squeak twice. Once when she feels my hand on her hip, and the second time when I press against her.

"About tonight," I say as I pull the basket down and hand it to her with a grin. "I'll spend any time I can with you, Angel, but I can't promise I'll be watching much of the movie with you around."

Her robe has fallen again, and my fingers trace around the tattoo on her shoulder. It's a distinct style from the others. Simple line art of a caterpillar rather than colorful characters.

"My sister and I have matching ones."

"What does it mean?"

""Sort of a Disney reference. A promise that someday, if I give myself enough time, I'll be a beautiful butterfly." She turns to face me. That mischievous sparkle in the corner of her eye has my mind in a haze.

"But Angel, you already are."

I stare at her because she's all I can see. I hold her face, my thumbs sliding over her soft skin as she looks through me and into my soul. The sounds of apartment life fade away to somewhere distant, and all I hear are the unsteady breaths we're both taking. My thumb slides over her parted lips and I know what I have to do.

"Oh, fuck it."

I cup my hand around her neck, pulling her in and we collide, savoring her in a long, deep kiss. I was right—she tastes like candy. We don't waste time on soft and slow, that can come later. Right now, we're too caught up in the moment. Tongues tangle as our mouths meet over and over, chasing each other like it's a game. I push her backward, grabbing her wrist as we hit the wall and swallowing her little chirps of pleasure.

Her back arches and her hips roll against me while I have her caged in my arms. I hear an unfamiliar moan from myself when her leg slides up mine, her body begging for more.

When we break for air, I hold her face to mine, afraid she'll run away if I don't because that's what I expect. I wait for her to pull away, to smack me for reading the situation wrong. But she kisses me back. Each time deeper than the last. Her arms slip around my neck and I pick her up and put her on the counter.

"James!"

We break apart just long enough for me to whisper, "I'll stop. If that's what you want. But you have to tell me."

"Don't." Her voice is soft and breathy, bordering on a moan that goes straight to my cock as she pulls me back for more. Our mouths slide together again as her legs wrap around my hips, holding me there. "Please. Don't stop."

It's not a request, it's a demand. Not a trace of doubt in her voice. The way she kisses me makes me think she's wanted this as badly as I have.

"Good, 'cause I don't think I can stop."

Her fingers play in my wet hair, nails dragging along my scalp and making me moan into her. Her robe is falling open and my hands slide up her thighs, finding her hips and squeezing hard. She's rocking against the growing bulge in my pants and I'm leaving bruises along her pale skin. Her whole body sings with every move and every touch while I feel like I've been bathed in lava. I need her, all of her.

"Tell me what you want. Tell me everything that you need. Let me fucking worship you." I can't stop my heart from hammering and when one of her hands drops and lays flat against my chest, I know she can feel it.

"You," she whines. "I need you, James."

Fuck, my name sounds good on her candy flavored lips. I kiss along her jaw and to her neck and all I can focus on is how badly I need to explore all of her. Biting just hard enough on her earlobe to pull a whimper from her, I whisper, "You have me, Angel. Always."

As her knees spread wider apart, she reaches for my hoodie, desperately trying to pull it off, but I stop her. She wants to argue, but the words never come because my fingers are already tracing over her soaked panties and teasing her clit.

"Fuck, Lexi, you're so wet for me. What would you have done if I didn't follow you here? Was that your little plan? Torment me all morning?"

Her back arches as I tease her clit, bringing the sweetest noises from her lips to my ears. "I…I was going to try sitting on your lap. I even wore this robe just for you."

"Atta girl." My hands find the tie of her robe, pulling gently until it gives way and slips down her shoulders. There she is. My beautiful fucking muse is bare in front of me, and she's even more breathtaking than I had imagined. She's like a feast and I don't know where to start. "I'll take care of you, baby."

Her hand is back in my hair, switching between pulling it hard and running her nails over my scalp. I move her underwear to the side and tease her clit with my thumb. I want to sink into her endlessly, and she's so fucking wet right now, I could. When I slide my finger through her folds, her hips buck, begging for me.

"I want to know everything about you," I hum against her ear, two fingers slowly pushing into her pulsing cunt. "I want to know about your fantasies and what turns you on. I want to find every spot that makes you scream. Say my name again."

"Oh god, James! Just like that!" She coos, her head rocking back when I curl my fingers and rub against her G-spot.

"Good girl. Now don't stop saying it until you fucking come." Our mouths slot together like they were made for each other.

HOLLYWOOD

Lexi

CHAPTER 18
FIRST DAY OF MY LIFE

BRIGHT EYES

IN A HAZE, I find only three words. So, I yell them out. "Please don't stop!"

His mouth takes hold of my nipple and he swirls his tongue. Before I can say his name again, he's biting down and I scream as I ride his hand. He's going above and beyond to make up for edging me at the bar. His teeth graze my breast and my back snaps hard while the most beautiful fireworks fill my vision.

When I open my eyes, he's licking his fingers clean with a smile of satisfaction. When he's done, he grabs my face and the kisses are long and lazy, neither of us in a hurry for them to end. Eventually, his mouth wanders again, this time finding my pulse point and sucking it while I recover beneath him.

"You okay, Angel?" His low, deep voice has me vibrating with even more pleasure. I nod, not sure if I remember how words work yet. "Can I get you anything?"

I shake my head, and he lays his forehead against my shoulder. I melt into him, letting my fingers slide under his hoodie and trace drowsy shapes over his warm skin. His heart slows as his breathing becomes more rhythmic than chaotic, the softness of my touch over his muscles making him relax against me. There's no way he doesn't notice my body go stiff when I trace over a large patch of rough skin and jagged scars along his side. I don't need to see them to get a sense of how terribly painful this must have been.

"Jamie?"

"Later," he whispers as his hands continue exploring all of me. His touch is equal parts therapeutic and sexual to me. Each time I tense or jerk away, he stills there against my skin, allowing me to breathe through it. Later will inevitably come for me, too. For now, we're just brushing the surface; enjoying the rush of a new…whatever this is.

"Should, uhm, should we talk about that?" I pry my fingers from him and pull my robe back up over my shoulders. "I mean, what we…what you…"

He stops leaving marks along my neck and looks at me, that deep, heartbreaking sadness back in his eyes. "Shit, was that not—"

"What?! No, it was… I mean… that was…"

We both sigh with relief, followed immediately by laughter. It's a sensation fueled by euphoria, genuine and beautiful. I brush his fluffy hair from his beautiful eyes. Even now, when he's happy, I can still see the sorrow hiding inside him. Could it be the scars or something deeper?

"You're pretty when you laugh like that." His fingers trace over my face, like he's mapping me out for future reference, which he could be. He is an artist. A shiver runs through me as I think of myself being painted in some weird mural someday. It makes me wonder if he does this with all the women who scream his name while they lose themselves to him. It's possible he has a collection of sketches or paintings of all his conquests.

"*Pretty*? I can handle pretty."

"Pretty is all I've got right now. I can't think of anything but you."

"Are we, uhm, are we really doing this?"

He glances around the room before he returns his focus back at me. "What? Standing in your kitchen trying to figure out how I'm here with an incredible woman like you?"

"Technically? I'm sitting, you're standing." I'm also blushing—hard.

"Barely," he grins, moving closer for another series of slow, languid kisses. This time, he breaks the kiss, sliding his nose along mine. "You're so soft and warm, I can't stop touching you."

"Oh, moving up the scale from pretty now?" I hook my fingers into the sweatpants. "My turn to hear you scream, pretty boy."

"No." He lets go of my face and grabs my wrists, pulling them away from him.

"What, really?"

"Really," his voice is a growl as the hunger reaches his eyes again. I can see that he's horny, and for a split second I worry that I've done something wrong. But the butterflies in my stomach are at it again as I realize this man is insatiable and I'm the meal he plans to devour. "I want to take you apart a thousand times before breakfast, and another thousand before lunch. I want to study every noise you make and every curve of your body until you're all that I know."

"What about you? Don't I get to do anything to you?" He doesn't answer and I worry again that I've crossed a line I didn't even know existed. Hundreds of possibilities start flooding my brain and he must see what's happening. "I mean, most guys, that's kind of all they want. Some women, too. And this is the second time you've turned me down when I tried to get into your pants."

"That's because I'm not done with you yet, Angel."

"James, if there's something wrong—"

"I just…fuck this is going to sound so damn stupid. I don't want to…I don't want to fuck this up. I don't want you to think I'm only here to get laid." His thumb runs over my bottom lip. "I want to make you happy. Show you how badly I want you…and this."

"This?" I slide my hand between his legs and he groans, his head dropping to my shoulder when my fingers dance over his cock. Christ, he's big. "What is *this*?"

"What do you want it to be?" He mumbles against my skin.

Unsure how what to say, I continue to tease him while my free hand plays in his hair. "Well, I guess—"

"You don't need to answer that right now," he says, raising his head up to let me see the worry in his eyes. "And you don't even have to put a label on anything. You can always tell me to stop or back off, and I will."

"That's the thing—I don't want you to back off or stop. I want you to let me have my turn." I squeeze gently. His fingers dig into my hips in response while another moan escapes him. "When do I get to take you apart?"

"Soon. I promise. Angel, I want to take my time with you, and when you can't take it anymore, I want to do it all over again. I want to worship you like you deserve to be worshipped."

I cup his face and bring it to mine. "Okay, how about we have breakfast on the beach? We can get the photos done, and after that, we'll take each other apart all damn night. Since you don't want to rush things anyhow."

Hunger morphs to worry, and back to familiar sadness. "Did I do something wrong?"

"No, James," I assure him. "I can absolutely respect taking our time to figure this out. I'm just a little surprised to know that you are a pleasure dom. I thought Dani would have picked that out of you and told me already."

"A what? Is that bad?" His shoulders drop, and his brows knit together in confusion and worry. "Are you trying to find a nice way to tell me that wasn't good for you?"

"It basically means you get off on getting your partner off," I explain, biting my bottom lip. "As far as what we did? It was *really* good. Unexpected, but impressive."

"Pleasure dom, huh? And impressive?" he kisses me deeply, leaving me breathless once again. "I'll take that, for now, so long as I get to keep kissing you."

My fingers play in the hair at the back of his neck and he moans deep against my ear before he buries his head against my neck. I've found a spot that makes him purr like a damn cat. I'll remember that for later.

It's a few hours of him distracting me from getting ready every chance he has, and me teasing him as far as he'll let me go. I finally get us out of the apartment and we leave for Venice Beach. We talk about music and work, keeping the topics light-hearted and fun. He holds my hand the whole way there, bringing it up to his lips at each red light and kissing my knuckles.

I blush every time.

For wanting to take it slow, I have a sneaky suspicion that he'd drive me to Vegas right now if he could. I don't know how to handle this kind of attention, because this isn't how my relationships go. Dani called the cops on one of my exes. My mom or stepdad have scared a few away. Mostly, though, they've been a trail of short-term hookups. That's not even counting the jerks my mom tries to set me up with.

I'm so used to pushing people away that my brain is struggling with the idea of having something more. I'm not sure how to handle a legitimate relationship, but James seems more than willing to give me the time I need to figure it out. It's scaring the shit out of me.

He parks the Jeep closer to the beach than I realized you could, and I'm surprised by the number of open spaces around, but it's still early for LA. There's a restaurant nearby with a crazy aesthetic and a cow's ass sticking out of the front, it looks like the perfect place to nurse a hangover, which neither of us have. We order and find a table in a corner. We share our food and his hand doesn't leave my thigh the entire time we're there.

While talking about the photos from yesterday, I reach over and snag a piece of bacon off his plate. He laughs as I pop it in my mouth and I stare at him. I glance down and realize both plates are empty and I've been picking his clean of crumbs.

"Shit, I'm sorry!" I'm mortified, but he's smiling at me. "You must think I'm—"

"Beautiful?"

"That wasn't the word I would use."

"I would, and did. If you're still hungry, I can get you something else. What do you want?"

"Hell no, that was…I shouldn't have done that." I can hear my mother's voice in the back of my head and I wish she'd go away.

He doesn't argue, simply leans over and kisses me softly between every few words. "On the way back to your place… we're going to a grocery store…and I'm buying one of everything you like." He squeezes my knee. "You're going to need it, because I can't stop thinking about how good you taste, and how much I want to devour you all night long. I'll mark every inch of you as mine. Every. Single. Inch."

He walks his fingers up my thigh at the last few words, then dips his hand between my legs. I stare forward, utterly dumbfounded. The ache in my core makes me want more, but my brain keeps screaming that we're in public. I wonder if I fell in the shower this morning and hit my head. Maybe I died. He teases me, his fingers pushing against me, making my hips rock as my body desperately cries out to let him touch me. Then he stops and stands up.

"Ready to go, darlin'?"

A shiver runs down my spine as I blink myself back to reality. As we walk, James snaps pictures here and there, both for the client and for himself. He's being sneaky about it, but I know some of them are of me. I don't mind because I can't stop thinking about what he said; the heat between my legs is still begging for him. It's strange, when you're this turned on, every alleyway looks less like a dingy hot mess and more like an opportunity.

"Hey, I'll catch up. I need to swap this out."

"Swap it—holy shit, is that film?"

"Yeah, yeah. I know. It's dumb. Film gives it a more authentic look—to me anyhow. More of an artistic edge to it instead of that perfectly crisp digital shot. There's a unique beauty in the imperfections that digital can't replicate."

"How do you do that?"

"Do what?"

"Make me feel really dumb and really turned on simultaneously by saying a bunch of smart, artsy words." He puts the camera down and takes hold of my hips, and I wrap my hands around his neck. I've barely touched him, but I can feel how turned on he is. I can hear it too in those soft little moans that sneak out of him.

"Yeah, well, you can talk me under the table in computer programs and design."

"That's all tech speak. 'Artistic edge' and 'Beauty in imperfections?' That's poetic!" He blushes and drops his head to refocus on changing the film. The way his fingers move so masterfully, I'm sure he could do it blindfolded. No wonder he shattered me so completely a few hours ago.

I need to get my mind out of the gutter. It's my job to keep us on task and I'm failing. All I can think about is this morning. His lips. His hands and how they played along my skin. He steps behind me, holding the camera out so I'll take it. His hands hold my hips tight as he kisses below my ear, whispering, "Show me what you can do, my perfect Angel."

He talks me through the settings and I hold the camera up and try to focus as he presses against me. Through the viewfinder, I catch our reflection. He has us lined up in front of a vibrant, happy mural with a shop window in the middle. Warmth spreads through my belly when I realize he wants a picture of us. Together. I shake the butterflies off and try again to focus.

"You're a sappy one, aren't you?"

"Nostalgic for parts of the past I never experienced, I guess. Besides, now, when I go home again, I can spend hours developing pictures of you." He laughs. "Jesus, I suck at this whole flirting thing."

"You do go from dirty to Shakespeare to stalker a little too quickly." He pinches my ass and I squeal and smack his arm. "So wait, you were being serious? You develop these? Like you do the whole red light in the darkroom situation?"

"Yep." He holds up the second camera. "This one is digital,

and to be completely honest, I still don't have the best relationship with her yet. She's excellent for things like client work and as a backup, but I'm too old school for her sometimes. I have a darkroom behind the house. It's one of my sanctuaries."

"That sounds impressive. I should set up a sanctuary in my place, but what would I even put there? Smutty romance novels and my computer?"

"If that's how you find your inner Zen, yeah. I have a friend who plays these horror video games to relax, and he has an entire room in his apartment with LED lights and everything."

"Oh, that sounds cool—I could totally do that. Not the horror video games, though. I love horror, but fuck those games."

"Yeah, we tell him he's a psychopath for finding that shit relaxing." He messes with the camera again and I'm reasonably sure it's because he's afraid to make eye contact with me sometimes, and I wish I knew why. "We could set you up an area for your sanctuary, but we'd need to fix your place first."

"Fix it how? What's so bad about my place?"

"Well, we need to hang that Rent artwork for starters. After that, add some stuff to make it more you—like you have in your office. Make it seem less like an IKEA catalog before you start forming some underground club you're not allowed to talk about."

"I have no plans to blow up a city, thank you. Was that for reference, or do you have issues with IKEA?" He picks me up and I yelp as he spins me around.

"It's boring, You're not."

"Yeah, well. I kind of hate the apartment sometimes. Maybe the sanctuary idea would help?"

"It's a Los Angeles secret." He puts me down, but doesn't let me go. "It's how people who have lived here their whole lives can still put up with a city like her. You have to have somewhere to go and remind yourself who you are and what you're doing. Otherwise, she's likely to chew you up and spit you out somewhere near Oklahoma with a splitting headache and no clue how you got there."

I laugh at the visual. "Oh, my god."

"Too much?"

"Honestly, not enough. I like the way you talk; it's... different."

"I listened a lot as a kid." His smile fades and he busies himself. He's doing it again, doing anything he can with his hands to distract himself from meeting my eyes.

"I'm sorry." I'm such an ass, stepping on every emotional land mine he's buried away.

"It's okay. I, uhm, I stopped speaking when I was five and didn't start again till I was around fourteen." He stops and looks up the street, but he's not really here. I wonder if this is part of the *later* he talked about when I found his scars, but I don't ask. "Went through some stuff and kind of shut down."

It's not the right time to ask him what happened and I'm not even sure I want to. We're not there yet. It's also not my place to ask about what kind of trauma a five-year-old experienced to go non-verbal for nearly a decade. He'll share when he can, if he wants to. "Can I ask what got you talking again?"

His eyes finally meet mine, and there's a slight pull at the corners of his mouth. Too many people want to talk about what caused the trauma because that's where the good gossip is. The recovery? If it works, everyone forgets about you. I want to know what helped him, how he survived, and I'm betting not a lot of people ask that.

"Kid in my class, Coop. He was new, recently moved here from Canada with his dad and his kid brother. He wasn't happy about the divorce and the move, so he was acting out. Some kids started shit with me on the playground, and he clocked them. They were going to throw him out of the school, and, well, someone had to speak up for him. Literally."

"Holy shit, that's kind of awesome of him. And you!"

"Yeah, he grew up around hockey, so he's got a hell of a left hook. We've been best friends since."

"Wait…Coop? Canadian? Hockey?! I mean, the odds are astronomical, but please tell me you're not best friends with Chase fucking Cooper. You're not, right?"

"Well, if I tell you I'm not, I'd be lying."

"FUCK! You've seen my office, too. Oh god!" I cover my face while embarrassment floods my body.

"Yeah, well, just so I'm not alone under the bus, he's friends with Dani, too. Personally, I would never stand in line for more than five minutes for the guy's autograph."

"Wait, I thought you were friends?"

"Yeah, if he makes me stand in line, I'll kick his ass. Well, that and if he knew you waited in a four-hour line, he'd apologize to you for about a year."

"Huh, so the brooding artist is besties with an A-list, legit Hollywood celebrity. That's kind of cool. I'm not freaking out or anything." I laugh at how unbelievable this all is. It's like the world tilted oddly on its axis or something and nothing has been normal since running out to get coffee in the middle of a Thursday. "Guess that's what you meant about contacts in the business, huh?"

I take off my shoes and let my feet sink into the sand. It's an odd sensation against my skin. I always think of beach sand as warm, but this morning the sun hasn't touched it yet. I'm surprised by the chill. I wiggle my toes and watch James take off his shoes and shove both pairs into his bag.

"Coop was the only person besides my dad who ever tried to

stand up for me. He talked for me, and when he wasn't, he gave me my space. He still does when I need it. Freaks people out sometimes because he and I can have an entire conversation without a word."

"I can do that with my sister, but ours is a twin thing, I think. Do you write, too?"

"Sometimes. It's not my favorite medium because I'm one of those people who doesn't think words are enough to really get an idea across. Some people can, but I can't seem to get them to be as deep and meaningful." He watches me wiggle my toes as my smile grows to a giggle into a laugh. It's freeing.

"Okay, when was the last time you came to the beach? Was it at least this century?" James is quick enough to catch the face I make on camera—so I stick my tongue out at him.

"Jerk," I push him playfully and he tucks his cameras into his bag. "The night my sister and I moved here, we drove across the country. We wanted to end our trip by saying we literally traveled coast to coast. So, I guess that would be almost fifteen years now."

"So you come to the beach on your first day in California, and it takes you fifteen years before you find yourself back on a beach? You do know that's kind of what we're known for, right? Beaches and sunshine? Alright." He sighs heavily and holds out his hand. I stare at it for a moment. "We definitely have to do this."

"Do wha—" He's leading me down the beach in a full run, headed right for the water. I should let go, but I don't want to. Instead, I scream and laugh like an idiot the whole way. He stops for a split second to drop our things in the sand, spins around, and lifts me into the air.

He runs into the water and the sting of cold hits us instantly. It's positively freezing. We both shout as the first wave hits us, pulling us along as he jumps into it, but he doesn't let go. He's in up to his chest and holding me up higher as he goes deeper.

I should be mad because I'm freezing, but I don't care. With each wave that hits us, I feel less and less of the chokehold life has had on me for nearly twenty years. I feel genuine happiness. I look down into his eyes as I slip into the water and our shivering lips meet.

Fuck, he's pretty. Why can't I stop laughing?

HOLLYWOOD

James

CHAPTER 19
PICTURES OF YOU
THE CURE

SHE'S PRACTICALLY CLIMBING me to escape the sharp bite of icy water, but she's still laughing. It's the most beautiful sound I've ever heard, and I know with every ounce of my soul that I want to spend the rest of my life making her laugh. She slips down into my arms. All I can do is stare into her eyes until the cold becomes too much and I race back into the sand with her.

"Oh my god, that was crazy, James!"

"If you're going to beach, beach properly," I say, chuckling and shivering as I put her back down on dry land. The wind is catching the loose strands of her hair as she looks out over the ocean. I've snapped more pictures of her than anything else this morning, but I can't help it—she's radiant.

"Come on, my hair is a mess and you're wasting film! Fuck, we need to find some new clothes before I die."

I wrap around her, trying to warm her up, but it's no use since I'm freezing, too. We hurry back up to the street, finding a tourist trap of a store with overpriced everything. She grabs a ridiculously enormous hat and matching sunglasses and directs me to sit in a display beach chair. Over the next twenty minutes, she models different hideous outfits for me by holding them up and spinning around or walking between the racks like it's a runway at fashion week. She adds her own soundtrack and even starts doing commentary in a goofy German accent. I've never laughed this hard—or felt this free—around anyone. I don't know how she does it considering she has every right and reason to be furious at the world, to be miserable and angry—like me.

Instead, she's snarky and full of life, curious and playful, and god is she sexy. She's effortlessly breathing new life into me every moment I'm with her.

"James, I simply cannot choose!" she says in an awful posh accent, dramatically holding her wrist to her forehead and giggling when the giant hat falls off. "What am I to do! I can't wear these to the ball! You must choose."

"Well, sure as fuck not that thing." I take the shapeless muumuu she's modeling and change it out with something I'd been eyeing. Standing behind her, I slip the hanger over her head, and we look in the mirror. It's a white dress with tiny pink flowers that match her hair. There's a deep v-cut front, and the bottom hits her mid-thigh. I wouldn't blame her if she smacked me for picking it out.

"Come on, there's no black in that. Are you trying to be my mother?"

My hand is on her hip, and I whisper against her ear, making her shiver. "Your mother isn't going to be who you think about when I get you so wet you'll drip down those pretty thighs."

"James!"

"I can't wait to rip this dress off you, cherry blossom."

The hand I've splayed over her belly slips down, bunching the skirt fabric so it rides up her thigh. She swallows hard, watching. All I can think about is bending her over in this thing later.

"I don't know, James. I can't wear these leggings under it since they're soaked. It's...that's not a lot of...dress," she laughs and turns to hang it back up, but I stop her.

"We could consider it payback for the tight grey sweats you gave me this morning. You know you were looking."

"I would never," she giggles while she blushes and holds up the dress again. She bites her lip and thinks it over before giving in. "Fine, I guess fair is fair. Don't think this is going to be a thing, though. I don't even like dresses."

"You might like them more, now that you've got me." I kiss her before she slips into the dressing room.

The woman at the register has been eyeing us since we walked in, so I can't sneak in after Lexi. So I find a cheap pair of board shorts and change into them. When Lexi comes out, she's clutching her wet clothes to her chest and has a dusting of pink on her cheeks. She refuses to let go of her things as I pay, and I'm dying to see how she looks.

"I really don't get how this is supposed to keep me warm," she grumbles as we head out. I feel a tug on my t-shirt followed by a groan. "Dude, we need to go back. You forgot to get a shirt and I should find something else to wear," she decides as we're almost to the Jeep.

I glance down at the t-shirt I borrowed from her. She tossed it at me this morning since it's the largest shirt she owns. It's tight, but the way she looked at me when I pulled it on was pure sin. I have no intention of letting go of it until she forces me. "No chance! It smells like you and no one could pry it off me now. I'm girlfriending this shirt. It will dry while we walk."

"Girlfriending?"

"Yeah, my idiot friend, Steve, calls it that when one of his dates permanently borrows his clothes or other stuff." I hold the bag open and nod toward it.

"If you tell Dani about this, I will murder you." She takes a deep breath and reluctantly drops her leggings and shirt into the bag.

"Tell Dani about what?" I freeze the moment I pick my head up and take her in. I can't stop staring.

"It's stupid, isn't it?" She glances down at herself and groans. "Shit. Let me go back in and pick something else. I'm too pale and no where near skinny enough for this thing, James."

I grab her arm, swallowing thickly as she turns away. I can't catch my breath. "Stay," is all I can manage as I step back and study her body. "You…you're…breathtaking."

"Breathtakingly dumb. This is why I don't wear dresses. Did you know there's a literal office pool for when I'll be seen in public in a dress?" With her arms outstretched, she spins carefully, making sure not to go too fast. "This is what you can't tell Dani about. Me. In a dress."

"Hey, unless she cuts me in on the office pool, my lips are sealed." I grab my digital camera, knocking a bag out of the back and accidentally spilling stuff everywhere. I go to pick it up and she beats me to it, holding up one of the small blue ducks that fell out.

"Rubber duckies?"

"It's a Jeep thing. I always keep them handy in case I see another Jeep around." I bring the camera up and snap a series of quick pictures.

"Fuck, James? Come on, I look like an idiot." She holds a duck up, trying to hide her face behind it even though it's tiny. Her nose scrunches and it kicks up a fresh wave of butterflies in my stomach.

I take more photos before handing her the camera, hoping

she can see what I see. She stares for a long time, and I'm concerned she's trying to delete it, but then her glistening eyes meet mine.

"Okay, it's a good picture. Whatever." She hands the camera back. Her cheeks are red and she's chewing on her lip. "Just, you know, don't send it to Dani. Or Kennedy. Or Sam!"

"Scout's honor."

She narrows her eyes at me. "You were never a scout, were you?"

"Correct." I tuck the bag of ducks into the back.

"How do you feel about bikes?" she asks as I help her into my jacket, sneaking a few kisses while I do.

"Bikes?"

"Yeah. We could rent bikes, and that way we could get more shots from different places down the beach without moving the Jeep." I hesitate and rub the back of my neck as she pokes at my stomach. "You do know how to ride a bike, don't you?"

"I mean, yeah, but…," I stammer and frown at the idea. I've never biked on the beach before. "Angel, I'm all for watching you bike around in that little dress, but it's the beach."

"Is…is that your grumpy face?" she teases, wrapping her arms around my neck.

"My…no…it's just my face."

"Okay, grumpy duck, if you say so. There's a bike trail, concrete. I saw it earlier while we were walking. We're not biking through the sand. We could see if they have any of those tandem bikes. I'll do the steering and you can see the sights. By 'see the sights' I do mean stare at my ass." I'm thinking it over when she drops her arms and hooks my pinkie around hers. She blushes again—fuck that's cute, I can't say no to that. She slips my camera off my neck and points it at me. "We don't have to. How do I do this again?"

I put my hand over hers and help her adjust the settings. She takes a burst of shots, then pulls the camera away and starts flipping through them.

"You have a wonderful smile, Jamie. Has anyone told you that?"

"I better. Those damn invisible braces aren't cheap."

She turns the camera around and shows me and I just stare. "What's wrong with it?"

"Nothing. I'm not used to seeing myself smile for pictures."

"Well, it's been nice seeing you smile then." She puts the strap of the camera back over my neck and kisses my cheek before skipping toward the bike shop.

Days ago, I stared at a stack of bills, mulling over how to pay off, rent out, and escape the house. I hated my life, and myself, to the point that I was ready to give up on everything. I've been begging for something to keep me here—and not just in the city I've always called home. Maybe I was just waiting for her. Life can be funny like that, or at least that's what people say.

Two kids are working at the rental shop and they're both gawking at Lexi through the window before we even step inside. Neither of them is even trying to hide what they're doing as they fog up the glass with their breath. They're probably straight out of high school and blazed out of their minds, but if I had to do this job, I would be, too.

Most days, I am.

"Hey, pretty mama," the blonde kid says as we walk in, making me wonder if they know the windows don't have a tint. It's like I'm not even standing there next to her as he continues to hit on her. "Are you looking for something fun to ride today?"

Her hand finds mine, and she smirks. "Oh, I've already got that covered."

"Dickhead!" the other kid with braces whisper shouts,

smacking his buddy in the head then turning back to us. "What he meant was, do you guys wanna rent a bike?"

"Do you have tandem bikes?" Lexi asks, and the kid with braces offers to take her outside to see them.

I hang back, and as soon as they're out of earshot, I turn the blonde jackass. "You need to apologize to her."

"Oh, come on, it was funny! Bro. Chicks love that line," he snorts, clearly amused with himself as he plays on his phone. "It was, you know, like a compliment, man. I had to shoot my shot with a thick ass piece like that."

"Apologize to her for acting like a primate in heat." I keep my voice low as I step forward. "Or I'll rip your fucking nose ring right out of your face. Bro."

The kid's eyes are wide and I'm not sure they've ever been open this wide before. He sizes me up, which is hilarious considering I doubt he could lift a pencil, let alone stand up for himself. I'm not a fighter, I never have been, but he can plainly see that I haven't missed a gym day in a while.

"Yo, bro, chill. Fuck, I'm super jealous that you're hitting that, my man! High five? Those tits are banging, and that round ass—"

Before I can move toward him, a familiar warmth slides up next to me. "They have a tandem bike. I think we should rent it."

"Alex, you're gonna get us fired, dickwad!" the kid with the braces scolds his friend.

"Whatever, Todd. Your dad owns the place!"

"Uhm," Todd stutters, looking at us. "I could give you a discount if you don't say anything to the owner about Alex being a douche. I kind of need this job. So does he."

I'm staring Alex down, and he's starting to sweat. He shoves his hands deep into his pockets and mumbled, "Uh, so, like, I'm sorry I was acting like a primate in heat." It sounds like he's reading off a script. "Please don't complain to my uncle. He's already pretty pissed at me because I never show up on time."

Lexi has to fight back a giggle. "Apology accepted. How about we call it even and you give us the bike for an extra hour?"

"No shit? Yeah, totally! That doesn't even show up on the log, bro!" Todd takes us outside to the bike and gives us both a quick rundown on safety as Alex gets distracted by a group of teenage girls with accents.

Lexi waits till they're both back inside, then turns to me, laughing. "How badly did you threaten him?"

"Barely. Kid's just a dumbass. He did say you looked lovely in that dress, though."

"Lovely isn't in his vocabulary," she hums as her hand slides over mine on the handlebar.

"Yeah, you're right." I lean into her. "I agree with his assessment, though; your tits are banging. I'm sure he was about to be just as eloquent in describing your ass."

"Oh my god, you're both idiots." She grabs my shirt and pulls me in for a soft, slow kiss. I could kiss her all day. Someday I will. Someday, I'll do nothing but make her come until she begs me to stop. I'll listen to those intoxicating moans while she digs those nails into my hair. "So, would it be okay to walk it around the corner before hopping on? If I make a fool of myself, I'd rather it not be in front of those guys."

I can't stop looking at her and realizing that I'm finally seeing the real her. She's sassy and brilliant with enough confidence for me to forget how fragile she can be. The combination of strength and beauty while she stands beside me takes my breath away. She's letting me in to see her authentic self, the woman she's meant to be, the one I fell for with a glance, and I don't think she even knows it.

This is my Lexi. Brilliant and unbroken. She doesn't hide behind sarcasm and wit; she wields them like blades. Her parents tried to force this version of her into the darkness because they know this is the one they should fear. This is the phoenix that will burn their empire to the ground and dance in their ashes.

"What are you thinking about?"

"How badly I hope to be by your side when the world begs your forgiveness, and you unleash that raging fire inside you."

"Wow, okay," she snorts, pulling the bike around the corner. "I was expecting something about me falling off this bike and onto my ass, and a little less deep there, pal."

I could tell her I love her right now. I'd mean it, too. I love her.

We take a couple of tries to work out our timing and for Lexi to get comfortable steering for two, but eventually, we're on our way. We cruise nice and slow down a beach that's emptier than I've seen since the lockdown a few years ago. Even the gulls aren't out in force, probably because there's no one to swipe food from. We stop at a handful of street vendors and check out Muscle Park, and I get some fantastic shots that even the clouds can't ruin.

We've been going for a while when Lexi brings us to a stop and puts her feet down. She spins around, eyes wide with surprise and child-like excitement.

"Wait! That's the fucking Ferris wheel!"

"You know, if you'd come down here more than once every fifteen years, you would know that Venice Beach and Santa Monica Pier aren't too far away from each other."

"But I thought it was, like, miles!" Her expression changes as she pouts and bats her eyes at me.

If she asked me to jump into the water and fight a great white shark with my bare hands right now, I'd absolutely do it. Good luck, Jaws. I'm here to win the heart of my beautiful bike mate and muse. I'm unstoppable!

"Do you think we could go on the Ferris wheel? We couldn't go on when we got here because it was already closed."

That sounds much better than fighting a shark. "Absolutely, Angel. In fact, it's a Los Angeles requirement that you're 15 years behind on."

My phone rings and as I'm pulling it from my pocket, a giant beach ball knocks into the side of us. Neither of us is ready for it, so we go down with a crash, bags, equipment, and both of us hitting the ground hard.

"God fucking damnit! Lex, are you okay, Angel?" I hop up and pull the bike off her as she winces. Blood is pouring out of a long, hopefully shallow gash. Without hesitation, I pull off my shirt and grab the bottle of water from her bag so I can wash the sand and blood from her leg. Two kids run over, grab the ball, and then take off in the opposite direction, not an adult anywhere to be seen. "Idiots. This is why I like about five kids in the whole world."

"The cameras!" she shouts and winces at the same time.

"What?"

"Make sure the cameras are okay."

"You matter way more than a camera, Angel." I pour some water over the cut, then wrap the shirt around her calf. "It's not perfect; I can probably get a first aid kit from somewhere."

"I'm fine. I fell off a bike in front of the hottest guy on the beach. I'm more embarrassed than anything." She snickers, but I can hear the underlying pain. "Now I'll never get in your pants."

I don't even hear the last words because of where her eyes are. I took off my shirt. Shit. I turn so she doesn't have to stare at the disgusting scars. I'm not ready to ruin our day with that conversation. My hands shake as I clean the blood, bracing myself for the questions I don't want to answer. When her words finally replay in my head in slow motion, I realize she said nothing about my side or the jagged disfigurement. In fact, she called me…hot.

She's smiling through the pain, giving me a shrug. I feel like an absolute moron. Panicking over something she's not concerned about at all. I'm blaming myself for the crash, too. I should have been paying more attention and not fucking with my phone. "Damnit, I ruined your shirt. Fucking assholes. I'm sorry I dragged you out here. We should have stayed at your place and gone over pictures."

She reaches over and touches my arm so softly I almost don't feel it. "I'm the one who suggested the beach and the bikes. You didn't do anything wrong, James."

"Sorry, I…uhm… guess I got a little upset. It's not deep, so you shouldn't need stitches."

"Hey," She tilts my head up with a finger and I can't breathe. "Don't let it ruin the morning. We still had a really wonderful time, and we got some work done. You should check out all the texts I'm getting from my sister and Dani because of a few pictures I posted."

I take a breath and try to relax. "Posted? Should I be ready for round two with your mom later?"

"No, I keep my account super private. Want to help me back up, tough guy? Let's find out if I can ride this thing or if I have to walk."

"You're not walking back like that," I say firmly as I help her to her feet, then lean in next to her ear and whisper, "Would you prefer to ride the bike back, or me?"

She covers her face and how the pinks and reds of her skin

creep through her fingers when she laughs. "Oh, my god. Are you taking flirting lessons from a bike shop kid?"

"Hey, at least you didn't slap me. Now wrap those pretty legs around me and I'll carry you back and walk the bike."

"James, you don't have to do that. I can—"

"I want to. I want to take care of you." I brush her hair out of her face, tucking it behind her ear. "Please?"

We strap the bag to the bike and I help her climb on my back, careful not to bump against the cut. She snuggles against my neck and plays with my hair. For the first time in my life, I never want to leave the beach. It takes us over an hour to get back to the Jeep after we stopped a few times to give us both a break.

"Alright, you stay here and I'll run the bike back. I'll try to find something to clean that up a little better, too." I start to move away, but she grabs my shirt and pulls me in for a deep, fiery kiss.

"Hurry back."

On my way back from returning the bike, I pull out my phone to check my texts to make sure Lexi doesn't need anything else. As soon as the screen lights up, I remember what distracted me before the bike went down.

UNKNOWN NUMBER

I went by the house, but you're not at home. Such a shame.

Don't ignore my calls again, dickhead.

She's cute in a boring way. How long before I get this one to leave your sorry ass?

[Image Attached]

Lexi and I eating breakfast this morning just down the street from where I'm standing now.

I think back over the last couple of days, trying to figure out how the hell she found me and how she knows about Lexi. It wouldn't surprise me if she hired a PI to follow me around before she came into town so she could have extra ammunition to hurl at me.

I shove the phone in my pocket, knowing I can't let her get to Lexi. No matter what.

HOLLYWOOD

Lexi

CHAPTER 20
TRUE LOVE

🌶 P!NK, LILY ALLEN

I STILL CAN'T BELIEVE he carried me. He not only carried me but also never complained or tried to back out. I'm starting to believe none of this is real and that somewhere between Sam's office and the boba shop, a bus hit me, leaving me either dead or in a very drugged out coma somewhere.

He feels real, though, and my leg definitely hurts. My phone chirps in my pocket and I remember I told my sister I'd get back to her and I haven't. Oops.

💀 BEXXUS 💀

You tell me you KISSED HIM and then LEAVE ME hanging?

I need updates!! STAT!!

I KNOW WHERE YOU LIVE!!

Girl, updates! Come on, you can't tease me with one picture of that specimen and then ghost on me.

I will hunt you down!

LEXI

Sorry! I fell off the bike, long story.

💀 BEXXUS 💀

OMFG, only you could do something as basic as falling off a damn bike in front of hotty mc hot pants at the beach. What did he say?

LEXI

HE CARRIED ME BACK TO THE CAR!!!

💀 BEXXUS 💀

WAHT?! OMG I CAN"T EVEN TYPE.

LEXI

Yeah, he uhm, he pushed the bike and carried me on his back.

It was like two fucking miles. He was shirtless!!

💀 BEXXUS 💀

Did you die? Keep him. MARRY HIM!

Think how much that would annoy mom!!

LEXI

He's really nice, Bex. Like, really nice.

💀 BEXXUS 💀

What does he do? Not that it matters. He could be a fucking cartel boss and I'm still going to be team SMASH THAT MAN and get a RING put on it...

Your finger or his cock, whatever you're into!!

LEXI

You're so ridiculous. Are you sure we're related?

My phone rings and I answer before her name even pops up.

"I couldn't type anymore. I want to hear it!"

"Hear what?" I giggle.

"THAT! Oh, you like him. I recognize that giggle! It happened with that kid in middle school. Devin?"

"Kevin. That guy was a dickhead, though. James is…he's…"

"Everything all the other people weren't. Yeah, that happens when you get out of the bubble and away from the queen dragon mother. You should cover him in fake tattoos and leather, send a pic to mom, and watch her spiral through her own private hell."

"So, about that, uhm, he already has tattoos. And he kind of, uhm, met mom."

The line goes silent for a while, and I give her the time she needs. Mom and I are blissful best friends compared to her and Bex, but Bex will be the first to admit that she never made it easy on Mom. Bex never thought she deserved anyone going easy on her, and someday, I'll admit she's right.

"How?"

"We're working on this project for work I told you about and when we got back from the convention last night, I invited him upstairs. It was innocent and at that point, I'd already told him I wasn't interested. We were just going to go through pictures and brochures."

"Please tell me you didn't give her a key?"

"No, but she was there waiting for me, I guess. She kind of stormed the apartment and played it off like she had no idea he'd be there. She might not have seen him come up, I'm not sure. Either way, he got a front-row seat."

"Was the asshole Jesus freak with her?"

As bad as my mother is, her holy roller husband is a thousand times worse. She needs a therapist and help; he needs jail time. I hope someday he gets it, too. I would give my life savings for a front and center seat to watch his cult collapse around him.

I miss Bex. She is my sister and my best friend. She didn't have a choice when she left, if she had, she wouldn't have left me behind. She tried convincing me to come with her, but I'd started my job at Sam's by then and I thought that would be the light at the end of the tunnel. She has always felt indebted to me since I couldn't continue living in our shared apartment and had to move back with mom for a few years.

"No. I would have sent James out of the fire escape or something if he were there." I search the lot to see if he's headed back, but nothing yet. "She went full rage on him, called him a lot of terrible things, called me a lot of terrible things, then she tried to hit me. James stopped her. Told her to leave and then he took me out for pie."

"Is that a—"

"NO! We went to the Pie Hole. That doesn't sound any better —fuck—it was just pie, Bex."

"Okay. Well, either way, I like James. You seriously need to think about a restraining order and cutting contact," she seethes through the phone. "I get that you want to see the good in her still. You like to think it's there somewhere, buried under all the bullshit, hate, and religious crap, but it's not. Even before dad died, she was a shit mother. I love you, Lex. I love you so fucking much, and I hope someday you get that through your head. Even Dad couldn't help her."

"She's been worse lately. Calling me at work and practically stalking me. She keeps telling me to get my priorities straight and saying my job is pointless. She wants me to move back in with them."

"Not fucking happening. Next time we talk, it better be less about that bitch and more about how big his dick is and how many times he made you—"

She's still talking, but I've stopped listening. I watch James walking down the parking lot and I have to wipe the drool off my face. The sun chose just this moment to come out and glisten off his shirtless chest. I had no idea the sun did that outside movie sets. He has muscles. His muscles have muscles. He's got that deep V in his hips that makes me shudder. God I want to lick him like a fucking lollipop. And the tattoos. He doesn't have tattoos all over his torso, but the few he has complement his physique.

"Yo, Lex? Are you still there?"

"I gotta go, Bex."

"I love you, now go get your man," she laughs and the call ends. I hate hanging up, since I'm never sure when I'll hear from her again. I'm trying to count his abs when he opens my door.

"So, the dickhead at the bike shop had this," James says as he holds up a medical kit like he just won it at a fair. "Little shit also wanted me to remind you that you have great tits. I still hate him, but he's still right. Mind if I take another peek?"

"At my tits?"

"I meant your leg, but I'll take either." He blushes and smiles like a little boy who just told the girl next door he loved her. Fucking adorable.

I have no control over my eyes as they bat. "Absolutely, Doctor Barton. I'm all yours." I shift for him, spreading my legs and letting the short skirt spill between them. His eyes grow dark as he watches, mesmerized by the motion.

He pulls his eyes away and crouches in front of me. I can tell he's trying not to stare, trying to be a gentleman. I, however, have no plans to be a lady.

"I, uhm, I'll just…" he stutters until I take his hand, guiding it up my leg and under the skirt. His chest is already heaving when he glances up at me, then drops his eyes. "I guess you were right. You might not be shy after all."

"Shy has no place around a hot shirtless guy who asked me to ride his co-OUCH!"

"Sorry! Shit!" He pulls away, focusing on my leg again. "I

need to make sure the sand is all out and get this bandaged better." He hides his face while he laughs so hard his shoulders shake.

"What?"

"Nothing, it's stupid."

"What! Tell me."

He looks up, meeting my eyes with a big, dumb grin on his face before he replies, "Ride his couch, huh?"

I slap his arm. "Don't ruin the moment, jerk!"

"I think it's cute." His free hand slides back up my leg without me leading this time, and I bite my lip. "I'd absolutely let you ride my couch."

A yell down the beach grabs my attention, then I gasp when his hand dives deep under my skirt. There's a devious gleam in his eyes and I expect horns to grow out of his head any minute now as he teases me.

"Angel, you're all wet." His fingers drag down my panties.

"Yeah, I guess I am."

"Lift your hips." I do, and he pulls my underwear off and down my legs, tucking them in his pocket with a wink. He leans in, kissing from my knee to high up my inner thigh, then goes back to cleaning my leg. "I'll take care of the leg, then you."

"You will?" As he looks down to wrap my leg, I pull off his hat and run my hand through his sweat-dampened hair. My nails drag along his scalp and he moans deep and needy. "How's it going, Doctor?"

"Alright, that will have to do till we get you home, since you won't stop teasing." He shifts so his body blocks the open door, and he flips the skirt up and grins. "I'm half tempted to throw your bratty ass over my shoulder, walk you down to the bike shop, and show that little prick that you're my girl."

My girl. I love how sounds with that hint of a possessive growl.

"Oh, going full caveman on me, huh? Careful, I might take you up on it someday." There's a group of people headed our way and I nod toward them as I sit up and push my skirt back down to cover myself. "Should we head out to one of the other shot sites? We might get ahead on all of that today, and then I could go home and start putting things together."

"I'd rather start taking you apart," he says with the slightest edge of confidence creeping into his voice.

"I told Sam I'd start the project this weekend and send him some samples before Monday. That was before I realized any of this was going to be happening."

"Angel, you're gonna burn yourself out if you keep working like that. You really need to take a day off, especially with your banged up leg."

I reach out and take his hand, pushing it between my legs as our lips hover dangerously close. "Come on, we can hit one or two more spots and still be back at my place before dark—and then I'll ride whatever you want, big boy."

"Oh, you are evil. I like it. Alright, fine," he finally says, shifting my legs into the Jeep again and closing my door. He looks at me as he starts the engine. "Okay, GPS says we can get to the Grove in under an hour, which is crazy. Lunch?"

"Oh, we can pick up some food for the apartment there, too. Uhm, can I have my underwear back though? This dress is pretty damn short."

"You have to earn it back."

The surprised expression on my face must be priceless, because he gives me a wicked laugh. "It's broad daylight, and this is an open Jeep. I'm not sucking your dick while you drive."

"What? Not what I had in mind, my little cherry blossom.

Close though, sort of." He grabs my thigh and pulls it up onto the seat, turning me sideways. "Scoot a little closer."

His husky voice has my head spinning as I do what he asks. Once he has me where he wants me, he pushes the skirt up again and licks his lips while his finger slides through me. It's like my body recognizes him from this morning and knows what's coming next, and fuck do I want it.

"What are you going to do, James?" My voice, airy and unfamiliar, and the torturous anticipation in my skin, begging to be touched.

He leans over and cups the back of my neck, pulling me to him for a kiss that promises me the world, and as he breaks it, he whispers, "I like it when you tease, Angel. It means I get to pick your punishment for being a tease."

"Punishment?" The word should scare me. It might even be a red flag. But all it does in his gravelly voice is turn me on more. I want this man to punish me. I want him to make me scream until I have no voice left. I want him to pull me out of the seat, bend me over the hood, and fuck me while everyone watches.

I want him to ruin me.

His mouth closes over mine again, but before I melt into him, he's pushing two fingers inside me. My back arches and just as I feel the moan building, he pulls his fingers out and sticks them in his mouth, sucking them clean. I glance at his pants and I can see the outline of his cock straining to be let free, but he's ignoring it, too busy tormenting me with his thumb. He's kissing me again and I feel the delicious pressure of his fingers pushing inside me again, quickly curling to find my G-spot. If this man is half as good with his dick as he is with his fingers, I'm in for a very long night.

Before we can get any further, his phone vibrates, sending it skidding across the dash and falling to the floor. He panics as the screen lights up and he goes to grab for it, but before he can, I see…me.

"What the fuck?" I yell and pick the phone up, looking at myself in the kitchen.

"Lexi, it's not—"

"Yes, it is! That's me! Were you fucking recording us this morning?"

"No!" He looks scared.

"That is a picture of me, half-naked and on top of my kitchen counter with your fucking hands between my legs! How did you do that? Why did you do that?" I'm freaking out, but I can't stop. I want to cry, I want to throw up. "Is this why your phone is blowing up all the time? Are you fucking sending people pictures of me?"

I grab for the handle of the Jeep and I've got the door half open when he yells out, "It's not what you think!"

"What?" I spit the word out and glare at him.

"Alexis, she's fucking stalking me, okay!" He opens his phone and shows me a string of text messages from an unknown number, all of them time stamped from the last half hour. The last one has the image attached to it, which is bad enough, but the message underneath turns my blood to ice.

UNKNOWN NUMBER

Your new whore has got cute tits…she could lose some weight, though

I bet her stepfather would love to see some of these videos. Maybe her boss, too?

Open her legs wider next time. I'm sure the internet will pay extra for that.

I stare at the screen, the taste of bile hitting the back of my throat. "Take me home."

"Alexis—"

"Now," I snap back, slamming the door shut again and leaning against it to get as far away from him as I can. He pulls away from the beach in silence. My mind races from rage to humiliation and I need to be alone.

When I raise my head again, I see we're only two exits from my apartment and he hasn't said a word since we left the beach. The panic is building. It's moments like this when I wish my sister were here, pushing me out the door to live life rather than letting me stay tied down to my work and spending my whole life pleasing others. She was my constant support, always there to anchor me in chaotic times. She might tell me to walk away, tell me not to give him the chance to explain himself. She's not here, though.

The click of the blinker is deafening, and I force myself to blurt out, "You said she's stalking you. Who is she?"

"It's...complicated." He slows the Jeep as we come to a red light. His jaw is tight and his heart is racing, I can tell by the pulsing vein in his neck.

"Holy fuck, are you married?"

"No, Alexis, I get how this looks and I understand if—"

"No, you're a fucking asshole." I reach for the door and he grabs my wrist.

"She's... she's my sister."

"Oh, bullshit."

"Her name is Elle. She's my kid sister and she hates my fucking guts. I swear that's the truth, and I didn't know...fuck... I didn't... I didn't know." He runs his hands through his hair and when he closes his eyes, I can see they are wet with tears. "She...she's been texting me for a few days. This morning she sent a picture of us eating breakfast. I thought I could ignore her, but—FUCK! Just...you should go."

I should. My brain is screaming at me to get out of the car, go upstairs, and tell Sam to find someone else. My heart, though, is reminding me how he held me when I cried last night. How innocent and sweet he looked this morning as he stood in my kitchen trying to make coffee. How warm his lips are. My heart is so much louder than my brain sometimes.

"James, look at me."

He shakes his head, "Don't. It's… it's better for you to not be involved with me. I'm sorry."

"James." I shut the door and move closer to him, catching his hand before he slams it into the steering wheel. I let my heart take over and kiss his knuckles softly before wiping the tears streaming down his face. He has no reason to lie to me, and if he'd just wanted to get into my pants, he would have done that already. "Take a deep breath, and count to four…do you know how to box breathe?"

He nods, and it takes a minute before I feel the tension in his arm loosen a little. He stares at me with those sad eyes I can't get enough of and all I want to do is hold him.

"She's threatened me for years. Cost me jobs and friends because she said I ruined her life. She blames me for our parents' divorce and every time something good happens in my life, she's there to blow it up."

"Boy, we sure have some fucked up families, don't we?"

His eyes meet mine, and he's undoubtedly confused. I've never seen a man look so fragile before and for me, it's like looking into some kind of bizarre mirror. Everyone has pain, but finding someone with pain that you truly understand on its most raw level isn't something you expect when it cuts so deep. I see him with his fear and panic and I know how all of that feels, even if it is for different reasons. The pain is the same. This isn't healable. This is the hurt that will stay with you until you die and you either learn to live with it or you lose the fight.

"In the last forty-eight hours, I've lived more than I have since my sister left and I was alone." I caress his cheek. Some people have this innate need to fix someone. It's an entire writing hook that authors routinely lean on. I'm taking this step because I know I can't fix him, and I'm hoping he knows he can't fix me, but maybe we don't have to be alone. That would be enough for me.

"Park the Jeep. Come upstairs."

"I can't."

"You can because I believe you, James." I squeeze his hand and nod to him.

He wipes his eyes on the back of his hand and takes a shaky breath before driving up the block and finding a spot. He shifts into park, and I notice the deep worry crease in his brow.

"Lexi, you don't have to do this. I understand."

"Do you want to come upstairs?" He nods with a sniffle.

I smile, "Good, then stop arguing with me and let's get past this."

HOLLYWOOD

James

CHAPTER 21
JUST LIKE HEAVEN

THE CURE

I CAN'T BREATHE, I can't control my thoughts, I can't stand. I'm a fucking mess.

I don't understand what's going on, because I should be on my way home to sulk for the rest of my life. I should be letting Elle win so I can keep her away from Lexi. Lexi should hate me for hiding this from her. She should run as far away from me as she can. None of that is happening, though. Instead, I'm sitting next to her in the Jeep, and she's taking me through breathing exercises because she asked me to come upstairs. I'm not even sure how I got the Jeep parked.

"Okay," she coaches, stroking my arm gently. "Last one. Can you tell me one thing you can taste?"

I take a deep breath and slow my brain down, just like she's been telling me to do. "You? I still, I think I taste your lip gloss stuff."

"Cotton candy. The judges will accept your answer. Feeling any better?" I nod and press my forehead to hers, closing my eyes. "What are you thinking about?"

"I think I have a date tonight. She's a pretty girl with whiskey-colored eyes." When I look at her, the brightest, most brilliant images of the stars and galaxies can't even compare. "We're supposed to watch movies and fall asleep on the couch together again. I want to show her she's special while I can. She's the best thing that's ever happened to me, and she's perfect. I'm just hoping I'm not too late, hoping she hasn't changed her mind and realized what a fuck up I am."

"She hasn't, so let's get up there and hit the reset button, okay?"

I grab all our things from the Jeep and help her onto my back. She only fought it for a minute when I insist on carrying her at least to the elevator. The world is moving strangely and too fast for me to keep up. I'm not sure what the fuck I'm even doing, but she's not giving up on me.

"Alright, put me down, Prince Charming. I think I can handle it from here."

The gate hasn't even closed and I've already got her pushed against the wall, losing myself as I kiss her upper lip in a deep, slow, deliberate kiss. We met two days ago, been kind of together for six hours, and already we've shared more of ourselves than some couples do in a lifetime. We've seen the raw emotion and shared some of the torment that haunts us both.

I need to touch her; I need to know she's real. This is real. Her skin sends waves of warmth through my body and it almost... tickles. Just touching her is enough to make me happy.

"I want you," I say before our mouths collide again in a hot and uncontrollable need.

I grab her hips and push her against the wall of the elevator. I nip her bottom lip, and my hand slips up the back of her shirt and pulls her closer. The driving need for more consumes me as I lift her, and her legs wrap around my waist.

I wonder how like me she is. I wonder if she's ever had a chance to just relax and let go. I want to be that for her, like she just was for me. Be the one she can always be herself with. I need her to let go for me in more ways than one, but that means I'll need to let go for her, too.

I carry her through the hall, briefly stopping to unlock the apartment, then I bring her directly to the bedroom. I don't give two shits if her mother is watching again. She can knock all she wants. We're busy.

I lay her on the bed and she shimmies away from the edge on her elbows. I crawl my way to her, nipping at her legs and stomach through her dress and listening to her breath catch each time I do.

"I promise I'm not going to hurt you."

"What if I want you to?" she asks in an airy whisper. Her hands grip my arms, squeezing tight as I dip my head down to hers, brushing her lips with mine.

"I'll do anything you want, Angel. But first, I want to sample every part of you. I want to make you writhe and moan for me."

She practically lunges for my mouth, and when I slide my hand up her thigh and between her legs, she gives me the softest whimper. She's already throbbing, begging to be touched. I press against her and her hips respond, bucking against me. The way she writhes under me, the way her whole body responds to every touch, is intoxicating. I want—no; I *need* to devour her.

I trace down her collarbone with my tongue while I slip her bra down, exposing the most perfect pebbled nipples. She's the goddess I want to spend the rest of my life worshipping. I want to take her to the highest highs and give her everything she could ever want. I close my mouth over her nipple, sucking and biting while I roll the other between my thumb and finger. The noises she makes are a song to my ears, like the chirping of a morning bird, and it drives me on.

I release her breast with a gentle pop and move further down her body, paying extra attention to her soft, beautiful belly. My sister made a dig at her weight, and I want Lexi to know I think she's fucking perfection. Easing her dress up, I leave a trail of kisses across her skin and slide my nose under her belly button and she giggles. Fuck, I want her so badly it hurts.

The moan she pulls from me while her hands play in my hair drips with animalistic desire. The more she claws and pulls, the louder I am for her. Only for her. I'm memorizing every inch of her body with my tongue and my hands, biting lightly at her tender thighs.

"Harder, James," she coos, holding my head to her. Her back arches off the bed when I bite down again, and she's no longer humming my name. She's fucking screaming it.

I press my tongue into her folds and my nose bumps against her swollen clit. The perfect combination of sweet and tangy explodes in my mouth, and I'm practically drooling to be inside her when she falls apart for me.

It's hard to go slow when all I want to do is ravage her, to listen to her screams echo off the walls as she comes all over my tongue. I lick a stripe over her clit, then suck in pulses while two fingers push into her. Her grip tightens and her hips roll when I hook them upward, thrusting steadily against her g-spot.

"Oh, my god. Oh, my god. Oh. My. God!"

"Use my name. Pray to me, Angel, because I'm about to make you come so hard you'll think you're seeing god."

Her body is dancing on the edge of the cliff, waiting for one last flick to push her over the edge. When her orgasm hits, she screams my name, and it's never sounded better from any other lips. I don't stop, thrusting my fingers a little faster and a little harder into her as my tongue writes her name over and over because it's the only name I ever want on my tongue again.

Her body convulses, and she's still riding the wave as she

squeezes my head between her thighs. Fuck, it feels amazing. Honestly, I'm not sure if it's one continuous orgasm or if she's sailed right on into another because I'm too busy destroying her. I break for air as her body slows, and she releases my head, gasping for breath herself.

"You alright, Angel?" My head is spinning from the speed I went from panic attack to sucking on her pussy, but I admit, it's one hell of a way to recover.

"I...I've never..." She gestures vaguely and then covers her face.

"Baby, if you tell me no one has ever gone down on you, we're in for a very long night of my head between your beautiful legs."

She giggles, "Oh god, I'm so embarrassed. I can't believe I screamed like that. What if the neighbors heard me?"

I climb up her body and her legs wrap around me almost by instinct as I sink into her neck, biting and sucking. She tastes like the beach—salty and sun kissed. "I'm going to make sure they hear you again and again. They're going to know my name and what I do to you. You're so fucking perfect, my angel. And those noises you make are driving me mad."

"James, that was... I mean..."

I pick my head up and run my nose along hers, smiling at the sex-drunk expression she's giving me. I've only just started on her. "Now, what exactly did you mean *you'd never*? Never had someone's tongue make you scream for god?"

"Not once before today."

"And?"

"I've... I've never had someone make me...or... orgasm more than once before." She closes her eyes. "I mean, I have a toy, and sometimes I use that, and I can make myself—"

"Get it."

Her eyes open wide as she stares up at me, and I kiss her deep and hard. She's moving her hips again, desperately grinding against my raging hard-on. I roll my hips in response, thrusting against her and growling in her ear, "Get the fucking toy."

She wriggles out from under me and moves toward her nightstand. I watch her ass while she bends over in the disheveled dress to look in the back of her bedside drawer. While she searches, I pull my shorts off, giving some much needed relief to my cock. I toss my shorts off the bed and she gasps; I turn back to her and laugh. She's staring at me with her mouth open and shock on her face. Judging by the way she's staring, she's both hungry and worried. Then I see the tiny bullet vibrator in her hand.

"Come here," I keep my voice soft and steady. I'm in no hurry. "Lay back down. I want you to show me how you use it."

"What?! I…I can't…I'm…" she yelps then stutters. She turns her back to me and drops to the edge of the bed with her shoulders slumped.

"Hey, hey, Angel. What's the matter?" I shift over, so I'm sitting behind her just as her shoulders start to shake. "Alexis, sweetheart, talk to me, please?"

She sniffles and jumps a little when I put my arm around her, my hand across her belly. I nuzzle against her head, trying to help her, but she shakes her head, "You probably think I'm some kind of freak."

"Because you have a vibrator?"

"Because I'm boring! I'm in my thirties and all I've ever had is okay vanilla sex. I know everyone thinks I'm wild and fun, but I'm not. I mean I don't know if I am. I'm just…just…I've never had—" She takes a big breath. "You're the first guy I've even brought into my own bed, James."

"Alexis, can I ask you something?" She shrugs and nods. "Do you trust me?"

"I...yeah."

"No, I need to know that you trust me. If you don't, then we need to start there, not here. So, do you trust me?"

"Yes, James. I trust you."

"You don't have to be so formal, Angel. Jamie is fine," I offer, kissing across her shoulders and sliding the straps down her arms. "You have nothing to be embarrassed about. All you need to do is relax and I'll take care of you. If you're not comfortable, we take it slow and find your boundaries. If you don't want to do anything else tonight, that's fine too. You're not boring. You could never be boring."

I should have known better. There's no way she would risk really letting herself go with just anyone, not with her helicopter mother lingering around. It's why she's wild and free at the clubs, and reserved here in her own home. My gut tells me there's more, though, and I shiver at the thought of how much more we still have to uncover. Both of us.

I have an idea.

"Stay here, okay?" I say between kisses along her neck.

I wait for her to nod, and then I climb off the bed and pull on my boxers. I head for the bathroom and search for something I'd spotted earlier. There's a small basket with snowmen and Christmas decorations, and inside are a handful of bottles and bath bombs she's never touched. I grin at the bottle of bubble bath; I've never been happier that someone has a clawfoot tub in their apartment. I pop the cap open and immediately my head is swimming in cherry blossoms. Perfect. Then, I rush to the living room, gathering all the candles and a box of matches. I'm about to check the fridge, but stop and swear under my breath when I remember it's empty.

"Where's your favorite place to eat?" I ask, heading back into the bedroom. I do the math and figure I should still have a little wiggle room on one of my credit cards. This isn't work, and I'm not having Sam pay for this.

She gazes motionless at the candles, then at my outstretched hand.

"Sweetheart, tonight—and every night hereafter—you're a goddess and I'm going to take care of you like one. We'll move at your pace. We'll only try new things after we've discussed them, and the second you change your mind, we stop."

She continues to stare at my hand. "Why are you still here? I've yelled at you, you've met my mother…why aren't you running away?"

"Rent," I answer and she stares up at me, confused. "Your baggage goes with mine." I see the recognition to the play's reference and crouch in front of her. "Angel, I'm not trying to pressure you into anything. If this is a one-night thing, that's fine, and I'm going to do my damndest to make it a good one-night thing if you'll let me. But to be really honest with you, I'm kind of hoping we get at least a few nights before you tell me to get lost. Maybe even longer if I'm lucky enough and don't fuck this up beyond repair."

She blinks at me as she sits there. "Why me? You're too hot and too smart to be with someone like me."

"Someone like you?" I frown, trying to keep down the anger. How badly has her mother fucked her up? "You are bold and brilliant, the most amazing person I've ever met before. You're also captivatingly gorgeous and—"

"No, I'm…none of those things."

I swallow hard. "Why do I want you? Because something inside you has set me on fire. Something that makes my heart skip a beat and my knees get weak when you smile at me. I don't just want you, Alexis, I fucking crave you. To touch you and be near you. To hear your voice and your laughter." I tuck a strand of hair behind her ear, put the candles in her lap, and scoop her up as she squeals. "I'm also about to flood your bathroom out if we don't get back in there."

I put her down and turn off the water before I slip the dress off her shoulders and let it pool around her feet. Stepping back, I take her in. Each time she tries to cover herself, I move her hand away affectionately. Licking my lips, I hoist her up onto the counter and hold her face. Our mouths slot together and we kiss until we're breathing for each other. I lift her again and carry her to the tub, letting her get accustomed to the water while she giggles over the bubble bath. I light the candles and turn off the bright fluorescent lights, then kneel by the edge of the tub.

"Tilt your head back. I'll wash the sand out of your hair." She closes her eyes. I gently take her hair down and let it fall into the water. "You look like a mermaid."

"Are you really going to wash my hair?"

"Every opportunity I get, my Angel."

When I'm done, she scoots forward and pats the water behind her. She looks away and blushes as I slip my boxers off and climb in, careful not to splash the water over the edges. I leaned back, taking her with me, and once we were comfortable, I move my hand between her legs while the other cups her breasts. I leave trails of kisses over her shoulders, and trace my finger up and down her slit, teasing her playfully. The anticipation has her heart racing so hard I feel it.

"I've been going about this wrong, Angel. How about you tell me what you have done instead of all the things you haven't? Show me where the starting line is, where you're comfortable, so I can carry you well past it if you'll let me."

"I can't concentrate with your hand…down there." She laughs

and takes a sharp breath as the tip of my finger glides through her folds. "I, uhm, I'm not a virgin, if you're worried about that. I've had a few partners in the past—men and women. I'm not a total prude. I just, it's always been a quick fuck in a bathroom or car, sometimes back at their place. I haven't even had or wanted any long-term relationships since high school, really."

"Because of your mom."

"Among other things, yeah."

"Well, just so you're aware, I never thought you were a prude and I wouldn't be worried if you were a virgin. Virginity is some made up, meaningless standard that shouldn't be important. The people you dated or hooked up with are your past, and now it's my job to help you forget them. To help you understand that whatever they made you think about yourself, it's wrong. And to show you my devotion as often as you'll let me. You taste divine, Alexis. I really hope you liked that as much as it seemed you did; I want to do that every single night to you."

"You don't have to worry about doing that again or pretending you liked it. I know most guys don't like it."

"Did *you* like it?" She nods and even though I can't see her, I know she's biting her lip. It's what she does when she's nervous. It's also adorable. "Then I'll continue licking that beautiful pussy. Because I'm not most guys and I love it. I can't get enough of how you taste. You're a million times better than any of those pies from last night, and I could eat you for breakfast, lunch, and dinner."

I take her hand and guide it between her legs, slowly tracing up and down with her hand. "We're going to break through every one of these things that you think is embarrassing, and later, we're going to wake up every one of your neighbors with your angelic song."

"I…I don't…"

"You can do it. You can make every person in this building jealous."

"Ja…Jamie. I think… I think I'm going to come again."

"Good." She squirms against me and I groan. I'm not sure how much more I can take. "Let me see you play with yourself. Just like that, Lexi. Fuck you're beautiful."

"Please, I want you. Please?"

"What is it you want, darlin? You've gotta tell me."

"I want you inside me. I want you to fuck me. But… shit, you're so big."

"Let go for me, Angel. Then we'll see how much you can take. I have a feeling my girl can take every fucking inch of me," I whisper. The way she's sitting, my cock is right against her ass, and if she keeps moving like she is, I'm going to come way too soon.

She unravels on top of me, and I can't wait any longer. Not worrying about towels, I pick her up and carry her to the bed. I'm enamored with how her soaked body looks, the bubbles and her pink hair clinging to her soft skin. I'm beginning to think I might have a mermaid kink. I realize she's staring, too, and when I pry my eyes from her body, I notice again that she isn't looking at my scars.

"Wow," she chokes out before licking her lips as she watches me stroke my cock. "Holy shit, you're…pretty."

"You're fucking exquisite." She rolls her eyes and scoffs, not believing me. "Do you know how many museums I've been to or sculptures I've seen of beautiful women that don't even hold a candle to you? You're…have you ever been to the Philadelphia Museum of Art?" She shakes her head, still staring at me while she wets her lips. "There are these terracotta sculptures there—

from the 20s, I think—and one of them is Aphrodite. You're her —but so much better."

"Jamie," she sounds hurt, and I shake my head as she pulls a pillow over herself next. "Don't be an ass."

"No. No, I mean it. You're more beautiful than the ancient goddess of beauty, and if she wants to come down here and smite me for saying that, she can, because I'm standing by this."

"I don't remember her smiting anyone."

"Then I guess I'll be the first." She giggles, and the sound travels down my spine and into my cock. "Fuck. I love that sound."

I grab my pants off the floor and fish out my wallet. "Fuck, well, shows how often I get laid. Expired months ago."

"I've been tested and I'm on birth control."

I crawl into the bed, between her perfect, thick thighs, "I've been tested, all good. Your call."

She bats those long, beautiful lashes at me as she nods. Our mouths meet like it's the first time again, shy and uncertain. "Spread your legs and relax for me, Angel."

I push just the tip inside of her, and already she's gasping, writhing against me, and whimpering with need. I slide in further but keep it slow as I look between us and watch how well she's taking me. She clenches tight around each slow, shallow thrust, pulling a deep moan from me.

"Damnit, Lexi! You feel so fucking good."

"Oh fuck, Jamie!"

"Eyes on me, pretty girl. Let me see how good I make you feel." It's a fight to keep my eyes from rolling back in my head when my hips are flush with hers and I bottom out. "Oh, fuck, you were fucking made just for me, baby girl."

"Shit, you're big!!"

"And you're taking all of me, just like I knew you could." I run my nose up her jaw and nibble on her earlobe. Her hard nipples press against me when her back arches, and I lean down, taking one in my mouth.

I pull all the way out and thrust slowly back in, letting each loud, desperate moan wash over me as she gets used to my size. Once she does, I let my head drop to her shoulder and groan against her ear as her hips roll. I'm sucking hard on her skin, marking her neck as I find a slow, steady rhythm that makes her sing while her nails claw at my arms. My senses are flooded by everything that is Alexis. Her scent, the way she feels, the way she moves, each sound she makes for me and only me. Everything about her is perfect.

She pulls my head to hers, catching my bottom lip and biting down as she stares right into my eyes with those big, dark doe eyes. Suddenly, she's taking over, rocking her hips and trying to push me deeper into her.

"Take everything you need from me, Angel. All of me. Because I'm yours."

I already know that I'm gone. I already know that she fucking owns my heart, and I'll hand over my soul if she asks for it. I already know I want her, this, us—I want it all. I want to come home to her and bend her over the counter. I want to wake up next to her naked body against mine as she sleeps in my arms. I want to be with her every day because she's a fucking drug, and I'm never going to get enough.

"Lexi, please," I gasp as she holds me tight inside her. "Be mine. Be my girl, my Angel, my muse. Be my forever."

"You mean it?" She pants, hooking her feet behind my back and digging her heels in.

"You're all I want, Alexis. All I need."

"Yes! Yes, Jamie!" she sobs, her nails raking over my shoulders.

I grab her wrists and push them over her head and into the mattress, leaning back so I can watch her face as my hips snap faster, harder into her. "Is this what you wanted, Angel? Christ, look at you, you're so fucking beautiful." Her legs clench around me like a damn vise. She tries to bite back her screams, and I shake my head. "I need to hear you, baby. Let everyone hear you. Let go for me. Let it all fucking go, my sweet angel."

"James!"

She begs, cries, and pleads for more as her body vibrates under me. I feel like a damn god as she comes apart for me and I follow right behind her. My release mixes with hers in the most intense orgasm I've ever had, aftershocks rolling through both of us until I can't hold myself up any longer. I try to collapse beside her, but she holds on, pulling me down on top of her and guiding my head to her neck.

She holds me inside of her after my hips stop and I go soft. When the world stops buzzing, I wrap my arms under her back and roll as she unlocks her ankles. I have no idea how long we lay there holding each other wordlessly, our bodies still humming.

I love this woman. The sex being amazing is just an extra perk.

HOLLYWOOD

Lexi

CHAPTER 22
CHERRY BLOSSOM

LANA DEL RAY

"YOUR TONGUE IS MAGICAL," I slur as if I'm six shots in at one of Dani's parties. I've totally lost track of how many times I've orgasmed in this all night sex marathon we've been having, but I definitely am going to need another nap soon. He chuckles against me as he kisses up and down my torso. I want him between my legs again, but I'm pretty sure if he even blew on my clit right now, I'd come again.

"Don't ever shave your beard."

"Longer hair, keep the beard, anything other requests, my cherry Blossom?"

I finally have the strength to crack my eyes and see his beautiful face. The scruff on his chin glistens, and I'm not sure why that doesn't embarrass me. Instead, I'm extremely turned on at the sight.

"Why do you call me that?" My voice is sleepy, like I'm in a dream, which I very well could be with how amazing I feel. "Cherry blossom?"

His hand comes up, and he twirls some of my hair between his fingers. For a second, I wonder if those were the fingers that damn near made me black out. "Your hair is the right color, and your body wash is cherry blossoms. I smelled it when you walked away at the cafe that day and I haven't been able to get that scent out of my mind since."

"What if I change the color?"

"You'll always be my Cherry Blossom, no matter what you do to your hair."

"Is it crazy that we haven't even known each other for 72 hours yet?"

"I think it's more crazy that I went thirty-three years without you."

"Are you always this smooth-talking when you're in bed?"

"Absolutely not." He wraps me in his arms. It's been like this since we got home—sex, talk, nap, and the cycle repeats. As we're drifting off to sleep again, he mumbles, "There's just something about you. I think you're my muse, Alexis."

I wake up sometime later, still tired, but with a dull ache between my legs. There's an arm around my waist and a hard chest at my back. Luckily, the memories of everything Jamie did to me last night come flooding back when I recognize the tattoo below his thumb. Giddy butterflies are dancing like it's a nineties rave in my stomach, and I've never smiled this much in my life. I check the clock, carefully move his arm, and try to slip away slowly, but he grumbles and pulls me closer. It takes three more tries before I manage to escape. I duck into the bathroom, and a few minutes later, I slip out the front door in a pair of sweatpants and his shirt. I figured it was the easiest way to keep him from sneaking out before I could get back.

I drive a few blocks, knowing I'm early enough that I should be able to find a spot and only have to wait fifteen minutes or so in line. I love it when I'm right. I find a spot that's about as close as you can legally get, and, thanks to it being a drizzly Saturday morning, I'm through the line and headed back to the car in almost no time.

I sneak back in the front door and tiptoe into the bedroom, listening to him softly breathing. I'm inches from his face, watching him sleep, when he sighs.

"You smell delicious," he mumbles before one of his eyes opens just enough for me to make out the sparkling grey, "but I'm betting you also *look* delicious in my clothes."

"So you noticed I snuck out? Shit, I was trying not to wake you. I brought breakfast!" I place the two coffees and paper bag of food on the nightstand, and as I go to stand, he grabs me around the waist and pulls me into the bed. He's showering my neck with kisses, and I can't stop giggling. I think this is my new favorite way to wake up.

Second favorite. When he woke me up with his head between my legs after I gave him permission to, *that* was my new favorite way to wake up.

He rolls me onto my side and kisses all over my shoulders. "God, you have a beautiful laugh. It's like that perfect first ray of light that manages to break through a cloudy morning."

"I think I sound like a hyena."

"Well, I guess you're one sexy hyena, and I'm happily tone deaf."

I sit up, straddling his hard abs, and stare at him. I run my finger over his lips, and he kisses it. "You have the prettiest lips for a guy. Breakfast is getting cold."

He pulls me down and attaches to my neck again. My hips grind against him with a mind of their own as he sucks on my pulse point lazily. His hands slide under my shirt as he lifts it over my head, tossing it across the room. His mouth travels up my jaw and all over my face until we're both laughing.

"What, didn't you say breakfast? I was planning on having more of you."

"You are bonkers. I ran out and got Eggslut," I say, swatting his hand away from my boobs. "I figured we should probably eat before we start working again."

"Ehwhat?" His brow raises as he looks up at me with sleepy eyes.

"Eggslut, oh my god, how do you not know them?" I climb off him and sit cross-legged while I pull out the food. "They're super popular. I got bacon, egg, and cheese sandwiches with chipotle ketchup, truffle hash browns, orange juice. Oh, and a thing called the Slut that is to die for. It's eggs and some kind of potato thing in a little jar."

"Jesus, you're perfect." He leans over and kisses me twice, deepening the kiss slowly while his hand squeezes my thigh.

Leaning on his elbow, he holds the food to my lips and feeds me. After a piece of bacon, I stop his hand and turn it over, tracing the tattoo on this thumb. "What is that? It looks so damn familiar."

"Lord of the Rings. I was obsessed with the books as a kid, and the movies too. I was absolutely sure I wanted to grow up to be a Ranger of Ithilien."

I expect him to be looking at his tattoo, but he's staring into my eyes.

"You know, when you stare at me like that, I'm pretty convinced you're like that serial killer from Silence of the Lambs. Trying to get me to the right size before you slit my throat and wear my skin like a dress." He starts laughing uncontrollably until I shove a hash brown in his mouth. "Oh, or maybe you want to eat me!" I scream and cover my face when I realize what I said, and he smacks his lips.

"Cherry Blossom, you have the mind of a true creative. A dash of paranoia and a heavy dollop of very dark humor. You caught me though, because I definitely plan to eat you right after breakfast."

"After last night, you still want more?"

"Oh Angel, I do. As a matter of fact, I think this morning I'd like to have dessert before I finish breakfast." He winks and throws the covers off as I try to grab for the food. He hooks his fingers into my sweatpants and starts yanking them down to my ankles as I go between laughter and trying to yell his name sternly.

His strong hands pulling my thighs apart and the cool air slips between my legs as he moves my panties to the side. "Shouldn't have even bothered with these things, Angel." There's pressure, the snap of material, and I see my panties fly across the room.

"You owe me new—OHMYGOD!" His tongue and fingers dive deep inside of me without warning, and my back is arching high off the bed. I slap a hand over my mouth when I realized how loud that came out. I'm right back where I was last night. Floating in a galaxy of bliss. He reaches up and pulls my hands away from my face.

"I wanna hear you call me god while I worship you." He stops, his hot breath sending sparks up my spine. He raises his head from between my legs again, adding, "Besides, I think I like your hands in my hair way more than over that pretty mouth of yours."

His mouth destroys me not once but three times before his kisses and soft touches pull me back together again. He calls me angel, beautiful, and sweetheart, and for the first time in my life

I'm not immediately turned off by the words because they sound real. I say, scream, and moan his name so much that I'm sure the entire neighborhood knows it by now.

When he's had his fill of me, he curls back into the mattress and pulls my naked body to his bare chest. We share more gentle kisses and sweet words as we lay there. His arms are warm and safe. I don't worry about work, my mother, or what anyone thinks of me. Not a single intrusive thought can penetrate the barrier he builds around me as he feeds me breakfast and whispers poetry in my ear.

Until the knock on the door.

"Nooo, but I'm so comfy!"

"I take it you're not expecting company?" I shake my head, and he moves me over before he slips out of the bed. "If it's okay with you, I'd like to answer. I figure I'm about due for another round with your mother."

"That's a terrible idea, and she doesn't knock that lightly. It's probably a neighbor here to complain about the noise. "

"Even better reason for me to answer instead of you. Especially since you're still naked." I giggle, realizing he's right as he pulls his pants on and heads out of the room. I jump up and start gathering some clothes, listening in case I'm needed. I've got Jamie's shirt half on and freeze when the slight southern drawl hits my ears.

Oh, no. Oh no no no.

"Well, by the sounds of it, that's a lovely service you're holding for the lord in there. Was it James? I believe that's what she said—or screamed."

"And you are?"

"Oh, she's expecting me." He speaks loud enough to make sure I can hear him from where I hide in the bedroom. "Her lovely mother asked me to come check in on her. Name's Ronnie."

I step out as he's offer Jamie his hand, glad to see James doesn't take it.

"There she is. You should think about joining the choir, Alexis. You've got a beautiful singing voice."

"It's not what you think." I bolt into the room, standing between the door and James.

"Darlin, I am sixty-six years old, and I'm not dumb. Your mother said you might have had some unsavory company loitering nearby." My stepfather looks me up and down, pausing at my bare legs and again at my chest. I quickly cross my arms, instantly regretting not putting pants and a bra on before coming out here. "Guess I can tell her all I found was you being brought to your knees and worshiping in God's name." He nods to James. "And also his."

"What? No, I—"

"I told her she was riding you too hard; all I see here is this upstanding young man whose shirt you appear to be wearing. I take it today is laundry day?" He reaches out with a grin, touching the sleeve. I cringe, feeling his finger slide along my arm. I'm certain James can't see it from where he is, so I stay still and say nothing. I don't need James getting in trouble, and Ronnie is clearly trying to bait him. "I do wish your mother sang as pretty as you do."

"Lex?" James's hand is on my lower back, and I lean against it.

"James, this, uhm, this is my stepfather, Ronnie."

"James, the coworker? Ah, yes. You met my lovely wife the other night. She told me about you, but I can't blame a man for working so hard on the weekend. Especially when the work dress code is so…distracting."

"Ronnie, I don't—"

"You joining us this afternoon, darlin'?" I cringe at the name. From James, it's soft and sweet. Ronnie's voice is like old motor oil. He makes it clear he wasn't planning on listening to anything I had to say. "The board sure is looking forward to seeing what you've made for us. They told me to ask real nice since they know I can make you come."

"The fuck did you say?" James tries to move past me, but I block him, shaking my head.

"Oh, he's a bit jumpy, isn't he?" Ronnie winks at James before leering at me. "You should join us later today. There's someone very special I'd like you to meet."

James tenses even more, and I know he's ready to snap.

"I told Mother I would be there like we planned. I've already emailed her all the designs, and I'm sure she's shown you." I stare at the floor, avoiding looking at him. "I will be there when the meeting starts, but why are you here?"

"Well, I'm here to protect my precious little girl, of course. And introduce myself like a proper gentleman to the man who's brought you to your knees and put a bit more than prayer in that pretty little mouth of yours."

"What the fuck is your problem?" James tries to step toward him again, but I stand firm and thread my hand into his, squeezing hard.

"Calm down, son. Complimenting your technique is all. Perhaps next Sunday you could give us a live demonstration? Get her to sing like that in front of the whole church?"

"Daddy," I wince as I spit the word out. I hate calling him that, but I know it will make him happy, and he'll leave us alone if I do. He'll think I'm giving in to him, which is exactly what he wants. In a way, I am. "Please, go home. I'll be at the meeting later."

His grin is as wicked as he is, and his eyes have gone dark like his soul. "That's my good girl; all sugar and no spice. You're going to love the surprise I have for you tonight. I promise."

"Goodbye."

I close the door and breathe a sigh of relief as I turn the deadbolt, letting my head fall to the cool wood.

"Shit. I thought your mom was bad." James is enveloping me in his arms and pressing his lips to my temple. "Angel, are you okay?"

"Yeah," the response is weak, and I'm not really listening to what he's asking. I'm too busy shaking. I think I'm going to be sick.

"Alexis, I don't only mean right now, at this minute." He lets me go and turns me around to caress my face, tipping my head back so I meet his gaze. "Angel, has he touched you? Ever."

"No!" I answer too quickly, dropping my head back down. "Well, not…it's complicated. He makes passes all the time when my Mother isn't around—sometimes when she is—he holds my hand too long, stares, things he can easily pass off as innocent gestures. He hasn't tried anything beyond that in a while. He's never talked to me like that when someone else was around, though. No one but Mother." I'm biting back tears at this point. I hate lying. I should be used to this one by now.

"Your mother knows he talks to you like that?"

"She tells me it's my fault," I shrug, trying to shake it off. "I'm a temptress and a whore sent here to ruin a worthy man of god. I mean, I'm answering the door in your shirt and nothing else. Who does that?"

"Hey, no. I answered the door, not you. It doesn't matter what the fuck you're wearing, he shouldn't talk to you like that. Ever. How long has—"

"Only since I turned eighteen, thankfully." I let the half truth slip out so easily now. "I mean, I don't know how much better it is that he waited, considering it was the day of my eighteenth birthday when he grabbed my ass, kissed me, and offered to turn me into a real woman in front of Jesus himself."

"Woah, what?" I can see the anger building again, but I know what comes next. Maybe it's for the best that he's met them both now, so we can end this before we get any further. "He's not going to touch you again, Angel. I won't let him. I'll do everything I can to keep you safe. From both of them." He kisses my forehead, lips lingering long enough to make sure I know he's telling the truth. "You're sure you're okay?"

"I don't understand. You're… you're still not leaving?"

"Lexi." His face drops and I can see the pity in his eyes. "Shit, those two should be poster children for why religion is bullshit." He brushed the side of my face with his finger. "Sorry, I don't mean—"

"I'm not religious. Completely faking it to—hell—I don't even know. Keep in contact with my mother, who has spent the last fifteen years being a terrible human being, I guess. She wasn't always like this. She's…she's all I've got now that my sister is so far away."

He tilts my chin and his lips ghost mine. "You've got me now."

As we kiss, I push him backward until he hits the wall. "James, I want to forget again. I want it to be you and me and to forget about what he said, or that he was ever even here."

I kiss a trail from the center of his chest down to the top of his pants, which I pull down. He's not hard, but who would be after all of that?

"Lexi, you don't have to do t-this," he stutters a little as I kiss along his thighs before I tease his cock.

"I want to. I want this." I need him to understand. I need him to let me take back some control in my own way. He takes hold of my face and rubs his thumb over my bottom lip.

"Okay," he whispers, eyes locked onto mine. "I am so glad I don't have the Daddy kink."

His face contorts while I continue, leaving soft kisses along the shaft and watch him harden in my hands. I like the way he tastes as my tongue slides along the thick vein, making him groan loudly. As the first drops of pre-cum form, I lick at them like a lollipop, eyes focused on his.

He lets out a deep moan and I grip the base in response, squeezing it as I slide him down my throat as far as I can. I have to take it slowly. I've never been with anyone like James before, not even close. It's not like his cock needs to come with a warning label, but it's certainly not average, either.

He pulls the pins out of my hair, fluffing it softly before he wraps my hair around his fingers. He doesn't push, doesn't force me down, allowing me to take the lead.

"Fuck, Angel. Just like that. It's like you were meant for me, my beautiful muse." There's a high-pitched whine from him when he hits the back of my throat. I gag, choking a little, but I don't stop. "Atta girl, looking so fucking pretty on my cock."

I glance up, watching his head rock back and hit the wall as he rambles nonsense.

There's another knock at the door, and I try to pull back, but he stops me. "Keep going, Sweetheart. Let him hear what you do to me. What he can't ever fucking have."

I hum the most sinful moan I possibly can, and the strangled noise he makes falls somewhere between a keen and a whimper. I cup his balls gently, rolling them with my fingers. His shattered breaths are the signal that he's losing control, giving it over to me. It's my turn to take him apart and put him back together. It's my turn to claim him like he claimed me.

"Shit. I can't…you feel so good. Angel, I'm gonna…"

His grip on my hair tightens as he holds me there, fucking my mouth deep and hard. Saliva drips down my chin, and I'm struggling a little at the size of him, but I don't give up.

"I wish you could see how pretty you look on your knees. How beautifully and thoroughly ruined you look with that mouth on my cock. My perfect angel," he pants out, wiping the tears from my cheek. "Fuuuuuck," his body finally stills, and he fills my throat.

I swallow every drop, and when I release him with a soft pop, he falls to his knees in front of me and cups my face. His kiss is deeper and stronger than any before. Like I've sucked his soul out of his body, and he wants to see if he can get it back. It surprises me at first, but his hands are grabbing my ass and pulling me toward him before I can think too much about it. I wrap my legs around his waist and he stands, holding me, tongue still down my throat.

The knock comes again, followed by a different voice. "Are you assholes finished in there yet? It's been like three hours!"

"Dani?"

"No, it's the porn police. Put his pants back on and open the stupid door already."

HOLLYWOOD

James

CHAPTER 23
TIME AFTER TIME
IRON & WINE

"DANI, WHAT ARE YOU DOING HERE?"

"Okay," she barges into the apartment with a tray of coffees in one hand and a box of donuts in the other. "So I was coming here to play matchmaker and hook you up with this guy. Not Jamie, actually," she looks at him and winces, "one of your buddies that I dated."

"Coop?" I yell from the bedroom.

"Stevie," she shrugs. "I never dated Coop!"

"No!" I say sternly as I come out with the coffees Lexi got us earlier and head to the kitchen to find bigger cups.

"Oh, come on, he's not that bad!" I poke my head back around the corner and glare at her. "Anyhow, based on the sounds that were coming from this apartment, it doesn't matter." Dani tosses the donuts on the table while I hand Lexi a cup.

"I'm off the dating market," Lexi answers with a grin as I kiss her.

"Clearly. You both look utterly fucked in the best way possible. And that man over there is smiling. Legitimate smiles!" She watches me combining my coffees and recognizes the logo. "You got him Eggslut?! Wait, is this like a cute inside joke thing between you? Does he call you a slut while he sticks it in? Jamie, you dirty dog!"

"I do *not* call her that." I lean against the couch, shaking my head.

"You should. She and I read the same books. Seriously." She flops onto the couch next to Lexi, offering her a bite of her donut. "You two are so fucking cute together. I set Jamie up before and it never really worked out."

"Dani, it's not—"

"I mean, he got laid and stuff. A few even got a second date before he ghosted them."

"What?! I didn't ghost anyone. You're making me sound like a dick."

"You are, I mean, not Stevie level dick. You're more of a grump. He's a man whore."

"You wanted to hook me up with a man whore next? Wow, thanks," Lexi jokes, taking a bite of a donut.

I'm relieved to hear Lexi laughing. Both because of the way Dani is talking about my dating life and how awkward the last half hour has been. She goes into the room and grabs some clothes before heading toward the kitchen, but I stop her, wrapping an arm around her waist and pulling her toward me for a quick kiss.

"Doing my laundry again? You don't have to do that, Angel."

"Wait, again??" Dani yells and kicks her feet like a kid. "So this isn't the first night? Have you been home since Friday, Jamie? Wait! Angel? Oh my god, what have I been missing?"

I ignore her rambling and press my head to Lexi's, "You're beautiful." It means more than that, but I can't say what I really want. Not this soon, and especially not with Dani around. She'd be planning a wedding before she left. I wouldn't stop her, either.

Lexi winks at me, and to my surprise, like she understood the meaning behind the words. She replies, "You're beautiful, too." She slips out of my arms and into the kitchen and I wish Dani wasn't here, so I could take Lexi apart a few more times this morning.

"Dani, why are you really here?" I ask as I take a sip, frowning at the amount of sugary syrup in the coffee Dani brought.

"There's a party Tuesday—"

"No!" Lexi rolls her eyes as she slides back under my arm. "Absolutely not. That's a work night."

"Uhh, since when? I roll in whenever I feel like it, and you two aren't even working from the office," she says around a donut. "It's not a wild party, it's a fancy party! Rich people, champagne that costs more than my car, free bougie food. Besides, when has Sam ever cared if we show up hungover?"

"This sounds terrible. Why would we want to go to that?" I growl and slam back half the cup of coffee as fast as possible.

"It's an art gallery party, and we all got invited, sort of." Lexi and I both cock our heads to the side, eyeing her. She's hiding something; I don't think it's something bad, but it's something. "Okay, so it's a guy I met the other night, and he wants me to go to this stupid art show. I don't want to go alone and you guys are my artsy fartsy friends!" She pouts. "Okay, well, Jamie was my artsy fartsy friend—"

"Wingman," I interrupt to correct her, pulling my laptop out and sitting it on the coffee table so we can go over the pictures we've got so far.

"Same thing…which is why I texted this morning, but then I figured out there's this whole thing with you guys and so I came here to beg you to go to the party…and of course, give you a hard time."

I narrow my eyes and stare at her. "There's more, come on."

"You come on! Oh wait, you already did! Haha." She rolls her eyes and takes another giant bite of a second donut, spilling powdered sugar all down the front of her shirt, but she doesn't seem to care. She's far too wrapped up in our sex life now that she knows it exists. "Okay, so, fair warning, I'm inviting you because I really like this guy and I want to hook up with him. But it's a fancy party and we can get Lexi in a skimpy, hot dress!"

"Fuck you," Lexi yells from the kitchen.

"What? Jamie looks stupid hot in a suit, so you get your eye candy, too!"

I laugh. "I'm going to take a shower." I kiss Lexi's head as she passes by me before I pull off Dani's knit cap and toss it on the floor. This is why we couldn't date. We're too much like siblings.

"Wait, but what about the party?" Dani whines. "Come on guys, he's really cute, and he's, well, probably rich or whatever. Seriously, I need this! He said he'd do some bad ass cover art for my next album!"

"It's up to you, Angel." I head for the bedroom and stop. "Jesus, I'm sorry. I'm acting like I live here. Is it cool if I—"

"Yes, you have earned the right to my shower."

"I would hope so," Dani mumbles, picking sprinkles off her donut and popping them in her mouth. "He's earned the right to your pussy."

"Dani! Keep that up and I'll say no to the party!" Lexi yells, throwing a pillow at Dani's head while I laugh. "Why did we even let you in here?"

"Because I brought donuts! And coffee! And there's never food in this house!"

I lift my cup to her in salute and then turn to head into the bedroom.

"Wait," Lexi calls out while flipping through the picture files on the laptop. "Can we get some of these printed out today? I was thinking of setting up a giant visual mood board we could present in next week's meeting. A mixed media thing. I can throw in some graphics and a few pieces from the flyers and leave behinds I picked up the other day, too."

"Oh, thank god! I thought she was going to ask you to shower together, and I was going to throw up a little. I told you that you'd like her, didn't I?"

"When did you tell him that?" Lexi teases, sticking her tongue out at me, then turning her attention back to Dani. "How about I tell you by tomorrow? Let us get the week planned out and if we can work it out, then we might go to the party. Might!"

"Yes! I'll bring a dress over for you tomorrow so you can try it on! I promise, it won't count toward the office pool."

"We can pick out some prints to send off and I'll pick them up later." I set my cup down and move back to Lexi, rubbing her shoulders. "Since the idea is out there now, why don't you come shower with me? Let's leave Dani out here to take care of the neighbors when they come knocking."

"Yeah, yeah, you two lovebirds go get it on in the shower or whatever you kids do these days. I still have some errands to run, and if I'm not home before my sister wakes up and she finds out I drank the last of the coffee, I'm going to be unalived! I'll text you the details about the party later."

"Pretty sure we're both older than you are, Dani. But don't change." I move the laptop, scoop Lexi up off the couch, and toss her over my shoulder, slapping her ass as she screams in laughter.

We're huddled under the warm spray of water, unable to keep our hands or mouths off one another. I'm licking the small trails of water that cascade over her shoulders and she's playing with my hair and giggling. As badly as I want to be inside her, I can't get the things her stepfather said to her out of my head.

"Lexi, can I ask you something?" I nibble that spot just below her ear, and she digs crescent shapes into my ass in return.

"If it's, can we have sex again? Yes."

"No. I mean, I want to, but it's not that." I step back, feeling the cool air against my exposed skin. "Your stepfather, your mother, I don't get it. Why do you even talk to them when they treat you like that? You're this magnificent ray of happiness and light, and all they want to do is snuff you out and turn you into a shell of yourself. Or worse."

She tips her head back into the stream of water, trying to cover up the tears, but it doesn't work. As her eyes redden and she sniffles, I lean back into her and kiss just under each of her eyes, tasting the salt against her soft skin.

"You don't have to tell me, Cherry Blossom. I only want you to have better. You don't deserve any of that, and they don't deserve you."

"My mom has always been a bit, I dunno. Strange," she starts in a whisper. "When Dad was still around, it wasn't this weird obsession with religion, but there were still other things. Dad tried to be the fun parent. He worked hard and was home late, but always made time for us. Sometimes, he'd get home, and we'd be asleep, and he'd come in and wake us up to hear about our day, sometimes giving us candy or presents. Mom hated that so much. Those were the nights we'd lay in bed hearing her scream at him and throw things."

"She could be fun, though!" She pivots quickly, trying to convince herself as much as me. "On her good days, she'd take us to the park, and we'd meet Dad for lunch there. On her bad days, she wouldn't leave her room, and we would have to fend for ourselves until Dad got home. We didn't understand it, but he did. He'd always tell us that no matter what she said or did, our mother loved us, but sometimes she just had a hard time and needed a break."

"Did she ever go to a doctor or try to get help?"

"He tried to convince her, but she wouldn't go. She'd always have some excuse." She wipes her face and straightens, trying to put on a brave front, even though she doesn't need to with me. "Anyhow, just before he died, he started to tell us to make sure we always took care of our mother. It's part of why my sister, Bex, thinks his death wasn't an accident. It was, though; they investigated it. We spent a few years with an aunt so we could finish high school. As soon as we graduated, we moved to California. Mom and Ronnie were already married by then, and they moved here because she claimed she wanted to be closer to us. More like to control us."

"So, you're trying to fulfill a vague promise you made to your father when you were a kid?"

"You sound like my sister now," she groans, kissing my neck while I hold her.

"I don't mean it to hurt you. It's what it basically boils down to, isn't it?" She nods reluctantly. "Where is your sister?"

"She moved. When my dear old stepdad set up the new branch of his church, I'd hoped it would fail, and they'd have to go back east. The opposite happened and, in a way, they chased Bex off."

"You two are twins, right? Lex and Bex? Who's older?" I change my questions up, not wanting to upset her more.

"Bex by an entire minute. Rebecca, but she goes by Bex because Bex and Lex together is fun. Plus, Mom wanted us to go by Becky and Ali or some shit—she still calls us that. Well, when she's not calling us other things."

"That must have been rough when she left."

"Yeah. My sister is ridiculously smart. Like a full scholarship to UCLA smart, but she's also a party and fun-times kind of girl. She got pregnant—it wasn't the first time—but this time, mom found out about it, called her every name she could think of, and my sister didn't take it. She packed up, left me some money, and moved. She put the kid up for adoption, got a really excellent job that allows her to travel, and right now, I think she's still in Europe, doing an 'architectural tour of the world', as she calls it."

"So your mom doesn't want you to be like your sister because your sister is smart, successful, and has her own life? Looks like you're failing in that regard because you're just like her."

She chuckles, but I can tell she doesn't believe me. "Mom thought we'd follow her and Ronnie into this whole religious devotion. No drinking, no drugs, no tight clothes, no dancing, and most definitely no boys. Failing there, too." She smiles, but it's sad and distant. "But I still go. I still try to make her… happy…proud."

"I'm coming with you," I growl possessively in her ear. She giggles, and her arms wrap around my neck as her nose rubs mine. God, the things this woman does to me.

"Unless you mean you're about to fuck me stupid again, I don't think that's a good idea."

"I mean, I'm going with you to your parent's. Tonight and every other night. And if she tries anything, I'm going to bend you over that dinner table, hike up your fucking skirt—because that's what you're going to wear there—and shove my cock so deep inside you that your mother is going to know exactly who you pray to."

"She'd die. Ronnie would watch, sick fuck."

"I'll just have to knock his ass out."

"This is exactly why you're not going with me later. I don't want to start a war, James. I am going to go, do what I have to, and leave. If you're there, I can't control what's going to happen and I wouldn't put it past them calling the cops on you." She takes my face in her hands, her nails lightly scratching at my stubble. "There will be plenty of people around tonight, so they'll behave. Besides, you're the one I get on my knees for."

"You looked so pretty on your knees for me," my voice cracks as I think back to her how incredible her mouth felt all over me. My hands wander over her soft skin. "Fuck, Alexis. You're extraordinary. I want you all to myself. I want to never leave this apartment again."

"You're a menace."

"I can't help it, you bring out this absolutely devious side of me." Shit, I'm already getting hard again just thinking about all the ways I want to make her mine. "You…you remind me how to be happy and your strength gives me hope."

"Strength? Yeah, I don't have any of that."

"You do. You might not see it, but you do. You haven't let them win, you haven't given up your life for what they want from you."

"Barely, but, uhm, thanks I guess. I tried to warn you that my life is chaos and drama. Even told you I'm not the girl for you."

I close my eyes with a heavy sigh, but she stops me, putting her fingers over my lips. I love this woman. I've fallen madly and hopelessly in love with everything about her. My father used to call it the Artist's Trap because he knew far too many who fell into it. You meet someone, think they're your muse, and fall hard within hours of meeting them. Usually it only lasts a few days or weeks and they snap out of it, but sometimes it's how you find your soulmate. I want to tell her everything, pour my heart out and lay my soul bare for her right here.

Her fingers play against my skin, slipping over my hip to the scars, and suddenly I feel like I can't breathe. I don't talk about these to anyone—not therapists, not my best friends, no one. The people who needed an explanation get a story about falling off my bike or car accidents. The weird thing is, I want to tell someone. I just can't ever get the words out. I owe her since she's already poured her heart out to me, but I don't think I can offer her the answers she thinks she wants. Not now, not yet.

"Jamie?"

"I—I—I can't. I can't." She moves her hand around my back and away from the scars, holding me close to her. I take a minute to realize she's rocking me as she pulls my head to her shoulder.

"It's okay. You don't owe me anything."

"I—I wanted… you told me…shit. I'm sorry. I'm so sorry."

"Where'd you grow up?"

I lift my head and look at her like she's got two extra sets of eyes. "What?"

"I only told you what I could, and I don't expect you to rip open old wounds just to tell me about your past. Just tell me the simple things, the things that aren't going to make you freeze up and freak out. I'll figure out your tells, warning signs, and triggers, and with any luck, learn how to help you through the rough patches."

It baffles me, because it's exactly what I just did for her.

"Here… I grew up here. My, uhm, my dad raised me after he and my m…m…" I can't say it.

"It's alright, you don't have to say anything, I promise."

Thirty fucking years later and I still can't say it. I can't talk about her without shutting down, but Lexi doesn't push me. I've talked about my father around her before, told her how he took me to our breakfast spot and took care of me. She knows I can talk about him. Just like at the beach when she didn't ask what made me non-verbal for so long. She's leading me down paths I can open up about, the same way I did for her. She's better at it, though.

I kiss her forehead, holding my lips there for an eternity before I pull away just enough to whisper, "Thank you."

"We should get out of here before we run out of hot water."

We spend the next few hours talking and getting a little work done in between short make out sessions and long gazes into her eyes. I tell her about my dad and his art, but I keep it all surface level stuff, nothing deep. It feels good to talk about it, and by the way she listens and the questions she asks, I can tell she cares.

By the time she needs to start getting ready, we have half of the presentation ready to go. She's mocked it up on the computer and has placeholders for the remaining images on the physical board. I didn't even realize how much she'd done. I just took pictures, but she's turned them into fucking art. There are samples of brochures, trade show displays, and even packaging options.

I stare at her screen and my heart sinks. I've been distracting her and getting nothing done, while she's been busting her ass.

"Call me tomorrow? We can go over everything else we need and make a plan of attack." she says as she stands between my legs while I sit on the edge of her bed.

"I'm sorry, Angel."

"For what?"

"You did all this work, and I didn't do a fucking thing. I feel like shit about that."

"This? Oh, this was all easy. Besides, you took the pictures, you ordered the prints, you're going to develop the film. Don't worry, when this is done, the work will be pretty even. Promise."

She kisses the end of my nose before she pulls a band t-shirt over her head, trying to get dressed. I'm not making it easy, kissing her neck and running my fingers over her body.

"I'll make it up to you, sweetheart. Anything you need." I cup her breasts and play with her nipples through her bra.

"I can't, pretty boy. I need to do this so Ronnie and my mom fuck off for a little while."

"Or we could just stay here all day and ignore them. I'd even let you work on your other stuff for a few minutes just so I could interrupt you."

"As much as I would love to, I think I need a break." Her hair falls over her shoulders like a pink waterfall as she flashes the cutest smile. "Besides, didn't you say you had to go somewhere today?"

Shit. I almost forgot Coop was coming home today. He'll ride my ass hard if I don't show up for a standard pizza and beer decompression day. Last time I missed out on it, he didn't get a call back from an audition and he blamed me for it—I'm pretty sure he still does. I also promised him I'd help get the place ready for his brother to move in with him.

"Yeah, I kind of do. I can pick up the prints tomorrow morning and bring them over. I'll get the other shots developed, too." Letting go of her is hard and I think it's harder knowing that she's headed straight into the lion's den. I wish she'd let me go with her and be by her side, but she's right to tell me to stand down. Her parents are evil and I can already tell they'd do anything to keep their hooks in her. We have to tread lightly until we figure out what to do next.

At our cars, it takes twenty minutes to stop kissing and trying to start new conversations, holding back the inevitable goodbye that's coming. When we run out of time, I close her door, telling her I'll miss her and reminding her to call me when she's home. My stomach twists as I climb into my Jeep and watch her drive away.

HOLLYWOOD

James

CHAPTER 24
BEVERLY HILLS
WEEZER

HE'S WATCHING me like a hawk, waiting for me to break. We've played this game for years and still he thinks he'll get the better of me. I'm the guy that didn't talk for nine years. I'm not giving him even the smallest satisfaction of acknowledging his game.

"Come on, man!" he finally yells. "You're not seriously planning on sitting here in *my* home, smoking *my* fucking weed, and eating *my* food while you pretend there's nothing going on, are you? Really?"

I take another slice of pizza and lean back in the giant chair. There's a hockey game on and the Cooper family is the only reason I watch any sports at all, other than Steve dragging me to the bars on Sundays during football season. These guys are my friends—my family—but they're also bigger than that. Coop is everywhere, from talk shows to red carpet events, and now little Devin Cooper is on national TV. Steve is on billboards, social media, and podcasts. These can't be the same assholes I roughhoused with as teenagers. Yet, here we are. In a fucking mansion in Hollywood Hills, eating greasy pizza in front of a TV that cost more than I make in three months.

"When does Dev get here?"

"Don't fucking change the damn subject! Who is she? I want names! I want addresses! What does she look like?"

"Also, I paid for the pizza. So, technically, it's not your food." I continue to deflect, hearing the annoyance in his voice. It's rare that Chase doesn't get his way, but he says that's why we're brothers. I keep him grounded. Thankfully, he's not a rich brat, he's just very convincing and puts in the work to get what he wants. "We could rework the second guest bedroom to have a private entrance so he can bring his…what do they call them?"

"Bunnies. Puck bunnies."

"Yeah, he can bring them in through the back." I take a drink of my beer, trying not to laugh at how annoyed he is. Coop picks up the nearest pillow and throws it at me. I'm not surprised by how hard it hits me, but sometimes I forget he could have been a pro pitcher instead of a big shot Hollywood actor.

"What are you laughing at, Bart?"

"Don't call me that, dickhead." I throw the pillow back lazily. "I'm laughing at the thought of one of your little sleepover girls running into Dev's *puck bunny* in the kitchen at three in the damn morning."

"Fuck no! Wait, shit, it really could happen," He yells, then stops and snickers. "Dude, remember that time that smokin' hot redhead came home with me after an audition and accidentally went into Steve's room instead of mine while Andy was over?"

"Yeah, I'd never heard Andy scream so loud. I have no idea how the three of us survived that roommate situation. I love you guys, but I sure as hell don't miss living with you. Plus, your little brother has that whole cute puppy dog thing down, so if you lose a date in his room, she's not coming back to yours. No chance."

"Oh, whatever, he'd probably take her to breakfast and drive her home after she sees his race car bed." He laughs loudly. Poor kid is in his twenties now and we still don't let up about the race car bed. "Besides, I haven't had a date in—SON OF A BITCH! Stop changing the subject!"

He turns off the TV, tosses the remote to the side, and stands there with one hand on his hip and the other holding a beer. He points the beer bottle at me. "Fuckface! I'm gone like a month and I come back to you being…you! Like old you! Grouchy but fun, whatever, YOU! I want phone numbers. I want pictures! I want ring sizes! Please tell me who she is!"

"Chase, fuck off! I'm trying to watch the damn game! Besides, what if therapy is working, and it has nothing to do with a woman?"

"You're a terrible fuckin' liar!" His eyebrows shoot up. "Wait a fuckin' minute! Is she one of my exes? Are you railing one of my exes and that's why you won't tell me? I mean, I don't mind if you are or whatever but—"

"You couldn't name the last five women you slept with, let alone pick them out of a lineup." I'm treading on dangerous ground here. If I'm honest, Chase hasn't had a girlfriend in two years, but there's a reason for it. Steve sets him up with women all the time, but it never goes anywhere because Steve isn't the best judge of character. His idea of getting someone back into the dating game is having him fuck anything with a pulse. It failed for me, and it continues to fail for Chase. He takes them to dinner and tells them he had a terrific time, but he's not interested. A few slip through his defenses and come home with him. As an apology for not being ready for a relationship, he always sends them gifts. "To answer your question, no. She's not one of your exes. There are still a handful of women in Los Angeles that haven't gone to bed with you or Steve."

"Yeah right!" The shout comes from the front of the house as the door slams shut. "Wait, who's sleeping with who? Sharing is caring. We discussed this!"

"You're disgusting, Steve," I shout back. Some days I wonder how the hell we're all friends.

"Stevie, get the fuck in here. This prick has a girlfriend and he won't tell me anything! I need backup!"

"She's not…my girlfriend!" I yell back, but I'm not sure if that's true or not. We didn't give each other titles, at least not officially. It seems unnecessary with everything we've done already. I pull my phone out and check for messages—nothing from her. My fingers hover over our text exchange and I wonder if I should message her and ask. Maybe we're friends with benefits. It could be a temporary hookup. Neither of those outcomes is ideal, but I told her I would be okay with whatever she decided. I asked her, but that was in the middle of fucking her brains out. I'm overthinking this, and I'm way too high.

"AH HA! She! A *she* who fixed you! I wanna meet she—uhm—her. Shit, that sounded cooler in my head." Coop paces the room as he shouts.

"Dude, you're fucking wasted," Steve imparts his incredible wisdom as he joins us with two more packs of beer. "Move over, Barton. I need to catch up. What's going on and why isn't the game on? Did they pull Dev already?"

"No, Columbo just shut it off so he could drill me."

"You're not old enough to be making Columbo references, man," Steve laughs as pops the top on a beer and starts setting up a fresh bowl to smoke. "Alright, put little Coop back on TV!"

"Hollywood," Coop says from across the room. "As soon as people found out he's my brother, the team started calling him Hollywood, and it stuck. He's getting a mask done up with a Hollywood theme."

"Well, then turn fucking *Hollywood* back on!"

"Hollywood? Come on, Mini Cooper is way cooler and would get him an endorsement deal," I grumble, handing my lighter to Steve in exchange for a fresh beer.

Coop turns the TV back on and drops back onto the couch, disrupting Lulu, who was sleeping peacefully and is now just staring at him with her tongue sticking out. I love that dog, but she's the biggest derp I've ever met.

The three of us settle back into our longstanding tradition. Coop goes off to a shoot or a ceremony and when he comes back, I remind him he's a normal person by eating pizza, getting blazed, and watching Devin play. If Devin wasn't playing, it would be video games. Steve reminds him he's a playboy by trying to get him to go out and fuck every woman in LA. It's a very delicate line, and we're here to push him off the high wire and laugh when he falls. Brothers.

I check my phone again, and there's still nothing. If she's not texting, she's presumably okay, still I can't help but worry after meeting her parents. I pull up a local flower shop I've used on photo shoots before because the owner is nice. I found them a few years ago while I was working at a wedding. As I scroll through, I realize I have no idea what kinds of flowers to get her.

"Dude, are you…NO SHIT! FLOWERS? Oh, fuck!" Steve screams with laughter. "We've got flowers, Coop!"

I watch the end of the game while my two best friends annoy the living shit out of me, then I go out to the back patio. It's still early, but I'm getting antsy, so I call Lexi and leave her a voicemail. I feel like an absolute idiot as I talk, trying to listen and make sure the guys don't come out and interrupt. She doesn't need to hear these two morons—not yet, anyhow. When I hang up, my phone vibrates and my heart leaps out of my chest, but then I see it's only the flower shop confirming that they dropped off the delivery.

"Hey man." Steve pokes his head out, clearly buzzed. "We're going to the bar. Come on. We should bring Pongo! PONGO! HELP US PICK UP CHICKS!"

"Coop has a bar," I remind him as Pongo trots in from the other room. He's a huge Pitbull with a heart of gold. He's also Coop's therapy dog—only about five people in the city know that. Steve constantly wants to take him out to the bars to attract women, but since Coop doesn't need the world knowing he had a fucking breakdown two years ago, it's hard to get the dog in. Money doesn't always keep people from spilling your secrets for more money.

"Yeah, but we're going to the other bar to pick up some lllllllladies."

"That's a terrible idea. You're both high as fuck right now." I'm going to lose this argument, and I should go home. It doesn't matter, though, because even when I'm high, I'm the responsible one.

"Duh, that's why we're calling a rideshare, bro."

We end up in this bar that's not high end, but not a total dive either. For a Sunday night, it's pretty packed, and the second we open the door, I can hear why. Loud, off-key warbling is coming from a small stage as some poor drunk pair try hard to sing Bohemian Rhapsody. I've never been so glad that Freddy Mercury is dead.

"Stevie!" a voice screams from across the bar as soon as we walk in. He's got his arm wrapped around my shoulder, pulling me along. He spins toward the voice just in time to catch the petite blond who's launched herself at him. I'm half surprised they aren't making out already, but then I'm also a little surprised she jumped at him like that and wasn't worried about breaking her implants. It's never been my thing, but Steve is here for the boobs. Real or fake doesn't matter, so long as they're big enough to smother him.

"Becky! Holy shit! Are you working here now?"

"Yeah." She leans back in his arms, pushing her hair over her shoulder to present her name tag—and her boobs. "Oh my god, you can sit in my section and I'll totally hook you up." She turns to me. "Who do we have here?"

She gives me a wink, and I return a tight-lipped smile. When Coop stumbles in behind us, her eyes go a little too wide. His hat and sunglasses aren't as good a disguise as he thinks they are.

"Becky, do me a favor, put us where no one is gonna bother us, okay?"

I glance around and shake my head. At this rate, it will only be a matter of minutes before someone clocks Chase. He's hard enough to miss at 6'4" with long hair and a solid build, but he wasn't even sober enough to grab a hat *without* the insignia of his brother's team on the front. The bar is pretty small, but luckily she's able to tuck us into a high-top table toward the back. She slides onto Steve's lap with her arm around him like she's here with us and not working.

"So, you going to introduce me to your friends, Stevie?"

"Oh, Mr. Angst and Brooding over here is James." He winks and I just give him a glare that immediately says no to whatever he's planning. "James, this is Becky. We met at one of the other bars closer to the college. Be nice."

"Hi," I offer, but she's not looking at me—which is normal.

"And this dashing guy right here is—"

"Hi, Becky, was it? I'm Antonio Banderas. Nice to meet you."

"I totally knew you were someone famous! Oh my god! You look so much taller in person."

"Younger too, I'm told."

"Becky, babe, can you go get us a round of beers and shots

of… whatever's expensive and good?" Steve leans over and kisses her neck before whispering something. She hops off his lap and skips toward the bar, where she giggles and points us out to friends of hers.

"Dude, if you fuck this up, I'm not taking you out anywhere anymore," Steve threatens, leaning over the table and pointing at me. "Girlfriend or not, try to fucking enjoy yourself!"

"Is that a promise? Because I'd really like that in writing."

"Come on, man." He grins. "Becky's gonna hook us all up. Please don't be an asshole. I just wanna get my dick sucked and play with her tits."

I nudge Chase's arm, and he looks up from his phone at Steve. "Uhh, whatever Barton said." He flashes us a tooth grin and looks around the room.

Being out with the two of them is like wrangling cats, or very annoying toddlers. Chase will talk to anyone about anything. He'll sign autographs, let people take pictures, and anything else to please a fan. He's a genuinely nice guy, but he's been struggling with some pretty debilitating anxiety and tries to keep a low profile when he can. Steve is a fucking terror. I've known him for almost fifteen years and he wasn't always this playboy man whore, as Dani calls him. One wants to hide, the other wants to fuck, and I'm stuck in the middle.

Sure enough, Becky comes back a few minutes later with a bucket of beers, six shots, and two friends.

"Stevie, this is Amber and Tiffany." I'm already willing to bet those aren't their real names, but who the fuck uses their real name now, anyway? Amber comes around the table next to me and Tiffany slides up on Chase. And here's the reason Steve hates taking me places where he's trying to hook up. I'm an excellent wingman, unless it involves actually sleeping with someone just because my buddy wants to get laid. Steve's people expect to be doing something sexual within the next ten minutes.

Steve and Becky excuse themselves almost immediately, ducking into the nearby bathroom.

"Hey, I'm sorry to disappoint you lovely ladies, but we're both spoken for," Chase says, which surprises me, but it means I'm not the evil villain tonight. The women let out a huff and storm off, mumbling something about Antonio Banderas. Chase tips back his beer and dumps his shot into a nearby plant that looks fake. "I have got to stop letting Steve convince me to come out to these places. So, you gonna tell me her name or what, man?"

"Alexis," I sigh, sliding my phone over with a picture of her pulled up.

"Digging the hair. She's fucking cute, man!" He looks around again as a new group takes over the Karaoke and it's some twangy country song. "Did Dani set you guys up?"

"Sort of. It was a little of Dani's matchmaking, weird timing, and a gig from Sam all coming together. We're actually working together on a project."

"Ooof, I hope that goes better for you than it has for me. How long have you been going out?"

He's hurt that I didn't tell him sooner, like I've been going behind his back or something. "Uh, let's see, tomorrow will be," I make a show of counting things out on my fingers, "Five days since I met her. If you count the first day. We're around eighty hours in right now." I only know because she made the comment this morning about it not even being seventy-two hours. "Dating or whatever we're doing started yesterday morning."

"Wait, what? Seriously?" He smiles, realizing that I wasn't hiding this from him for as long as he assumed. "Alright man, spill it. Don't skip shit either, I want the full artist in love breakdown."

I can't help but smile. A warmth I'm not used to runs through me, I feel it every time I'm around her or thinking about her. Which is near constantly. I tell him about the coffee shop meeting, the weirdness of the club, and the beach, and he listens intently, like it's the best story he's ever heard. I avoid personal matters, and unlike Steve, I don't discuss intimate details.

"She's a designer, and a damn good one. She's got some mixed media pieces in her apartment that are just…they're amazing. You should commission her to do one for you. It would look epic in your place."

"Amazing, huh? Like her."

Blush creeps up my face and I nod, biting my lip. "I feel like a fucking teenage idiot. She's just, I dunno, incredible."

"Downsides?"

"Crazy parents. They already both hate me, but it's a mutual feeling. They fucked up her confidence, probably more. Culty nut jobs in my opinion."

"Well, look at you go, Romeo. Wait." He glares at me and I can't hide from what's coming next. "There's something else, isn't there? Does she have like eight kids? Two heads? A tail? There's something, otherwise you'd be gushing more about her. I've listened to you in love before. There wasn't enough prose and flowery words in your description for me to fall for it."

"Well, we already had a fight."

"Oh, shit…that's quick."

"Elle texted me. She's following her, or me. Probably both of us." I take a drink while he lets out a whistle. "She sent a picture of Lexi and I in a…compromising position. Threatened to send it to Lexi's family and our boss. Said she'd post it online. I hadn't told Alexis about her yet, so it kind of blew up in my face."

"That's rough, man. Elle's a fucking bitch and a half."

"Yeah, except we talked through it. I mean, I had an anxiety attack and fully freaked out, but Alexis stayed."

"That's actually healthy, shit. As for Elle, dude, you need a lawyer." He finishes his beer and pats me on the back. "Did you tell your new lady about your family yet? Show her what you've got in common?"

"A little about when I was a kid, all vague stuff. I told her about you, too. She hasn't pushed and I'm not ready to go deeper into that."

"She sounds amazing, man. It's good to see your happy grouch face back, and I can't wait to meet her."

"You already have, technically. She waited in a four-hour line for your dumb ass autograph."

"Oh fuck you, man! You know how nuts that shit makes me! Tell her I'll sign anything she wants and I'm so sorry she waited so long." He pushed my arm. "Speaking of signing, did you open the envelope of doom yet?"

"No. I'm thinking about signing the papers and just being done with all of them, though."

My father's death was hard enough to deal with, so my surprise when my estranged sister and her lawyer showed up at my door the day before the funeral was palpable. The deal sounded straightforward enough until I realized she was lying about everything just to get me to sign the papers. My father's art is worth a small fortune, maybe a medium-sized fortune now that he's dead, and he left it all to me. He left me the house and shares in a company I didn't know about—enough shares for majority control. Majority control over my mother's company.

My mother and sister are both terrible human beings, but they're not dumb. The problem is, neither was my dad. I always thought his income was from the art, but it turns out, he was living off his shares of the company and giving his art away. So, now I'm in legal limbo, I'm broke, and I'm trying to figure out how to handle all of this without letting go of dad's art. If I take the company, I relinquish all rights to my father's art, his name, all of it. If I keep my dad's art and give up the company, I give up a four million dollar and counting trust he had set up in my name that I'd inherit as the main shareholder.

I'm not a numbers guy, none of it makes sense to me and the only person close to a lawyer that I know is Steve. He went to law school until he burned out, then became a personal trainer. He checked out the paperwork and said it ranked in the top five craziest contracts he ever read.

The paperwork mainly involves my parents, but Elle also has a stake depending on my choice. If she doesn't get the company, she gets dad's art. If she gets dad's art, she's going to destroy it. If I pick dad's art, she'll have enough money to make my life hell. I know why dad agreed, so I can't pretend to be clueless, but that doesn't mean it sucks any less.

They've made counter offers, all of them worse than the last. I haven't even bothered to read the latest one. There was always one part of the contract Elle focused on most. In the event of my death, Elle gets everything. I don't think she'd outright kill me, but she doesn't have too far to push me before I'm at the end of my rope. With dad gone, I've taken a few steps closer to the edge. All that changed on Thursday morning, though.

"You won't sign, you can't."

"If I don't, she'll go after Lexi."

"If you do, she'll fucking rip *you* apart. There won't be a need to go after Lexi because there won't be a Jamie. You know I'm right."

There's laughter and the sound of plastic cups clattering to the floor as Steve and Becky make their way back out of the supply closet and over toward the table. Chase leans in closer. "Stop fighting this alone and let me help. I'll call some people. I'm sure my agent has contact with some decent contract lawyers at this point."

"Even the really bad ones cost more than I have. I had to fucking get a loan on the house already just to pay the funeral expenses and other shit. I couldn't even go through the bank for that."

"Yeah, and that was fucking dumb. So shut up and let me help you this time, you prick."

"Hey! Why'd you scare the girls off, *Antonio*?" Steve's laugh interrupts us, then he looks over to the stage where someone is murdering Hozier. "When does Dev get here? I wanna do karaoke and you fuckers won't do it unless he's here to make an ass out of himself."

"His stuff is getting here next week; he'll be here as soon as their away stint is over." Fun Chase had slipped away somewhere during our conversation. He's pulled his hat down lower and he's hunched over his beer, making it harder for people to see him. Elle scares the shit out of him, mostly because she hasn't messed with him yet. That's partly because of his amazing agent who watches out for him. He's had one scandal in his whole life, and it wasn't even his fault, but the media storm after it happened was more than he could take. His agent wants to keep it from happening again.

Steve orders another round of beers, then he notices Chase hiding from the crowd. "What the fuck? Why are you two all serious and messing up my blow job high? Paparazzi again? I'm self-employed; I'll go punch that motherfucker in the face."

We look at each other, not sure we should even bring it up, but someone has to warn him, and it's *my* sister. "Elle is in town. She said she went by the house the other day."

"What?!" He yells it so loud that several people look our way to see if a fight is about to break out. The color drains from his face and it's like he becomes a different person as he falls back against the wall. "What the fuck? When did she get here and why am I only just now hearing about it?"

It's completely justified for Steve to be mad. The last time Elle was in town, she nearly got him arrested, sent his then fiancé to the hospital, and cost him a huge client all because he kicked her out of my dad's funeral. It's the other reason we put up with Steve's crap. He stuck with me through all of that. We also recognize that he acts like an absolute dickhead because of the mess Elle made of his life. It's his way of coping, pretending he doesn't care about anything or anyone. That way, they can't get close enough to hurt him again. I hate that it's my fault. The guilt is part of why I keep playing along with his game.

"I'm going to make some calls in the morning and get a lawyer to check this contract shit out," Chase answers. "If she's stalking you and sending pictures, we should probably get out of here. This bar is a little too public. It might be good for you and your girl to get out of town for a while."

"Already working on that. Luckily, it's part of the job."

HOLLYWOOD

Lexi

CHAPTER 25
SYMPATHY FOR THE DEVIL

THE ROLLING STONES

SCREAMING '*MORE*' sounded good when James and I were in bed, but now? I can't even walk right. The dull ache and emptiness combine to make it almost unbearable. He's broken through so many of my walls in the best possible ways and he's all I can think about. We can count our time together in hours, but he's not sitting next to me right now, and it's pulling my heart in a million directions. I need this to slow down, but someone cut the brake line when we met. Now, we're picking up speed as we careen down the mountain together. I miss him. The way he talks, the way he smells, the way his tongue does that—

"Ali? Are you paying attention?" My mother's voice is sharp, as if she knows what I was thinking about while I wasn't listening to her. "Mrs. Harper asked you a question."

"What? Oh, I'm so sorry. I swear my mind wanders sometimes."

"Well, Ms. Harper wanted to know if we should hold off on the printed brochures until the deal goes through on the new church?"

"New church?" I furrow my brows. I don't remember anyone mentioning that.

"Oh, right, you missed that meeting because you were… working." My mother's voice is nothing but disappointment and shame. If she could, she'd slap a scarlet letter on my chest letting everyone know I'm an embarrassment. "Your father is expanding the church. We've just put an offer in this week on a lovely piece of land in Orange County to enlarge our congregation. He's even found another pastor to help him spread the good word and recruit new members into our humble arms."

Humble, I fight back a laugh when she says that. Psychotic cult is more like it. Although Orange County could be a exactly the thing to keep them busy. "Oh, uhm, then yes. You could wait for that to be final before we run those."

"Fantastic. Oh, I nearly forgot, we'll need you to go to the new site this week. We'll need signs and other elements you can help out with. We agreed you should be there in person to let the beauty of the Lord's work really speak to you when you decide on the colors and other decor." Her mouth curves into a wicked grin. I've told her more times than I care to remember that I'm not an interior designer. She never listens. My degree doesn't mean shit to her other than getting me to do free work for them. "You'll be accompanying your father there on Thursday. He should be by shortly to introduce you to Pastor Noah."

My blood runs ice cold, and I have to steady my breathing. "I will have to check my schedule. I can always go over another time without him if my availability isn't convenient."

"Oh, darlin', I'm sure we can work something out." My stepfather steps out from one of the back rooms with a grin that turns my stomach. My memories of James are gone, tucked away where I can protect them. "I wouldn't want you to drive all the way out there by yourself. You might get lost. Besides, it would be nice to have your company on that long ride. Our new pastor even offered us a place to stay the night so we don't have to rush."

Another man, younger but not by much, follows him into the room. His plaid shirt and short, all-business hair screams *divorced father of four and devout follower*. My stepfather is walking him right over to me, and the closer he gets, the more I recognize that gleam in his eyes. It's the same one my stepfather has. There's no way in hell I'll be in a car—let alone a house—with these two alone.

"Darlin', this here is Pastor Noah. He's going to be heading up the new church."

The new guy sticks his arm out. I'm hoping he's just going to shake, but the second my hand touches his sweaty, clammy palm, he's pulling my hand to his lips. I want to throw up. "My, my. You are even lovelier in person than Pastor Ron described you. An absolute angel, to be sure."

Using James's words against me is cruel. I look at my mother and she's busy fussing with her nails and a part of me wonders what they're planning, because they are clearly up to something.

"Thanks." I force a tight-lipped smile, pulling my hand back and shoving it in my pocket.

Ronnie moves behind me, putting his hands on my shoulders so tight I wince. He kisses the top of my head as I stare at Noah. "She's a *good* girl. I'm sure you two will get along once she settles down."

"Settles down?" I try to turn toward Ronnie, but he tightens his grip, keeping me facing forward. Facing Noah.

"Darlin', help your mother. I'll finish showing Noah around and then you come by for dinner after. It's time you and Noah became better acquainted."

Noah licks his lips, staring at me like I'm a slab of meat being served up to him. Ronnie releases my shoulders and the pair of them walk out of the room. I glance around the room, aware that people witnessed what had just happened. Conveniently, they all seem to be busy and unable to make eye contact with me. The few who look at me have a jaded happiness in their stares, as if what happened was normal. So I drop my head and bite the inside of my cheek to fight the tears. I say nothing, and as the meeting wraps up, my mother marches over to where I'm packing up my things. She fists the collar of her sweater closely against her neck as she talks to me.

"We'll be very disappointed in you if you try to avoid the trip. It's all for your own good." She turns to leave and then glances over her shoulder. "Come on, it will be easier for all of us to get this over with now."

I can't even respond before she's marching the other way. I look around the room, noticing everyone has left. I scoop up the last of my things and shove them into my bag. I can straighten it all out in the car later. I'm still confused, but even my false sense of safety has vanished. I pull my phone out, planning to text my mother that I can't stay for dinner once I'm in the car. I'm practically running out the door when I nearly trample right over poor old Ms. Harper.

"Oh, excuse me dear. I forgot my reading glasses on the chair."

"No, it was my fault. I was in a hurry and not paying attention to where I was going." She can't possibly know how happy I am to see her. "I'll wait and walk you out. It's late. I wouldn't want you out there in the dark on your own."

"You're such a sweet girl, and so good to your parents." She picks up her glasses and stuffs them into a tattered purse. This woman can barely afford food, but somehow my parents have convinced her to give all her money to the church. It's sick. "And that Noah! Oh, he's a fine young man. I'd envy you if I were still in my younger years. This must be so exciting for you. We've all prayed for this day."

"Yeah, exciting, that's one word for it," I mumble as we continue walking out to the parking lot.

"Thank you for walking me out, dear. Now, make sure you come see me at the house before you move. I have some nice dishes that I was hoping to pass down to my daughter someday for her wedding, but she said she didn't need them."

"Move?"

"Oh, I'm rushing things, aren't I? I'm just giddy for a wedding, is all. You'll be so lovely, dear." She slaps my arm a little harder than I would have thought she could. "I'll make sure to pack up those dishes so they don't break. You send Noah by anytime, dear. Don't come yourself. We can't have you lifting in your condition."

The second I'm in the car, I lock the doors and start the engine. I don't even take the time to buckle my seatbelt before I'm pulling away, desperate for a large crowd of people. I don't stop until I'm miles away, parking at a nearby mall.

I close my eyes and take several deep breaths, fighting back the panic. It takes about ten minutes before I get myself together and I'm not about to burst into tears. It's not surprising to me when I think about it. That's the terrifying part. My phone hasn't stopped buzzing in my bag the entire way here, and I check my mirrors to make sure my mother hasn't followed me. When I unlock my phone, I find four missed calls and a long string of texts from her, along with a few from my stepfather.

Another name appears on the voicemail list, and my heart leaps.

New Voicemail from James

I press the button and close my eyes.

"Hey Cherry Blossom, I hope your meeting went well. I wanted to check in on you, so if you don't mind letting me know when you're safe and at home, I'd appreciate it. That probably sounds cheesy, but I've been worried about you since we left this afternoon. Is it weird that I miss you already? Yeah, probably. Ignore my dumb ass. Sorry. I'll talk to you later, beautiful."

I listen two more times. His calm voice helps me come down from stress and panic. I understand now what he meant when he said he craved me, because right now I crave him and the reassurance he brings me. I want to call him, but I can't. This isn't his problem to deal with, it's mine.

I turn the phone off and head home.

I'm just slipping my key into the door when someone down the hall calls my name. I smile, hoping it's enough, but he's still staring at me.

"You got a delivery earlier, and I brought it in here for safekeeping. Let me go grab it."

He's tall with salt and pepper hair and a friendly smile. He moved in about a year ago and we haven't interacted beyond polite hellos, so I'm not sure what to expect. I think he's a doctor of some sort, but he bakes a lot and it always smells delicious near his apartment. Once, after a fight with my mother, I found a small box outside my door with the most delicious eclairs I've ever tasted. I wonder how much he's heard from the last few days with James.

He comes out of his apartment with a giant bouquet of pink and white flowers and a card. Carefully holding the base, I almost drop it while opening the card—I need to stop juggling so much. My neighbor is nice enough to hold the flowers again while I read the card. I know who I *hope* sent them, but today I need to be certain.

Angel-

You never told me your favorite flowers the other day. These are as close as I can get to cherry blossoms, so I hope they're okay.

-JB

"Thank you, uhm—"

"Dr. Clay. You can call me Theo. Nice to actually meet you." His smile is warm and friendly, and I wonder if he's a pediatrician or someone who works with kids a lot. "Do you need a hand with these?"

"No, I can get them from here." He nods and watches me walk back to my door. Before I reach for the handle, I turn back around. "Oh, uhm, thanks for the pastries a while back. They were delicious."

"No problem, I hope it wasn't too weird or forward of me. I'll make sure I drop more off next time I'm up doing an all night bake-a-thon."

Closing my apartment door, I'm finally met with silence. It's weird now, empty. I feel that way when Bex visits town randomly, stays briefly, and leaves too soon. I look at the clock, surprised to see it's already after midnight. I must have sat in the mall parking lot longer than I thought.

I play the voicemail one more time after I get changed and crawl into bed. I've put the flowers next to my bed so I can stare at them as I fall asleep. As I settle in, I pull up our text thread, hoping I don't wake him.

LEXI

Finally home.

The flowers are beautiful, thank you.

[Image Attached]

📷 PRETTY BOY 💕
I'm glad you like them.

His reply is almost immediate and I can't stop the wide smile spreading across my face, or the warmth growing between my legs. God, this man has ruined me.

📷 PRETTY BOY 💕
Did everything go okay tonight?

Should I tell him everything or simply lie about it? I don't want to lie. James is the lighthouse in the stormy sea that I've been struggling to navigate. I often considered giving up, surrendering to the waves and crashing onto the shore. Letting my mother have her way and letting go of the few things I have left to cling to. My father was my first anchor, but after he died, Bex took over. She couldn't handle being around my mother and Ronnie, so I was alone.

I can't lie to my last hope.

If I can just keep my head above water a little longer, James can pull me to shore before I drown. Although he's fighting his own sea monsters. It's in his eyes and the way he reacted when I touched his scars. Someone has hurt him horribly. Maybe I'm putting too much hope and faith into a man I barely know, but I'm willing to take the risk in the hopes we can fight our monsters together.

My hesitation to respond must be enough for him, because the phone buzzes in my hand and his name flashes. I don't even get to say hello before he's talking.

"Lexi, are you okay? What happened? Should I come over?"

I'm scared it's too soon and too much. I'm scared that I'll wake up tomorrow and realize he's only here for the sex. Deep down, I know that's not true. I want to scream yes—to tell him to come over and never leave because I want someone to hold me. I want him to hold me.

"No, I was figuring out how to respond."

"Oh, shit. Am I overreacting?"

"No, it's… it's kind of sweet, really."

"Or stalkerish. I just, I was worried about you."

"You're the sweetest, Jamie," I hope he doesn't catch the shake in my voice as the memory of my stepfather's hands on my shoulders and the look in Noah's eyes comes back.

"You're sure? Because I'll drop everything and come back right now."

My face is blushing bright red; I can tell without seeing it. He can't even begin to understand how at ease and safe I feel having him on the phone with me. Or maybe he can. It's crazy to have feelings this intense for someone so quickly, but it's nice to let go for a few minutes.

"No, I was headed to bed. I didn't wake you, did I?"

"Nah, about to head home, actually. Uhm. Not to derail the conversation, but I was looking over our shot list. Would you be interested in taking a three-day trip up the coast this week? Wednesday, Thursday, and Friday. You can totally say no if—"

"YES!" I scream into the phone. Three days away means three days I won't be able to go with my stepfather. James Barton swoops in with the save yet again, and he doesn't even know it.

"Wow, uhm," he laughs, *"I wasn't expecting that level of enthusiasm, but I'm glad it matches mine. I can work on getting us rooms at the hotel once I plan out the trip."*

"Rooms?" My heart sinks a little.

"Yeah, we'll be in at least two hotels, and I didn't think you'd want a single room showing up on the expense account when Sammy sees it."

"Oh, valid point. I should talk to Sam at some point. We, uhm, we could go longer if you want."

There's silence on the line and I'm terrified I've scared him away. I don't want him to call the whole thing off and because I'm too weird. Too clingy.

"Lexi, I would absolutely love to take you away for an entire week—hell, longer if you want—but first, you have to be honest with me. What are you running from? Did something happen tonight?"

"It's... it's nothing, really. I... I haven't had a vacation in a while and, I mean, this isn't even really a vacation, it's work, but I—" My lungs lock up and the words hurt to say. The hot sting of the tears burns my eyes even though I'm fighting hard for them to stay away. I just need to get through this phone call. But my body won't let me. "I can't. I can't lie to you. Why can't I lie to you?"

"Breathe for me, Cherry Blossom."

I stop rambling and start counting and breathing. His voice is coaching me through each breath like he's here, holding me. It's exactly like I did for him yesterday. I don't do this. This isn't me. I don't fall for guys after just a few days. I don't cry in front of people. I don't break down on the phone. I bury my secrets; I always have. I don't tell them to people who are practically strangers, hell I don't even tell friends. No one believes me when I do, so why should I tell anyone?

"You don't have to lie to me, sweetheart. You have nothing to be ashamed about, okay? That's the first thing I need you to know. The second is that I'm not going anywhere. When you feel like you can tell me, tell me. Until then, just know that I'm here for you."

I've already told him more than I've told anyone else.

"Ronnie is trying to take me to Orange County. He says we're visiting a new church they bought. It's all bullshit though, because there's a new pastor and I think..." I close my eyes and say the one thing I've been screaming inside for so long. "James, I'm... I'm scared. I'm scared to go with him, but I'm scared not to. I'm scared he's going to force me into...that they'll try to..."

"Keep your phone with you in case you fall asleep. I'm headed over."

"No, it's late. I'm okay, I—"

"You don't need to be alone right now. You have every reason to be scared, and I want to be there for you so you know you don't have to go through this alone. Do you want me to bring pie? Ice cream? Burgers? Anything from anywhere?"

"I'm serious, James. You can't come over here just because I'm a little insecure."

His muffled voice yells something, and another voice replies, but I can't hear their words. He's moving around and shuffling like he's packing stuff up.

"I can, will, and am. Be there in twenty plus time to grab stuff. If you don't text me what you want, it's pie."

"James, you're with your friends and I—"

"Stop arguing. Be over in a bit. I—"

He stops moving around and there's a silence; it's almost deafening.

"I'll see you soon, beautiful."

HOLLYWOOD

James

CHAPTER 26
JUST THE WAY YOU ARE

BILLY JOEL

I PUT my bag and the pie on the ground before I knock, and then I wait. I almost told her I love her on the phone and ever since then I've been a jittery mess. It's like my brain and my heart are arguing over what the hell I'm doing. I can't tell which one is winning. The second she opens the door, I wrap around her, lifting her off the floor and holding her as tight as I can. At first, she hesitates, but it doesn't last long and soon she's got her arms around my neck and she's holding me just as tight.

We say nothing because it's not the time to. Right now is the time for her to know I'm real and I'm here. She doesn't need to fight these demons—real and in her head—alone. Once she understands that, it will be time for pie and probably tears. I walk her in and sit her down on the couch.

"Forensic Files?" I roll my eyes playfully as the overly dramatic voice tells me about some egregious error made by a guy in the late 80s.

"Comfort television?" Lexi shrugs.

I chuckle as I go through the house and turn off the lights, making sure the blinds are all shut. Before she can close her laptop, I catch a glimpse of the screen. "What's that?" At first I figured it was part of the project when I saw my name, but then the graphic caught my eye.

She bites her lip as she turns the computer toward me so I can see it better. "Your business cards kind of suck."

I don't even try to hold back the laugh. "Yeah. Yeah, they do."

"Sometimes I design things when I'm stressed out. It helps me focus and relax. What do you think?" She redesigned the whole card, and it's beautiful. Instead of the boring, basic card I had, she's got colors, graphics, and better fonts. "I can change the logo if you want, but I thought it was a nice personal touch. Might help market yourself better." It's a camera aperture with a blue rubber ducky in the middle, just like the ones that fell out of my Jeep at the beach.

"I fucking love it, Angel. It's brilliant." Her giant smile makes my heart flutter.

She closes the screen and goes to put the laptop down, but there's no room. A whole pie, forks, two wine glasses, a large iced coffee milk tea with boba, and two unmarked bottles of wine cover the table and she looks up at me, confused.

"Pie and a horror movie?"

"Yeah, I think I need that."

I take the wine bottle and unscrew the top. I'd make some joke about screw top bottles and being a classy guy, but this stuff isn't cheap. I hand her the bottle so she can check it out while I flip through movies. She sniffs at it and instantly her lips purse and pull to one side while her nose scrunches up. I can't tell if she hates it or just isn't sure what the scent is. "It's blackberries. I have a thing for sweet wines. A friend of mine makes it. Well, he was a friend of my dad's and once a month he still drops off a couple of bottles. These were for Chase, and I had to promise him the next batch to pry them away."

"So I'm about to be drinking Chase Cooper's bottles of free homemade wine?"

"Sort of free. Carl has it in his head that he still owes them to my dad for some job my dad did for him or something. I've told him he's got nothing to worry about, but he insists. It's his way of keeping the tradition going. I get free wine dropped off once a month. He gets to sit on the back porch, reminisce about my dad's life, and complain about his kids for an hour or three while we get high."

"Reminisce about your dad? I don't understand."

I sit beside her and caress her cheek, working myself up to say the words I try hard to avoid. "Lexi, my dad…he died six months ago. Car accident."

"Oh my god! Jamie, I didn't…oh I should have, though. I should have known by how you talk about him. I thought…"

"It's okay, Angel. I'm shit at talking about it still, and tonight I'm here to take care of you, not me. So drink up and scoot over."

She takes a cautious sip. As I watch, her eyebrows shoot up and her tongue slides across her lips. I should focus on how fucking hot that is, but I realize that's the second time I've talked about my dad without feeling like I'm walking the edge of a downward spiral. Both times have been when I'm with her. I tuck a piece of her hair behind her ear, letting my fingers linger on her neck.

"This…this is really good."

"Glad you like it, beautiful." She blushes. I desperately want to kiss her, to taste that blackberry wine on her lips. Instead, I turn back to the TV and pull up the movie we started the other night. "Wanna watch this again since we fell asleep last time?"

"Yeah, it's kind of my comfort movie. I've seen it like ten times."

"Comfort movies go well with pie and wine on crappy

nights. Even if they are about a cannibal abducting women." We laugh together as we snuggle on the couch. I bought a whole damn pie, and it's sitting on her lap as I feed both of us while we watch. It's about halfway through the movie when she's finally comfortable enough to talk.

"I've never actually told anyone about him. Well, I did, but they assumed I was lying, so I've never told anyone like friends or anything." I nuzzle the side of her head and she sniffles. "Can…can you tell me about your dad? He just sounds like such an amazing guy. I'd rather listen to you tell me about him than go through my issues right now. If that's okay."

She hands me the bottle and I take a long drink.

"Well, I, uhm, I haven't figured out how to talk about him and the accident yet. Not really."

"I shouldn't have asked that. I'm not sure why I—"

"It's alright, Lexi, I promise. I get it, you're in a shit spot and you need some kind of comfort. And me telling you about my dad might bring you some. He'd have been honored. Helping people was his thing."

"You don't have to say anything. I know what it's like, losing someone like that."

"No, it's…Angel, I can't tell you that you and your secrets are safe with me, or that you can trust me with your experiences if I'm reluctant to do the same with you. That's not how relationships work. Or at least I hope not." I take another long drink before handing her the bottle, afraid I'll drink too much before I get this out. "I should be able to talk about it now. It's been six fucking months."

"Why? There a time limit on grief and grieving that I never learned about?"

That gets me to smile, which helps me relax a little. She pauses the movie and turns around so she's facing me, giving me all of her attention. It might have been easier when I wasn't staring at her, but I can't say that.

"He was on his way back from a charity art show. He did a lot of those, this one for Carl, actually. Dad had donated a bunch of paintings to an auction for kids who needed mental health treatment. Usually, I went to the shows and helped him setup, but this was one I didn't go to. He was leaving the studio to go get cleaned up and ready, and when he noticed how focused I was, he told me to stay home and keep working. He said I was too in the zone. He probably came back out to tell me he was headed out, but I never heard him."

"He texted around midnight to say the event was a big hit. He said there was a guy he met there who might be interested in working with me on an installation. I didn't see the text because I was still working on that piece. I worked on it till I couldn't keep my eyes open anymore and crashed out on the couch. I did that pretty often."

"I was sleeping in the studio when someone started banging on the front door so loud I could hear it all the way in the back of the house. It's all a little surreal, like I knew it was going to be the last time I locked up the studio somehow. I could tell something was off because Dad wouldn't be knocking at 2 in the morning. If he did, he'd have knocked on the studio because he'd have known I'd still be out there."

I don't even realize I'm crying until she wipes the tear from my face. That breaks open the dam, even though I try to hold it back. I struggle through the rest of the story, trying not to break down any further.

"He, uhm, got hit on the freeway. A semi truck driver fell asleep. Carl wasn't far behind him and saw the whole thing happen. I think that's part of why he still brings the wine over, guilt. I never blamed him or anything; he even got out and tried to help, but there wasn't anything he could do. Once the cops got there and took his statement, he came right to the house to tell me. He wanted to make sure someone was there for me, since he knew about my past and was real tight with Dad. He didn't want me finding out from some random badge that pretended to care."

My fingers trace down the bottle of wine. "I remember the look on Carl's face when I answered the door that night. I'll never forget it. I haven't been back in the studio since."

It's the first time I've been able to tell the entire story to anyone. I gave Chase bits and pieces along the way, the same with Steve, and they pieced the rest together. It's something of a relief to get it out, like a piece of the burden has lifted. I just hope I didn't give that piece to Lexi. She has enough on her own. I guess that's the point, though, sharing it so someone else can do the heavy lifting for a bit.

"What was your dad like?"

"You know how people are always saying how the deceased was always a nice guy and everyone liked him? Then you dig into the story more and realize they were assholes who never did a damn bit of good their whole life? Dad was the guy who actually was nice and everyone really did like him. He did his best taking care of a kid who was basically mute for almost ten years, was always there for me, and I sure as hell wasn't ready to let him go."

"He sounds like he would have gotten along great with my dad. Although that's just me remembering him as a kid." She presses her forehead to mine. "Your dad got to see you grow up, and I bet he was, and still is, proud of you for growing up to become such a warm, caring, wonderful man."

I shake my head slowly. "He liked to say he was. Every day before I leave to go somewhere, even to the kitchen, he'd stop me and tell me he was proud of me and he loved me. Not many people do that. I don't understand how he could be proud of me right now, though."

"What? Why not?"

I stare holes in the flooring, not sure how to say any of this. Lexi is like truth serum in human form. Whenever I'm around her, I get this deep desire to tell her everything I can. I guess my brain wants to see if she's ready for what my heart wants to tell her. Give her the opportunity to run away. Let her go before she realizes how much she regrets ever meeting me. The problem is, I'm not ready to lose her, but I can't stop telling her about me.

"What's there to be proud of?"

"Jamie." Her voice pulls at my heart. I glance up and meet her eyes. "I promise I won't go anywhere. I don't think there's anything you could tell me that you've done that would make me change my mind because…because…you're a wonderful guy and I really, really like you."

"You're the only good thing I've got going for me." She holds my hand and I decide it's better to tell her now than to draw this out. It won't be getting better. "I've essentially lost every dime I have because of my mother and sister. I'd have lost the house by now if Carl, Chase, and a few other people Dad knew didn't come to my rescue. I'm close to giving up on…everything—or I was till I met you. I've already given up on painting, drawing, everything to do with art, except the photography. The passion I didn't share with dad is the only one I can keep doing now that he's gone.

"If it wasn't for Sam throwing me a job now and then because he feels bad for me, I'd be living in my Jeep. I, uhm, I had started to make plans to leave. No idea where I was going. Not sure how long. I won't sell his art, even though it would make enough money to pay off the house and more. I won't donate it, like he asked me to if anything ever happened. I've stopped working with every charity he was part of. I've… given up."

"Sweetie, Sam doesn't throw jobs at you because he feels bad. You're a damn talented photographer. Everything you're describing? That is all part of grieving."

"No, I've always just been a cranky, anti-social, mentally unstable fuck up. Haven't done anything right since I was born, except to ruin one life after another. After he died, I found out he basically sold his soul to the devil for me. All that talent, all that light, hidden away because of a fuckup like me." I take a shaky breath and add, "I should have been in the car with him."

I close my eyes so I don't have to see her. "I understand if you don't want to keep seeing me. I can… I can talk to Sam, get you someone else to work with. Someone who isn't a useless asshole. I shouldn't even be here. You have a beautiful mind and so much potential, you shouldn't be wasting your time on a broke loser like me."

"A broke loser wouldn't have come here to comfort me after I told him not to."

Her hands are cool against my face, and I want to sink into them. "I'm sorry," my voice is barely a whisper, "I'm sorry, Lex. I came here to help you and I made it all about me and my shit. I didn't mean to—"

"When I was eighteen, we were living with my aunt and she threw us a little party with some of our friends. She invited my mother, who, of course, brought Ronnie with her. At some point, I went upstairs to get something from my room—I don't even remember what it was now. I could hear noises coming from inside—whispering and other noises I didn't understand. When I stepped in, I found Ronnie. He had my best friend—my fucking *girlfriend*—bent over my desk, her pants around her ankles and his hands up her shirt, fucking her. I tried to run, but he caught me by the hair and pulled me back."

"I heard my girlfriend telling me over and over that it was no big deal and not to tell anyone while Ronnie dragged me over to the bed. He threw me down and climbed... he climbed on top of me. He told my girlfriend it was okay, and that he had a special present for me and to...to hold my hands down. He...he—"

I pull her head down on my shoulder and rock her gently.

"Bex came upstairs later and found me in the bed crying. He told me he'd do it to her next if I told anyone."

"You didn't tell anyone because you wanted to keep your sister safe."

"I tried to tell. I tried to talk to a counselor. That's when I realized what kind of reach Ronnie had as a preacher in such a big church. I couldn't trust anyone. I dropped out of the college I had applied for and begged Bex to move with me, so we did. He's made more passes at me since then, groped me, threatened me." She swallows hard and lowers her head. "I never kicked him in the balls and he never really stopped."

"It's not your fault, Angel. None of it," I try to assure her, although I'm not sure she believes me. "After the move, did you tell your sister?"

"No. I told her what I told you, mostly as a warning to stay away from him. She's my twin, though. She probably knows I'm lying."

"Does he still...touch you?"

"It stopped after he found out I was in therapy—well, stopped for a while. A few months ago, I was at their house and a migraine hit. I have medication I take for them and my mother got it for me. He wasn't home, so I went into the spare room to lie down for a few minutes. I ended up falling asleep, and when I woke up he was...he was standing over me and the blanket had been pulled back. I'd been asleep for three hours. My medication never did that before."

"Alexis—"

"Tonight...one of the older women at the church said there was going to a be wedding. She was so excited about it, saying how lucky I am and how wonderful this new pastor is. Jamie, I think my parents are going to try to force me to marry the new pastor somehow. How would they...how could they do that? She...she made it sound like I was pregnant, talking about my condition."

Rage like I've never known fills me, but before I can react, she moves against me again, curling up on my chest and pulling my arms around her. "I don't want to work with anyone else, Jamie. I don't want to see anyone else. We're still learning about each other and I'm sure there are more skeletons hidden away for us to find, but at least we got some of the big ones out of the way. I hope."

"There's got to be something we can do. A restraining order or something."

"I'm not sure what to do because I'm fucking afraid of him. Of both of them. I didn't want to lose my mom, but if she's part of this..." her voice trails off. "Can...can you just hold me for a little while?"

"Always, Angel." I hug her closer, leaving kisses against her hair. "Alexis, you're my muse. You're the light I never expected to get back in my life. I'm going to do everything I can to protect you, take care of you, and make you happy. I promise. I promise I'll try not to fuck this up like the loser I am."

"You're not a loser, Jamie. To me, you're a beautiful person, with too much care and worry in your heart. Your father would have been proud to see you still here, still trying. He'd be proud of you for listening to me. He is proud of you, and so am I."

She blindly wipes the tears from my face, then laces her fingers into mine. "Lexi?" my voice cracks.

"Yeah?" She looks up at me, and instantly, I'm drunk on those whiskey eyes and there's no doubt left in my mind.

"I… it hasn't been… I mean, I know we're still—Fuck it. Alexis Strauss, I have fallen madly and totally head over heels in love with you and I don't care if I'm a hopeless romantic or jumping the gun. I don't care that it's only been days. I love you, Cherry Blossom."

"You do?"

"I very much do. You're so beautiful and brilliant and kind. You're perfect, and you're more than I've ever wanted and way more than I deserve. You don't have to—"

"I love you, too, James!" She shouts, twisting her body so she's hovering over me. Her lips brush against mine. "I wasn't sure, but after tonight, after all this…I'm in love with you. You're beautiful, too."

The wine on her lips tingles against my tongue as our mouths slot together. It's soft and sweet. It's slow and meaningful. Each time our lips touch, it becomes a little more intense, a little harder, until I pick her up and carry her into the bedroom.

HOLLYWOOD

Lexi

CHAPTER 27
THE SHARPEST LIVES
MY CHEMICAL ROMANCE

LOUD MUSIC from a party fills the air as we travel down the obnoxiously long driveway toward the obnoxiously large house. Dani is in the back seat, fixing her makeup and hair. Jamie is driving with knuckles so white I'm surprised he hasn't broken the steering wheel. I'm still trying to figure out why the fuck we agreed to this. Dani owes us both. Big time.

We should have bailed, but we spent all day Monday and Tuesday working hard and getting ready for our trip. We thought we could use the break. This entire party is a mistake.

"So, remind me again why the fuck we're here?" I rest my hand on Jamie's thigh, giving in a gentle squeeze, hoping to ease some of his tension.

"Okay, so like, Rafael is the guy I'm meeting here. He's the artist. Anyhow, it's some big engagement party thing that they're writing off as an art exhibit." She spreads bright lipstick over her lips and makes a loud popping noise. "Rafael has a few pieces in it, of course, and he asked me to come out and to bring friends. He went to school with Tommy or something. So, maybe I have a legitimate shot with a cute, potentially rich artist. He also makes movies, and I kind of want him to do a video for my band."

"Great," James grumbles. "Tommy isn't going to leave you alone once he finds out you're my girlfriend."

When Dani sent us the address, James said it sounded familiar. As soon as he pulled up the map, I knew tonight was going to be a shit show. His face paled, then hints of red started poking up from under his shirt collar. Tommy Halpine has been an issue for James since he was a kid. It took some prying, but evidently, Tommy is the prick that tried to beat James up in school when Chase Cooper came to the rescue. In some ways, he's the reason they're such close friends, but he's still a bully and a dick, so they don't give him that credit—rightfully.

"Aww! You two are official in less than a week. Cute." Dani opens the camera app on her phone to check her makeup and applies even more lip gloss. "Less than a weekend, really. I can't talk though. If Rafael asked me to go to Vegas and get married tonight, I would. Mostly because I know kick ass divorce lawyers exist in LA. Wait, how do you know Tommy?"

"We went to school together. Don't you remember? I'm the one who introduced you to Raf." He looks at her in the rearview with a scowl. He's trying to keep his emotions inside, but that anger is fighting hard to escape. "He used to date Steve?"

"He did? Wait, Steve is gay? Your Steve dated my Raf?"

"Steve is…complicated."

"Oh, I kind of remember that now! So glad I didn't invite Steve!" She lunges forward, pointing. "Hey look, that's Rafael's car! Park here!"

"How can you tell? There's ten cars just like it." I reply.

"Because I know his bumper stickers? Anyhow, we're just here to mingle and get smashed on free booze and rich people food. Like we're crashing it, but we have an invitation. So everyone needs to stop stressing out and try to have a good fucking time, okay? Do not cock block me!"

"Literally the opposite of crashing it, Dani." James groans and parallel parks into a tight spot on the side of the road. He looks in the mirror. "If either of these cars could just, you know, tap the Jeep—"

"They'd have four lawyers find ten witnesses saying it was you who hit their car." I smile.

His shoulders drop, and he runs a nervous hand through his hair. "Yeah, you're right. Let's get this over with."

When I step out, I take a deep breath and smooth down the front of my dress that I had to borrow from Dani. She said she'd let me have it if I let her win the office pool. I'm now eye level with Jamie and towering over Dani thanks to the four-inch stilettos she found. They make my legs look damn good—which might be part of why we're running late. Jamie *really* likes them.

We're walking up to the house, Dani practically running at this point, when James slips his hand into mine and pulls me to a stop. His free hand grips my hip with a squeeze as he pushes me up against a garish column that serves no purpose other than flaunting wealth.

"You—you look like you belong here, in a house like this. You're a damn knockout, and I can't believe you're here with me. I can't believe you're mine." His eyes are drinking me in for the hundredth time tonight, and I can just make out the bulge in his pants. "Please don't leave me for Tommy. He's a prick."

"Yeah, but he's rich and I'd never have to work another day in my life…" I tease, using the most sultry voice I can manage. I let out a soft moan and watching his eyes darken. "Mr. Barton, you should fuck me right here on his daddy's lawn and show him who I belong to."

"Tempting. We might get lucky and find one of the cars unlocked." He nips at my bottom lip, pushing against me with a wicked grin. "Besides, you might be my girl, but if anyone in this relationship belongs to someone, it's me belonging to you."

"I love you, James Barton. Now, just bend me over the hood of that Maserati, baby. Who cares about car alarms?" I take his tie, slowly pulling it through my fingers. "I should probably keep hold of you while we're in there, so some rich cougar doesn't try to drag you away to her den."

He kisses my bottom lip, and when he pulls back, I reach up and wipe the lipstick from his mouth with the pad of my thumb. He's got on a tight black suit with a blue tie that makes his eyes sparkle—or it could be me doing that. His pants would show off his perfect ass if it wasn't for the jacket.

My arms wrap around his waist and I give his butt a squeeze while he smiles down at me.

"When we're done here, I want you to take me home, hike up my skirt, and eat my pussy like it's your last meal on earth." I smirk, watching his pupils react to my words as his mouth drops open. "Then I want you to fuck me from behind while I wear these stupid heels."

"Promise to keep those heels on, and you have yourself a deal, Ms. Strauss." He cups my ass and grinds against me. "I'm gonna peel this dress off you with my teeth and have you screaming my name."

"The way you say my name, it almost sounds like mistress. I think I like it. Oh, we should pretend we're rich and famous. I should tell everyone I'm from the North Carolina VanDerVanders."

He laughs and pulls me closer, nipping at my neck.

"Mmm, unfortunately, I actually know the douchebag whose family lives here. He's well aware I'm about as far away from rich or successful as an artist because he's the one who's managed to pull the rug out from under me on at least two clients and a grant." He takes my hand, and we move toward the front door again just as Dani calls to us from the doorway. "You, however, are the Countess der VanDerVander, and everyone should bow before you and shower you with riches. Speaking of, where the hell did that kid go that I hired to sprinkle rose petals at your feet?"

"You fucking would." I giggle. "You know, if I was the Countess der VanDerVander, I'd still let you be my aloof boy toy that fucks me stupid every night."

"A position I will gladly accept, mistress."

We walk in, and my mouth tries to drop, but I manage to hold it in place. It's the most idiotic, gaudy, ugly place I think I have ever been. It could be the designer in me, but I don't understand some of the people who get hired to decorate these places. I guarantee this place has at least one gold toilet. I hate everything about it. As we walk toward the crowds of people, I shake my head and laugh.

"What?"

"This, all of it. The house is beyond ostentatious, and the first painting we're about to see already has me wanting to run out the door and pour bleach in my eyes."

He leans forward to read the plaque next to the art. "Well, don't say that too loud. It's one of Tommy's." He frowns and lets a heavy sigh escape. "And it's worth more than my car and home put together."

"It looks like a vagina. Painted by someone who has never actually seen one." His nose scrunches up as he laughs, trying to hide it behind his hand. "What?! I've got one and I've been face first into one. This man has never satisfied a single person who identifies as a woman. Platinum card gay men have drawn better pussies."

"I love you."

"I know," she answers with a wink. "So, when do I get to see your paintings? You've got to be way better than this guy."

"I'd have to dig them out of a closet. Or the dump." He moves on to the next frame and purses his lips. "I stopped painting a while ago."

"Because of your dad?"

"Sort of. All my supplies are in the garage. I tried to buy some and work in the house and ended up tossing all the canvases into a barrel and having a little bonfire. Liking something doesn't mean you're good enough at it to make it a career."

"That doesn't mean you should give it up. I don't believe you're a bad painter for a second, pretty boy." I smooth his hair back and look into his eyes. "You just need to find some fresh inspiration. Something new to paint."

He takes my hand and squeezes. "I already have. I just can't seem to leave you alone long enough to put the brush to the canvas."

Someone runs up behind Jamie, wraps him in a hug, and kisses his cheek all in a blur of motion. James looks stunned for a second and then cracks up. I nearly drop the drink in my hand when I realize who is standing in front of me.

"Duuuude, I am so fucking glad you're here. Did you see that first painting? Fuck, man. A blind man could paint a better—" He lets go of Jamie and stops dead in his tracks, staring at me. It's not lewd, it's more that he's surprised. "You! You…must be Alexis. Please tell me you're Alexis."

Jamie sighs and pulls me in for a kiss on the head. "Yep, she is. Lexi, this is the Oscar winning idiot extraordinaire, Chase Cooper, but you can call him dickhead. Coop, this is the more brilliant and talented than you love of my life, Alexis Strauss."

"Before I answer this asshole, allow me to apologize. I heard about the line you waited in and I feel terrible. Also, anything he's told you about me is probably a lie." He takes my free hand, kissing my knuckles and sending electrified butterflies through my whole body.

Never meet your heroes, unless your hero is Chase Cooper. He's beautiful, like the goddesses themselves chiseled him out of marble. Jamie rolls his eyes when I giggle, but it's not my fault. It's not every day your favorite Hollywood crush is kissing your hand like you're a princess.

"He's said nothing but nice things about you, Mr. Cooper," I say with an unsteady voice.

"Chase. And in that case, they're definitely all lies."

"Alright, quit ogling my girl, you fucking troll. Why are you here, man?"

"My agent made me come. Tommy's dickhead dad is marrying some equally rich woman and there's talk they'll open a movie studio. I told her this was a waste of time and how much of a prick Tommy is, but she sent someone to make sure I'd be here—and be seen." He waves to a woman across the room who is twice his age and glares at him. He says it all with a smile, as if he's saying the nicest things about everyone. "They wouldn't even let me bring Pongo because that lovely woman is allergic to dogs. I think I hate her."

"A movie studio?"

"Chase Cooper?" A loud voice interrupts us from across the room, calling attention to our little group. "It *is* you!" A man around our age, in a full tux and slicked-back blonde hair, heads toward us with his arms outstretched as if he's welcoming the masses. I can already tell he's a smarmy weasel. He even looks like the guy from American Psycho. I half expect him to tell us he's got video tapes to return.

"Yeah, you know, so Tommy boy here can try his hand at

acting, since he sucks at everything else," Chase says under his breath. He's still beaming, but even I can see it's totally fake. He leans in by my ear and whispers, "Watch this, he fucking hates being called Tom."

Chase steps forward to take Tommy's hand, matching his loudness as he says, "Tom Halpine, what a surprise. I thought you were in China working on that big real estate deal? How's your dad taking that hit? I heard it was in the billions!"

Seeing the sneer that Tommy tries to hide almost has me doubling over with laughter, but I keep it all inside. They shake and I notice Chase wipe his hand on his pants after he lets go and takes a step back. I think I'm going to like Chase once I get over the fact that he's the guy who plays my favorite superhero. It helps that he's in a suit and not *THE* suit. It also helps that I'm already madly in love.

"Wait, is that? You brought Barton? Wow, you're looking… yeah, anyway." He oozes money and hair gel. He doesn't even bother to shake Jamie's hand. Dick. His voice drops and has a slight hint of annoyance when he addresses Jamie. He never actually talks to him, more like at him. "What in the hell are you doing here, man? I hope this isn't about the grant email last week. Damn shame. I really thought you'd have me beat by now."

"Guess it just wasn't in the cards," James gives him a tight-lipped smile that drops quickly when Tommy turns his attention to me.

"Chase, I didn't realize you came with such radiant company. Are you going to introduce us?" His eyes rake over my body and he has the nerve to lick his lips.

"I'm James's girlfriend, Alexis." He holds out his hand, but I just tuck mine around Jamie's arm.

"Alexis? That's a lovely name for a lovely woman. I'm

Thomas Halpine." He leans in, "But I hope you'll call me Tommy when you scream it in my bed later."

I laugh. Not a polite, soft laugh or a chuckle, but I straight up laugh in his face. "Not for all the money in your daddy's bank account, little boy."

I feel the squeeze on my hip and catch the corner of James's lip twitch up.

"Feisty! I like it. James, good luck holding onto this one. Hopefully, it works out better than the last, but when it doesn't, I have no problem picking up what you can't handle." He pulls his lip between his teeth and I'm certain I'm about to throw up as he stares at me. "When you change your mind, I'll be more than ready to ruin you when you come begging for it."

I feel the muscles in Jamie's arm tense, but I keep a firm grip on his arm. This isn't the time or the place to throw punches. Tommy tries to talk to Chase, and I lean into Jamie's ear and whisper, "Your name is the only one I'm screaming tonight, my pretty pool boy."

Somehow, Chase finally gets Tommy to leave, joining a boisterous crowd where he wastes no time at all, grabbing the ass of some skinny young thing with dollar signs in her eyes.

"What a douche," I mumble.

"I like her, Jimbo," Chase laughs, then ducks down a hallway, saying something about avoiding his handler.

"Jamie! Lexi!" Dani yells out as she drags a surprisingly good looking guy over to us. "Raf has another opening next week! I told him I have an artsy friend, and he wants you to be in it! If you are cool with that. He just needs to see your work. Do you have pictures of it or anything?"

"Minor correction," the guy who must be Raf beams as he holds a hand out to Jamie. I like him more than Tommy boy already. "Now that I see who she's talking about, it would be fucking awesome if you wanted to show with us next week. Your shit is fantastic, man. It always has been. I hope there are no hard feelings after Steve and I."

"Yeah. I mean, uhm, no." Jamie shakes his head. "No hard feelings." I'm grinning up at James like he's made of stars and he looks a little stunned, rubbing the back of his neck as he answers, "Uhm, tha-thanks. Really. I'll see if I have anything and get back to you if that's alright."

"Fantastic, man. Have you done anything recently? I caught the piece you did for that studio a year or so ago. Seriously mind-blowing. I haven't seen much of you since, though. Working on something big?"

"No, it's been, uhm, slow. Haven't really been able to do much on a canvas recently."

"That's right! I've seen your photos. It's a mixed bag kind of show—bring those, too." He pulls out a card and hands it over. "Oh, bro, sorry to hear about your dad. He was an inspiration and the times he talked at the art school, his message really got to me."

"Thanks. It's nice to hear that now and then." He flashes me a bright smile as Dani and Raf head off to find more champagne. "Okay, maybe he's not that bad of a—"

"Jamie," Chase's voice is a low grumble of panic as he hurries toward us, grabbing Jamie by the arm. "We need to leave. Now!"

"Why? What's going—" Jamie's smile drops into a scowl as he looks across the room to the ornate staircase.

The couple of the hour make their grand entrance in the most over-the-top, rich people's way—including a music change by the string quartet.

She's young and beautiful, with dark hair expertly pulled into an updo and a dress that's old Hollywood but completely sheer. I half expect a flock of crows and a fog machine as she descends the stairs like an evil queen. I can't help but think she looks familiar, but given the crowd she's running with, she's probably been in a commercial or something.

She's on the arm of what Dani would call a Silver Fox, and what I just see as an older version of Tommy the Douche. Somehow, he has softer features—like he hasn't spent his entire life being an asshole—but he's still smug as hell.

"Shit," James mumbles under his breath.

"What's wrong?"

"Come on, this way," Chase says, pulling Jamie's arm.

"That's my sister."

Before Jamie can turn and run, which is what he and Chase are trying to do, the woman glares right at him with a malicious smile.

"That's Elle."

HOLLYWOOD

James

CHAPTER 28
SEASON OF THE WITCH

LANA DEL REY

—6 MONTHS AGO—

"WHAT DO YOU WANT, ELLE?"

"What do I want? Oh, James. I just wanted to relay how sorry I am that your father passed away. I know you were close."

"*Our* father, Elle. He was our father." I had hoped that this was the olive branch. That we could move on from whatever hatred she's built toward me and start acting like family. As soon as I laid eyes on the lawyer, I realized I was alone—I had no family left.

"It's hard to think of him that way when I never knew him." She's smug, dressed like she's headed to a board meeting in some tall tower downtown, and looking at me like I'm dirt.

"That wasn't his fault. You're the one who refused to see him. He tried, Elle. He tried all the damn time and you know it."

"He loved you more."

"Jesus," I say under my breath, rubbing my eyes and looking around the living room. "What the fuck do you want?"

The lawyer hands me an envelope that's stamped with a red Confidential and Urgent across it. It looks like something you'd see out of a spy thriller, and I have no idea why this asshole is giving it to me.

"*Our* mother wanted you to have this." I stare at it blankly and, after a pause, her eyebrow raises and she cackles like some kind of cartoon villain. "You really are clueless? Oh, that's fantastic! This is better than I thought! What a fucking moron!"

"What are you talking about? What is this?"

"Ask me what I want again." Her maniacal laughter sends chills up my spine, while she pretends to dab tears from her eyes. I don't think she's ever shed a tear in her miserable life.

"What do you want?"

"Everything, James. All of it. I'll get it, too." She pulls open her phone and reads from it, but I don't understand the legal terms and can't think straight at the moment anyhow. "All of that boils down to: *you're fucked*. You'll find it all in the contract that your dearly departed father never amended after the divorce. You've got one year to contest it before it becomes legally binding. Good luck finding a lawyer though, because as of this morning, you're broke."

"Why the hell would I be broke?"

"Because you don't have access to dad's money. His insurance money and bank accounts, all of it goes to Mother. You paid for the funeral already, and you're not getting any of that money back from his estate. The funeral is non-refundable, I checked."

"No. No, he…he took care of that."

"I was going to tell Mother to take the house too, but I think it would be far more fun for you to struggle to save it, fail, and watch as the bank forecloses on it—or you're forced to sell. Anyhow, I need some new clothes for the funeral. See you this weekend…don't you wish you'd gone with a pine box and wild flowers?"

I drop onto the sofa and stare at the ceiling, daring the roof to collapse on me. Why not? The rest of the world already had. Steve and Coop sit on either side of me. They heard the entire exchange and they're both seething.

"I'll cover the funeral," Coop offers after the silence lingers too long.

"You can't." I glance up at my dad's oldest friend as he sips his coffee and frowns at us. "Jamie, your father had a plan. We just thought we had more time to make it happen. We can still make most of it work, starting with you signing the house over to me. It keeps it over your head and there's no way I'm selling to your sister or your mother. We'll figure the rest out. We just need to be careful of how it's all handled from here on out."

"Why…why didn't he change his will? Why didn't he tell me?"

"This is hard to hear. Hell, he never wanted you to find out, but it's time you do. The only way he could save you was to give her everything. She owns him, but she wasn't allowed to touch you or any part of the contract that had to do with you. He protected you from your mother, but it never occurred to your dad that your sister would come after you."

—NOW—

"James, what a coincidence to see you here." Elle glides over to us, she offers a glass of champagne to me like it's just the two of us in the room. "I wasn't aware you owned clothes that weren't covered in paint and fit for the homeless. Did you steal them? Borrow them from a friend who took pity on your poor soul?"

My mouth is dry, but I'm not taking a damn thing from her, not even a glass. If I did, I'd throw champagne in her face and smash the glass against the wall. My mind is running, trying to get ahead of whatever she's doing here. I'm going to lose this race. I always do. She's smart, conniving, manipulative; she's probably a psychopath. I'm here because she *wants* me here. This is all some wicked plan she's set in motion, and I won't have a clue what to expect until it's too late.

"Chase, why don't you scurry along? I'm sure you'll trip and fall dick first into someone as soon as you turn around. I guess it's better than the alternative. How did you get the blood out of the grout?"

Coop stares at her with a snarl.

"She was too homely for you anyhow. Wasn't that what the press called her? Homely? Tell me, is Steven here, too? I miss having all my playthings in one house."

Coop takes a step closer to me and I can see the vein in his neck pumping as his jaw clenches. He would risk his entire career for me if it meant tearing her down from her pedestal.

"Not here, Chase."

She chuckles, and it sounds like poison. Her eyes flick next to me and she sizes up Lexi. I pull her between Coop and me, almost daring Elle to try something. "Oh, you must be Alexis. The latest pair of legs to spread for my idiot brother. Tell me, do you charge by the hour or by the pound?"

"Shut the hell up, Elle."

"Careful, James. You're a guest in my fiancé's house."

"Your what?"

"Fiancé, James. It's a French word that you wouldn't understand." Her claw-like nails tap against her champagne flute and I'm sure she's picturing gauging my eyes out with them. "Oh wait, maybe you would. You had one once, didn't you? How is Natalie these days?"

"Don't, Elle."

"That little boy of hers has some very pretty eyes. Blue-grey, like yours. I'm curious. Are they both yours, or is it only the one bastard you put inside her behind her hardworking husband's back?"

"Oh, fuck you, Elle."

"That's rude, disgusting, and illegal. We're related." She drains the flute and sets it on a tray of a waiter passing by. "If you're going to continue to be crass, I might send Natalie's new hubby that paternity test you took."

"I never took—" My face drops and my stomach follows. "Leave Natalie and her family out of whatever the hell this is."

She eyes Lexi again and hums as she steps toward her. "She looks like healthy breeding stock with those hips. I bet you're a *daddy's girl,* aren't you? I've seen your Daddy. Maybe when I'm done with this one, I'll find Jesus."

"What the hell do you want?" I snap.

"Me? Oh, how could I possibly want anything from you? I'm rich, I'm about to marry into even more money, and you're a penniless pauper who won't do what he's told." She turns her wrists, examining her nails. "Sign your name and then curl up in a ditch and cry."

"He's not signing a fucking thing," Coop growls.

"Fine by me. The longer it takes, the more it hurts poor little Jamie in the end." She bats her eyes and uses a baby voice, "Will widdle Jaime stop talking again? Curl in his widdle shell and die?"

"Come on, we're leaving," Coop says.

"Before you go, is daddy's art still in the studio? Oh, you probably wouldn't know. You don't go in there anymore, not since his brains splattered all over the fucking five." As she talks, I half expect to see a forked tongue and razor-sharp teeth in her mouth. I'm at the end of what I can handle, and she knows it. I'm shutting down, following every step of her plan. "Just be careful if you decide to take your chubby little fuck toy here into the studio so you can fuck her up the ass while she looks at your pathetic art. Wouldn't want you to ruin your father's legacy."

"That's enough." I step between her and Lexi, going toe to toe with Elle. She takes a half-step back so she can look up at me again. "What the fuck do you want? What do you *really* want?"

She walks two fingers up my chest while she cackles, "The usual. You. Gone. Leaving me everything."

"Go back to Europe, then. Go back to where you and I never see each other."

"Oh, but that isn't enough, and you know it. I want what I'm fucking due. I want all of it. I want *my* company, *my* art, and *my* house. I want to ruin you over and over. I want you penniless and on the fucking street." She curls her lip. "You were born first and with a dick and now you get whatever your little heart wants? Fuck you. You don't deserve it."

"Elle, darling, is this man giving you trouble?" Mr. Halpine steps beside her, wrapping his arm around her waist and pulling her in. I glare at him. He's got to be forty years her senior, if not more.

"No, love. In fact, I think he was just leaving. Weren't you, James?"

"You look familiar, James. Do I know you from one of my son's gallery showings?"

"No, you don't." I turn my head toward Coop but leave my eyes fixed on Elle. "Chase?"

Without missing a beat, he moves to the other side of Lexi and we turn to walk her out. She seems just as confused as me about this situation. I would never have walked in the door if I'd known Elle was here to blindside me. Now I'm hoping we'll be able to walk out.

"Wait," Tommy's dad says just before we get far. He's holding up his champagne glass toward us with a look of recognition in his eyes. "Chase Cooper. That means you're Barton's boy, right?"

I just stare at him, then he gestures across the room. My eyes follow his gaze and I my stomach lurches when I'm staring at an all too familiar piece on the wall.

"I really appreciate you donating that to the show tonight." He smiles with his too white teeth. "Your father was very talented. I think he would have been honored to show here tonight with my boy. Shame he threw it all away to charity cases."

"Jamie!" Coop whispers as I drop Lexi's hand and rush through the crowd to the painting until I'm standing a foot in front of it. Anger is making me see red and my hands clenched into fists.

"Jamie, you didn't donate that, did you?" Lexi asks when they catch up to me.

"No. No, I fucking didn't," I snarl, still staring at the canvas in front of me. "This was in his room. This was in his fucking bedroom."

"What?" Coop looks around. "Dude, how the fuck?"

"She stole it. She's been in my fucking house and she stole my father's—" I close my eyes, trying to calm myself down. I storm back over to Elle and her idiot fiancé. "Why?"

"For this exact moment. Come along, dear. Let's mingle." She smiles and they both walk away from me.

"Let's get out of here, Jamie. We can call the police or something," Lexi suggests.

"We can't. She's too good to leave loose ends," Coop explains as he pushes us toward the door. He knows I'm shutting down. "I guarantee she has all the documentation saying she owns it and anything else she took and no one will question how authentic those papers are."

"But she broke into his home."

I drop my head to my chest, "They won't believe me, I'm nobody. She's got power and influence. I'm just a fucking idiot loser."

Coop turns to Lexi, "Get him home."

"Dani came with us."

"I'll make sure Dani gets home and I'll call later. Don't let him leave."

"What do you mean, *don't let him leave*?"

"Trust me, keep him with you," he answers her before disappearing back into the crowd. I'm glad he didn't explain any further.

I shake my head and stride toward the door, but before I can open it, Lexi's hand is on mine. I glare at her. This is her out. Her escape from my fucked up life. Something tells me she isn't going to take it.

"You're not an idiot or a loser." Her voice is stern, and the rage drops from my face. I'm not angry with her. "You're also not leaving without me."

Her lips are on mine before I can respond. When she breaks the kiss and has my full attention, she whispers in my ear, "Take me home. Let me take care of you this time."

I nod and look back at the painting before we leave. This is my fault. I haven't been in the studio or Dad's room since he died. I don't know what she's taken from the house, from me. But as I walk away, I realize there's one thing I can never let Elle take from me. I need to protect Alexis, no matter the cost.

Lexi shoves me against the Jeep and her lips crash against mine. Her hands are frantic and all over me, but I'm so surprised that I'm stuck in molasses. She goes to unzip my pants, but I grab her shoulders and swap our positions. My hand dives under her skirt, and I smirk when my fingers brush against her bare skin. She's already hot and wet just for me, and she's just the distraction I need right now.

"I wanted to surprise you later with the whole no panties thing. Especially after you ripped that pair off me the other day." She bites her bottom lip and looks up at me with big doe eyes.

"Oh, Cherry Blossom," I coo. Fuck Elle and her stupid fiancé. Fuck this whole stupid mess. I have everything I'll ever need right here. "I am very surprised. Can you guess what else I am?"

"No," she moans as my finger slides through her slickness.

I open the door, lift her into the passenger seat, and pull her dress up as I lick my lips. "Fucking. Hungry." I drop in front of her. I don't care who sees. Anyone who catches us is going to learn two things. She's mine, and I'm driving her fucking wild. I'm the one making her writhe against my tongue as she holds onto the roll bar. I'm the one she's moaning for. I'm the one who made her this fucking wet.

"Louder, Angel. Let 'em all hear your pretty song."

I hoist her leg up over my shoulder, and as I feast on her like a starving wolf, she's fucking my face and singing my name. Her hands find the back of my head and she's gripping tight and pushing me deeper. The second my fingers curl inside her, she tightens around me, and two strokes later, she's coming apart hard.

"Oh god, James!"

I slide another finger into her as she squeezes my head with her thighs and swears like a damn sailor. Her heel is digging into my back and the pain is making me fucking hard. I seriously consider pulling my cock out and claiming her right here. Before I can, she's coming again, harder and louder. As she comes down, I lap at her glistening pussy and thighs.

Panting and hard as a rock, I stand and she grabs my hand, slipping my slick fingers into her mouth and cleaning them as she stares into my eyes. I kiss her hard, letting her taste more of herself on my tongue.

"So, get you a little hot under the collar and the sex gets a little more…intense."

I quickly scan the street, just now realizing where we are. "Shit. I'm sorry. Probably shouldn't have done that."

"Oh," she sighs with a pout. "I was hoping you were sorry you stopped before you fucked my brains out."

She grinds against me. The whine that comes out of me is almost embarrassing. I slide my tongue over the shell of her ear and whisper, "I'm going to make you come so fucking hard for me tonight, so many times, you're not going to walk straight tomorrow, because you're *my* fucking Angel."

"Good, because you have no idea how badly I want you," she replies as her hand dips between us and grabs my cock. "Take me home. Forget this place and these assholes. There's no one in that house that could ever satisfy me the way you do."

"You're mine. They can't even fucking touch you."

"I thought you'd be too nice to be this possessive. I think I like it."

"Fuck," I breathe out, kissing up and down her neck, "I want to take you back inside, bend you over that railing and let Tommy watch what he will never fucking have. I need you. I need you so bad."

I'm rutting against her hip. I need to stop. I need to calm down enough to drive us to her place. Then I remember why we left the party and my head finds her shoulder. My arms wrap around her and I hold her to me as I fight with the rage and the pain and the tears.

"We'll get it back," she whispers, her hands stroking my hair. It's like she can read my mind already. Like she can see the pain I feel and give it a name. "Give me your keys, pretty boy. And before you ask, yes, I can drive a stick. Just not in these heels."

I pull my head away from her, sliding her shoes off and tossing them in the back. She cups my face and sees into my soul. "I love you, Alexis. I'll never let them take you from me. I'll never let them hurt you. I can't let her hurt you."

"I know, James. I love you, too. Come on, let's go home."

"You *are* my home."

HOLLYWOOD
Lexi

CHAPTER 29
HURT
JOHNNY CASH

AFTER LEAVING THE PARTY, I tried to do what I could to keep James's mind off of his sister and what she said. We made out during a movie, had sex in the shower, got high, got drunk, and even worked on Sam's project for a while. It seemed like everything I tried only worked for a short time before he'd slip back into staring blankly at nothing or looking lost and helpless. The entire night was like one long roller coaster ride.

When I roll over the next morning, I find a cold pillow and a half-empty bed. Last night comes back to me in steady waves, which I appreciate. My head hurts from the drinking and I'm exhausted, both physically and mentally, so I need to ease into the morning. I learned that while typical Jamie fucks like a god, when Jamie gets angry, he fucks like a demon. I'm a little sore and I'm sure I have random bruises all over me, but I regret nothing.

I check the time; it's later than I expected, but I appreciate the extra time to sleep before we're on the road and headed up the coast. He has at least three days planned out, but I'm hoping to convince him we need at least five to see everything. The longer I'm away, the better. The same goes for him.

"Jamie?" It's a half-hearted moan that he might hear if he's in the bathroom. I lay there waiting for him to come back to bed when Chase's words come back to me.

Don't let him leave.

"Jamie?" I yell out drunkenly. He's probably in the kitchen or out working on his computer.

No answer.

I sit up, my head throbbing and mouth dry from the alcohol and weed. When I search around the room, I see no sign of him, so I yell out again, panic seeping into my voice. "James?!"

Don't let him leave.

His suitcase and camera bag are gone, leaving only my bags by the bedroom door. I hobble out to the living room and he's not there, either. His computer isn't on the desk, his phone isn't on the charger, and I can't find any notes that he's left telling me where he's gone. Dread sets it as I run to get my phone.

Eleven missed texts, all from my mother. No new voicemails.

I call him and let it ring through to his voicemail, then hang up and call again. The fourth time I get his voicemail I leave a message, "Uhm, hi, it's me. Where did you go? I, uhm, I thought we were going on our trip today but your stuff is gone and... James...Uhm, can you call me and tell me you're okay? I love you. Please call me."

I hang up and text him. Maybe I'm being a little extreme, but I keep hearing Chase in my head telling me not to let him leave. What the fuck does that even mean?

My phone rings and I answer it without even looking at the caller ID. "James?"

"Hey, no, sorry, it's Sam." My heart sinks, and I let myself fall onto the edge of the bed. I'm relieved that it's Sam and not my mother. *"Everything okay? Were you two at that party with Dani last*

night? Cause man, that's one hell of a hangover she's got. Sounds like maybe you've got it, too."

"Uhm, yeah, yeah I was."

"Damn, how late were you and Jamie up?"

"What do you mean?" Dani's probably already told Sam about us, but this is a pretty forward question from Sam.

"Don't get me wrong, these are stellar. Love the direction you guys are going. But you didn't need to drop the prints off at four in the morning. That's not what I meant when I said work whatever hours you want."

"Four…four in the morning?"

"Well, that's according to the timestamp on the video. Were you not with him? I just assumed you and he dropped them off together. Dani says you two are damn near inseparable since you met. I'm happy for you guys, by the way. Both of you."

"Sam, stop. What are you talking about? What video?"

"The security camera. It shows Jamie swinging by and dropping these off this morning. The Jeep is just off camera, so I figured you were in there." His voice changes from jovial to worried. "Lex, is something going on?

"I…No. I think it's a hangover, like Dani's. I guess James couldn't sleep or something."

"Alright, get some rest and get some coffee or whatever you drink." I'm about to end the call when I hear him speak again, "Oh, and have fun in Frisco. It's really nice this time of year. Tell Jamie to take you to the Cherry Blossom trees. They match your hair."

"Yeah, yeah I will. Bye Sam."

I pace the apartment. I call his number. I pace more. I try to work, but my mind is too worried to think straight. I pace more.

It's three in the afternoon before I decide to call around to the local hospitals. I'm not sure if they can tell me if he's there, since I'm not family. I lie to a few and say I'm his sister, but no one has him or anyone fitting his description that they know of. All this calling around might be bullshit I saw on television shows, but I'm trying it anyhow. The next thing I realize is that I don't have his address or a clue where he lives other than Pasadena. I don't even know how to get a hold of his friends to check on him. Then I remember Dani. How could I forget Dani?

I frantically call the office, but someone else answers and tells me she's gone home for the day with a stomach bug. Dani's hangovers are pretty intense, so that doesn't surprise me. I call her cell and it goes to voicemail, so I text her. And wait.

A few hours later, I stop my pacing and nervous cleaning and take a deep breath. "He's a grown man with his own life, and he doesn't need to check in with you all the time. He's probably with Cooper dealing with a lawyer." I say to the empty room.

I'm lying to myself. If he had left and intended to come back, he would have called me or left a note. I don't know if it's something I said or did last night, but there has to be some reason he left me. I don't understand what the hell is going on, so I break down and cry on the couch.

I'm up too early the next morning after sleeping with my phone and checking non-stop. I've been lying on the couch trying to will it to ring all night. The problem is, it *has* rung. A lot. I have almost forty missed calls and texts from my mother and a few from Ronnie. I can't stay here today because they'll come looking for me, so I pack up my stuff and head down to the office to get my mind off things.

Dani isn't at her desk when I get there and I'm feeling like no one is where they're supposed to be anymore in my life. I see Sam in the back by the coffee machine and head for him.

"Hey Sam, have you heard from Jamie since he dropped off those prints?"

"Hey, my star designer!" He beams when he sees me. "No, I haven't. Why? Lose him?"

"Honestly, I'm not sure. I can't get a hold of him. He isn't returning my calls or texts. I'm worried about him, but I don't have any way to get a hold of him. So I came here to work and try to clear my mind." My eyes burn the longer I'm rambling until Sam pulls me in for a hug and I realize I'm already crying. "I…I think he left me. I don't understand what I did."

"Hey, no. Jamie isn't like that. I'm sure there's an explanation."

"He just left in the middle of the night. I know things were weird after he saw his sister at the party, but I didn't expect this. He took all his things and didn't leave a note. We were supposed to go on that trip, but now he's ghosting me."

"His sister?" Sam's face darkens, and I can tell he's hiding something from me. "Lex, uhm, give me a minute. Stay here, try to find a way to calm down."

"What?" The panic hits my stomach hard and my knees buckle. "Sam?"

"I'm gonna go call him. I'm sure he's fine. He's been through a lot lately, so I'll check in."

He hurries off to his office, taking the stairs three at a time. I'm standing there holding a cup of coffee I hadn't even realized he'd handed me, wondering what the hell I've gotten myself into. Something is wrong and no one will tell me what. "No, fuck this."

I run back to Dani's desk, relieved to see her there. "Where have you been? I texted you!"

"Chill! I dropped my phone in the fountain at the party and was way too hungover to go get a new one. Why?"

"I need to do something reckless, and probably stupid. In fact, I'm pretty sure it's illegal, or it is on TV."

"Oh, I'm in. Whose house are we burning to the ground?"

"I need an address. I need James' address. He's not answering, and there was an issue at the party. Chase told me to not let him leave my place, but he snuck out."

"The party from two days ago? That's fucked up. Say no more, I'm on it."

In what seemed like seconds, Dani hands me a slip of paper with an address scribbled on it. I recognize the street name, but other than that, I have no clue where this is. I don't exactly go to Pasadena very often.

"Do you have Chase's number?"

"No. I only hang out with him when I'm with Jamie. It's not like the guy wants his number floating around. You're really freaking out, huh?" I nod. "Alright, go! Eat that after you get there, in case someone tries to arrest us for it!"

"I'm not eating paper, also, I have to put it in my GPS. I love you, Dani, but you watch way too many crime dramas."

"I watch them with you, dummy!" I'm halfway out the door when she adds, "Oh, and if he's ghosting you to break up with you, tell him I'm going to beat his ass!"

I bolt out the door, not bothering to wait for Sam as I plug the address into the GPS and speed away the second the directions pull up. The screen says forty-five minutes with traffic and when I finally pull into the driveway, I'm a mess. I've thought of every terrible thing that could have happened to him, not stopping at an alien abduction.

Chase said Elle was powerful.

Jamie is terrified of her, even though he doesn't want to admit it.

If she hurt him, I will hunt her fucking ass down and shove those stupid, pointy fingernails into her damn eyes.

I spot his Jeep parked in front of a large, two-story home. It's a simple house, set back off the road but in decent shape for how old it probably is. Next to his Jeep is a silver SUV that looks brand new. As I walk past, I see two car seats in the back.

James told me he didn't have kids. He said Elle was lying about all of that. The back of my brain taunts me with what ifs. What if he lied? What if he has kids? What if he has other girlfriends? My heart is in my throat as I head up the stairs to the porch and knock. When there's no answer, I knock once more and I check my phone. I hear hurried footsteps and the door flies open, revealing an absolutely stunning woman I've never seen before. She has long, blonde hair pulled up in a messy bun that looks slept in, so does the shirt she's wearing. I recognize it as Jamie's. I had it on just a few days ago.

Fuck. I think I'm going to throw up.

"Shit sorry, I thought you were Chase," she says to me as if we've met before. "Wait…Chase doesn't knock. Fuck."

"I uhm. I'm…sorry," I stutter, then turn around, ready to bolt for my car. When I hear my name. I stop, teetering dangerously between rage and confusion over a man I met a week ago who isn't returning my calls but is telling his other girlfriend my name.

"You're her, right? You have to be. I mean, Jamie showed me the pictu—Oh Jesus fuck, I just realized how this looks. We didn't!"

"What?" It comes out a distant squeak as I turn back to stare at her. I was aiming for '*strong woman who doesn't need a man in her life if he's going to cheat on her*'. Nailed it.

"I'm Natalie, but you can call me Nat. I'm guessing he hasn't gotten around to me yet; he did say it was a kind of whirlwind relationship between you two." She's talking so fast and waving her hands. I'm not sure what to make of the situation. She stops to take a breath, but then more of an information dump follows. "I'm his ex-wife who's happily remarried with two children that are absolutely not his. Jamie's. I mean, they're my husbands. The kids. We're not sleeping together. Not the kids, Jamie and I. I'm just a friend!"

"I...don't think I understand."

"I don't blame you. I'm not explaining any of this well." She takes my arm and pulls me back toward the door. "J is upstairs. Coop and I finally convinced him to take the good drugs last night, so I think he's coming out of it. Do you want to come in for coffee? Coop will be back soon. He's taking Pongo and Lulu home."

"Uhm, I... okay?"

"I promise, I don't bite; I just talk too much."

Stepping inside transports me right into Jamie's mind. Art decorates the walls, with books stacked on shelves, the floor, and any flat surface available. The art ranges from portrait sketches to beautiful landscapes, most of them leaning in stacks against tables and chairs. I want to flip through them and see the rest. It's not messy in the traditional sense, it's like everything has a place, but it has the trademark takes of an artist's troubled mind. Chaos in organized form.

"He really likes you." I'd almost forgotten Natalie was there. I remember the name now, and what Elle said about her. She's right, we haven't gotten around to talking about her at all. Until last night, I assumed when Jamie talked about '*the divorce*', he was referencing his parents' divorce. "He said it hasn't been long for you two, but I know him better than most people. The other night I was here dropping some stuff off and he was a tornado tearing through this place and getting packed up. He was so excited about the trip you two were taking. I've only ever seen that twinkle in his eyes twice before. The day we met, and the day we said I do."

She sets a cup of coffee on the table by the milk and sugar. I wonder how many cups she's had already. The scent of bacon hits me, making my stomach growl as it reminds me I haven't been eating.

"How do you like your eggs?"

"Uhm, I'm not really hungry. I think I'm still a bit confused." It's strangely easy to open up to her. I explain about the missed calls and what Chase told me while I glance around the room. Stacks of papers litter the table along with bills and financial documents. Under those, I discover sketches in various forms of completion. I shift the first one, an apple, to the side and find one of a cat, enormous eyes staring up at me with only half the face finished. Below that is an attempt at a shop interior that looks a bit like the boba shop next to work. He must not have liked it though, because this and the next few sketches below it have scratched lines through them.

"This all seems bonkers, I'm sure. Trust me, though, you don't have to worry about James Barton cheating on you. He's as loyal as they make them. He's just—there's a lot of baggage and he's still learning how to deal with it all."

"We've been comparing patterns," I say flatly.

"What?"

"Not important. I should probably go. I kind of got his address from a mutual friend and I feel like I'm invading his space and—"

"Alexis!" Chase comes in from the back, runs over, and gives me a bear hug, lifting me off the chair. "Fuck, I've been trying to find your number, but his stupid ass has you programmed as something other than your damn name." The lightbulb goes off in his head. "Shit! Your hair. You're Cherry Blossom! I thought it was the flower place! God, I hate him sometimes."

"Oh. I uhm, I got his address from Dani."

"Son of a… I've been calling her since I dropped her off after the party to try to get a hold of you." He sighs and drops onto the stool next to me with a soft smile. "You must be losing your damn mind."

"That's…an understatement." My head is spinning and I understand absolutely nothing that's going on. I can't breathe and it's too hot in here. I'm starving, and to top all that off, no one has told me a damn thing yet.

"Hey, do you want to bring him breakfast?" Natalie asks me, holding up a small plate and a travel mug.

"What?!" I snap. I didn't mean to. I'm so confused, and they're acting like this is normal. If this is James's normal, I'm going to need some time to adjust to the chaos. What the hell have I done?

"Hey," Chase says, taking my shoulders in his big, firm hands. "Breathe. He had a slip, emotionally. Elle does that to him and sometimes it takes a few days to get him out of it. If that's not going to work for you, we understand and I'll break it to him later. If you're everything he's described you as being, then bring him breakfast. It's a lot to take in right now, we're just… I dunno… used to it, I guess. It's easy for us to forget you haven't even known Jimbo for that long."

Unsure of my answer, I stand and stare at the plate.

"Don't tell him I called him Jimbo. He hates it. I do it to annoy him." He shuffles through the stack of sketches and pulls one out, handing it to me. "When James lost his dad, it was like a giant piece of him died right along with him. He started letting go of everything else he cared about. He's scared and a little lost. But I think I know what he's looking for."

I'm staring at my eyes, my face, and my mouth on paper. I almost don't recognize it's me. Not because it's bad, no, it's the opposite. This isn't who I see in the mirror every day, it's how he sees me. The smiles instead of the stress, the relaxed look in the corner of my eyes instead of the worry. This is how I feel when I'm around him.

I grab the plate and coffee and stare at Chase. "Upstairs. First door on your left. Don't knock, just barge in. Don't let him give you any bullshit, either. He's a mess, but he's our mess."

Standing in front of the door, I soak in the house, smells, and people. I'm second guessing everything, thinking I shouldn't be here. As I consider leaving, I hear a muffled sob on the other side.

His room is dim, making it difficult for my eyes to adjust. However, I can still make out a lump of blankets on the bed. I set the coffee and plate on a desk, careful not to put it on anything that might be important, and climb in next to the lump. He groans, clearly annoyed. After almost two days, I finally relax. He's home, and he's okay. But are we?

"Chase, I don't fucking—strawberries?" He pulls the covers down and I can just make out his red-rimmed eyes and his messy bed head. "Angel?"

"Hi," I whisper back, brushing the hair from his eyes.

"Why…how did you…?"

"I was worried. You just…you left." He stares at me for a long time before he pushes the blanket back and I crawl under them and cuddle next to him. "Natalie asked me to bring you breakfast."

"Alexis…I—I'm sor—"

"No, don't worry about that. Let's get you better before you start worrying about explaining or apologizing. I'm not mad, I was just…worried."

He stares at me until his fingers find my face, tracing tender shapes along my skin like he's seeing me for the first time—even though he can barely see me in the low light. I can make out the dark circles under his eyes and what was stubble is now a full beard. I don't think he's slept since he left my apartment.

"It's okay. We're okay, if you still want us—"

"I do. I do want us. But, it's not okay. I'm not okay." He pulls me closer and I tuck my head under his chin. "I don't know how, but you found me."

"I had Dani get me your address. I'm sorry if that's too much. I didn't want you to be alone."

"No, I mean…I don't mean that you came here, I mean that you found me. There's finally something that isn't darkness trying to swallow me whole." His voice is gravelly and low and I wonder when the last time he spoke was. "You were sleeping like an angel…my angel. I'm sorry I left. I should have told you, but I didn't want to scare you."

"Are you going to be okay, Jamie?"

"I don't know. I really don't know, but… I think I'll at least be better now. I should have called, but I didn't think I could handle the disappointment in your voice." He kisses my head softly and I can feel the wet tears in my hair. There's heartbreaking pain and sadness in his voice.

"I'm not disappointed, not at all."

"I don't know how to protect you. I want to, Alexis. More than anything, I want to protect you, but I don't know how. Between your parents and my sister, I just don't know how."

"I don't want you to protect me, Jamie. I want us to be there for each other."

He loosens his grip on me and rubs his eyes. "There's more you should know. A lot more."

He shifts and sits on the edge of the bed, then looks at me over his shoulder. Leading me into the bathroom, he flicks on a light. The room fills with a yellow glow as James opens the medicine cabinet full of tiny bottles. I'm not sure exactly what he's showing me at first, but then I notice they're all his. Every one of them—and there are at least fifteen—are his prescriptions. I'm unfamiliar with some of them, but there are a few I recognize from my own medicine cabinet.

I reach into the cabinet and pull down a bottle, holding it out to him. "Teach me," I say, lacing the fingers of my free hand into his. "What should I know? What one helps with what thing and how can I help?"

He stares at me again, blinking like I'm speaking German.

"If we're going to do this, I need to know how to help you, Jamie."

"Alexis, I'm a fucking wreck!" he yells, but he doesn't mean to. His voice drops to a shaky whisper, "Even on the days I remember to take this shit, I can't…I can't function. I can't hold down a job. I can't do my art. I can't fix the house. I can't even get out of fucking bed."

"You're out of bed now."

"What?" He falls back onto the edge of the counter, dropping my hand and covering his face. "You can't want this, Lexi. You can't. You deserve someone who can—"

"Make me happy? Because you do, Jamie, and I do want this, and you, and us."

I cup his face, stroking his beard with my thumbs. He wants to argue with me again, but I cut him off.

"You *can* function, but some days are harder than others. You *can* hold down a job, because Sam still hires. You *can* fix the house, because I was able to walk up every one of those stairs to get to you. You *can* get out of bed, and on the days you can't, there's nothing wrong with that. You're a man, Jamie, not a superhero." I take both his hands in mine and kiss his knuckles. He doesn't fight me when I take the hem of his shirt and lift it over his head.

"What are you doing?"

"Helping you take a shower."

"Why?" Pain and confusion lace the question.

"Well, for one, you're still wearing the clothes you had on at my place two days ago. Also, because I wasn't lying when I said I love you. This is what love is, Jamie. Good days are magical, but shitty days are going to happen. They'll happen to me, too. If we're lucky, they won't happen on the same day, but if they do, that's what food delivery and streaming is for." The crease between his eyebrows deepens, and I take hold of the sides of his head and pull him down enough to kiss it.

"You've done more in the last week than any of these bottles have done in months."

"Doesn't mean they can't help you. You need to take them or they won't work." He turns me around and stares at me through the reflection in the mirror. "Oh, and you *can* make art. I saw that sketch of me downstairs."

"I drew that when I came home. The house was cold and empty, and I needed your warmth. I hoped that drawing you would help, but it wasn't the same. I couldn't even draw you right."

"The sketch is beautiful, Jamie. I don't think I've ever seen myself like that, through the eyes of someone who cares about me."

"I do care about you, Lexi. I care so damn much. But I'm going to fail again. I'm going to fuck this up. I always do."

"You've hardly given us a chance, pretty boy. Now come on, we'll go one step at a time. You got out of bed. Now let's shower and see where we can go from there. It may just be back in bed to eat your cold breakfast. I'm here, James, and I'm not leaving."

His chin quivers and his eyes well with tears once more. He hugs his arms around me and holds me with his head buried against my neck as he cries tears he's held in for too long.

"I love you, Alexis."

HOLLYWOOD

James

CHAPTER 30
ALL I NEED
AWOLNATION

I STAND OUTSIDE the door for a while, her hand in mine. I'm not back to my level of normal yet, but I'm getting there. Between ghosting her, the pills, the depression cocoon in the bed, and everything else, I expected her to run away. No one should want to stay with someone as broken as me, but her strength and resilience push me forward. She keeps asking if I want to stop or if this is too much. I can't remember the walk out here, but I'm standing in front of the garage studio door.

"Why haven't you opened it since that night?"

"I'm too scared. Too afraid that if I do, maybe I'd let out whatever was left of him. I'd be accepting he was really gone. If I kept this door shut, I wouldn't have to let him go."

"Is that why the room upstairs is shut, too? Was that his room?"

I nod as my hand slides down the weathered door, tracing the cracks and imperfections like I'm reacquainting myself to a long-lost lover. My *real* sanctuary—the place where I could flourish and create in peace. I turn to glance back at the house and I can see Chase and Natalie standing by a window, watching.

"I tried to clean out his room after the funeral," I reply as the texture of the door brings back memories. "I got through his closet and put the things downstairs so I could work on getting a collection put together to donate. It's what he wanted. He always said when he died, I shouldn't keep anything but the art that I wanted."

I take a deep breath and slip the key into the lock, half wondering if it will even open and only a little disappointed at the telltale click as the key turns.

"When I went back upstairs and saw the empty closet, I lost it. I didn't leave the room for three days. Natalie came to check on me and found me. She said I had passed out at the foot of the bed; she was sure I was dead. I spent two days in the hospital."

"You have a support system, now we just have to learn how to use them."

"*We*?" I whisper, the hint of a smile pulling at my mouth as she nods. She squeezes my hand as I put the key back in my pocket.

"I was like that too, kind of." She shares. "When my dad died, I wanted to keep everything. I would sneak into their room when my mom wasn't around and take his shirts and hats, anything I could get away with and shove them into my backpack. I kept it hidden in the back of my closet. I didn't want her to throw him away. That's what it felt like when she donated his stuff after the funeral."

She doesn't need to be here, doesn't need to go through this with me. She should be at home or out with friends, out living her life. Yet here she is, clutching my hand and ready to walk right into the room that holds my grief. Ready to take it on with me. One step at a time.

"Lexi..."

"Come on, don't back out on me now, pretty boy. We can do

this. If you want to take a break, we can. But we have to do this someday, so why not today?"

We. She really means it.

Behind the door, time stands still in the room. A cup with brushes sit on the bench he worked at, waiting for his return. Tubes of paint lay beside it at the ready. His palette is on the floor, probably knocked there by a rodent of some sort.

"Oh my god," Lexi whispers next to me, staring at the painting on my dad's easle. "Who is she?"

"His sister. That's the last thing he ever worked on, didn't even get to finish it. She passed when I was a kid."

"She's beautiful. The way he painted her eyes is just…it's incredible. So lifelike."

I walk into the room to my station, and that's when I remember why dad's palette is on the floor. Cans and brushes litter the area, violently scattered around the room. Splatters of paint go up the wall, some even reaching the roof. The piece I was working on that night lays shredded on the ground, the frame broken like a toothpick. The rage and grief come rushing back to me, crashing against me like waves in a hurricane. I can't hear anything but the blood pumping through my body while my heart races and I fall to my knees.

Dad.

"I forgot. I forgot I came back. I—" My lungs are tight and I can taste the paint in the air. I'm hyperventilating and I need to get out of here. I shouldn't be here. Then I see her. She steps in front of me and her hands cup my face, thumbs softly stroking my grown out beard.

"Look at me, not everything else. Focus on me. Tell me what you were making that night." I stare at her, unable to answer. "It grounds you when you talk about it—about the art and the process—so tell me about it."

"It was…it was a painting. It was supposed to be for him, a gift. I'd been working on it and kept it covered. He used to tease me that he was going to peek when I walked out of the room, but he never did. He never got to see it."

"Did you get to finish it?"

"I finished it that night." I pick up a jagged and splintered piece of wood, running my fingertip over the end as the memories come back in another powerful wave. "We kept wood pieces in a bucket across the room. I'd picked out some that were still in good shape and wanted to make a frame. I'd been working for fourteen hours straight. I was so tired, I passed out on the couch."

Lexi helps me stand and I toss the wood onto the pile of rubble that sits on top of my bench. I used to keep it so clean, like dad taught me. I blow out a breath and start straightening up the things on the bench. Her hand closes over mine as she picks up the brushes and places them in a nearby cup that—miraculously—hasn't broken.

"I had trouble when I was a kid, with a lot of things. When I stopped talking, my…my moth…" I take a deep breath, counting slowly down from ten and breathing with her. "My mother wanted to ship me off to some specialist. The night before I was supposed to go, dad found me in his art room, painting. That was the night he packed my things, and we left."

"He just took you?"

"The paintings he found, the ones I'd done that night, were of my mother. They were of some of the things she did to me. It was my last silent scream for help. She, uhm, she didn't want a little boy, and she made sure I knew it. She hit me with things, anything she could find. She would…do things to humiliate me in public. Traumatize the shit out of me. When she got pregnant with Elle, things got worse. Mom had a brother, sick fucker, and she let him—" The brush in my hand snaps and I drop it, jumping from the noise.

"You're safe. I'm here. You only need to talk about what you can. Don't force yourself, Jamie."

"She got pregnant right before their divorce and she did it on purpose, to trap my dad. She had all the papers drawn up and was just waiting to spring on him as soon as she knew the baby was healthy. It was all about her fucking company. I still don't understand it, something about shares that would go to her heirs or something."

There's a sniffle from somewhere behind me and realize Chase and Natalie are there. Not to judge me or force me to move on, but to show their support and be there if I need them. Lexi is right. They're my support system and it's a damn good one.

"Dad realized she was the reason I stopped talking. He found the bruises and scars just after we left. I think I was six, and no one knew because Mom was good at hiding them or blaming me for them. She was trying to use me to get leverage in the divorce. Courts tend to side with the mothers and she could lay it on thick, but around that time, the cops found out about her brother. Dad finally had the upper hand, even though he hated why. He could have taken the money and had power over the company. Instead, he made a stupid agreement with her that basically gave her everything she wanted so long as he got to keep custody of me. He tried for Elle, too. He tried so many times to get Elle. Especially after he found out mom had shipped her off to some fucking boarding school in the middle of nowhere…Switzerland, I think. I don't know."

"You're doing great, Jamie. Take your time."

"After Dad and I moved, he found me a doctor who worked with me while Dad started studying more about art therapy. Eventually, they taught me how to paint my feelings." Muscle memory has taken over as my hands move around the table, putting things where they once belonged, orderly and neat. "My father was also the one that taught me art was messy, like life. He saw how calming it was when I'd start putting everything away. I was methodical about it, like it was soothing. Everything had a place, everything but me."

She doesn't ask me directly, but I can sense the question when her hand runs along my side, over the scars. I nod and she gives me a tender smile that says I've said enough for now. I don't have to tell her which household items became weapons in my own mother's hands or the words she wielded just as sharply. I've opened the door; it doesn't mean everything needs to rush out at once.

Tears run down my cheeks, but I turn to her anyway, cupping her face for just a moment before I pull her close and sob into her shoulder. It doesn't hurt the way I thought it would. I know it's because of her and the way she helped me through this. She's given me a safe space, somewhere I'm allowed to feel what I need to. She's my safe space.

I pull back and look at her, and that's when it hits me. In a frenzy, I rush around the room, looking under everything until I spot the pile of canvases, already mounted and ready to go. I find one that's undamaged, then I scrounge through drawers and boxes until I find a full set of charcoals my dad gave me. I drop to my knees with the canvas and rip open the pack, mumbling to myself.

"James?"

"The eyes."

"What?"

"EYES! You said her eyes, the way Dad did her eyes. I fucked up the eyes. Every time I draw you, it's the eyes I get wrong. It's too much light!"

She kneels next to me, her hand on my back as my hands race over the fabric. I hear her breath stop as she watches me work. As she watches *herself* appearing on the canvas.

"I couldn't see it before. I couldn't get it right."

"See what?"

"The darkness."

"They'll be shrouded in the night sky that matches the shadows of my soul." Natalie's voice whispers the words with me from the doorway. "They'll be the reminder that the brilliance of stars can only be seen in darkness."

"Martin Luther King, Jr?" Chase whispers.

"Inspired by, yeah." Nat replies. "Jamie's take on the words."

I wrote them not long after my divorce. Natalie had been texting me almost daily at that point, trying to encourage me to date again, but I said I hadn't found the right person. That was my answer when she asked me to describe the right person. I'm a little dramatic when I'm depressed, but I was right. Lexi knows the dark, but she doesn't hide from it. She embraces it as her own and that's why she could always see my darkness. It's why I was so drawn to her from the start.

I grab Lexi's face and pull her to me, our mouths crashing together like freight trains that have run off course. I want her. I need her. Not just now, always. She breaks the kiss and leans back. Her face is a mess with streaks of charcoal from my fingers and somehow, it's made her more captivating.

"You're not a single light in the darkness. Your my gothic muse. You are the darkness that makes the light more brilliant." I trace her bottom lip with my thumb. "I'm not afraid anymore. I'm not afraid of love or life so long as it's with you. All I want is to drown in you. You're my ocean. My air. My home."

Lexi stares at me and I worry I've gone too far, said too much. Then she grabs my face and kisses me back, matching my ferocity.

"Ooh, I know where this is going. Come on, Coop," Natalie says softly as she shuts the door behind her.

We're all over each other in an instant, pulling and tugging at clothes—so many clothes. Our mouths can't seem to leave each other as the kiss intensifies and deepens. We're drinking from the last fountain on earth while the world burns into oblivion around us.

"James?" Her voice is airy and beautiful.

I pull back, holding her face again. I can see her worry, her fears. I can read it all now, like a book written only for me to decipher.

"I will never leave you. I will never let you go. I will never hurt you. I'll stand next to you forever." I run my nose up hers and close my eyes. I want to feel this moment. "I want your tomorrow, your yesterdays, your nows…I want you always."

"I want you, too."

I smile against her lips and kiss her again while she grabs my face and leans backward, pulling me down to the floor with her. I trace kisses along her jaw and to her ear while I settle on top of her.

"Open your legs for me, Angel."

She's so wet that I slide into her with one deep thrust, and we moan together. I lock eyes on hers as the soft squeak slips through her perfect lips. Already she's blissed out and we both know this is not a marathon session. I'm still as we look at each other, feeling each other for the first time. Her body tightens around my cock and I let loose a high-pitched whimper. I don't think I've ever made that noise before. This woman is a sledgehammer, breaking down long-standing barriers and dragging me to her heart. She's my escape from the prison I've built myself. She's my freedom. She's the one who will slay my monsters over and over, and all I want is to worship her for eternity.

Her fingers curl in my hair and her legs wrap around me, pulling me deeper. She sounds primal and exotic as I pull all the way out and thrust slowly back into her, releasing her own demons that have held her captive. I watch her find her strength and her power as she takes all of me.

"Say that you're mine," I whisper in a shaky breath. "Say it, Alexis. Tell me you want me."

"For as long as you're mine to have, James. Yes."

"Always. I'm yours forever."

Heat builds rapidly inside me and we're dancing on the edges of bliss. Her back arches as my hips take over on their own. Our voices echo nothing but our names, clashing and tumbling together. My head falls to her shoulder as we gulp the dusty studio air, and she holds me there, whispering promises until we both fall asleep.

Waking up, I feel her fingers tracing over my scars. In my dreamy haze, I can see night outside the window, stars if I squint hard enough. I kiss her forehead and smile before I get up and head across the room to my dad's bench. Clearing the clutter, I open an old record player to find *Rumors* still sitting there waiting to be played again. My dad was in love with Stevie Nicks and even said she was his muse. As "Dreams" fills the air, I grab a couple of blankets from a trunk and walk back to the woman who forever holds my heart. Unlike dad, I have my muse here in more than just music.

"Fuck, you're beautiful."

She looks at herself and laughs. "I'm naked on a dirty garage floor and covered in art supplies."

"Exactly. You have no idea how badly I want to run into the house and get one of my cameras." I hold out my hand and help her stand, pulling her into my arms where I want her to stay forever.

Her fingers dance over my face and I can see the tears she's trying to fight. "James? Is this…is this what happiness feels like?"

"I sure hope so, Angel. I don't think I could take anymore without dropping dead right here." Her eyes glisten, and mine do, too. "I love you and I can't get enough of you."

"Not to ruin your perfectly romantic moment there, but yeah, I can tell." She glances down and then winks at me.

I wrap a blanket around her and I'm about to lead her over to a couch toward the back when she stops me and pulls me back. Dropping the blanket, she wraps her arms around my neck. "Dance with me?"

"How could I ever say no to you? You saved me, Lex."

"It's not over."

"It never will be, but at least I'm not alone in the dark anymore."

We dance for an eternity, with me running over and changing the records when they'd end. Every time I run back to her, she's full of giggles and kisses and warmth. I'm in my studio and for the first time in my life, I know what it feels like to be genuinely happy. I've found the darkness where I belong, the shadows that will highlight the beauty around me and let me fall in love with it over and over. In love with her.

"I wish my dad was here to see this. Not the sex or us naked—"

"I know what you mean. I do."

"Oh, wait!" I lift her bridal style and carry her over to the couch. I pull on my jeans and dig through a couple of boxes until I find what I'm looking for. "If we're celebrating in the studio, we have to do it right. Do you prefer scotch or whiskey? Or I can run into the house and find some wine—if Natalie hasn't drunk it all yet."

"Whiskey!"

"That's my girl." I curl up with her on the couch and we take turns drinking straight from the bottle, laughing and falling deeper in love into the early hours of the morning.

HOLLYWOOD

James

CHAPTER 31
ACROSS THE UNIVERSE

FIONA APPLE

WE STUMBLE out of the house and into the ride share. It's been a rough few weeks with me fighting the depression and getting back into our work, but Lexi has been there every step of the way. She's spent the time in the house with me, avoiding the apartment whenever she could and not answering her phone. The only time she leaves is to drop things off with Sam.

We've spent almost every night in the studio, sleeping on the couch until I had Chase come over and help me move a spare mattress. The time has been about healing and getting to know each other. What could have easily torn us apart has brought us closer together. Our demons, it seems, have a way of playing well together.

I've set her up at Dad's old station so we can work together, too. It's like she's always belonged there. I also have roll after roll of her covered in paint or other supplies after we've had sex. While I'm eager to develop those, my favorite part is lying in bed together while we work. Sam was right. Her designs and my photos are coming together to create a beautiful thing, like us.

"Hey, good morning. I'm your Lyft driver. There's water under the seat there if you want it and plugs for—"

"Oh my god, yes," Lexi grabs for the water like it's gold, ripping the cap off and guzzling half of it down before handing it to me.

"Hey man," my voice cracks and sounds like gravel from smoking more weed than usual. We're thinking of switching to edibles simply because they hurt less. "I promise we'll be the easiest ride you have all week and a cash tip for you if you turn the music down a few notches."

"Oh, yeah, sure, no problem." He turns the dial down and pops the center console open, handing a pair of cheap sunglasses back. "Looks like she might have forgotten hers."

"Five stars all the way, man, and a ten-page novel of a review about how excellent you are," I say as I slide the glasses over her face. "Here you go, beautiful."

She doesn't say a word, just curls up against me and drapes my arm over her. She's soft snoring before the car leaves our driveway, so I kiss her head and stare out the window, watching the buildings merge into one another. Because of everything going on in our lives, we didn't get to do as many trips as I'd hoped. Sam loves what we've gotten around town, though, and promised us more work together. This day trip is the last one before we hand everything over for the big presentation next week. Lexi wants to head to San Francisco after we're done—no phone, no laptops, and no work, only us. I haven't told her, but I already booked the rooms and have the entire trip planned out. I spent half of the bonus Sam gave us on it, because fuck bills.

I also spent some of the money on a ring. It's not diamonds, but it's more Lexi—cherry blossoms and pink gems.

We pull up to Union Station and exit even less gracefully than we entered the car. We somehow get inside without tripping over each other, and we both stop, staring up at the large signs that try to tell us which way we need to go. Hieroglyphs might be easier this morning.

We get lost three times before we find the right train, but still get a table with a set of seats on either side. Since the train isn't as busy as I had expected, we put our bags on one side of the table and sit on the other. Lexi makes me sit against the window to block the sun, then she cuddles against me and falls back asleep before the train leaves the station.

I work on Lexi's laptop, making quick work of sorting the images we have from our other shoots and getting the next wave of files labeled and set up. It's about five stops into the ride when Lexi finally straightens up and stretches her arms above her head, so I sneak a kiss on her cheek.

"What the…" she pulls the sunglasses off her face. "Where the hell did I get these? Please tell me I didn't buy these from one of those overpriced gas stations?"

"Oh, absolutely not. No, you stole them from a homeless guy after smacking his ass. After that, you ran like a squirrel across traffic, screaming something about the Mandela effect. Don't worry, I recorded it and uploaded it to YouTube. You're a viral hit. I've booked you on the morning news show."

She stares at me with eyes wider than any anime character I've ever seen and I can't hold it in. She smacks me hard, and I deserved it.

"Asshole."

"Yeah, but I'm a fun asshole, and you love me," I hum as I tilt her head toward me and press my mouth hard to hers. She tastes like toothpaste and coffee with a hint of whiskey and, as I'm about to pull away, her hand glides up my leg, pressing against my cock. I gasp when it catches me off guard.

"That's for being an asshole. Actually, it's because I wish this thing had a privacy car so I could suck your cock."

"Listen to that perfectly dirty mouth on my girl."

"You like my dirty mouth. In fact, I bet you want that dirty mouth all over you, don't you?" She leans over and whispers in my ear as she squeezes again, "Tonight, I want you to spank me and call me your dirty slut."

"What did you drink last night? What happened to that sweet, innocent girl I was dating?"

She winks at me. "You must have confused me with someone else. I'm the girl who dragged you into a bathroom stall the first night because I wanted your cock."

"If you don't let go of my cock, I'm going to make a mess. Are you going to explain why you're kneeling under the table with your head in my lap cleaning up that mess when they ask?"

"Wow, Mr. Kinky is on it today, isn't he? I like it."

"Alright," I say as she slides her hand away and I pack up the computer. "Switch places with me so I can put this away. Then we'll have some fun if that's what you want."

"It's about time you figure out you're dating a wild woman who's begging for a good time." We swap seats so she's not totally exposed, and immediately she moves down, putting her ass on the edge of the seat. I slide my hand up her leg and into her shorts. She's not wearing panties, she rarely does anymore.

"Oh, you came prepared to be a brat, did you?" She bites her lip and nods. I nibble her earlobe as the tip of my finger flicks her clit. If she wants to play dirty, I can surely give it my best.

"I love you, Alexis."

"I love you too, James." She gasps softly, gripping my thigh and digging her nails into me. "Fuck, we should have had sex before we left the house."

"You have to be quiet for me, baby. Can you do that? You didn't wear any panties, so I can't shove them in your mouth, and if any of these people hear you, they're going to want a taste of this sweet little pussy."

"I'll be good, sir."

"Mm, I think I like that."

Two fingers slip into her as I bite down on her earlobe. She arches her back, but stays silent. I take a quick glance around. No one has an eyeline of us and the closest person is ten rows up. Pretty sure he's wearing headphones, too. If they don't look too hard, we're nothing more than a couple huddled together and making out. I love California.

"Good girl. How bad do you want to come for me, pretty girl?" Since she's been staying with me, she's embraced some of her kinks. One of them is public places, and the train is a perfect place to play a little.

"I want you to make me soak this fucking seat, sir." She bats her eyes at me, and I move to kiss her and stop, letting my lips ghost hers as soft moans spill from her lips.

"You keep being a brat and I'm going to edge you the whole way there," I whisper, curling my fingers so they're hitting her G-spot. That's when she lets out the cutest little squeak I've ever heard, but cuts it off by slapping her hand over her mouth.

The rhythm of the train and the thrust of my fingers have her biting back screams. The faces she's making are beautiful—works of art that I want to paint and hang all over my house so I can remember every one of them. The train slows for its next stop, and I match pace with it, bringing her down before she's finished.

"Don't stop, I was so close."

"Gotta stop, Cherry Blossom. People are going to be passing through. Besides, the more the train and I edge you, the harder you're going to come for me." I lick my fingers and she slumps in her seat with a whimper.

She watches the passengers milling about, wishing they'd hurry. Someone tries to take the table across from us before they realize it's broken and I laugh at the luck. It's not long before we're rolling again and I take another quick glance around. Just as I start sucking on her neck again, her phone rings. I see the screen and groan loudly. It's not surprising that they broke her down and she's once again answer these calls.

"Answer it, Angel. Let me play with your perfect little cunt while you talk to her."

"Seriously?"

"Fuck yeah, Angel."

"Hello, Mother," she answers, her hand guiding mine between her thighs. She moves the phone away from her mouth and whispers, "Now you have to be quiet, too."

"I bet she'd like it. Hearing you come apart for the devil. Maybe just moan my name once, huh?"

"Eww," she giggles before kissing me quickly.

The second that phone is back against her ear, I've got two fingers shoved inside her and I'm sucking on her neck like a thirsty vampire. My thumb traces tight circles around her clit, I'm done holding back. I hope she fucking screams now.

"Oh! Uhm, no. We, uhm, we hit a bump," she tries to cover for her own gasp. "No, the train. Yes, Mother."

My thumb is working her swollen clit and I can feel her tensing around me. Edging her can wait for another day. I wish I could lay her on the table and devour her in front of everyone while her mother listens.

"M-Mother, I don't think—Oh god! No, I just, I dropped something."

She grabs my arm, squeezing tight as she closes her eyes and opens her mouth in the most incredible silent scream I've even witnessed. Not a peep from her as her cunt pushes against my hand, pulsing as she slides into oblivion.

"Sorry, Mom. I gotta go," she practically slurs the words. "Tunnel.... recep...bad..." She hangs up and tosses the phone on the table. I hold her closer while she comes apart and her body shakes.

"Someday, I'm going to sketch the face you make when you come for me, pretty girl." She gives me the most adorable smile. I hold my fingers up to her lips and she opens her mouth and sucks them clean. "You're a dream come true, Lexi."

"Because I'm as disgusting and dirty as my mother thinks I am?"

"Because you've reminded me how to live." She moves closer and cuddles against me again. "And why I want to."

"I think she invited you to dinner tonight."

"You're kidding."

"Nope. Don't think too much about it. She likes to do that: get my friends to come over so she can embarrass them or me to where they no longer speak to me. She'll probably have Noah there so he can swoop in and save my soul after she berates me for how horribly I treated her or how I gave my body to Satan."

I hold my hands up, giving myself devil horns and flicking my tongue at her until she laughs. "Let's go. Let's show them you're with me and you're happy."

"You think they care if I'm happy?"

"I promise I'll stay calm and we'll have a pleasant conversation. If it goes south, we'll leave. They'll either respect that we're together or we both walk." I kiss her cheek. "Or I could go full neanderthal and fuck you on the dinner table. Tear your pretty clothes right off your body while you scream my name so loud your mom has a heart attack."

"No, I want you all to myself. No one else needs to see how

pretty you are when you fill me up, but we can absolutely play that out on the kitchen table before we go."

We get to our stop and spend a few hours meandering around the small historic town. We start at the Mission first, since it's the farthest spot from the train station. I snap pictures of the exterior, the bookstore, and even get permission to take pictures of the interior. We got a few interesting looks from the caretakers. I guess they didn't think Lexi screaming when I snuck up behind her and grabbed her ass was as funny or cute as I did. We head back outside and I turn the lense on Lexi. She's still so shy around the camera, but fuck, is she beautiful. She's changed my damn life and I can never repay her, but I'm going to do my best.

Lunch is at a small cafe near the train station. It's nothing fancy, but it's calm enough at this time of day that we can get a little more work done. I touch up a few images and send them off to the shop so we can pick them up tomorrow and wrap this part of the project up.

"Can I ask you something?" She holds the sandwich up to me.

While staring at the screen, I take a bite and finish typing the email before closing the lid. "Always, Angel," I reply, giving her my full attention. I can sense the seriousness in her question as she nervously chews her nail.

"Why does your sister hate you so much? What's her deal?"

I take a deep breath and sit back in my chair, trying to think of how to tackle this question. I'm actually surprised it didn't come up sooner. "The short version? Because I was born first and a male. Mom resented that, and passed that on to Elle because it was what she knew. That's the hardest part; I don't blame either of them for how they feel. I just wish they knew that I don't want to take anything from them. I never have."

"Sometimes I think my mom resented Bex and I. Do you know why your mom resented you?"

"Well, for starters, she was convinced I was going to take credit for her work. Like because I was a guy, I would swoop in and take her company once I was old enough. She was born in Russia—I don't even know what part—but her father was…well, kind of a tyrant. When she got older and tried to speak up about it, her father would hit her and tell her it wasn't her place."

"Wow, that's fucked up."

"Yeah. Dad said there was more, but she wouldn't talk about it. While trying to escape him, her sister died of some illness and her brother was killed in a mugging. My dad met her in New York shortly after all of that happened, took care of her, and they got married so she could stay in the country, although he really did love her."

I blow out a slow breath and shake my head. I've never shared this with anyone or fully processed it myself. Dad only told me this stuff a few years ago, shortly after trying to contact my mother and Elle to 'mend bridges', as he put it.

"She said she had feelings for dad, too. I don't know if she ever did, though. Dad put her through college since she was a damn genius on computers. Her father somehow found her and sent another brother to collect money from her. Basically, her father said any money she made was his, and that she *belonged* to him."

"Did they pay him off?"

"Sort of. Money at first and a place to stay." The lump finally forms in my throat. I can only tell part of the story. I thought I could tell her all of it, but I'm not ready. Not yet.

"Is this the uncle the cops caught?"

"Yeah. I heard he died in jail, but I never followed up."

"Hey," she takes my hand, lacing her fingers into mine before

I can hide inside myself again. She was right, she's learned my triggers and tells—or at least most of them. "You wanna go to a petting zoo?"

Sure enough, there's a nearby petting zoo. I take a million photos of Lexi feeding every animal she can. She even threatens to take one of the guinea pigs home, and I have to compromise by promising we'd get a dog. When we get back on the train, I'm exhausted. The late night and early morning finally hitting me and the next thing I know the train lurches to a stop and we're back at Union Station. Lexi is asleep, her head resting on her crossed arms on the table, and I'm wrapped around her protectively.

"Morning, beautiful."

"Afternoon, handsome. Ugh, I think my back is permanently fucked from that position."

"Lucky for you I know some positions to loosen you right up," I laugh, and she elbows me in the ribs. I still can't get over how good it feels to laugh, to honestly laugh. "Okay," I check my watch, "I think we can go to your place and pick up your stuff, have sex, go to my place, have sex again at least twice, and then mess around in the shower before we head out to Hell on Earth —I mean Malibu—for dinner with the Satans."

"You are a menace! Don't forget, we're dog sitting at Chase's house tonight since his brother is on a road trip."

"You just want to fuck in his pool." Before I can kiss her, my phone goes off, nearly falling off the table. I grab it just before it goes and flip it over. Steve's calling me. He never calls.

"Hey Ste—" I don't even get the rest of his name out.

"Dude, I'm in jail. You gotta come get me."

"You're *what*?"

I talk Steve down and finally figure out what's going on, then agree to meet him as soon as I can. I hang up and shake my head. "I need to cancel all the fun we had planned. Steve got pulled over last night on the way home and the cops arrested him. They impounded his car, and he's a fucking mess. They just let him out."

"Why did they arrest him?"

"He said they let him go, claiming it was a mistaken identity issue or something. Fucking Elle, more than likely."

"She can do that?"

"She can…and she already hates Steve. I wish I knew what the fuck she was up to."

"I'll text my mom that we can't make it."

"No, it's fine. We'll go back to my place, I'll go take care of Steve, and meet you at your parent's place."

"Are you sure?"

"Yeah. We'll get through dinner, go feed Lulu and Pongo, and after that I'll do all kinds of dirty things to you in that stupidly big shower of his." I kiss her and get up to gather our things. "It will be payback for him not being in town to help me with Steve."

HOLLYWOOD
Lexi

CHAPTER 32
PAINT IT, BLACK

CIARA

I CHECK my phone again for what has to be the hundredth time, and I know my mother has noticed. James said he'd be here by now, but he's not answering his texts or calls and it's making me nervous. I don't have Steve's number and calling Chase is useless since he's in Atlanta. I'm not worried he's having another episode, but I am worried something else has happened.

So many people have lied to me, this shouldn't surprise me. Broken promises to be there and failed to show. My father promised he'd see me after school. My ex promised he'd help me move out of my parent's house. My new boyfriend stands me up for dinner with my parents. The problem is, this time it doesn't feel right. Not after the time we've been spending together. It doesn't make any sense.

"So, I invited your new…friend. Where is he?"

"He had to work late."

"Mmmhmm. So he stood you up?"

"No, Mother. He had some important photos that had to be processed tonight so they could be delivered to the client first thing in the morning." I lie.

"Sweetheart, he's pushing paper around in some tubs of foul-smelling liquids, not performing open heart surgery." She drains her third glass of wine and is eyeing the bottle. "Besides, the way you're checking your phone tells me he doesn't even care enough to tell you he's running late. He's not showing up. Got his free sample and now he's gone."

"Would that make you happier?" I hear myself say the words and regret them when she slams her hand on the table.

"Alexis, I only want what's best for you. An artist with no stable job who can't show up for dinner is not the right kind of man for you. You should pray that God will forgive you and not leave you with a reminder of your poor choices nine months from now."

That's all I am to her. Bex and I are nothing but reminders of her poor life choices.

"Ah, hello ladies! Dinner smells as delicious as you both look." Noah kisses my mother on the cheek and goes to do the same with me, but I pretend to check my phone and move across the room. He and Ronnie move over to the sink and wash up before heading to the table.

"Catherine. I think you're being too hard on our girl," my stepfather interjects as he sits down at the head of the table. Before he's even finished speaking, my mother is on her feet and running to check the food. "The young man is doing what comes naturally. Someday, you'll be absolutely radiant with a big, round belly, but it should be from a servant of God."

"I don't, we're not..." I take a few breaths, trying not to be sick from the way he's glaring at me.

"Well," Noah pulls out a chair beside my stepfather and motions for me to sit, and reluctantly, I do. His hands fall onto my shoulders with a squeeze. I smell iron and see cuts and bruises on his hands, but I don't say anything. "I think I'll side with Catherine on this one: a good man should be mindful of wasting God's time. Catherine has worked hard on this supper. He could at least be here when he says he will. I'm here right on time, aren't I?"

It seems like a strange question, but I'm still messing with my phone. It's acting strange and I wonder if I've downloaded a virus or something.

"We want to make sure you're taken care of, sweetheart." The lingering attention he gives me sends goosebumps up my arms and legs. There's something on his shirt and his hands are a mess, even though he washed them. "Shouldn't you be in the kitchen, helping your mother serve the meal?"

I stand up, hesitating when I remember I've worn a skirt. Shit. I thought James would be here, so it would be safe, but he's not. He didn't show up. He's not coming. I hurry into the kitchen, but my mother isn't there. Grabbing the nearest dish of food and bring it out to the table, stopping at the side opposite of Ronnie.

"You can't exactly serve the meal if you're going to stand all the way over there, darlin'. Now, come over here and let me see what's for dinner." He's like a snake, coiled and ready to strike, and I know I've fucked up. "Unless you want to skip right to dessert."

I swallow hard and walk over toward him in half steps, trying to take as much time as possible and hoping my mother will be back soon. Hoping James comes through the door.

"Good," he hums. Instead of moving his plate closer to me, he pushes it away, ensuring that I'll have to lean across the table. "Now, do your old man a favor and dish out whatever delicious surprise that bowl has in it."

I take a deep breath and stop for a second. I'm in my head. I'm overthinking everything that's going on and I'm in my head. He won't touch me, not with my mother flitting about the house somewhere, ready to burst in at any minute. Surely not with Pastor Noah right here in the room. I take the spoon with a shaky hand, and as I scoop the mashed potatoes onto his plate, I feel something move over my skirt and grab my ass, pushing me against the table. My stepfather grabs my arm, twisting it so I can't move. There's a quick pull and I hear fabric tear as Noah rips my underwear off.

The sound of the dish shattering and the spoon clanging against the floor would be deafening if it wasn't for the blood rushing through my ears.

"We're doing this for your own good, Alexis. With a child, you'll learn responsibility and how to keep a respectable house for your new husband," Noah whispers harshly in my ear. "Of course, by that, I mean me."

"I do wish I could be there later when you explain to your little boyfriend why you left your daddy's house with no panties on. Listen to you justify why another man's fingers squeezed you so tight you bruised." He leans in, but I turn my face away. He grabs a handful of my hair and yanks it. "Even better will be when you explain to that pretty boy why someone else's cum is sliding out of your pussy and how the baby growing in your fat belly ain't his?"

"Good thing we already took care of that, huh *Angel*?" Noah says, grinding against me and shoving his hands into my shirt. "No more whoring around, you're all ours now."

I'm fighting back sobs because it's all I can do. I don't fight. I can't run away. There's only me, frozen. Scared. Alone.

"Oh you're being such a good girl for us, baby. Just like on your birthday." Ronnie grabs my face and turns it toward him. "Now, as soon as we're done, you're going to sign some papers for us. Make this binding more than just in the eyes of god."

"No," I whimper. "Please, no."

"You'll learn that I am a very patient man," Noah whispers, making sure I feel his erection through his pants. "but even patience has its limits. Once we consummate our union, you'll learn to serve us, like your mother does. I can't wait to have you barefoot and pregnant. We're gonna keep you that way."

I close my eyes. I'm not here. I'm not here. I'm anywhere but here.

I try to move, to get away, but Ronnie pushes me down, holding my face against the table. Noah lifts my skirt and kicks my legs open and I try not to move anymore, not to make a sound. I know if I struggle, it will make it worse. I feel the tears start, but I make no noise.

"Alexis, what is all this commotion?" My mother yells from down the hall, her footsteps coming closer. She comes back into the room in time to see them release me and pull me off the table. For a split second, I think she's seen them. "How could you?"

My heart leaps. Finally! She's finally caught him and she'll believe me this time. She'll help me and she'll understand everything that's happened. She'll see I wasn't lying and I'll have a mother again.

Then, everything shatters like the plate on the floor.

"That was your grandmother's china, Alexis! What in the name of the lord himself were you thinking?"

I want to scream.

"I'm sorry, Mother! It slipped." She couldn't have missed that. She was right there. She had to have seen what he was doing. She had to have seen him holding me down. Bex was right, she's never been our mother.

"It's alright, Catherine. She's simply excited about the news.

Now, go back to the other room and we'll discuss the dish later. Pastor Noah and I need to finish up."

"You should have put it down before you started serving! This is why we have to save you from that loser. How are you going to serve God and Pastor Noah if you can't even serve dinner?" She crosses her arms over her chest, cinching her sweater shut.

I blink back tears and realize that whether or not she knows it, she's given me the chance I need. I race for the door, grabbing my bag and my keys as I go. I can't get to the car fast enough, and when I do, I slam the door shut and lock it. My mother yells and she chases after me, but as I turn back, all I can see is Ronnie and that smirk as he leans against the door frame, licking his lips. I hold back another wave of tears until I'm far enough down the street that they can't see me from the house. I pull over and release a sob that seems to come from every inch of my body.

I drive home in a haze, not realizing I've made it until I glance around and find myself in the parking lot of my building. I'm scared to get out of my car. I am scared to move. I know they're not here, but that doesn't make it any better. I pull my keys out and hold them between my fingers, staring at the dark hallway I have to go down to get to my apartment. They could be there. They could have gotten here before me easily. Shadows move and I almost scream when one of the other tenants steps into the light, headed toward their car.

I sprint across the parking lot and to the elevator, looking over my shoulder every few seconds and trying to listen to every noise. But I can't because his voice is an echo trapped in my mind.

When I'm finally in my apartment, I lock the door and turn on every light I can—kitchen, hallway, bathroom, and even the closet. A fluorescent glow floods my apartment. No one could hide in here, not that I think anyone is. It doesn't matter though, because I can still feel him, smell him, hear him. I strip off my clothes, shoving them into a trashcan in the kitchen, and run to the bathroom. I don't even wait for it to heat up before I'm covered in soap, but it's not enough. When the heat finally hits my skin, it's scalding and still not hot enough simultaneously.

While I'm in the shower, there's a loud knock on my front door. I stand still, unable to move. Maybe I can scream. Maybe the doctor next door is home and he'll hear me. My mind races through every scenario where Ronnie or Noah have a key to my apartment. Every way they could come in and finish what they started. When I hear the door open, I'm sure it's them. They'll hear the shower. They're going to find me. I crouch down, making myself as small as I can, sobbing silently.

"Lex?"

I cover my ears with my hands and let the water flow over them, trying to block out all the noise. I should grab my phone, but when I look over, it's fallen on the floor on the other side of the room.

"Alexis?" there's a soft knock on the bathroom door. "Lexi? Answer me, please. I can hear the shower."

I don't move. I can't.

"Fuck this—" There's a loud thud, and a grunt followed by a rush of cold air as the door whips open.

"No. Please, no!" I'm screaming and close my eyes tight against what's coming. But it doesn't come.

The hands aren't rough, they're gentle and small. The voice isn't demanding, it's comforting and familiar. The smell isn't turning my stomach. It's sweet and safe.

The cold air sweeps over me as the pelting, burning water

stops. I'm staring at Dani's confused brown eyes when she drapes the towel over me.

"Hey, I've been trying to reach you for like three hours." Her words are barely making sense to me yet. "Guess you already know, though. Come on, Coop is there with him and I told him I'd bring you."

"W-w-what?" I manage through clattering teeth and tears. "W-w-where?"

"Where? To the hospital. Wait, that's not why you're in the shower crying? Lex, where have you been? What happened to you?"

"My…stepfather…and…they…" I try to remember, but my mind won't allow me to. It wants me to melt into the safe arms around me and sleep for days. I think harder, and it all comes flooding back. The table, the dish shattering, the hands.

No escape. No hope. No one was there to save me.

"Hun?"

"N-n-n-o! No, don't touch me!"

"Shit, I'm calling the cops," Dani reaches for her phone. She knows what he's capable of.

"NO! You can't. He knows too many of them. T-they didn't believe me." I couldn't say anything more, so I cry again. Sobbing between the words. "They'll say I lied. They'll all tell them I'm a worthless whore."

"Do you want me to call your sister or Sam? Anyone?"

My brain is too slow to catch that she hasn't listed James as someone to contact. Too foggy to wonder why she wants me to go to the hospital. Does he know? Was he somehow a part of it? Is that why he wasn't there?

"James…he was supposed to meet me there. He never showed up. He left me there, alone." I sob while she rocks me. "He promised. He promised he'd protect me."

"Shit, this is too much." she sighs under her breath and cups my face, forcing me to look at her. She's crying, too. Sadness and pity fill her eyes. "Lexi, James is in the hospital. There was some kind of fight when he went to help Steve pick up his car."

My heart drops through the floorboards, shattering several floors below. Maybe this is all a nightmare. Maybe I'm still asleep on the train, in his arms and safe. I'm not though, I'm still trapped in hell and now I've endangered James.

"Come on, let's get you dried off and over there. It's safer than being here alone. I know someone there you can talk to. He's really sweet."

HOLLYWOOD

James

CHAPTER 33
ALL APOLOGIES
SINÉAD O'CONNOR

YOU BOUGHT HER A RING? *Ain't that sweet? Too bad you'll never see her again.*

We're gonna end you, then we're going to break her. When we're done, she won't even whisper your name. She'll be our whore, and you'll be six feet under.

The voices in my head pull me out of one nightmare and into another. Fists and pain. Blood fills my mouth. I'm trying to yell and fight back, but I can't. I can't get any air, no matter how loud my lungs scream. The voices won't stop. It feels like a gorilla has used my body as a punching bag.

My mouth is dry and everything feels strange. I can't open my eyes yet, but I catch noises in those brief moments when I'm conscious. I recognize Coop talking to someone, but I can't make out words, only the sound. More sounds follow, lights going by, and more voices. I can't actually see the lights, only the change from bright to dark as we pass under them. I must be in a hallway.

We stop and there's more commotion. I want to get someone's attention; I want to know what's going on, but it's like I'm stuck in the dark. Fuck, I can't think or move. I'm cold.

Alexis.

"See, JimJamJabber, I told you I'd get you a better room." I can tell Coop is pacing from the sound of his shoes on the tile. Click clack click sniffle clack. It's like a metronome and it keeps putting me to sleep over and over. My throat hurts so much, but I feel a cough building. When it finally comes, it's like I'm being hit by a train. I can't fight it, but I can't take the pain much longer. Coop yells, bringing more commotion, and far too many hands.

I wake up and I'm breathing normally again and Coop is back to pacing. I can see him now, or at least some of him. Everything is still hazy.

"Hey! JimJab! Welcome back, buddy. You gonna actually wake up?"

There's a moan, and I think it's me because it hurts.

"Works for me, but dude, seriously, don't talk." He turns and pulls a chair over. My brain can't process what's going on, so it looks like he's moving at double speed. Sometimes, there's three of him. I wish he'd stop before I throw up. "You had us scared out of our heads, man. We thought you were dead."

He's freaking out, but I'm still not sure what's going on. He's having trouble looking at me, which is fine since I still can't make him out clearly. Eventually, his rambling turns into what I want. Information.

"You were with Stevie, picking up his car at some crazy ass junkyard impound lot. Steve went with a guy to pull his car up from the back and when he got back, you were knocked the fuck out." He smooths his hair back and takes a long breath. "Asshole at the junkyard says he's got no cameras and everyone's claiming they didn't witness anything."

"Steve's downstairs giving a statement." He winces. "Do, uhm, should I tell you the damage?"

It's barely a nod, but the pain shoots through me and my head erupts. I must black out because when I open my eyes again, Coop's on the other side of the room and I'm pretty sure Steve is with him.

I'm forgetting something. Something I can't remember, but I'm sure it's important. The words I recalled when I woke up have slipped back into my mind and I can't pull them out, but they were important, too.

"Hey, you're up again," Coop bounces back over to my bedside. He needs to stop moving like that.

I remember a name and mouth it to him when he stops me from trying to talk.

"Dani has her. She's bringing her here when they're…when they're done." His answer is too blunt, too unsure.

"Shit, Jamie, I'm…" Steve's face has no color as he looks at me. In all the years I've known him and all the pain I've seen him go through, not once have I seen him cry. Until now. "I'm sorry. I'm so fucking sorry. I didn't know."

I try to talk again, but Coop is in my face. "Stop! Seriously!" He's more worried than angry. "You're not supposed to talk because they… fuck, man. They really tried to kill you. They tried to crush your damn windpipe, Jaim. They had a fucking noose around your neck!"

Coop slumps into the chair behind him and starts listing off injuries. Broken orbital bone, broken ribs, skull fracture, collapsed lung…he keeps going, but I can't concentrate on what he's saying until he leans back in and waits for me to look at him again after Steve rushes out of the room. "He's blaming himself for what happened to you and…shit. Jamie, you were supposed to meet Lexi after you were done getting Steve's car. Do you remember that?"

I nod.

"Jamie, they, uhm, Dani's got her in the ER to get checked out. She, uhm." When one of the five billion monitors I'm hooked up to starts screaming, Chase tries to keep me calm. "Breathe, buddy."

Coop's crying and having trouble finding the words.

"I can't—I don't know how to—" He wipes his eyes and then closes them. "They tried to rape her, Jamie. Her fucking stepfather and some other guy named Noah."

I can't process what he's just said. It's like the words don't make sense except for one. Noah.

Hold him down, Noah. I'll get some rope.

I'm trying like hell to move my hand, and it's like learning how hands work all over again. One won't move at all and it feels like it's strapped down, the other I'm inching toward the edge of the bed, biting back the pain. I finally reach Coop's hand, and he jumps, then looks down at me. I mouth the name over and over again until his eyes light up.

"Noah?" I nod, fucking exhausted. I have to stay awake, though. At least until Coop figures out what I'm trying to tell him. "Do you know him?"

I pinch my index finger and thumb together and do the best I can to pull my wrist up. It's the closest I can get to signing. I learned ASL when I wasn't speaking and Coop learned it because he's my friend, but we haven't used it in a while.

"Wait, shit, I remember this one." He snaps his fingers and hits his forehead with the palm of his hand as he tries to remember. "FIND!"

My hand drops back down to the bed as he shouts the word again and Steve comes in, trying to figure out what's going on.

"He signed 'find'. I told him about Lex and—wait, Dani

found Alexis?" He stares at me and I roll my eyes. "Don't be a dick. This is hard!"

"What else did you say?" Steve asks, joining the most frustrating game of charades ever.

"Find…find… I don't know… find…he said…*NOAH*! Find Noah?" He looks at Steve after I nod and then back to me. Some days I think I can see the wheels turning inside Coop's head when he thinks hard enough. Right now, I'm watching his face go from complete confusion to realization to rage. He and I have always had this kind of connection. "They did this to you, then went after her? Jesus fuck."

"Shit, I'll get the cops. They're downstairs with Alexis," Steve yells as he runs out the door just before I pass out again.

I was supposed to protect her. I promised her.

There's a distinct scent in the room. It's what wakes me up the next time. It breaks through the cleaners and antiseptic hanging so heavily in the room I can pick them out with a broken nose. It's a sweet scent that makes my heart monitor race. As badly as I want to open my eyes, I'm too scared to see the pain in her eyes.

"Hey," Steve whispers, "Chase and I are going to grab a coffee. Do you want anything?"

"No. I'm okay, thanks."

"Text us if anything changes and we'll come running."

I hear the door close, then her voice again. "You can open your eyes now. I know you're awake again."

I force my one working eye open. When I see her, the pain disappears, replaced by broken butterflies trying to fly with torn wings. She leans over, her lips grazing mine, and I whimper as she pulls away from me.

"I'm sorry, did I hurt you?" she asks in a panic, but I shake my head and try to smile. My eye never leave hers as she moves to the other side of the bed and picks my hand up. The second she does, I squeeze as hard as I can since I'm fairly sure a baby has more grip than I do right now. She pushes the hair away from my eyes, careful not to brush against the one I still can't open. "Guess you were tired. You've been out for two days."

I open my mouth, but she covers my lips with two fingers. "No talking, pretty boy. Besides, I already know what you're going to say."

I want desperately to hold her, to tell her how sorry I am. I want to tell her I'm here for her, that I've got her now and she can fall apart if she needs to. She needs to, I can tell, because the stars in her eyes have gone out.

"Wakey, wakey! No eggs and bakey for you, James, sorry man," Sam sings as he comes into the room three days later with bags of food. There's some guy in a suit following him and carrying coffees. I'd kill for a coffee right now. "Where's Lex?"

"Therapy," I whisper, and Chase smacks me. He rolls his eyes when I add, "Sorry."

He hasn't left the hospital since I got here, taking turns with Lexi to make sure someone is always in the room with me but also giving each other breaks from the boring room and that fucking beeping that never stops. It's why they keep people drugged in hospitals. I swear, how else is anyone getting any sleep in here? I wonder how much the studio and his agent hate me right now.

"Alright, we can at least get your part of things started. This is Stan Morgan. He's a lawyer, a damn decent lawyer, and I've hired him for you and Lexi. Stan, this is James Barton and his buddy Chase Cooper."

"Nice to meet you, Mr. Barton." He shakes my hand, carefully. I'm not sure what to make of all this. I still have a lot of pain medication running through me and it's made me more than a little loopy when I can stay awake. "Mr. Cooper, my kid, loves your movies. Before I start, though, I have to ask James if he wants you and Sam in the room for all this."

I nod. If I can't trust Sam and Coop, then I'm beyond fucked.

"I don't have all the details yet since it is an active and ongoing investigation, but they have arrested both Ronald Miller and Noah Jones for their assault on both you and Ms. Strauss. James, I've tried a lot of cases, and looking at the police reports, these two are going away for a long time. There was evidence all over them, their vehicle, and the house. They were so sure they'd get away with it; they were both still wearing blood stained clothing when the police showed up."

Lexi slips in behind him and sits on the edge of the bed, holding my hand while Morgan goes over more of the details and his plans moving forward. It's a lot to take in, especially right now, with everything so raw for both of us. Lexi is blaming herself for all of it. I'm blaming myself for all of it, and neither of us is ready to have the conversation we need to have about the situation. We sign some forms to get things rolling after Sam insists on paying for all of our legal fees. He said we could pay him back after we sue the living hell out of that mega church Lexi's stepdad was running.

He's packing things up when Lexi finally asks her burning question, but I also know she's afraid to hear the answer. "Did the police say anything about my mother?"

"They brought Catherine Strauss-Miller in for questioning. There's a chance the prosecutor will offer her some leniency if she testifies against them, assuming she has anything to offer. It looks like her lawyer is going to take the battered wife defense."

When he leaves, Lexi climbs into the bed next to me. "How was therapy?" I ask as I kiss her forehead and put my good arm around her. We've found the one or two positions I can hold her in without getting her tangled in medical equipment or me doubling over in pain. We're making it work, which is kind of our thing anyhow.

"Fine."

Before I can ask her more, the spitting image of her—except with brown hair and a tan—bursts through the door.

"Lex?!" That has to be Bex. She strides over and the pair embrace.

"I got here as fast as I could. Dani called me, but I didn't have my phone on and I'm so sorry! I got the first flight I could and then a bunch of other flights after it," Bex mumbles into Lex's sweater as they rock back and forth, crying together. After a few minutes, Lex pulls away and turns back to me. "Uhm, Bex, this is Jamie. Jamie, this is my sister, Bex."

"Holy shit, who did a number on you?!"

I smile, then wince. I forget that smiling still hurts like a bitch.

"Ronnie," Lex answers, then looks at the floor. "Ronnie and another guy, Noah. Then they came to the house. They acted like nothing was going on. Like they hadn't just beat someone to the brink of death because of me."

"NOPE! This is *not* your fault. Where is that son of a bitch?" Bex shouts. I like Bex already. "I'm going to shoot that fucking bastard in his goddamn dick." Lexi grabs Bex's arm as she tries to leave and pulls her back. "What? I'm serious! I'm not letting them get away with this shit. Where are they?"

"Jail. They arrested both of them for what they did to Jamie… and me." Lexi looks so small. The therapy is helping her, but I'm not sure I'll ever get the old Lexi back. "I'm sorry, Bex. I should have listened to you. You were right about mom, she knew what they were planning."

"I'm sorry. I'm so sorry. I should never have left you."

"You were doing what was best for you."

"But I should have been doing what was best for you, too!"

Over the next few hours, they shed more tears and hug each other tighter. Watching the two of them is like staring into the sun and the moon. Even as twins, Lexi still looks up to Bex. She is strong and independent, but there's a softness in Lexi that Bex doesn't have. They're so alike, and so uniquely themselves. At some point, I doze off and when I wake up, they're sitting across the room with Chase talking about superhero movies. I can see a bit of Lexi coming back with Bex around, and I hope it sticks.

"Dinner's up!" Steve announces as he comes in with three bags of the most delicious smelling burgers ever. I have got to get some solid food soon or I'm going to lose it. "Sorry, pal." He tosses a handful of Jell-O cups onto the tray next to me as I frown. I stare up at the ceiling as a fresh wave of depression hits. It seems so dumb, getting depressed over burgers, but it's not the burgers. It's the hospital, it's meeting Lexi's sister and I can't even speak to her, it's the pieces of Lexi littering the floor around me that I can't do a fucking thing about.

"Open your eyes."

She's standing over me with her beautiful brown eyes and her half smile. Somewhere in my self-wallowing, everyone has left, and I didn't even notice. She holds out a spoonful of toxic green gelatin and shrugs as I scrunch my face up.

"Come on. Eat this and then I'll give you part of the burger I saved for you, but only a very small bite, mister." She feeds me a few spoonfuls and fuck, this stuff is awful. She scrapes the bottom of the cup and shovels it into her own mouth and laughs as she chokes a little. "Eww, sugar free? That's just rude. You want some company up there?"

I nod. She climbs up and carefully squeezes in next to me, then reaches back and fishes out a bite of her burger from the greasy bottomed bag. She holds it out for me, but I shake my head. There's something else I want more, no matter how tempting burgers are.

"Thirsty?"

I smirk, "Only for you." I sound like someone strangled a fucking frog.

"Nice to see you still have your cheesy pick up line game going strong, pretty boy," she giggles. It sounds like angels, and I catch that tiny glimmer of hope blooming in her eyes.

She kisses me once, softly, on the lips. Twice a little harder to see if I can take it. Then my hand slides over her ass and her tongue into my mouth. She tastes better than a thousand burgers and is as sweet as all the sugar in the world. The beeping finally stops and the world slows down for us again.

"I like Bex." I whisper.

"Yeah? She's pretty great."

"Now I know what you'd look like with dark hair."

"And skinny," she says with a frown.

"But I want you just like this, Angel. Just the way you are. Perfect."

"Yeah? You know, you're not supposed to talk until your vocal cords heal. I won't tell Chase though." She smiles, it's a shy smile that hides how broken she is. "He's supposed to teach me a few signs tomorrow. I didn't know you knew sign language, but I guess that makes sense since you did the whole mute kid thing."

She kisses me again, and it's slow. Like she's trying to tell me everything will be okay even if she doesn't believe it herself.

"I love you," I whisper against her lips. She lays her head on my chest and I drift off to sleep again.

HOLLYWOOD
Lexi

CHAPTER 34
TILL FOREVER FALLS APART

ASHE, FINNEAS

I'M CLEANING up the tornado that is Bex staying in my living room when there's a knock at my door. It's so soft I almost don't hear it over the music. I open the door to find James, struggling to hold a box between his hip and good arm. I take the box from him and put it on the table as he stands by the door. He looks like a lost puppy, and it's likely because I've been distant lately.

"You know you can come in."

"Yeah, I…didn't want to bother you."

"You're not. Sam gave me some time off to deal with things."

He walks over, sitting on the other side of the table. "It's, uhm, it's for you."

I open the box and it's full of painting supplies. Jars and tubes of paint, brushes, things that I'm not even sure what they are. "You might have brought the wrong box." I mumble and hold up one of the jars.

I feel bad pointing it out to him because he's been trying so hard—a little too hard at times—to act like he's fine. I can see how much pain he's still in and every time he winces or moves strangely, I just remember that I'm the reason this happened. How do you tell the man you're pretty sure you're hopelessly in love with that he's a daily reminder of the worst night of your life? Every new scar on his body is there because of knowing me.

"No, that's the right box." He pulls out a jar of red paint and holds it up. "We can start with the wall behind the Rent art piece you did."

"Start what?"

"Our therapy?" He puts the jar down and runs his hand through his hair. It's grown so much, it's almost to his shoulders. Natalie has offered to come over and cut it, but he declines every time. "Your therapist helps, I can tell. But, I thought we could work on painting the walls here. Maybe a gigantic mural or even just a solid color. Something we could do together. Something, to…" his voice trails off and he mumbles the rest, "Are you leaving me?"

"What?"

"You're pulling away. You don't mean to, I can't even blame you. I wanted to do something special for you, with you. I want to help you get yourself back. Get us back." He frows at the box of paints. "I don't even know if it will work, but it's the only damn thing I've got."

He's right. I'm a shell and I have been since that night. I don't laugh unless it's fake. I haven't done a single design since Sam pulled us both off the project without an explanation beyond '*it's nothing personal*'. I'm not me anymore. I'm even doubting if I love James, which is stupid because I do and he's done nothing wrong.

"Oh, uhm. Painting might need to wait. Mom wants to sign the place over to me, but that's in limbo and, frankly, I don't want to stay here. Bex and I are going out tomorrow to look at apartments while you're at your physical therapy appointment. She said she found a few I can afford and might like."

"Oh."

I didn't even tell him I was moving out—I guess I'm pulling away from everyone faster than I thought.

"Yeah." I take the jars and put them carefully back into the box, sealing it back up. "The lawyer is looking over the paperwork and trying to see what can be done. If I keep it, I'll rent it out. I've always hated it here because they owned it; it was never mine."

"That makes sense. It's probably weird living next door to your new therapist, too."

He's picking at the cast on his wrist, not wanting to make eye contact. He's two feet away from me and it feels like we're miles apart. The silence is no longer comfortable, it's deafening. I stand and go to pick the box back up when he says something I don't catch. "What?"

His glistening eyes meet mine when he lifts his head. "Stay with me."

"Like, right here where I'm standing? James, I need to—"

"No, that's not what I mean. I mean, move in with me."

"James, I don't…that's probably a terrible idea."

"Why? Because we've only known each other for a few months? Fuck that, we've been through more than most people go through in a year…or a lifetime, and we did it together." He stands up and takes the box from me, struggling a little to do it one handed. "Move in with me. You can have your own room—I'll clear out dad's room for you. We can convert the dark room to an office for you to work out of when you're not at Sam's. Hell, you'll have a whole art studio at your disposal if you want to go back to making your pieces."

I close my eyes and purse my lips.

"Please? We can bring your furniture if you want. If it's the drive to work, I'll drive you. Every fucking day." He sighs when

I don't answer, shifting the box on his hip. "Just think it over, okay?"

"Why?" I asked as he heads to the door. "I'm miserable and angry, and I'm the reason you're in pain. Why would you want me there reminding you of that every damn day?"

He puts the box on the couch and comes back over to me, holding my face in both hands and completely ignoring the sling he's still in. "Because I was miserable and angry until I found you. Because I was in so much more pain before I found you. Because I want to wake up to the smell of coffee and cherry blossoms for the rest of my life. Because I didn't blame you then, I don't blame you now, and I will never blame you for the decisions fucked up people make. But more important than all of that, more important than anything at all, is because I love you, Alexis Strauss. I love you so much and I hope that someday, when I ask you to marry me, you'll be able to see past all of this, say yes, and let me love you, anyway."

"Yes."

"What?"

"I would say yes if you asked me to marry you right now. Broke and broken. I would say yes, if you'd have me. So yes, I'll move in with you, James." I expect him to kiss me. I expect him to change his mind. I expect him to realize he doesn't love me and just leave. I don't expect him to drop to one knee right there in the living room.

"Alexis, I am broke, but I am not broken because you are the glue keeping me whole. I don't have a ring, but…marry me? Right now. We'll go to Vegas."

"Vegas?"

"Let me call Coop and Steve. You can call Bex and Dani." He stands with a wince and starts pacing around, planning the trip out in his head. "I need to grab some stuff from the house.

How fast can you—Wait, you're serious, right? That was a yes?"

"If that was a serious proposal. Yes. Yes, James *I don't know your middle name* Barton. I would marry you today."

There's a hard knock on the front door just as James is about to say something, and my whole body goes numb. It could be one of them. They could have posted bail and now they're here to finish what they started. I've been terrified of every loud noise, every shout, every police siren—in Los Angeles, those are all everyday background sounds. People love to talk about fight and flight, but they always forget those of us who just freeze and shut down. Dr. Clay says that I am stuck in a cycle. He's working to find something that works for someone like me to break the cycle of stress I'm putting myself through. So far, it's only helped temporarily.

"Hello, I'm Humberto Diaz. Is Ms. Strauss home?" The man at the door introduces himself to Jamie. He looks back at me and I nod, so he opens the door and lets two men in. "Good morning, ma'am. We promise this won't take long. Mr. Stan Morgan, your lawyer, hired us. We're private investigators and we've found some new information regarding your case."

He then turns to Jamie. "You wouldn't be James Barton, would you?"

"Yes, I am."

"Good, this involves you, too."

My stomach does more than lurch and I can taste the bile climbing up my throat until Jamie steps behind me and takes my hand. "Let's sit down, okay?" he whispers in my ear and then leads me over to a chair while the two PIs sit on the couch. "I'll go get you some water."

"Ma'am, we've learned that your stepfather and Mr. Jones may not have been working alone." Diaz explains. He's older and has a light Hispanic accent. "We dug into their finances after we got a lead and we found several large deposits made to each of them. Have either of you heard anything about a company called Cynosure?"

I shake my head. James calls out from the kitchen that it sounds familiar. The second PI holds up his phone, showing me a picture. Before I can say her name, the glass James was carrying drops to the floor and shatters. I jump and scream at the sound, and Jamie rushes over to me to calm me.

"I take it that you know her?" The second PI asks as he grabs a towel and cleans the water for us.

"Elle. Her name is Elliana Petrov. She's my sister."

"Your sister? What can you tell us about her?"

"Not much. In her whole life, we've spent a grand total of a week around each other." Diaz makes a rumble noise and I take Jamie's arm and hold it tight. "What does she have to do with this?"

"Well, I'm not sure how to tell you both this, but what we've found leads us to believe she paid Miller and Jones to attack you. It's just a little odd that she's got a familial tie to—"

"No, it makes perfect sense. My sister was following us, stalking us, just like we told the cops. She hates me and apparently I'm in her way of some big fortune from my mother's company. That's Cynosure, isn't it? Fuck."

"Oh, my god." The world spins as it all makes more and more sense. "How? She couldn't have done this all that fast."

"Well, we may have an answer to that as well," Diaz answers. "You both work for a Mr. Sam Greene, correct?"

"Yeah, I freelance. Lex is a full-time designer there. Why?"

"Because your sister created a number of shell companies and used them methodically to get you fired from all of your other jobs." The second PI answers. "She wanted to push you into a position with Mr. Greene's company. Now that I know who she is, I'm guessing that was because Mr. Greene was close to your father. She's been working on it for months, and in the meantime, she was searching for the right target."

"Fuck, she was going after everyone."

"Sorry, I haven't introduced myself. I'm Joe, Joe Mills. I work in cyber security issues mostly, which is why I'm here to learn about Ms. Petrov. The cops have a file on her already, and I've been following her for a while now for various cyber crimes."

"The cops weren't getting anywhere and neither your step father or Jones was talking." Diaz explained. "Which isn't a surprise, but once Mills went to Mr. Morgan with what he found, they took it to the detectives on your case and the District Attorney's office.

"Now that we have more info on them, Mr. Jones has started singing. He thinks if he talks, they'll go easy on him. He's already confessed that Elle approached him months ago."

"We'd only just met. That doesn't make sense," Jamie says as he sits down on the arm of the chair, still rubbing my back.

"Actually, you hadn't met Ms. Strauss yet, according to the timeline." Mills clarifies. "She had files on you, Ms. Strauss, and several other coworkers of yours. It looks like she was narrowing the search down and looking for the…right victim. She approached your stepfather first, and that set the plan in motion. We believe she discovered his extramarital affairs with numerous young women, and likely uncovered his past violations again you."

Diaz hands me a folder, and I flip through it, finding pictures of Kennedy, Dani, and a few other women in our office. "The plan was to assault you and frame Mr. Barton. She arranged to have you working that job together to guarantee out-of-town travel so it would be…easier to go through with the plan."

"The text. She threatened to send some…videos of me to my stepfather. She said he'd like them." This is all so surreal, but James doesn't even seem surprised. "That's where they got the money for the new church, isn't it? She's the big donor?"

"Yes, ma'am." Diaz answers. "Noah Jones and your stepfather have a pretty fucked up past. Elle Petrov found out about it and used it to her advantage. Once your relationship started, they adjusted the plan. Jones said it was Miller's idea to lure Mr. Barton out and kill him. Then Petrov would sabotage your career, Ms. Strauss. Leaving you nowhere to turn, except your mother, your stepfather, and Jones."

"So they did all of this for more fucking money? They have a fucking beach house in Malibu! They have a giant fucking cult!"

Mills sighs and rubs the back of his neck, "It wasn't just money, ma'am. Based on multiple emails involving your stepfather, mother, and Noah Jones, it was planned that once Elle was finished, you would be given to Jones as a twisted, messed up reward. We've got a mountain of emails to back it up."

Jamie stiffens, I can feel the rage building in him and then ebb into sorrow. He blames himself because he wasn't there for me. I don't.

"There's additional evidence against your stepfather in those emails as well. Images." Mills added with a sympathetic look while Jamie squeezed my shoulder. "Your mother is claiming her email was setup by someone else, but I don't think that's true.

Diaz pulls out his phone. "Mr. Barton, we found a record of you and a young lady being brought to the hospital in San Diego. Do you remember this incident?" He holds up his phone, showing James a picture of a pretty blonde woman I've never seen before.

"Yeah, I do."

"Petrov's backup drives had an invoice for a sedative usually reserved for large animals. It was found in your system, and the system of the young lady."

"Fuck. She almost killed us."

"We're dropping all of this information in a pretty little bow to the DA's office soon. He'll be going after her for the attempted murder of both you and the young woman on top of everything else."

"That all seems so…extreme."

"She wants the money and fame and power, just like mom," James said in a distant voice. "If the plan had worked, this would have been a win-win from her perspective."

"How?" I ask him. This all sounds like some far-fetched plot of a crime show and I'm just waiting for some quippy one-liner before some song by The Who starts playing. It's insane.

"Because, in one plan, I'm in jail for assaulting you. In the other plan, I'm dead. She doesn't care who she hurts, so long as I get hurt along the way, too. If I'm dead, she inherits all of Dad's shares and mine. She'd get everything."

"James…I…" I squeeze his hand, unable to find the words.

"Cynosure is currently worth over three billion dollars. They announced yesterday that they were making some higher level staff adjustments. They're covering their asses," Mills informs us. "When, not if, you get an NDA in exchange for a large sum of cash, let us know. You have more than enough to bring that entire company to its knees with a scandal this bad."

I sit on the couch, staring at the floor while they continue to talk, until I felt someone beside me pull me toward them. I glance around and realize it's just James and me now.

"You want me to start a bath for you, Angel?"

"No," I whimper. The walls I'd built over the years have all crumbled to dust and I can't tell if it's a good thing or not. Ronnie and Noah are going to prison—maybe my mother, too. I try not to speculate about what they had planned to do with me or why they really believed they could get away with it. It reminds me of the true crime shows I watch with Dani where the culprits are always so surprised they get caught. I wonder if they would have gone after Bex to keep me quiet. It would have worked.

Jamie's playing with something in his hand, but I can't see what it is until he holds it up to me. It's a ring.

"Mills said they found it at the scene. They got the cops to release it from evidence, since all it did was prove I was at the junkyard, which was obvious." He takes my hand and rubs my ring finger. "I was going to propose to you at Chase's place that night. I had the whole house decked out with cherry blossoms and roses. Dog sitting was kind of a lie."

"James…"

"I wanted it to be perfect."

I glance up from the ring and into his beautiful eyes, glad I can see them both again. Even banged up and bruised, he's absolutely gorgeous, but more importantly, he's mine. I have to help him get on one knee this time, and I can see it's painful for him, but he insists. He wants to do this right.

"Alexis, I'm not rich—I don't even think I have a job—and I'm a pain in the ass. I can't promise you anything more than all of me, and I hope that's enough. Will you marry me?"

"Do you like Alexis Barton or James Strauss better?"

"How about Countess Alexis der VanDerVander and her aloof boy toy?"

"So, is that a yes?"

"No. It's a hell yes, pretty boy."

I'm crying, but I'm also laughing for the first time in weeks when my phone rings and I see Dani's name pop up.

"Hey."

"Hey, is Jamie with you? Are you crying?"

"Yeah and yes, but it's not sad tears. Why?"

"Cool, can you guys come down to Sam's? The cops are here and they need some info from you both. I'm not here to fuck with cops. Ugh, please come down here and get this sorted so Sam can get back to work and stop being a pain in my ass."

"Yeah, okay. We'll head there now."

HOLLYWOOD

James

CHAPTER 35
TAKE MY BREATH AWAY

EZI

THEIR TIMING COULDN'T HAVE BEEN WORSE. Just as I thought I was getting her back again, she's hiding in her bunker once more. She's so fragile now, not the playful, wild woman I know. I take her hand and hold it, even though it's a little awkward to reach over. I'll deal with awkward so long as it means I get to feel her. It doesn't matter to me who she is now because I still love her. People change, but no matter how much she changes, I will never give up on her.

I park behind Sam's building and they're both there waiting for us, but I don't see any police around. Dani hugs Lexi when we get out and Sam comes over to me.

"How are you feeling?"

"I don't know."

"Well, come on. I've got them waiting for us at the coffee shop, so they stop freaking everybody out at the office."

As we walk, I tell Sam about the PIs and some of what they found. I keep it general because as much as I appreciate everything he's doing for Lexi and me, some things just aren't his to know. By the looks of it, the line for the coffee shop is out the door. Lexi won't handle a crowd well right now, but she hasn't noticed yet since Dani has been talking almost non-stop. I reach over and take Lexi's hand, and just as I do, Sam steps in front of us.

"Before we go in, I want to talk to you both real quick."

"I'll meet you inside," Dani says before taking off.

"Guys, I know you've been through a lot and I don't expect answers today, this week, or any time before you're ready to make these kinds of decisions." Lexi squeezes my hand as Sam looks at her first. "Lex, I want to take the office remote and I need your help to do that. I'm thinking maybe hybrid at first and then transition everyone to fully remote. I'll still keep an office setup and have desks for any time we need to meet in person, but I want you and everyone else to have a little more freedom—including myself."

"Uhm, okay, sure."

"Great. James, how would you feel about a full-time job?" He checks the time before I can answer. "Shit, let me tell you about it inside. We should get going."

"You'd like remote work," I say softly to Lex as we walk. She nods, still staring her feet instead of looking ahead. "We can talk about where you want your office later. You can have any room in the house. I'll paint you a beautiful mural. How does a cherry blossom tree sound?"

"What if…no that's stupid."

"What?"

"What if we put it in the studio? So we can work together. Depending on what Sam wants you to do."

My heart does double dutch against my chest. "That's not stupid. That's the best idea ever." I lean over and kiss her head. Maybe there's still hope for her. For us. I need to get this over with so I can call Chase about Vegas.

Lexi and I step into the shop and we both freeze. Instead of police or detectives, there's Chase, Dani, Steve, and Bex, all standing there like they've been waiting on us. Great, apparently we need an intervention. I groan and go to move out of the doorway, but Lexi isn't moving. Fuck.

"Angel, are you—"

"James, look."

"Huh?" I stare at our friends again and Coop laughs, pointing toward the wall. Like one of those Magic Eye posters from the old malls, things come into focus. Instead of the quirky decorations that were here before, the walls are full of paintings. My paintings. My dad's paintings. Lexi's posters are up, too. "What the fuck?"

I glance around at the people, and I realize I recognize some of them. There's a dean from a college I applied to for a teaching position. There's a handful of people I've met at my dad's charity events. In the back corner, there's a group of guys my dad played poker with and Carl.

"Surprise?" Dani says with arms wide, with Raf next to her.

"What is this?"

"It's an art showing, dumbass." Coop pulls us into the shop. "Haven't you been to enough of those to know that yet?"

"But, why? How?"

"Well. Dani and Steve did most of the work. Bex and Sam did all the networking, and I told the shop if they shut down for a day to do this, I'd do a commercial for them. Which, when I say it out loud, makes my helping sound super lame."

"Okay, but that doesn't answer the why?"

"Because," Dani chimed in, "You two need a reset button like nobody's business. Also, Sam gets to use it all as a write off when he opens the new cent—"

"Woah! Haven't told them yet."

"Told us what?" Lexi spins around to ask him.

"Well, we're going remote because I want to repurpose the building. Jamie, the job I want to offer you is head of my new organization—an art school."

"Art school?"

"Yeah, that's why I pulled in the dean over there. I want to come up with a way for local artists to work with therapists in an arts center for at-risk and disadvantaged youth. Locals helping locals kind of thing. We're going to name it after your dad. If you'll let us."

My mind is only retaining half of this conversation, so I hope Sam will have it again later. There's so much going on all at once.

"Why is my art here?"

"Advertising mostly. We're handling all the donations and registration here since there's food. Right now, my office has twelve local artists' pieces, and at last count, over four hundred guests bidding on them. A small portion of the sales goes toward the new art grant my lawyer is in the middle of writing up."

"Jesus, Sam. This sounds like a lot," Lexi mumbles before letting go of my hand and wandering toward the art.

"It is. You've got some particularly convincing friends who also have my home telephone number. There's a small catch. We need a big donor for this to kick off. I was thinking of you."

I search behind me to see who he's talking to and realize there's no one there. "Me?"

Sam steps aside and the lawyer, Mr. Morgan, is standing behind him with a handful of paperwork.

"Mr. Barton, I contacted Cynosure and I've spoken to their legal team. They're ready to offer you fifteen million dollars and the retained rights to your total shares, as well as your father's, if you don't take legal action against them. Now, that means we could always reject the offer and go after them for more, but that seems pointless if you're in charge of the company."

I stumble backward, luckily finding a chair behind me. Lexi rushes over and I can see that she's talking, but I can't hear the words. My mind is racing, and it's several minutes and two shots of whiskey before I'm able to make any sense of the world again.

"You good, man?" Coop asks.

"When did this place start serving whiskey?"

"So what do you say?" I study Sam's outstretched hand. "Partners?"

"All I have to do is sign the papers?"

"Yep."

"Sam, can I borrow your car?" He looks at me strangely, probably wondering if I hit my head when I fell. "I need to do something before I sign those. I promise I'll sign them as soon as I'm back."

"Why my car?"

"Because I need to fit six people in it and drive to Vegas. I want to marry Lexi while I'm still a broke ass idiot artist."

We get to the hotel and it's almost one in the morning, which is early for Vegas. But we need a marriage license and the office closed at midnight. We filled out the forms online while Chase drove and Dani booked hotel rooms for all of us. Now we're supposed to get some sleep before we pick up the damn license in the morning and find Elvis. That's seven hours from now.

"Wow, Dani really knows how to pick 'em, doesn't she?" Lexi asks as we survey the small motel room. "I mean, I know we're living the broke artist dream for another day or two, but this is a little—"

Before she can finish, I pull her against me and she lets out one of her little squeaks. I fight with the stupid sling until she helps me take it off, and then I'm cupping her face and practically shoving my tongue down her throat. It's not romantic. This room isn't romantic. The whole situation isn't romantic. It's desperate and dirty and absolutely us. We're making it work.

She helps me pull my shirt off and I pick her up, not giving a shit about how much it hurts to do so, and carry her to the bed. She crawls back on her elbows and looks up at me. I'm sure she's just looking at a wild, insatiable stare. Then she giggles.

"What?"

"You."

"Me? What did I do?"

"You have your arm in a cast and your ribs still aren't healed and you're trying to throw me onto the bed and have your way with me?"

"Yeah, that did kind of hurt." I rub my side. "But…we haven't…I mean. We haven't done more than a little making out since…fuck. I don't even know when."

She gets up on her knees and reaches out, balling my shirt up in her fist and pulling me toward her. "Take off your fucking clothes and get in the damn bed." She moves away from me and off the bed.

"Where are you—" There's a knock at the door and she winks at me as she goes to answer it. I hear a voice; It sounds like Bex. Someone passes a small bag into the room and my eyes narrow suspiciously when Lexi hides it behind her back. "Do I want to know?"

"You'll never find out if you don't get the fuck on the bed."

She disappears into the bathroom, and I start desperately trying to undress. It's not easy with my wrist still fucked up and when she pokes her head out, I'm fighting with my fucking fly. I stare up at her in a desperate plea.

"I tried!"

"I know. It's close enough. I'll take care of the rest later. Lay down on your back."

I throw myself onto the bed. Not the best of decisions, but that seems to be the role I'm playing. Lexi crawls up from the end of the bed in this absolutely jaw dropping, hard on inducing lingerie. It's got lace and straps and things I can't even comprehend. It pushes her tits up in these perfectly overflowing cups and makes her ass look phenomenal. I wipe my mouth, convinced that I'm drooling.

She stops right over my cock and smirks. "We'll take care of that next. But first…you look hungry, Jamie."

I can't even speak, and the moan she rips out of me when she traces my abs with her tongue. I hope none of our people are sharing walls with us tonight. She continues up my body as my hands explore all of her I can reach. She's fucking amazing and if she keeps this up, I'll be coming in my damn pants.

My head rocks back onto the pillow when her tongue slides over my nipple and she palms my cock. I'm not exactly quiet in bed. I never have been, but fuck—I've never been this loud before.

"You're so fucking beautiful, angel."

"So are you, pretty boy." The nickname has me seeing double as my head spins. "Tonight, I'm going to make you sing for me."

"I will always sing for you, Cherry Blossom." I see the flicker in her eyes. "Every damn day. But first, why don't you come up here, straddle my head, and let me taste that perfectly sweet pussy."

She moves over me carefully, clearly unsure of herself. "James, what if I…"

"Baby girl, if I suffocate while eating you out, you just tell everyone I died a very, very happy man. Now, hold on to that headboard and let me feast on you."

I lower her right where I need her, and her whole body shivers when I lick a slow strip through her. It's not long before she's riding my face and singing my name like a bird. It's beautiful and breathy and it's all I'll ever need. I get her to the edge and she's about to climb off of me, but I wrap both arms around her thighs and hold her down as she grinds harder, coming apart on top of me.

Tomorrow morning, I'm going to marry this woman. Then I'm going to do this to her every day for the rest of our lives. She's screaming my name, and I feel her tight pussy pulsing around me. She's all I want. All I ever need in this world.

"James…right fucking there, baby. Oh, shit!"

My cock is straining against my pants and I'm so fucking lost in her ecstasy that my hips thrust into nothing. She throws her head back and arches her back as she releases the most primal scream I've ever heard before. She looks down and her eyes lock on mine. We've only just begun and already she looks fucking ruined.

"Don't stop, James!"

She comes undone, squeezing my head with her thighs and grunting as my tongue fucks her right into a second orgasm, not letting her come down before I'm done with her. She reached down with one hand, gripping my hair hard and riding my face like she's at a rodeo and I couldn't be happier.

"I can't, oh god, I can't!"

I let her go, and she collapses down next to me on her back, gasping for air. I roll over, gently nipping at her neck, a mantra of I love you's between every kiss. When her breathing finally slows, she looks up at me with a drunken smile.

"You okay?"

She looks at me for a while, as if she's contemplating her answer, then tucks my hair behind my ear and purses her lips. "I will be, because of you."

"What do I call you tomorrow?"

She giggles as she says the word, "Wife."

"You know what I mean. Are you going to change your name? Am I? I will happily be known as Mrs. and Mr. Alexis Strauss from here on out. James Strauss has a ring to it. Or Alexis Barton."

"I think for once we do things a little differently."

"Like what? I'm not taking Coop's name."

"No you goof. I mean we take it slow and figure it out later."

"Well, that's not a very us way of handling it, soon-to-be-wife."

"Which is exactly why we're going to do it, soon-to-be-husband."

"Graham."

"What?" she giggles.

"My middle name. It's Graham. Named after my grandfather."

"James Graham Barton. It's pretty. Mine's Riley because mom shot down Sophia. It's probably the nicest thing she ever did for me."

"I mean, ASS or ARS." She swats at me playfully. "I love it. Alexis Riley…whatever we decide."

I brush her hair through my fingers and stare into her beautiful, broken soul. I wish dad could have met her and seen just how happy I am. My angel. My muse, who shrouds me in her darkness so we can watch the stars burn.

"Thank you."

"For what?"

"Dropping your phone."

"We would have worked together even if I hadn't."

"Yeah, but our story would have been so different. I wouldn't have told Dani about my pink haired goddess. I wouldn't have ignored almost everything Sam said because I couldn't concentrate on anything but how I could find you again." Carefully, I climb over her and she undoes my jeans, pushing them down as we exchange soft, sweet kisses.

"We have to be at the courthouse in a few hours," she reminds me as her fingers play in my hair. "We should probably get some sleep."

"Yep." I rock my hips and her legs open for me. She reaches down and I groan as she grabs me, lining me up. Electricity shoots through my body as I slowly stretch her. I watch between our bodies as she take me in until she cups my face.

"I love you, James. I wanna watch your pretty blue eyes. I want you to see what you do to me."

"Oh, Cherry Blossom, I already know."

HOLLYWOOD

James

EPILOGUE- LOVING YOU

PAOLI NUTINI

—ALMOST TWO YEARS LATER—

"AHHH, WATCH OUT! LEX!" I shout as I run through the house chasing the little shit. He's faster than I had ever expected at this age. So far we've knocked over two easels, a can of paint, and a table all in under two minutes.

"James, what the—Oh my god, seriously? You're just letting him run around like that? He's got paint all over his feet!" She steps into the doorway right in time to grab the wriggling puppy from the floor and shower it in kisses. "Oh, what's the matter? Was that big cranky daddy chasing you again?"

"He fucking likes it." I drop onto the floor and sprawl out, utterly beat. "He ate your shoes. He also redecorated the floors upstairs." I get out between gasps for air.

"Oh, look at those little red toes!" I watch her inspect the paws, spotting the remnants of red paint. "So I'm guessing it looks like a crime scene up there and our number one suspect fits your description, doesn't it, Mr. VanDerVander?"

She sits on the floor next to me and the puppy stops its

wriggling and relaxes in her arms while a smile spreads across my face.

"James, we've been married for two years now. Are you ever going to stop looking at me like that?"

"if I do, it's because I've died." My hand slips up her leg and I growl, "Now put *Count* VanDerVander down!"

"He'll run through all the paint again."

"Let him." As soon as she releases the dog, he trots over to his bed and passes out. Meanwhile, I grab her arms and pull her down on top of me, covering her face and neck with kisses while she squeals in laughter.

"James! Seriously, there are paint cans all over the floor!"

I roll us over so I'm on top of her and her legs wrap around me. Her hands find my hair and I smear wet paint on her as I pull her sweater over her head. I kiss between her bare breasts and move further down as she continues to laugh.

"You're so beautiful."

"You're so cleaning up this mess!"

"Right after I make a mess of you, Cherry Blossom."

"The windows are open!"

"Mm-hmm." I slide her leggings down, kissing her thighs.

"Someone could see us!"

"Mm-hmm." I run my flattened tongue over her soaked panties and listen to the breathy ramblings of a woman being driven mad with lust. "Why do you bother to wear these things?" I rip them off and toss them over my shoulder.

"Y-you…. you… oh god!" Her tight grip holds my head against her as my tongue slides into her, coaxing a sweet song of shattered moans mixed with my name.

She tastes as sweet as the first time I had her, but now, the hesitation is long gone. She thought at first it had been a joke, a flippant comment that I made about worshiping her every day.

Now she knows I was serious, because every damn day since I put that ring on her finger, I've listened to her sing my praise to a higher power while I worship her. While I devour her. While I shatter her around me, put her back together, only to do it all over again.

My name echoes in the mostly empty room, and she claws at my scalp. I can't help but smile against her and know that as soon as she's back down to earth, I'll bring her right back to the top of the mountain so she can scream to me once, twice, three times more.

I barely hear the doorbell and I certainly don't register what it is—too focused on her voice and the way her body responds to me.

"Shit, James!"

"Mmm," I hum against her clit and her back lifts off the floor like a bolt of lightning surged through her.

"Door. Someone… door."

"Are you asking me to stop?" She reluctantly nods as I grin at her with a glistening beard. "Should I go answer it like this?"

She laughs and pulls up her pants. "Oh, for fuck's sake. Damn it. I was so close!"

"Who said we're done? Stay here. I've got it." I get up, grab a towel from one of the ladders, and wipe my face before I head to the front of the house. When I pull open the door, I can't fucking believe it.

"Hello. Is my daughter in? I would like to speak to her."

I check my watch, realizing that today is the day the restraining order lifted. She wasted no time.

"She's busy." I didn't mean for it to come out like a growl, but I'm not mad that it did. I cross my arms and stare at her.

"Yes, I uhm," she lowers her head and stares down at her feet, "I heard. It won't take long, I promise."

"If you so much as raise your voice to her, or say a fucking thing to upset her in the slightest, I will end the conversation, drag your ass out of our house, and have the cops haul you off our fucking property. Do you understand?"

I walk her to the back of the house where Lexi is holding paint swatches up to the ceiling while standing on the larger of two ladders in the room.

"Lex, shit," I run over and hold the ladder for her. "I told you I'd do that. I don't want you up there."

"Oh whatever, I'm not—" She looks back and forth between me and her mother a few times, and then accepts the hand I offer her while she climbs down. She shoves her hands deep into the hoodie she stole from me years ago when we first started dating.

"Alexis…I," her mother starts, before her face twists up and she looks like she's about to have her own nervous breakdown. She takes a deep breath and my hand finds Lexi's as we wait to see where she plans on taking this conversation.

"I didn't expect you to come here," Lexi says when her mother still hasn't spoken.

"Yes, well, I didn't expect to come here either. Not after how we left things. Is all of this…" She motions around the room, ending with Lexi. "Alexis, are you…?"

Lexi snorts out a loud laugh, and a second later I realize where her mother is looking at her and I laugh, before kissing her on the head. This is not my dance; she knows I'll follow her lead.

"Yes. I should be delivering the antichrist any minute now. We just found out last week, and I forgot how quickly a demon spawn grows!"

Her mother glares at her. "That isn't funny, Alexis. Are you actually pregnant, or are you trying to fluster me?"

"No, mother. Jamie and I are not having a baby." She pauses before adding, "Ever."

"Oh, well, that's a shame. It's a woman's—"

I clear my throat and level my gaze at her. She knows this will be the only warning she's going to get.

"Anyhow, I wanted you to be aware that your fath—I am moving. To New Mexico."

"His transfer finally came through? Wow! So is this the trial with the sixteen-year-old or the mother of two?" Lexi asks and squeezes my hand.

"Alexis, I wish you would think about what you're doing."

"Well, that was fun, time to go," I step toward her and she takes a step back.

"I just mean that, well, you've ruined his life enough, haven't you?"

"Get the fuck—" Lexi stops me by putting a hand on my forearm. I see the flame in her eyes go from a flicker to a raging inferno as she stares her mother down. It's the same look she had a year ago when she had to testify against her stepfather and the defense attorney tried to twist the events and victim-blame her. It's a look I hope she never gives me, but god does it turn me on.

My phoenix, my queen, my wife. She tore down the empire they built to imprison her. She stood in the flames, and I was beside her every step of the way.

"You could have stopped this. You could have spoken up and said something, could have listened to me or Bex. You don't get to blame me, mother, because *you're* the reason he ever came into my life. I can't wait—" I step between them and hold Lexi's arm to keep her from getting too close. She knows what I'm doing, and that I'm in no way protecting her mother. I don't trust her mother and wouldn't be surprised if she ran out of the house claiming Lexi attacked her, given the chance. Lexi stays calm, which is more terrifying. "I can't wait till they get you into that courthouse and behind that table, because they will. They're going to make you listen to everything he's done, every other woman he's assaulted, and they're going to know that you could have stopped it. They'll know you stood there and watched him do this to us."

"I don't believe you! Ronnie is a good man! He only wanted what was best—"

"He's a fucking rapist! Now get the fuck out of our house and don't ever come back here. You had your chance. I did everything to try to make you happy. Everything but let your sick, depraved, disgusting husband touch me ever again!"

"You're okay baby," I whisper after I pull her into my chest and rock her. "Slow breaths, breathe with me, beautiful."

There's a shuffling behind me, and I close my eyes. "I'm going to pretend that's the dog and not your fucking dumb ass still in our house. Don't say another word. Get the fuck out." I hold Lexi to me, blocking her view as her mother leaves again and for the last time.

We'll call Morgan as soon as Lexi is alright again. He's been in touch with us a lot since Sam hired him. He's become more our friend than our lawyer. He even came to my birthday party a few months ago. Lexi's stepfather is trying to appeal. But when twenty-three other women came forward, we weren't worrying about him anymore. Equally surprising was finding out that Noah Jones wasn't the other dickhead's real name. In fact, he had five other names he used. Each of those is associated with a different family. Some of those families were with underaged women.

"Knock, knock," comes a familiar voice, and Lexi giggles in my arms as Chase comes into the room. "Woah, sorry. Am I interrupting?"

"No, Chase," she answers. She smiles up at me, grabs my face, and kisses me like she's feasting on my soul. She can have it; it's hers anyhow. When she pulls away, she winks, and I can't help but smirk. This beautiful woman is going to fuck my damn brains out the second Coop is gone. "We're fine."

"Cool. So, what are we taking with us?"

"I've got it all organized in the other room." Lexi stands on her tiptoes and kisses Chase's cheek. He hands her a giant iced coffee milk tea, and she heads out of the room. The puppy right on her heels having finally woken up again.

Coop hangs back, handing me a second coffee. "Figured you'd need a boost before the event."

"Thanks for coming with me. I know it's kind of a pain in the ass and all after that last movie and the awards and stuff."

"Hey, you had me at *elementary school*. If the paps wanna follow me there and deal with all those lawsuits, they can fucking have at it. I brought like two boxes of those little figurines with the big heads that I'm gonna sign for them while you do your thing. Do you think four hundred is enough?"

"Yeah," I laugh. When we started the program bringing art classes and speakers to different schools, I never in a million years thought Chase would be interested. Not only is he interested, he's an active member and high-level donator. He brings toys to the kids, answers their questions, colors with them—it's a whole side of him I've never even seen before. "Dani said there are only about two hundred attending and her sister is a teacher there, so she should have somewhere to store them for any of the kids that didn't make it. You really don't have to do that all the time."

"Are you boys going to come help with this, or do you expect me and *COUNT* VanDerVander to do all of this on our own?"

Coop laughs, "Fuck, I can't believe you named my dog that."

"Our dog, now, buddy. She called him *mister* earlier like he's some common peasant." I throw my arm over his shoulder. "He's a descendant of the Great and Magnificent Lulu Cooper. He's a Count at the very least." We head toward Lexi and I yell out, "Coming, Angel!"

"Eww."

"Dude, shut up."

The Hollywoodland Series will continue with Chase & Ren in Love the Stars Fondly

MENTAL HEALTH RESOURCES

IT'S OKAY TO NOT BE OKAY.

This book deals with several instances of mental health issues. If you or someone you know is struggling, the following are free and confidential resources to help.

Suicide and Crisis Hotline
https://988lifeline.org/
Call or text 988 or chat 988lifeline.org

National Domestic Violence Hotline
https://www.thehotline.org/
1-800-799-7233 or text LOVEIS to 22522

Prevention & Treatment of Child Abuse
https://www.childhelp.org/hotline/
1-800-4AChild (1-800-422-4453)
text 1-800-422-4453

National Sexual Assault Hotline
https://rainn.org/
1-800-656-HOPE (4673)
online chat: https://hotline.rainn.org/online

From hrc.org:

Transgender Community
https://translifeline.org/ - 877-565-8860

LGBTQ+ Youth
https://www.lgbthotline.org/youth-talkline - 1-800-246-7743
https://www.thetrevorproject.org/get-help-now/ - 1-866-488-7386; Text START to 678-678

All Ages
https://www.lgbthotline.org/national-hotline - 1-888-843-4564

For International Mental Health resources:
https://dbtselfhelp.com/resources/international-resources/

ACKNOWLEDGMENTS

The specialist of special thanks to my mom. You listened to my silly ideas, read my books (yes, even the spicy ones), and commented/shared things online all for me. Also, you put up with my non-stop talk about Marvel/Bucky/A certainly actor who's name I probably shouldn't put in here. You're the best!

So, so much thanks to the people who made this book happen. Danielle, you don't even read spice, but you still volunteered to edit for me. Emily, for your time, your gluten nightmares, and your kind words that pushed me on with my silly story. Jenn, who helped me figure out my marketing and cheered me on, then convinced me to start a company with her. You're the one who introduced me to good old smut and fanfic.

Thank you to the alpha readers who became beta readers, Aly and Amy, your feedback made me feel like I had something good. Also, my street team, and all of you who share my social media marketing. My ARC team, you all were incredible with your speedy reviews and catching the small edits we'd missed.

An extra special thanks to the amazingly talented **Thea Lawrence** for their guidance, patience, and friendship. I hope someday we get to sign together at a book conference. I also hope our books take off and we can do this full time. You're an inspiration and an awesome person.

To AJ, Matty, Jeff, and Ashley, without you, I wouldn't have some of the amazing LA references for these books. AJ, it's really your fault, since you're why I moved to LA in the first place. Let's also not forget Janet, who spent years dragging me around to singles nights, gaming, and my first boba shop.

To Los fucking Angeles!! What an adventure you were. I hope I get to try it again sometime. I found myself out there.

I referenced a ton of restaurants in this book, and will likely do so throughout the series. These business don't sponsor me, or even know I exist, however, I highly recommend each one:

The Crooked Duck- Long Beach

The Pie Hole- Multiple Locations

Eggslut- Grand Central Market, Los Angeles

The Cows End- Venus Beach

ABOUT JORDYN

Jordyn Barnes is a graphic designer, nerd, elder goth, and now, a published author. She loves Halloween, creepy things, morally grey characters, and writing about the flawed and beautifully broken people she creates in her mind palace. When she's not writing or reading, she's rearranging the growing collection dedicated to her favorite Disney Princess: Bucky Barnes/Winter Soldier. She also enjoys designing, Marvel movies/shows, true crime podcasts and TV shows, and, occasionally, sports. She's a long time Disney adult who relates most strongly with Madam Mim's dislike of sunshine while envying her forest hag lifestyle.

For updates on upcoming releases, join Jordyn's mailing list at jordynbarnes.com. Don't forget to follow her on social media and Goodreads as well:

instagram.com/jordyn.writes.and.reads
tiktok.com/@Jordyn.writes.words
amazon.com/author/jordynbarnes
goodreads.com/jordynbarnes

THE HOLLYWOODLAND SERIES

Let Me Love You Anyway
Faith in Fools*
Love the Stars Fondly
Never to Suffer
Dream Only by Night*
In the Hatred of a Minute

*Novella

Printed in the USA
CPSIA information can be obtained
at www.ICGtesting.com
CBHW071532260724
12259CB00010B/128

9 798990 503410